The Chainmakers

"Oh, Clancy, dear...." Anna caught at his arm as
they reached the canal. The boat was already there,
and one or two passengers were climbing aboard.
The bargeman, recognising Anna, gave her a cheery
wave and indicated she should hurry.

"Clancy, I'm sorry, I have to go...."

"Yes. I just wondered if...what you thought
about it."

Clancy took Anna's arm as she clambered
aboard and then walked along the towpath to talk
to her as she settled herself at the rear of the barge.
He leaned towards her. "Ye didn't say, Anna. Ye
didn't say," he entreated in a loud whisper.

"What?" Her face was stricken.

The bargeman took the tiller and the canal boat
began to move away. Clancy walked alongside, eyes
locked with Anna's. "Are ye coming, darlin'? To
America? Are ye coming with me?"

She did not answer. The boat drew away and
she mouthed, "I'll see you next week."

Clancy raised his hand in acknowledgement
and watched the barge recede slowly. Then he
turned away and walked back along the canal path.
It was only when he reached the main road that
he realised he had not asked Anna to marry him.

The Chainmakers

by

Helen Spring

Authors Choice Press
New York Lincoln Shanghai

The Chainmakers

Authors Choice Press
an imprint of iUniverse, Inc.

iUniverse books may be ordered through booksellers or by contacting:

iUniverse
2021 Pine Lake Road, Suite 100
Lincoln, NE 68512
www.iuniverse.com
1-800-Authors (1-800-288-4677)

Originally published by Commonwealth Publications

Certain characters in this work are historical figures, and certain events portrayed did take place. However, this is a work of fiction. All of the other characters, names, and events as well as all places, incidents, organizations, and dialogue in this novel are either the products of the author's imagination or are used fictitiously.

Designed by: Jennifer Brolsma

ISBN: 978-0-595-44765-7

Printed in the United States of America

For Val Orton,
my Black Country friend.

ACKNOWLEDGMENTS
AND AUTHOR'S NOTE

All the characters in this novel are entirely ficti-
tious, but I am indebted to many real Black Country people who gave so generously of their time
and experience to help me put "flesh on the bones"
on the tales I heard as a child.

I wanted to tell a story about the people of my
grandmother's day, who, in spite of the harshness
of their lives (or possibly because of it), managed
to defeat the odds by a blend of sheer endurance,
hard work and stoic humour. These characteris-
tics continued to serve many of them well when
they faced new challenges in America, and when I
began the research for this book I found these vir-
tues still alive and well in the Black Country.

My deepest thanks go to the senior keeper and
staff of the Black Country Museum, Tipton Road,
Dudley, for allowing me access to their private library, and particularly to Marjorie Cashmore and
her book *A Feast of Memories*, which was a delight
and an inspiration. Also many thanks to Ron Moss
(who I am told has chain in his blood!), chairman
of the Industrial Archaeology Group of the Black
Country Society, who did so much towards the
restoration of the old chainshop at Mushroom
Green.

Many thanks also to Joan Edmonds for her
help with the New York research.

I am very grateful to you all.

Helen Spring

CONTENTS

CONTENTS

Prelude
Aboard the *Ocean Star* 1924

Three pairs of eyes swivelled in unison to watch the departure. As the slim, elegant figure reached the doorway to the starboard deck, a uniformed officer leapt to hold open the door, and Mrs. Neville sniffed, "I've never known anyone to get such attention. Grovelling, I call it!"

"Steady on, old girl," her husband remonstrated mildly, trying in vain to get his cigarette lighter to work. "She probably tips well."

"I should think so too!" Betty Neville was not about to be kind. "If she can afford a stateroom to herself, she can afford decent tips. What do you think, Colonel?" She pushed herself back in her chair, surveying Colonel Haines with what she hoped was a languishing look.

The colonel looked slightly astonished, and Aubrey Neville, having at last managed to light his wife's cigarette, smiled broadly. "Yes, come on, Colonel, what do you really think of our dinner companion?"

The colonel hummed and hawed a little, and mumbled something about "not discussing a lady, you know."

Betty Neville gave her "silvery and tinkling" laugh, a cultivated attempt at a Mary Pickford sound, that is, if you could ascribe a sound to a silent film star. She puffed at her long, gold cigarette lighter and gave the colonel another of her looks.

"Oh, no, Colonel, you aren't getting away as easily as all that! I'm not saying anything *bad* about Mrs. Sullivan, only that it's a little...well...ill-mannered, I suppose, to leave the dinner table even before dessert is served! Two nights in a row she's done it! Anyone would think she didn't like our company!"

"I'm sure not, my dear Mrs. Neville." Privately, the colonel reflected it was a bit rich to call someone else ill-mannered, as you lit up between courses.

"Betty," her tone was soothing, "Betty, please, dear Colonel Haines."

The colonel was not about to give away his own first name. "Quite so...Betty, quite so. Well, since you insist, I find Mrs. Sullivan quite charming, quiet, I agree, but quite charming."

"Good looking, certainly," Aubrey Neville chimed in eagerly.

His wife ignored him. "Handsome is as handsome does, I always say. How can you call her charming when she hardly speaks?"

"Being seated with us at dinner doesn't mean she has to tell us her life story," Aubrey remonstrated. "You're only annoyed because you can't find out the gossip about her."

Betty Neville was about to make a sharp retort but changed her mind. "What do you mean?" she asked quickly. "What gossip?"

Aubrey laughed. "None that I know of. I don't even know who she is."

As Betty began to fume, the colonel decided to pour oil on troubled waters. "Well, I do know Mrs. Sullivan is wealthy," he ventured.

"But why is she travelling alone? Is she a widow?" Betty interrupted.

"Oh, no, her husband is probably staying in New York to look after the business. Sullivan's, you know, the restaurant chain."

Betty's mouth dropped open in horror. "She's not *that* Mrs. Sullivan? The one in all the papers? Are you sure?" Her horror gave way to annoyance. "And they put her at our table! I shall complain to the captain."

"Don't get so excited, dear. What could you complain about? That she doesn't want to talk to us?"

"Aubrey, how can you?" Betty exploded. "Why the woman is...is...almost a gangster!"

"Nonsense, old girl," Aubrey soothed. "Just because her son happened to get mixed up in something...and if I remember correctly, he was the victim anyway."

"Victim? You need talk about victims!" Betty was outraged. "It is we who are the victims, having her at our table."

"Well, dear lady, I think that may be my fault," the colonel interposed gently. "You see, we single travellers are a bit of a nuisance. They have to make up four at table, and so she was probably put here to balance me out." He stopped and gave Betty Neville his most winning smile. "If you complain, I might be moved as well, and I am enjoying your company so much. Please, be at ease, dear lady...er, Betty. I'm sure no one else on board realises who she is, and as you so rightly say, she is hardly a problem, she speaks to no one."

Betty was slightly mollified. "Well, of course I wouldn't want to lose your company, Colonel," she sniffed. "But I'm cross with you just the same. Did you know all along she was *that* Mrs. Sullivan?"

"I recognised her," the colonel admitted. "I was dining in one of the Sullivan restaurants in New

York a year or so ago, and she was pointed out to me."

"Once seen, never forgotten, eh?" Aubrey joked.

"She certainly takes the eye," Colonel Haines agreed. "And from what I hear, she has brains too."

"But surely her husband runs the business?" Aubrey put in a little petulantly.

"Yes, of course, although I believe it was Mrs. Sullivan who started it all." Colonel Haines looked around cheerfully, anxious to change the subject before Betty Neville got angry again. "Where on earth is our waiter?" he grumbled happily. "I want my pudding...."

As she wandered along the deck, Anna Sullivan smiled to herself. She knew she had put the cat among the pigeons by leaving the dinner table so abruptly, but she was unable to stand any more of Betty Neville's idle chatter. Her husband was almost as bad, and Anna felt no pangs of guilt about them, but she had not intended to be rude to poor Colonel Haines. Anna recalled how the startled old gentleman had struggled to his feet as she left the table, and she resolved to apologise when she next saw him. Reaching the sun deck, she looked around for a deck chair, and immediately the deck steward appeared.

"In just a moment, Mrs. Sullivan," he said cheerfully. He fetched a chair and opened it up. "Will this do? Would you like a rug?"

"Thank you. Yes, a rug is a good idea." Anna smiled and settled herself in the deck chair. The service was good aboard the *Ocean Star*, and she was beginning to enjoy the trip. It had been difficult for the first couple of days; her mind had been in such turmoil. But now that the ship was well away from New York, and she had woken on two consecutive mornings to face nothing but the vast Atlantic Ocean, her problems seemed cut down to size, and she was beginning to relax.

"There we are, madam," the cheerful steward said, tucking the rug around her. "Can I get you anything else?"

"No, nothing, thank you."

Anna smiled at the man and settled back comfortably. It was almost eight o'clock and yet she could still feel the warmth of the sun on her face. It had been a wonderful day and she had made the most of it. It was not usual to have such good weather crossing the Atlantic, even in mid-summer. Last time....

She could not really remember what the weather had been last time, it was so long ago, and her memory was hazy. It had been almost twenty years, she calculated, since she had travelled third class from Liverpool to New York, and there had not been a moment when she was not cold, uncomfortable and sick. What a young fool she had been then, and how unhappy. How strange that a chance meeting when she was ten years old was to have such a marked effect on her life....

PART ONE

SANDLEY HEATH

An Offer
1904

"A sweet little lass—such as Sir John Millais would have liked to paint—dancing on a pair of bellows for 3d a day to supply 'blast' to the chainmaker at the forge, and to put 3d a day into the pocket of her employer. As she danced, her golden hair flew out, and the fiery sparks which showered upon her head reminded me of fireflies seen at night near Florence, dancing over a field of ripe wheat...."

Robert Sherard, *The Chainmakers of Cradley Heath*, 1896

Anna Gibson was almost eighteen when she saw Robert Nicholson for the second time. She felt no pang of recognition; the handsome, fair-haired young man chatting to old Ma Higgins bore no resemblance to the spindly youth of his teens. However, Anna couldn't help but glance at him again, and as a result, she mis-hit the iron link she was closing. A frown flitted across her brow as she concentrated repeated hammer blows on the red hot link in a shower of fiery sparks, and then, satisfied the link was successfully forged into the chain, she turned to pull on the bellows. As she made to pluck the next glowing iron rod from the fire, she heard Ma Higgins call, "'Ang on, ma wench, this gentleman wants a waerd."

Anna stood apprehensively as they made their way towards her through the chainshop. They were watched by the other women, who had stopped their hammering and chattering to stare at the unexpected sight of a young man, clean and well dressed at that, picking his way through the debris. As they reached her, Anna's face hardened with suspicion.

"'E only wants a waerd," Ma Higgins wheezed, "but doe be tew long. Them cart traces is urgent."

"Good morning, Miss Gibson," the young man began. "I hope you don't mind my asking for you."

"What's it about?" Her voice was softer and more refined than he had expected in this hellhole. He smiled encouragingly, but she quickly added, "I ay done nothin'."

"Of course you haven't, Miss Gibson. I assure you there is no trouble of any kind." He smiled again before continuing lightly, "You don't remember me, do you?"

Anna eyed him narrowly. "No. Should I?"

"Probably not, but perhaps you remember my father, Andrew Nicholson." He waited for a glimmer of recognition, but seeing none, he continued, "Father sketched you several times when you were about ten years old."

"Oh, yes!" A look of delight passed over her face, and Robert Nicholson realised for the first time that perhaps his plan would work. When she smiled, her features were quite delightful underneath all that grime. He inspected her face closely as she added excitedly, "'Course I remember. And he did the paintings afterwards...and one of them was in the exhibition at Dudley Art Gallery and we all went to see it.... We had a real day out." She stopped suddenly, as if aware she was talking too much. Then, in a faltering tone, she said, "You'm Robert, his boy?"

"Yes, that's right. I'm afraid my father died last year, Miss Gibson."

"Oh." She looked nonplussed for a moment, and then said with genuine concern, "I'm real sorry, Mr. Nicholson."

"Thank you, and the name is Robert. I believe your name is Anna?"

"Yes." A slight suspicion reasserted itself and a questioning look came over her face.

"Well, Anna, you probably wonder why I have looked you up after all this time. The truth is, I came across Father's sketches the other day and thought how good they were. As well as being charming in their own right, there is a certain honesty, the same clarity of vision I admire so much in Chardin." Realising he had lost her completely, Robert added quickly, "Anyway, I thought it would be interesting to do some paintings of you now you are grown...a continuum...the child, and the woman she became...a triptych perhaps."

He had lost her again, but she asked quickly, "You want to sketch me? You'm a painter, too, like your dad?"

He laughed, and Anna thought he looked quite wonderful, better looking than any man she ever saw in her life, even Clancy.

"Father wasn't really a painter, Anna. He was a businessman."

"Oh, yes," she agreed quickly, "I know he owned factories and all that."

"Even so, he was very interested in art, and was quite well thought of for an amateur," Robert continued cheerfully. "I take after him, at least as far as artistic temperament is concerned. Business is a different matter. I have no head for business at all, and no interest in it, either, if truth be told." His easy smile made lack of business sense seem like a virtue, and he added in a confiding tone, "I'm going to be a real artist, Anna, not an amateur. I intend to make art my life's work."

"Oh, I see," Anna replied. She didn't see at all. How could painting pictures be considered work?

"Well, now I've explained, will you sit for me?" Robert asked.

"Oh, sir, I'd love to, but I'm working now, as you can see, and can't spare the time. I work from eight to six."

"And how much does that pay?" Robert interrupted.

"Well, this is number one size," Anna explained. "If I can make a hundredweight and a half, like I did last week, I'll get about eight shillings." She smiled at him openly and then added, "But I have to pay for my gledes out of that."

"And you don't work at weekends?"

"No." Anna did not mention that Saturday was the family day for the copper, and she spent it washing and ironing, cleaning and blackleading the firegrate.

"I'll pay you ten shillings to sit for me at weekends," Robert stated firmly. "You can travel to my home at Edgbaston on the Saturday morning, sit for three hours in the afternoon, stay overnight, sit another three hours on Sunday morning and travel back on Sunday afternoon."

Anna, stunned by the suddenness of the offer, could not reply. In her mind, two words resounded again and again. Ten shillings...ten shillings...ten whole shillings! Just for sitting around doing nothing. She gazed at Robert, but still was unable to speak.

"Everything would be completely respectable, of course," he hastened to assure her, mistaking her silence for distrust of his motives. "My mother will see you are allocated a room in the servants' quarters. We have more rooms than servants." He smiled, attempting to allay her fears.

Anna swallowed. What would her father say? And how would her mother manage without her at the weekend? In a flash, she had the answer. Pay old Mother Smithson to do the washing and ironing; she would be glad of the chance to do it for a shilling, and the blackleading too, and there would still be nine shillings over.

"I'd pay for your travelling costs, of course," Robert was saying. "There's probably a Saturday cart coming to Edgbaston, but if there isn't, you could get on the canal boat and be in Birmingham in two hours, and I could send our trap to pick you up there."

He looked at Anna expectantly, and although she was quivering with excitement at the prospect of earning so much extra money, all that came out of her mouth was, "I'll miss chapel."

"Well, yes, I suppose so, but you would be back on Sunday in time for evensong...if you have evensong in chapel," Robert responded quickly, "We are Church of England," he added almost apologetically.

"We have an evening meeting," Anna said quietly. "Yes, I'd be back in time for that." She pulled herself together and gave Robert her rare smile. "If my dad agrees," she said, "I'll be glad to do it. How many weekends were you thinking of?"

"I don't really know," Robert answered, pleased with his success. "Several I should think, up until Christmas, anyway. That will be about ten weekends, perhaps." He smiled briefly. "I have business in Dudley now, but may I call back this evening to obtain your father's permission?"

Anna smiled assent and gave him her address. Robert thanked her and made his way out of the chainshop, turning to wave his hand as he went. In a moment, Anna was besieged by the other women, who were demanding to know what was going on. Ribald comments flew around the chainshop about Robert's good looks, and when she had explained his errand, there was a great deal of screeching laughter and expressions of disbelief, and not a little envy. After Ma Higgins had scolded them back to work, the women continued to yell at each other above their hammering, and there was much laughter and speculation about models having to take off their clothes for dirty-minded artists to paint them.

"There'll be none of that!" Anna remonstrated, blushing furiously in spite of herself. "If he starts any of that malarkey, I'll come home. Anyway," she added, "I'm sure he won't ask any such thing. His dad never asked me to take my clothes off."

This was met with further gales of mirth, and old Betty Potts, making spikes at the forge in the corner, wiped the tears from her eyes on her sacking apron and cackled, "What a ninny yo' am, Anna Gibson. Yo' was ten years old then!"

This was met with more screeches of laughter and shouts of "It's a bit different now, ma babby!" and "You'm in for a shock!" until Ma Higgins came in and reminded them that if they didn't want to work for her there were plenty of others that did.

The sparks flew as they settled back to their hammering, and after Ma Higgins had left the chainshop, Betty Potts wheezed, "Miserable old glede. 'Er's the waerst fogger I ever knowed."

"No, 'er ay," shouted a young woman who had recently joined the team. "Yo' should waerk for old Stubbin's. 'Er's the waerst, bar none."

"Arr," several voices agreed quickly. It was a dread that haunted them, that they could lose their work and be forced to make chain for Ma Stubbings. Her wages were lower for every size of chain, so you had to work longer and harder to make ends meet. The laughter had died, and the only further comment came from old Betty, who shouted above the din that perhaps Anna's dad would not let her go. After all, staying overnight in a strange house....

"He'll let me go," Anna shouted back confidently as she pulled at the bellows. *If he don't, it's all the same*, she thought, as she took another glowing rod from the fire and began to hammer. *I'm going to do it, and he won't stop me.* Expertly she cut in on the hardy and twisted the red hot link, inserting it into the previous link of the chain and beginning to hammer again. *I'll meet Dad from work and get him home before he has chance to get to the pub*, she resolved. *Once he gets in the Sandley Arms, I'll never get him out. Anyway, it makes no odds if he's drunk or sober, I'm not missing out on a chance like this.*

Surprisingly, Anna had more problems convincing her mother than her father. Catching George Gibson when he was sober had been the right approach, and as she hurried him home, explaining along the way, she only had to mention the extra money and he readily agreed. He even put on a clean paper collar to meet Robert Nicholson.

Her mother was against it in principle, but wanted the money. "Why can't he come here and sketch you?" she moaned, in her soft, north Worcester accent.

"I don't know, Mom," Anna said with some irritation.

Anna had never been able to understand how her mother, a gentle soul who could read and write well, could have been so attracted to George Gibson that she had given up the comparative luxury of life on her father's farm and defied her parents to marry him. As she busied herself in the small back room, waiting for Robert Nicholson to arrive, the incongruity of her parents match flitted across Anna's mind again. She wondered what Robert Nicholson would make of them, her father, huge and sweaty, struggling to fasten the paper collar around his thick, bull neck, and her mother, frail now and largely confined to her chair by the firegrate, nevertheless managing to convey an air of delicate gentility amid her poverty-stricken surroundings. Anna felt a pang of sympathy and knelt down by her mother's chair.

"Mom, I don't know why he wants me to go to Edgbaston," she explained quietly. "I only know that, for ten shillings, I'd be a fool to miss the chance."

"I still don't see why he can't come here," Sarah said plaintively. "His dad sketched you at the forge, didn't he?"

"Well, we can ask him when he comes," Anna responded patiently. "But I think he wants to paint me, not just sketch, and anyway, he probably wants a different sort of background. I don't know."

"But how shall we manage for the washing? You know Saturday is our day for the copper, and I can't manage to do it...."

"Mother," Anna said sharply, her patience wearing thin, "I have told you already Ma Smithson has said she will do it for a shilling. I knew she would."

"Paying out a whole shilling for someone else to do our washing when I've got a daughter perfectly capable...."

"I can't be in two places at once. And the shilling will be paid from what I earn at Mr. Nicholson's. Do try to understand."

"Understand? I understand you won't be here this Saturday, and I've no shilling to pay Ma Smithson this week, and neither have you, I'll warrant."

"I've already thought of that. I'm going to wash Friday night, after Mrs. Ketts has finished. She says she'll be done by four o'clock and has promised she'll fill the copper again for me and make up the fire if you let her have the gledes when she calls. You can give her the washing, and she will put it in so it will be ready for me to dolly when I get home from work. I'll have to iron on Sunday when I get home."

"Iron on a Sunday? Not in my house!"

Anna sighed and got to her feet. "Then I'll have to do it on Monday night, won't I?" She was dejected. Her wonderful news was not producing the hoped for effect.

Her mother was about to raise some other objection, but to Anna's relief the back door opened and her brother Will arrived with his seven-year-old son Billy.

"Just called in with young Billy, Mom.... 'Ello. What's to do, then?" Will stopped at the unfamiliar sight of his father home from work early and wearing a collar above his flannelette shirt.

"We're waiting on a gentleman, wants to sketch our Anna," his mother explained, and Anna was heartened to detect a hint of pride in her mother's voice.

Anna turned to Will eagerly. "Mr. Nicholson. You remember, Will. He sketched me before...when I was little. He's dead now, but his son wants to paint me grown, and he's offering ten shillings for me to go and sit at his place at Edgbaston. Three hours Saturday afternoon and three hours Sunday."

"Well, I'm blowed! Theer's a bit o' luck!" Will's smile broadened in his handsome face. "Yo' mek the most on it while yer can, our kid!" Unlike Anna, he spoke with a broad Black Country dialect, which rolled off his tongue with relish as he turned to his son. "'Ow about that, our Billy? Yer Auntie Anna's gunna be rich!"

"So am I!" Billy responded immediately. "When I grow up, I'm gunna be rich as anythin'!"

"Start now, then," Anna said quickly, fishing in her pocket and pulling out two pennies. "Run to Mrs. Skitt's on the corner and get me a penny lump of Hudson's soap and a ha'penny blue. With the other ha'penny, you can get a bag of boilers for yourself."

"A bag o' boilers!" Billy's face was a picture.

"Yes, from your rich auntie. Go along now. Walk, don't run."

They all laughed as Billy sped away down the ginnel which ran between their house, number twenty-two Dawkins Street, and number twenty-four next door. Will said uncertainly, "Do yo' want me to go? I might be in the way like."

"Of course not," Anna said quickly.

"Tell yer what...when 'e comes I'll nip in the parlour till 'e's gone."

"If you like. There certainly isn't much room in here."

"It won't tek long," said George Gibson rather aggressively. "I just 'ave to make sure what's what, that he's all above board like. Let him know he don't have everything his own way for the askin'. And when he's gone, we'll go for a pint or two, our Will. I'm as dry as a lime burner's clog."

"All right, Dad, but I can only 'ave one. Got to get back." Will was not about to be drawn into a heavy drinking session with his father. One drunkard in the family was quite enough.

Ten minutes later, the visit was over and the two men were on their way to the Sandley Arms, Will asserting once again that he could not stay long, as he had to get Billy home. Robert Nicholson had charmed George and Sarah Gibson with his honest good looks and impeccable manners, and had left the small house having agreed upon everything within minutes. Will, listening behind the parlour door, had been astonished to hear his father almost grovelling in his efforts to please, and his mother's objections had disappeared as if by magic. As he and his father entered the Sandley Arms, Will remarked dryly, "I noticed the way yo' told him what was what!"

"Well, I dae need to lay it on thick," said George. "Yo' can always tell a gentleman. Anyway, yo' need talk, runnin' 'ome after one drink to report to Mary."

"I do' need to report, Dad," Will retorted sharply. "I 'appen to like my time at 'ome, and I've more sense than spend all my 'ard earned wages in the pub."

They caught the barman's eye and George ordered two pints and then turned to his son. "Yo' know what they say, lad," he admonished, searching through the change in his pocket, "'Never be 'ooman licked.'"

Will laughed. "I ay 'ooman licked, Dad, and if I remember right, they say, 'Never let yer navel get too close to yer backbone' an' all. If yo' do' save a bit an' stop spendin' so much in 'ere, yer'll find yer navel a bit close to yer backbone in a few years. You'm not gettin' any younger." He picked up his pint and took a deep swallow, and George snorted. His son, he thought, had become a real nancy boy since he got married.

As she lay in her narrow bed that night, Anna's mind was full of the adventure which promised for the weekend. She had never been further than Dudley, her few excursions being confined to the chapel outing on anniversary day and an occasional Sunday trip to the Clent hills with Clancy. She thought again of Robert Nicholson and wondered what he had thought of her home. That they were living on the bread line would be immediately obvious to him or anyone else.

They had always managed somehow when Will was around. His contribution to the family budget had made a big difference, and he would often bring home some small treat, perhaps a cake or some boiled sweets made by a neighbour and sold at her front doorway. When Will had married his Mary and moved into the next street, number twenty-two had become cheerless and quiet, except for the times when George Gibson got really drunk and raised the neighbourhood, which seemed to be happening with increasing frequency.

The poverty of their existence was foremost in Anna's mind as she lay in bed, hugging a hot brick wrapped in an old piece of blanket. As she recalled Robert Nicholson's visit, she consoled herself with the thought that everything had been as spotless as she could make it. She was proud of the shining blackleaded firegrate and its brass oven knob, carefully polished twice a week, and the cheerful homemade rag rug on the hearth. She tried to imagine what the Nicholson house would be like, and decided it must be grand if he could afford to pay ten shillings every week for someone to sit around and be painted.

I wonder what Clancy will think, she mused. There had been no opportunity to tell him about the offer, and she suddenly realised he might not like the idea. It would mean they would not be able to see each other for a while, and she would miss him. *But after all,* she told herself as she drifted into sleep, *ten shillings is ten shillings.*

It seemed only a moment later that she was woken by a noise in the street outside. "Oh no, not again!" Anna said as she quickly roused herself and threw her shawl over her flannel nightgown. She hurried downstairs, only stopping to say, "It's all right. It's only Dad," as her mother opened her bedroom door.

In the street, the situation was worse than usual. Her father, stupefied with drink, had started a fight with Bert Castle, a puddler who lived a few doors down. Bert usually did not rise to the bait, but tonight he had been drinking heavily himself and was almost as far gone as George Gibson. The two men were brawling and shouting, but doing little damage due to the inability of either of them to land a punch. Anna ran across to her father and caught at his arm.

"Come away now, Dad, come away...."

"I'll flatten the bugger!" George Gibson yelled, slurring his words and making a wild sweep at Bert. He put down his head and ran forwards, butting Bert in the stomach and sending him flying. The momentum carried George onwards, and he crashed into the side of the house just as Bert's wife came out of her front door.

"What on earth's to do?" Her stony gaze took in her husband attempting to get up on the pavement opposite, and then George Gibson, who had slid down the wall and now lay on his back, waving his arms like a stranded beetle.

She turned her fury on Anna. "Your father again, Anna Gibson! 'E's a disgrace to the street!" She crossed to Bert and helped him up. "'E should be ashamed, gettin' our Bert drunk!"

"I don't suppose Dad had to hold his nose and pour it down his throat," Anna countered crossly.

She tried to help George to his feet, but he had collapsed into a stupor and it was impossible for Anna to lift him.

"Get 'im off the pavement. I don't want 'im spendin' the night outside my front door," Bert's wife said angrily, as she cajoled and pushed Bert across the road and into the house. "Your ma need put on airs an' graces, Anna Gibson, married to a drunk like 'im!"

"No need to be like that, Millie. I'll move him as quick as I can. I'll have to fetch our Will."

Anna sighed. It was no use trying to wake her father once he had drifted off like this. She heard Millie's front door slam as she hurried down the street, trying not to notice the neighbours who had come out onto their front doorsteps or peered down from bedroom windows. The embarrassment was becoming too much, she thought, but there was little either she or her mother could do about it.

Reaching Will's house, she knocked gently. It was a prearranged knock which signalled to Will that she needed help with their father. Within a couple of minutes, the small front door opened and Will emerged, pulling on his jacket and cap.

"What's to do this time?" he grumbled. "I'd just gone off to sleep."

"He's on the pavement outside Bert Castle's. Fighting they were. I can't wake him."

Five minutes later, Will and Anna had managed to get George Gibson into the small back room. He was a dead weight and Will gasped as he lowered him gently to the floor.

"There." He held his father up so that Anna could remove his jacket, and then lowered him again to rest on the rag rug in front of the fire. "That's as far as 'e's goin' tonight. We'll never get 'im up the stairs." He glanced up at Anna as he started to undo George Gibson's boots. "Yo' shouldn't come out in your nightgown, Anna. It ay decent for one thing, an' yo'll catch yer death for another."

"I had my shawl on. An' Millie Castle wanted 'im moved quick."

"Let 'er wait," Will said shortly. "An' let 'im wait an' all." He looked down at his father, a mixture of anger and disgust on his face. "Better get a bucket, our Anna, in case 'e wakes up took short. 'E'd never make it to the yard."

Anna nodded and fetched the floor bucket from outside the back door. She turned a worried face to Will. "What about Saturday night, Will? When I'm not here? Mom won't be able to manage."

Will grunted as he pulled off George Gibson's heavy boots. "Do' worry, our kid. I'll mek sure 'e's safe inside on Saturday, even if I 'ave to yank 'im out the pub!"

"And Mom? You'll...."

"Do' worry, I said!" Will gave her a wink. "I'll mek sure they'm both safe an' sound."

He stood up and made his way to the back door, his big frame almost filling the space as Anna opened it. On an impulse, Anna reached up and planted a kiss on his cheek. "You'm a gem, our Will," she said.

Will cleared his throat, taken aback by this unexpected show of sisterly affection. "Arr, I know," he growled. "It's a wonder I ay bin knighted." And he set off down the ginnel, back to his bed.

High Cedars

Anna stared fixedly at the picture in front of her, which Robert had propped up on a low side table so that she could see it easily without lifting her head. "There," he had said, "You can sit and look at *The Chainmaker's Child*; it will help you keep still."

The picture was a painting of herself at ten years old, bouncing on the bellows at the chainshop where her Dad worked, but Anna found it hard to identify with the rosy-cheeked image. Had she ever really looked like that? Had she been so pretty? She remembered bouncing on the bellows day after day, but the child in the picture seemed to be enjoying it. Anna recalled the heat and the tiredness and the way the big, grey-headed man in the corner used to snarl at her if the blast to the furnace wasn't enough, and then she would have to jump on the bellows harder and harder and faster and faster....

And that pinafore. In the picture, it looked a soft, floating material, but Anna recalled it was made of thick crash, rough enough to take your skin off before it had been washed a few times. She had worn the pinafore for years, letting down the big hem every year or so.

And the hair too. As a child, she had often been complimented on her hair, which was a reddish gold colour and very thick and curly, but had it really had those lights in it? She studied the picture intently. The child's hair was streaming out, and through it, you could see the sparks flying from the shadowy figures of the chainmakers in the background. If her hair had ever been that colour, she thought, it certainly wasn't now. As she had grown, the reddish-gold tints had faded to a tawny bronze, like the colour of the big lion in the picture book of animals at school. Her hair still had a natural kink, however, and Anna was grateful that she never had to spend time putting her hair in rags like so many of her friends did in order to have a few curls for Sunday chapel.

She eased herself slightly in her seat; her bottom was stiff. She glanced across at Robert, and as if sensing her discomfort, he murmured "Not long now. Another ten minutes or so and we'll stop."

We'll stop. Another ten minutes and it would be over, her first weekend at High Cedars. Then she would be on her way home, which would be another adventure in itself, for Robert had said the groom would take her in the trap to catch the three o'clock canal barge. Anna had been in a trap only once in her life, and never on a canal boat, and at the thought of it, excitement gripped her stomach again so that for the tenth time that weekend she felt slightly sick. She swallowed and tried to calm herself. The boat would drop her only a mile or so from Sandley Heath, and she should be home by six o'clock. Although it would be getting dark, she would enjoy the walk after all this sitting about. She had so much to tell her mom and Will and Clancy. How the girls would lap it up tomorrow when she described the great house, and Robert's kindness, and his statuesque and perfectly groomed mother who had said Anna was not to call her "Ma'am" but "Florence," because "you are not a servant, my dear, and you must dine with us."

Anna's stomach clenched again as she recalled her horror at being confronted by the gleaming white tablecloth, set with beautiful silver, crystal glasses and spotless napkins. Robert had sensed her unease and had asked quietly whether she would prefer to eat with the servants in the kitchen, and Anna had been happy to agree until Florence intervened.

"No, Robert. I know Anna ate in the kitchen when she arrived, but that was because I was not aware she was here." She turned to Anna. "I realise you may not be accustomed to the cutlery, my dear, but I will show you which to use. It's very easy, and how will you learn if you don't try?" She motioned Anna to a seat. "Just relax, Anna. We have no guests this evening; Robert and I were dining alone. I want to get to know you better."

After a short time, Anna began to enjoy herself, especially the delicious food, which was brought to the table in large dishes from which they helped themselves. "We are very informal tonight." Florence smiled at her, and although Anna had no idea what was meant by this, she gathered that, if guests were present, it would be even more grand.

The courses followed one after the other, and Anna, clearing her plate each time, began to feel very full. When the pudding came, a delicious, spongy confection filled with apples, Anna blurted out, "It's lovely, but I'm as full as a gun!"

She blushed as Robert laughed out loud and told her she was wonderful, a breath of fresh air.

Florence, too, was laughing, and then said kindly, "Don't worry, Anna. We are not laughing at you, but with you. Robert is quite right, it has been a tonic to have you here this weekend, and I'm so glad you will be coming regularly. Now, let me give you a little advice for when we have guests, because then there will be more courses than we have had tonight."

"More?" Anna was astounded.

"Yes, six at least and sometimes more. But my dear," she leaned forward confidentially, "it is not strictly necessary to eat every last scrap!"

"Oh!" Anna blushed. "I see." She did indeed. She had noticed Florence Nicholson leave half her food on her plate and had thought it a criminal waste, but deduced she was perhaps not feeling too well.

"Just eat a little of everything to be polite, and a little more of anything you particularly like," Florence explained. "Then you won't be too full."

"And when I come here, I'll eat with you and your guests on Saturdays?" Anna asked nervously.

"Of course."

"But I'm not sure.... I don't know..."

"My dear," Florence put a hand over Anna's and smiled at her, "your manners are a credit to you and your mother. You have nothing to be nervous about. I shall always seat you where you can watch me. Your behaviour is far superior to that of some of the young ladies Robert sees fit to invite." She said this in a tone of admonition, but Robert only laughed again and said Anna would be a tonic in any company.

Anna wriggled slightly in her seat as she remembered the meal. Perhaps she shouldn't tell the girls too much about it. They might think she was showing off, especially if she told them about being put in what Florence called the second guest room instead of the servants' quarters. *If that was the second guest room*, Anna mused, *heaven alone knows what the first must be like*. It was so big, with a lovely fire lit, and a thick rug and an easy

chair and pretty curtains, which the maid had
come in to draw as Anna was getting ready for
dinner. That had simply entailed putting on her
Sunday chapel skirt and blouse, which was all she
possessed apart from the black alpaca she wore
to work covered by a big "baggin" apron made from
boiled sugar bags. Anna smiled gently to herself
as she remembered how the maid had brought
hot water for her to wash in the big blue and white
china bowl on the washstand, and the piece of
soap that smelled of violets. And then, after that
wonderful meal, when she had snuggled down into
the crisp, white, lavender-scented sheets, she had
given her body over to the luxurious softness of
the big bed, a softness she had never realised existed, accustomed as she was to the hard, straw
palliasse which had been handed down to her when
Will left home.

The only thing that hadn't been right was her
clothes. She had arrived in her black alpaca, intending to change into her best skirt and blouse
for the first sitting, but Robert would have none of
it, and was most annoyed when he found she had
not brought her baggin apron.

"Don't you understand, Anna?" he had said
quite crossly, pacing the big studio which ran
across the back of the house. "I want to paint you
as you are, as a chainmaker. That's the whole point
of the exercise, so I need you in your working
clothes. You've changed your hair, too," he added
accusingly.

"I just washed and curled it last night, so it
would look nice for the sitting," Anna explained,
unable to understand his attitude. "I just
thought...."

"Well, don't think!" Robert said firmly. "Remember, I want to paint you as a chainmaker, and I

want your hair just as usual, done up, but some bits straggling down...how it was when I saw you at the chainshop. Although," he added, his good humour quickly returning, "I don't object to your washing your face, or your hair either, for that matter." He reached across and took a thick lock of her hair in his hand. "Yes," he murmured to himself, "washing it will help the light. It's a lovely colour."

He smiled, and Anna trembled slightly as she tried to recover from the shock of his hand on her hair. No man had ever touched her hair like that, stroked it and caressed it, not even Clancy Sullivan, and they had been walking out these eight months. Robert seemed oblivious to her unease, and after saying he supposed he could do the domestic picture first, went out of the room. When he returned, he sat her down on a chair, gave her a tray cloth and a needle and thread and told her she was supposed to be sewing.

Now Anna gazed doubtfully at the tray cloth, wondering if Robert would mind if she brought some real sewing with her. It seemed such a waste of time to sit doing nothing, even though she was being paid for it, and she could have turned a couple of her dad's collars in the time she'd been sitting here.

The door opened and Florence came in, saying, "Sorry to interrupt, but I wanted a word with Anna before she goes."

"I'm finished," said Robert, laying down his brush. "At least for today."

"Can I see?" Anna hopped down from the chair and hurried over to the easel. "Oh!" Her face mirrored the disappointment in her voice. There seemed little change from the rough composition of lines and shapes from the day before, and certainly nothing which even began to resemble herself. "It's...er...." She stopped, nonplussed, and Robert laughed out loud.

"It's a very good start, Anna," he said, still laughing. "I'm really pleased."

"Yes," Florence agreed, "I can see the perspective is going to be right. You see, Anna, it won't begin to be a real likeness for some while yet."

"Oh, I see," Anna said, privately thinking it seemed an awful amount of time and expense just to have a picture on the wall. With all their money, they could easily have gone into Dudley and bought one.

"Anyway," Florence said firmly, "Anna needs a cup of tea before she leaves. Come along now, my dear."

Florence hurried out of the room, and Anna followed, but as she reached the door, Robert said, "Just a second."

He fished in his pocket and found four half crowns. "Ten shillings, as arranged, and here's another shilling for your boat fare. I'll see you again next Saturday."

Anna beamed. "Thank you. Yes, I'll be here. Goodbye, Mr. Nicholson...er...Robert."

She followed Florence down the wide staircase with a feeling of real excitement, the four half crowns and the shilling almost burning her hand. It had not seemed quite real until now, but already she was planning how she would spend the money.

Florence led her to the elegant drawing room, where the maid had already brought in tea, and motioned Anna to a seat. "My dear, I hope you will not be offended at what I am going to suggest," she said carefully.

"Well...I don't know until I hear it."

Florence laughed. "Oh Anna, you are such a treat. Don't ever change, will you?"

"I...I don't really know what you mean."

"Lots of young women these days are so false, so...so devious and artful. You say just what you think, and I find that very refreshing. Anyway," Florence continued as she handed Anna her tea, "I wanted to tell you about next week. We are having a dinner party on Saturday evening, not many, ten or twelve at most, but I thought you might be more comfortable, er...feel more at ease if you had something nice to wear."

"Oh. I have my Sunday skirt and blouse. You saw them last night."

"Yes, and they are very nice, but for a dinner party you need something a little more dressy. Nothing too frivolous, but...."

"I'm afraid I don't have anything like that," Anna interrupted, "but I shall be very happy to have my dinner in the kitchen."

"Absolutely not!" Florence responded quickly. "That is not what I meant at all. I wondered if you would mind if I bought you a dress?" Receiving no response from Anna, she continued quickly, "If you leave your measurements with me, I can get one made up for next weekend. My dressmaker is very good, that is, if you will trust yourself to my taste."

Anna still did not reply. She was completely overcome. A dress...and a grand one at that! She could never wear it at home, of course, but it would be so good to have a nice dress here, so she would not let Robert and his mother down. She swallowed and then stammered, "Oh! You are so kind. I don't know what to say."

"Oh good! Then it's settled. I shall have great fun choosing for you!" Florence took a sip from her teacup and confided, "I always wanted a daughter. I should have so enjoyed dressing her up! This will give me a chance to indulge myself."

"Is Robert your only child, then?" Anna asked. As soon as she had said it, she wondered if the question was impolite, but Florence smiled and said cheerfully, "Oh, no, I have another son, my eldest, Andrew, named after his father. You will meet him next Saturday; he and his wife will be coming to dinner. He looks after the business; he's very good at it," she added.

Anna smiled. "Robert told me he is not good at business," she said carefully. "He's going to be an artist, isn't he? A real one?"

Florence grimaced. "We must hope so. He could probably be good at business if he was the slightest bit interested, but he isn't, so we must hope he has talent in other directions."

She rose and pulled the bell cord. "I will get Mary to bring in a tape measure. We must make sure you don't miss the barge."

Ten minutes later, having taken a note of Anna's measurements, Florence escorted her to the front door, where the groom awaited with the trap.

"Goodbye, Anna," she said, smiling. "Climb aboard now. We'll see you next week."

"Thank you, Florence. Thank you so much for everything."

"Oh...Anna," Florence called as the trap began to move away, "just to please Robert, don't forget your baggin apron!"

It was just after five o'clock when Anna alighted from the barge to find Clancy waiting for her.

"How did you know I'd be here?" she asked, delighted to see him.

"Just a guess," he said laconically, as they began to walk along the towpath. "Your mam and dad said you might be coming back on the boat. I'll not be wanting you walking home alone."

Anna settled happily into step alongside him. She loved to hear Clancy talk. Although he had lived in Sandley Heath since he was ten years old, he still had a slight Irish brogue which she found attractive.

"Oh, Clancy, I've had such a time, you'll never believe."

Clancy smiled at her, and his blue Irish eyes twinkled. "I thought you might. You'd best tell me all about it, then."

They entered the dark lane which led up to the main road, where the soot-blackened tree branches straggled weakly against the leaden sky, and Anna shivered. Clancy slipped his arm around her waist, and they strolled together, deep in conversation, Anna extolling the delights of life at High Cedars. Just before they reached the road, Clancy pulled her to him and planted a light kiss on her lips.

"I'm so glad," he said, "so glad you've enjoyed it. I was thinking of you, so I was."

Anna remembered Clancy's words when she went to bed that night, earlier than usual because, as it was Sunday, her mother refused to allow her to do the ironing, and because she wanted time alone to think about everything that had happened. Clancy was such a dear, she thought. So reliable and kind, you knew where you were with Clancy. In spite of the fact that he and his mother lived in that miserable hovel in Deakin Street, with only one tiny room downstairs and a loft above, reached by a wooden ladder, there were not two more kindly people in existence. Things had been hard for Mrs. Sullivan since she was widowed when Clancy was twelve years old, but somehow or other, she had managed to bring up her son as a decent and hardworking lad, and Anna knew his interest in her was serious.

She let her mind wander again over the events of the weekend, thinking of the dress Florence intended to have made for her and wondering what colour it would be. This was the one thing she had not confided to anyone at home, not even Clancy. It would seem like showing off, she felt. Nevertheless, she let her mind dwell on the dress, anticipating the style and the width of the skirt, would it have a low neck and the new sleeves?

Just before she fell asleep, a last thought crossed her mind. Next week there would be another ten shillings.

Two Worlds

The baggin apron, as it happened, was not needed for several weeks. Robert decided to complete the domestic scene of Anna seated over her sewing, the tray cloth now having been replaced by a flannelette shirt which Anna was making for her dad. When she had asked with some diffidence if she might bring her sewing with her, Robert had laughed and said of course she must, adding with surprise, "You didn't really think I was going to paint you sewing a tray cloth, did you?"

"I...I didn't know."

"Anna, try to understand. Do you ever sit and embroider a tray cloth like that at home?"

"No. We don't have trays at home."

"Precisely. I have told you before, I want to paint you as you are. I only gave you the tray cloth to hold so I could get the position of the arms right."

"Oh, I see."

Every week when Anna arrived at High Cedars, she found her portrait a little more alive, a little more like herself. It was fascinating to watch the progress. During the week, while she worked at the forge, Robert would continue to paint from memory, but by the time Saturday came, he was usually frustrated and angry at his efforts, only beginning to calm down when he had Anna seated before him and could check what he had done. The Saturday afternoon session was therefore very concentrated, and Robert would rarely speak, apart from an occasional murmur of "of course!" or "ah, yes!" or "that's better!"

When he was so engrossed, Anna would often steal a glance at him, committing to memory the line of his head, the way his smooth, fair hair was clipped straight across his neck, and how a piece at the front sometimes fell across his eyes, to be flipped aside with a quick shake of the head. These memories Anna would resurrect during the following week, as she hammered at the red hot iron rods; as the weeks went by, the impressions became more insistent, until she saw Robert shake his head in the flying sparks, saw Robert's eyes in the glowing coals, and heard Robert's voice in the very air she breathed, cutting through the tumultuous din of the chainshop. She knew it was a useless fixation and was a little ashamed of it, particularly when she thought of Clancy. When these feelings intruded, she told herself there was no harm in dreaming as long as it hurt no one. It was like being in love with a hero in a story, wonderful to feel, but having nothing to do with real life.

Anna now knew several of the dinner guests who had been invited to High Cedars, and had met Robert's elder brother Andrew, a tall, elegant man with long, bony fingers and a kind smile. He talked to her at length about the family business and proved to have inherited all the sensitivity and kindness of his mother, explaining his views and encouraging her interest, without a hint of patronage. Robert Nicholson and his family, their lovely home and gardens, their friends and dinner parties, were so far removed from the drudgery of Sandley Heath that it seemed to Anna that she led two lives. In one, she wore a grand dress, spoke carefully, and drank wine from a crystal glass in the company of people who laughed a lot and were witty and interesting. In her other life, she emptied the chamber pots before she went to work, pushed her father up the narrow stairs to bed when he was drunk, and helped her mother in and out of the tin bath which was set in front of the fire every Friday night. At work she was hot, dirty and exhausted most of the time, but as soon as she left the chainshop, she was freezing cold in the raw December air which penetrated her thin shawl. It was a world of constant noise and blistered hands as she hammered as if to save her life, trying to shut out the screeching of Ma Higgins, who exhorted her to "gerron wi' it, Miss Toffeenose. No time fer yer fancy notions 'ere."

The only comfort which had crept into this second life of Anna's was provided by the extra money. She now bought an extra booster each day, and quite often there was enough of the big loaf left to be made into a delicious bread pudding, which her mother cooked in the oven at the side of the fire. The cold bread pudding was cut into thick slabs to be taken to work by herself and her dad. She had also been able to buy a piece of beef every Friday since she had been going to High Cedars, and knowing her parents were enjoying a good dinner on Saturdays and Sundays made her feel less guilty. For Anna certainly suffered from guilt, as being waited on hand and foot still did not seem quite right. The staff at High Cedars treated her as they would any other guest, although they knew her background. On one occasion, when the upstairs maid brought hot water, Anna had attempted to engage her in conversation, saying that she was not used to being served. The maid had smiled quite openly, and then had said simply, "Then I should enjoy it, if I were you," without any hint of rancour.

Although she endeavoured to enjoy it, Anna couldn't help but feel it was unfair for some to have so much and others so little. It was not her own situation which weighed on her mind, but that of several of her neighbours who lived in the most abject poverty. She often reflected on these contrasts as she sat huddled in a corner of the canal barge as it made its slow progress back to Sandley Heath on Sunday afternoon. She was not envious by nature and told herself repeatedly that everyone couldn't be bosses, but there was one aspect of life at High Cedars which she did envy, and it had nothing to do with material possessions.

Everyone seemed to know so much, and about so many different things. Anna's mother had always been proud that her daughter was intelligent and had done so well at school. Despite George Gibson's protests that "the wench should be bringin' in," she had insisted that Anna stay at school until she completed Standard seven, and had been proud to watch her daughter ascend the platform to receive her book prize at the end of term. Largely because of her mother's influence, Anna had been accustomed to think of herself as having had a better education than her colleagues, but at High Cedars she was out of her depth. She would listen avidly to the conversation around the dinner table, being persuaded by first one argument and then another, until she hardly knew what she thought.

Florence Nicholson was a witness to Anna's confusion. Having been married for so many years to a man who was both an industrialist and an artist, Florence now enjoyed the friendship of a wide variety of people, whose opinions ranged from the strictly traditional to the most enlightened liberal. After her guests were gone, she would often talk to Anna about the evening's conversation, discussing and explaining points which Anna had missed or misconstrued. As much as Anna enjoyed these evenings, they served as a forcible reminder of her own lack of knowledge.

After Christmas had come and gone with a succession of icy cold mornings and searching, bitter winds, Anna found she had saved enough for a long-craved, personal indulgence, a pair of boots from the leather and shoe shop in Dudley, and some thick, knitted stockings. Florence had provided her with some good leather shoes which were ideal for High Cedars, but Anna was loath to ruin them in the mire of Sandley Heath, and so left them in the wardrobe at High Cedars with the other clothes Florence had provided. When Will called one evening in late January, he was quick with praise for the boots.

"I'm glad to see you'm doin' summat fer yerself at last, ma wench. You'm earnin' all this extra, an' yo' ay 'ad a bit o' treat fer yerself. My, they'm bostin' boots an all. They'll last a year or two."

"Well, they should; they cost enough," Anna answered briefly, as she took a bread pudding from the oven. "I'm glad you've come, Will. This fillbally is for your Mary. It'll be cool soon."

"Don't call it fillbally, Anna," her mother admonished. "You know I don't like it, especially now you're mixing in good company so much."

"Aw, cum on, Mom. Our Anna talks like a lady, an' yer know it." Will winked his eye at Anna and leaned over to see the bread pudding. "My, that's a good un, our Anna, plenty a currants an' all. Call it what yer like, it'll be fillbally cum termorrer. We'm down ter bread an' find it at our 'ouse till Friday."

"Everyone all right?" Anna's mother asked.

"That's what I cum for, Mom. Our babby's

middlin'." Will's handsome face became grave; his eighteen-month-old daughter Dorothy was the apple of his eye. "Mary's at 'er wits end. 'Er's tried all 'er knows. It's a sort of bally gripe."

"Glede water doing no good?"

Will looked embarrassed. "Well, to tell you the truth, we'm burnin' ling. Mary hasn't been able to get to the pit bank wi' Dottie middlin'."

"Oh, our Will, if you don't take the cake...." Anna was quite annoyed. "No proper fire and a babby in the house...."

"Don't say babby, Anna," her mother put in quietly.

Anna poured some water from the kettle into a basin and pulled a red hot glede from the fire with the tongs. She dropped it into the water and they watched as it hissed and steamed.

"There, we'll take that with us; it'll last the night," said Anna. "I'll just do Dad's jolly boy for the morning and I'll be with you."

"You'm lucky to 'ave jolly boy of a Wednesday," Will commented, watching as Anna spooned tea and sugar onto a piece of newspaper, and then a spoonful of condensed milk on top. She covered this with more tea and sugar and then rolled it tightly in the newspaper. A ball of jolly boy dropped into a billycan of boiling water made a good brew. She started to make another.

"Here you are, our Will. I can't see you go without a jolly boy."

Will flushed slightly, but smiled as he said diffidently, "I didn't mean...."

"I know that, our Will. We've plenty to last till Friday." Anna gave him the screw of newspaper and added, "I'll get my shawl. If our Dottie's really middlin', we'd better call at Pearce's for a bottle of Infant Preservative. He'll be shut, but he'll open up for us."

As they left the house, Anna took the bread pudding from Will and balanced the glede water on top of it.

"Now, our Will, fill a bucket with gledes and bring it with you."

"It's kind of yer, our Anna, but perhaps Dad won't like it." Will was hesitant.

"Dad's not paying for it," said Anna sharply. She looked at Will, and her tone softened. "Anyway, if you're quiet, he won't hear you."

She hurried away down the ginnel and by the time Will caught her up, they were nearing Pearce's shop.

"I was quiet," he volunteered, swinging the bucket of coal.

"Right. We'll put the lot on to get a good fire going, and then I'll take the bucket to the pit bank for some sleck to bank up tonight." In Will's company, Anna was already beginning to slide into the slight Black Country dialect she used when her mother wasn't around.

"I'll get it."

"No you won't, our Will. It ain't a man's job."

Will subsided into silence, and looked on as Anna knocked hard on the shop door. Mr. Pearce soon emerged from his living room at the back and served them quickly, assuring them that Atkinson's Infant Preservative would do the trick, all right.

As they hurried along the street and turned the corner, Will suddenly said, "'Ave I done summat wrong, our Anna?"

Anna snorted. "What makes you think that?"

"You'm bein' mighty snotty nosed. I know you."

Anna stopped dead in her tracks and turned a furious face towards him. "All right, our Will, I'm angry. Don't pretend you don't know why!"

"I don't know why! Honest...honest! What's to do?"

"You, Will Gibson! That's what's to do! Burnin' a ling fire and our Dottie middlin'. I'll bet there's no milk in the house neither!" Will's sheepish look let Anna know she was right.

"You knew very well I had a bit o' money and would help! You'm too proud by half, our Will."

Will sighed and fell into step beside her as she started to walk again. "It ay that I'm proud," he tried to explain, "it's just that we can usually manage. But Mary ay bin able to work for a while."

"Exactly! So why didn't yer ask?"

"Well...I didn't like...."

"Exactly!" Anna said again. "Too proud." She stopped and caught at Will's arm. "Don't you understand, our Will?" she said, almost pleading. "There ain't no room for bein' proud, not in a proper family, and most of all not when a babby is sick. Babbies come first, Will. You know that. Our Dottie's surely worth a bit o' pride?"

Will's big hands fumbled on the handle of the coal bucket. "Arr, you'm right, our Anna. I'm sorry."

"Promise me, Will, if ever you're in trouble, money or anythin' else, you won't keep it to yerself. Promise."

Will smiled. "I promise, ma wench. An' yo' promise me an' all if you'm ever in a fix...."

"Yes, Will, I promise. Now let's see what's up with our Dottie."

An hour later, having helped Mary make up a good fire and spoon some of the Infant Preservative down Dottie's wheezing throat, Anna made her way through the dark streets towards the pit bank. She wasn't really allowed to help herself, but even if someone saw her, they would turn a blind eye, provided she only collected slack. Slack was a thin, broken coal, almost like dust, but if you banked up the fire with it at night, it gradually solidified into a mass, and in the morning, a few prods with the poker would break it into a good blaze.

Reaching the coal bank, she climbed a little way up, glad of her new boots, and dug the galvanised bucket fiercely into the slack. *I wonder,* she thought as she began to scoop with her hands, *I wonder what Florence and Robert would make of it if they could see me now?*

George Gibson took a swig from the bottle of "seconds," a beer made from the second fermentation of the hops, and then slung the bottle back into the bosh to keep cool. He pulled on the bellows and took a white hot rod from the fire. With a few well-directed blows, he shaped it into a horseshoe-shaped link, then inserted it into the last link of the chain before beginning to hammer again. The black thoughts had been at him again today and he would be glad to see the back of his shift. In summer, George often started work as early as four in the morning and finished at lunchtime in order to complete his quota before the heat became unbearable, but on dark winter mornings, when he didn't start until seven, the shift seemed to go on forever.

He splashed water from the bosh onto the hood over the fire and finished off the link by working the Oliver with his foot. The leaden weight in his chest would not go away, and no matter how he tried, the dark thoughts returned. His frustration lay in the knowledge of his own limitations, for there was nothing he could do for Sarah...his Sarah. The time for change was long gone; perhaps it had never existed. Their dream was exactly that, just a dream. From the moment they had been thrown off her father's farm with curses ringing in their ears, there had not been a time when there was enough money to last out the week. Their endeavours as newlyweds, when they had walked every day, slowly making their way towards the burgeoning industrial towns of the Black Country, existing on love and hope and little else, now seemed the height of folly, a youthful game played by ignorant children unaware of the cards stacked against them.

After several false starts, George had at last found work at Sandley Heath, with a gaffer who needed a fourth man to complete his team making cable chain for the ocean-going liners which regularly plied from Liverpool to America. It had only ever been intended as a temporary measure, to make enough money to last until he could find work on the land. Sarah had been taken on by a fogger who paid her a pittance, but by the time she had acquired sufficient skill to earn a little more, she was pregnant with Will. Two years later, Anna had arrived, and somehow every week there was never enough money to feed and clothe them all, no matter how hard he worked.

George Gibson still missed the countryside, mourned for the loss of fresh green fields and whispering woodlands, yearned deep in his soul for the closeness to living things he had known in his youth. He knew it was the same for Sarah, although they never spoke of such things. Perhaps it was worse for her, born to a better life. She had never had a chance, his Sarah, not after she married him. He could see her now, running across the lower field to meet him at Bennett's Copse....

George started another link. He didn't like this half inch chain, it was a struggle to make six hundredweight in a week, and even that didn't pay much after shelling out about four shillings to the blower. *Think about something more cheerful,* he told himself, *there was an order for big cable to start next week which should pay better.*

Sarah's parents had been right; he could see it now he had a grown-up daughter of his own. They had not wanted their beloved child to waste her life with a mere farm labourer, and they had been right. Only it had been worse than they could have imagined. Sarah had found the grimy back-to-back terraces of Sandley Heath depressing beyond belief and had never really settled. Her soft Worcester accent had earned her the nickname "Toffee" Gibson amongst her neighbours, the implication being that, because she was well-spoken, she was toffee-nosed. She was not lacking in backbone, however. She worked hard and was never slow to help a neighbour in trouble, and over the years, her nickname of "Toffee" Gibson became more a term of affection than censure.

Then there had been the really bad time, two sons, both stillborn, one after the other. Despite their grief, they had comforted one another, had stayed close. Then, as if in answer to their steadfast hope, little James had been born. His sweet, gurgling nature delighted everyone who saw him, and when, at one year old, he had been struck down by whooping cough, it was too much to bear.

George hammered at the link, trying to blot out the image of Sarah's agonised eyes as she pleaded, "Are we being punished, George? Surely the Lord is not so angry He would take my baby?" And he had held her and told her of course not, James would soon be better and everything would be all right; but the next morning, James had slipped away from them, as gently and lightly as the death of a butterfly, and Sarah had raised her racked face to him, crying, "It's true. I am being punished for marrying you, for defying my parents. I have broken the commandment."

"No, my love, no. It's not your fault."

But Sarah only repeated over and over again, "Honour thy father and thy mother, that thy days may be long upon the land the Lord thy God giveth thee."

After that, she had given up, and there was nothing he could do to stop it. He had watched her age; almost overnight she became greyer, thinner, hopeless. Her skin now seemed paper thin, and she had developed a bluish look around her mouth and a burning, haunted look in her eyes.

Guilt gnawed at George's thoughts, but he pushed it away. So what if he liked a drink? So did lots of other men. There had been too many years of going without. Even if he didn't drink at all, there would never be enough money to provide what Sarah needed. Come to think of it, money wouldn't help at all.

Dottie was better by the weekend, and Anna set off for High Cedars with a light heart early on Saturday morning. As she crossed the main road and walked towards the lane which led down to the canal, she was surprised to see Clancy sitting on a low wall. As she approached, he got up quickly.

"So there ye are! I thought I'd catch ye, so I did!"

His happy smile and the sound of his light Irish brogue caught at Anna's heart. Clancy was such a good soul, she would have to go a long way to find a better.

"Hello, Clancy. What are you doing here?" she greeted him.

"Now what do you think a fella would be doin'

down here at this unearthly hour, and on a Saturday morning, too?" Clancy chided gently. "Waiting for his sweetheart, I should imagine. Trying to get a few minutes of her valuable time, busy as she is, dashing around all over the place."

"Oh, Clancy, I know. We haven't seen much of each other lately, have we? But it won't be for much longer. I think this will be my last weekend."

"Is the painting nearly finished, then?" Clancy asked, falling into step beside her.

"There are two paintings. One is finished and one is nearly done. Robert is going to come over and make a few sketches at the chainshop next week, for the background."

"Oh, so it's Robert, now, is it? You'll be having me jealous."

Clancy's light-hearted smile faded to a quizzical look as he noticed a faint blush suffuse Anna's face, but she only said, "Don't be silly. He told me to call him Robert, and I call his mother Florence."

"Well, that's all right then."

They walked on for a few minutes in an uneasy silence. Clancy had the feeling he had done something wrong but had no idea what. He cleared his throat. "I wanted to talk to you, Anna. My mam isn't so good...."

"Oh Clancy, I'm sorry!" Anna was immediately full of concern. "I intended to call and see her this weekend but our Dottie's been middling...."

"No...it's not that. I didn't mean that." Clancy was having difficulty, and with sudden intuition, Anna kept silent, allowing him to take his time.

"Well, it's like this. You know Mam has been poorly a long time. Last week I got the doctor...."

"The doctor!" Anna was surprised. Doctors were rarely called at Sandley Heath unless you were on your deathbed. She could not help adding, "How much did that cost?"

"Two shillings and sixpence," Clancy said sourly, "But I had to do it; she's lost so much weight. Anyway, according to Doctor Lawrence, she's not long to go."

"Oh, Clancy, I'm so sorry. Was it...what you thought?"

"Consumption? Yes. Of course we've both known it for some time, but it's still a shock when the doctor tells you."

"Yes, it is." Anna felt a pang of guilt. She had been thinking of many things these last few weeks, but Clancy's mother had not been one of them. She squeezed his arm. "I'll help, Clancy, any way I can. As soon as spring comes, we can make an infusion of dandelion flowers; that helps the consumption."

"I doubt she'll be here when the dandelions arrive," Clancy said softly. He hesitated and then continued carefully, "I've been thinking about what I'll do...after Mam is gone."

"Yes, of course." Anna was sympathetic.

"I've been finding out more about America. You know I have two cousins there."

Anna suddenly had an icy feeling of foreboding. "Last time we talked about it, you weren't sure."

"I am now. I've definitely decided to go. There's nothing here for me except a life as a puddler or perhaps a forgeman in twenty years time if I'm lucky. And there's nothing back in Ireland. I could never go while Mam is alive, but according to Doctor Lawrence, she only has a few months at most." He made an effort. "Anyway, when it happens, I'm off to America to see if I can better myself." He looked a little sheepish, and then added, "I dream of it, Anna, of doing really well there."

"Oh, Clancy, dear...." Anna caught at his arm

as they reached the canal. The boat was already there, and one or two passengers were climbing aboard. The bargeman, recognising Anna, gave her a cheery wave and indicated she should hurry.

"Clancy, I'm sorry, I have to go...."

"Yes. I just wondered if...what you thought about it."

Clancy took Anna's arm as she clambered aboard and then walked along the towpath to talk to her as she settled herself at the rear of the barge. He leaned towards her. "Ye didn't say, Anna. Ye didn't say," he entreated in a loud whisper.

"What?" Her face was stricken.

The bargeman took the tiller and the canal boat began to move away. Clancy walked alongside, eyes locked with Anna's. "Are ye coming, darlin'? To America? Are ye coming with me?"

She did not answer. The boat drew away and she mouthed, "I'll see you next week."

Clancy raised his hand in acknowledgement and watched the barge recede slowly. Then he turned away and walked back along the canal path. It was only when he reached the main road that he realised he had not asked Anna to marry him.

"Have you any idea," Robert asked, his brush poised in mid air, "just how beautiful you are?"

Anna froze. His tone had been conversational, but he had never said anything like it before, and she did not know how to respond.

Robert laughed. "Modest, too, unbelievable in this day and age."

Anna gazed steadfastly ahead. Eventually she said, "What do you mean? What is unbelievable?"

"The fact that you are unaware of your looks. Most young ladies of my acquaintance who have any sort of beauty use their looks to get what they want."

Anna blushed. "If that is truly the case, I don't think they have a very Christian outlook."

Robert let out a peal of laughter. "Pious, too! Oh, Anna, you're priceless, really you are, even if a bit po-faced." He studied her seriously and then resumed his brushwork before he added teasingly, "Is that what they teach you in chapel?"

Anna blushed. "I have certainly been taught that vanity is a sin," she responded hotly. "There are many things more important than looks."

"Of course there are." Robert came across to her and smiled his warm, confidential smile, and Anna felt her heart melt. He turned her face slightly and said quietly, "Hold it just there. I'm almost finished." He went back to his easel and continued, "There are many things more important than looks, I agree, but beauty? Ah! that's a different matter. I speak as an artist, and to me, beauty is the most important thing in the world."

"And you are an expert on the matter, of course?" Anna could not help but reply.

"Yes, indeed I am, and before you belittle my expertise, let me ask you a question. Do you think, Anna, that everyone has such knowledge? Can every Tom, Dick or Harry recognise true beauty when he sees it?"

"Most people know what they find attractive," Anna said. "It is surely in the eye of the beholder."

"What they find attractive, yes, but that is not true beauty. One can find many things attractive, from a pretty girl to a good dinner...or the cut of a jacket." Robert waved his brush as if to emphasise his point. "The appreciation of beauty has to be worked at, studied and explored. Beauty is a rare thing, and sometimes found in strange places by those who understand what they seek. But it is not for everyone to pick up, like a pebble on a beach."

"I think you talk of a beauty I don't understand."

"Perhaps. And yet...with time, I believe you might. Beauty can be found in an aged face, or a workman's face which shows character, just as much as in one which is young. And beauty is in wild and dangerous things, just as much as in those which are good and pure...." He broke off as he concentrated hard on a few touches of his brush. "There. If I do any more, I shall ruin it. You can come and look if you like."

Anna went over to the easel, grateful for movement. She was filled with awe at the masterly way in which her likeness had been captured. She still had no idea why Robert had wanted to paint her in her black alpaca, against the background of the chainshop, especially as she now had an evening gown, a plain grey dress and a flowered dimity. But Robert had been adamant, and Anna was mortified to see the accuracy of his depiction, even to the brown rust stain on her skirt and the darn near the hem which she had hoped did not show. Her gaze travelled back to the face; it was her face certainly, and she supposed it had a certain beauty, even if there were wisps of hair trailing to her collar. It was the eyes that gave the portrait life. They held a look...a look of...what? She looked deep into her own painted eyes and felt a slight thrill of recognition. The eyes held a challenge, almost an invitation....

"What do you think?" Robert's voice was soft, as if he understood her thoughts.

"It is...very like," Anna said lamely.

"Well, it's finished as far as you are concerned," Robert said, cleaning his brush. "I have to put in some more background, and as I told you, I'll need to do some sketches at the chainshop. I'll come over on Tuesday, and as a thank you for all your patience, when you finish work, I'll take you to Dudley Castle for a late tea." He grinned. "A little treat for both of us, as we've worked so hard."

Anna was filled with a rush of happiness at the thought of spending more time with Robert. She had feared that after this weekend she would not see him again. "It sounds wonderful," she said. "Thank you. Oh!" Her face fell.

"What is it?"

"It will be dark."

"Yes, that's why I want to go then. I expect you have been before? In the daytime?"

"Yes, I went once in summer. The view is grand from the top."

Robert laughed. "Exactly. Your idea of beauty perhaps? Well, I want you to see the view at night."

"But we shan't be able to see, and as for tea, I think the castle closes early in winter."

Robert laughed again, but it was an indulgent sound. "What a goose you are! A guinea opens any door, Anna, even Dudley Castle."

Saying goodbye to Florence was difficult. During the weeks she had been visiting High Cedars, Anna had come to admire and respect the qualities of this extraordinary woman, and she knew she would miss her a great deal. Florence had taught her so much, had opened her eyes and made her look beyond the grimy confines of her life at Sandley Heath, and Anna hardly knew how to thank her.

"It's not just the dresses and shoes, and everything," she said, stumbling in her appreciation. "But our talks...the way you explained things, took so much trouble with a complete stranger...."

"A stranger? Never!" Florence rejoined, taking

Anna's hand and leading her to stand in front of *The Chainmaker's Child*, now back in its rightful place on the wall of the sitting room. "Look, Anna, look at yourself, dancing on the bellows at the forge, only ten years old. What makes you think you were ever a stranger here? I have lived with you in my house for over eight years, and when my husband was alive he often used to refer to you as his little girl. He loved this picture, thought it was the best thing he had ever done, which is why he would never sell it. So you see, Anna, you have been part of this family for a long time. I have seen you every day, and in an odd way, I felt I knew you."

Her voice softened as she observed the tears in Anna's eyes. "Come along," she said kindly. They walked together to the door, where the trap was waiting to take Anna to the canal barge, the pony's breath condensing in the cold February air. Florence kissed Anna soundly on both cheeks and tasted the salty tears which now ran unheeded down her face. "Don't feel sad, Anna," she consoled. "We shall keep in touch. You must write to me; I should like that. I shall always keep the picture, and so you will always be a part of my life."

Anna could not reply. She just nodded briefly and climbed up into the trap. The driver gathered up the reins and the pony began to walk on, and Anna wiped her eyes and turned to wave as the trap jolted away. She held the image of Florence until the last moment, waving until the trap rounded the bend in the drive and Florence and High Cedars were lost to her forever.

Escape

"I'm not sure I approve of all this." Anna's mother spoke querulously, and her hands shook as she passed Anna a small, neat collar, newly starched.

"All what, Mother? For goodness sake, I'm only going out to tea!" Anna carefully fastened the collar above the grey dress which had been a gift from Florence and paraded herself for approval.

"I must say it's a beautiful dress," her mother admitted. "Fits perfectly, and so well made...but, Anna," she hesitated and then plunged in, "are you sure you have told me the truth? I mean the whole truth?"

"What about?" Anna was surprised and concerned. She had no wish to be a worry to her mother. She knelt down and gently rubbed her mother's left arm, trying to ease the stiffness which she had complained of since a nasty turn the day before. "Is that better? Now what's worrying you? I thought you would be pleased to see me going out decently dressed for once."

"Of course I am, but it seems so odd. You say Mrs. Nicholson...Florence...bought the dresses and shoes for you, but are you sure Mr. Nicholson did not pay for them?"

Anna was aghast. "Mother, of course not! Surely you know I would not have accepted them from him? His mother is a kind person, that's all. I told you she wanted me to dine with the family, and you must admit I didn't have the kind of clothes that are expected...."

"Anna, Mr. Nicholson is not...has not...?"

Anna blushed. "Mother, Mr. Nicholson is a perfect gentleman."

"That's what I mean. Why would a gentleman like him take a chainmaker out to tea? I know you are a good girl, Anna, but you are very young, and men can be so...so...."

"I know how men can be, Mother," Anna answered sharply. "I've seen enough of Dad." The moment it was out, Anna regretted her words. She saw the hurt cross her mother's face.

"Your father was not always like he is now, Anna," she said quietly. "He...."

"I know, Mom, I know." Anna kissed her mother. "I'm sorry, but I have to hurry. Robert is waiting in the carriage."

She picked up her new shawl and felt some annoyance as her mother continued, "I'm only trying to point out to you what people will say."

"Well, what will they say?"

"What do you think? A gentleman in a grand carriage, waiting in the street, and you going off with him dressed in finery everyone knows you couldn't have bought. And they know you've been going to his home and staying there every Saturday for the last four months. What do you expect them to think?"

Anna felt her anger mounting. "They can think what they like. If their minds are so filthy, they will think the worst no matter what I do." She flung on her shawl. "After tonight, I shall not see Robert or his mother again. This tea is a little treat for me as a goodbye present. You had to spoil it for me, didn't you?"

"Anna, I only want...."

"I shan't be late," Anna said crisply and hurried away.

The gates of Dudley Castle were closed when the carriage drew up outside. Robert succeeded in attracting attention by rattling at the gate with his cane, and an old man appeared. Seeming not to mind the interruption, he opened the gates and led them up the thickly wooded hill to his small cottage, constructed from one of the Castle outbuildings. Anna remembered visiting the cottage years before with Will. They had brought bread and jam with them for a picnic, together with a jolly boy, and Anna had paid a halfpenny at the cottage for hot water. Visitors with more to spend were served teas outside the cottage in summer, but on this chilly, late February evening, they were shown into the small parlour, where a good fire was blazing merrily in the shining blackleaded grate. Robert's driver carried in a wicker hamper and put it down on the small round table. As he departed, an elderly woman, presumably the old man's wife, brought in two candles.

Anna looked round at the neat armchairs, the kettle singing on the hob, and felt completely at home.

"You have a cosy place here," she remarked.

"Arr, true enough," the woman agreed in a thick dialect. "God's good, an' the Devil ay altogether ta bad, as they say."

Robert stifled a giggle. "I haven't brought a teapot," he said, "But I believe we have everything else."

The woman smiled and returned quickly with a teapot, which she handed to Anna.

"No, this is my duty," Robert cried happily, taking the teapot from her. "You sit by the fire, Anna. Your job is to toast the muffins." Carefully, he unpacked the hamper, handing Anna a plate of split muffins and a toasting fork. Anna speared half a muffin and held it out to the fire. She watched as Robert carefully spooned tea into the teapot. He looked perplexed. "I have no idea as to quantity."

"That's plenty," Anna laughed. "But you should have warmed the pot first."

"Oh!" Robert looked bewildered.

"Don't worry. Just pour the water on." Anna turned the muffin over and began to toast the other side. "We should have brought a jolly boy," she said.

"What on earth is a jolly boy?" Robert made the tea and looked pleased with himself. His face was a picture as Anna explained how to make a jolly boy.

"What an extraordinarily good idea," he said. "I shall remember it when I next go on a picnic."

"I doubt if you would care for it," Anna laughed. "You have to be used to the taste of condensed milk."

"Even so. It probably would not go off in hot weather."

He took the muffin Anna held out to him and began to butter it thickly, while he commented, "It was fascinating for me today at the chainshop. Although I was working, I could watch all that went on. I enjoyed it."

"I doubt you would enjoy it if you made chain every day for a living," Anna murmured.

"I'm well aware of that. I should think it is a very uncomfortable life." He handed Anna the buttered muffin and took another from the end of the toasting fork for himself. "It's hardly my fault, Anna, that I was born who I am," he said wryly. "I can't help it if I'm more fortunate than others."

"Of course not; I know that. But you can't really understand by just visiting for a day. It isn't fascinating at all; it's hard, very hard indeed. It's hot, poorly paid and very boring once you have the skill. The same thing every day, hour after hour."

"But that is obvious. One only has to watch. God knows how I would cope if I had to do it. Before I arrived this morning, I walked 'round some of the other chainshops. I was amazed how many there were. Some quite big like yours, and then little ones at the back of the houses, with just one man or woman working. I watched some of the men at work. Those huge links...."

"For the big anchor chains, most of them. My Dad makes those, four inch," Anna interposed, with a hint of pride.

"Yes, such heavy work, even the medium sizes, where they work that hammer thing with their foot."

"The Oliver. It's called an Oliver."

"You can probably tell me why every so often they throw water at the fire. I should have thought it would put it out."

"They don't throw it at the fire; they throw it at the plate, that big hood over the fire, to cool it down."

"Why do they have to cool it down?"

"The plate is there to protect the man from the fire. It gets very hot, and if it wasn't cooled by flinging water at it occasionally it would take the skin off his face and arms."

"Oh," Robert looked thoughtful. "Another thing I noticed. Some of the chainshops still have those huge bellows, but they didn't have a child dancing on them like you used to do. A man told me theirs was worked by a pump."

Anna sighed. "Robert, I never danced on the bellows. That is simply how your father saw it. I jumped on them, and because I was small and the bellows were hard to push down, I had to jump hard, so it looked like dancing." She leaned forward. "Dancing is something you do for pleasure. What I did was work, very hard work indeed. I used to become very tired, so tired that when we stopped for the day, I would just fall down exhausted and my father would carry me home."

Robert was silent. After a moment, Anna continued, "I didn't do it every day, of course, but whenever I was not at school I had to work, and often for a few hours after school. You rarely see a child on the bellows now because it was stopped a few years ago. There was a fuss made about it; they called it child slavery."

Robert let out a long sigh. After wiping his mouth on his napkin, he took a small fruit cake from the hamper and sliced it carefully. Offering a slice to Anna, he said quietly, "How crass you must think us, Mother and I. We kept mentioning dancing on the bellows, and of course, you remember it so differently. We must have made you very angry."

"No! Not angry, not at all. Your mother has been kinder to me than anyone I ever met. You didn't understand, that's all, any more than I understood your life at High Cedars. We have had such different backgrounds."

Robert nodded briefly, and they ate appreciatively. The cook at High Cedars took great pride in her fruit cake. Robert poured another cup of tea, having been reminded by Anna to top up the pot, and eventually Anna announced she couldn't eat another thing.

"Nor I," said Robert. "I'm as full as a gun!"

They both laughed, and the slight tension which had arisen with the talk of their background evaporated instantly. Robert took her hand. "Come on, young lady. Time to walk off your tea." He looked at Anna's shawl. "Don't you have a coat?"

"No, but this is very warm." Anna put on the shawl and followed Robert out to the kitchen, where he thanked the old couple for their hospitality and asked for lanterns, explaining they were going to climb to the top of the hill.

The old man bustled about, sucking at his wispy moustache and checking the oil in the lanterns. His wife exhorted them to make sure they kept to the path. "There b'aint no danger," she assured Robert, "so long as you'm on the trail. No climbin' round the ruins, though, not i' the dark."

Robert assured her they would try no such foolhardy thing, and gave the old man some coins. He seemed delighted and escorted them to the start of the climb.

"If we're not back in two hours, send out a search party!" Robert joked, as they set out, holding the lanterns aloft. The climb was not difficult, but after a while, Anna became short of breath and stopped for a moment.

"You ate too much cake," Robert accused. In the dim glow of the lantern, Anna could see his eyes twinkling.

"Probably," she answered. She could hardly tell him that, in his honour, she was wearing a new pair of stays, the first she had ever had. They were very uncomfortable; she should not have laced them so tightly.

"I can't imagine why we are doing this," she grumbled, as they started to climb again. "It's too dark to see anything."

A few minutes later, Robert turned around and held out his hand. "Hold on to me for the last bit, it's rather steep. Now you will see why I brought you up here."

Anna struggled up the last few yards, and as

she emerged to a flat viewing area, she caught her breath in astonishment. Before them, the whole vast blackness was lit like a huge fireworks display from the crimson lights of hundreds of forges and furnaces which roared and twinkled below like so many great red mouths, lipped with white at the edges. Above them the clouds hung heavy and purple, lightened with crimson and gold from the fires which spanned almost twenty miles.

"There, Anna," Robert breathed, "the Black Country's own Aurora Borealis!"

Anna was transfixed. Her eyes roamed the horizon, trying to make sense of it. "No," she said slowly. "The heavens have nothing to do with this; this is made by man. It seems to me like a great battlefield, with all the armies firing huge guns at each other."

"You are not the first to have seen it that way," Robert conceded. "Look, Anna, over to the left there, that's Wolverhampton, and then Coseley, Wednesbury and Bilston. There on the right you have Dudley, Albion, Oldbury and Smethwick. They are in the battle too. And in the distance you can even see Walsall. A great deal of your battlefield is owned by the Earl of Dudley, the land and the mines underneath it, and of course, he has the rents from the factories and foundries and chainshops. To think of owning so much."

"Like your family do in Birmingham?" Anna could not help the remark slipping out, but Robert did not seem put out.

"Touché, my dear. But we were never on such a scale as this, and not such heavy industry. Our factory makes small items, japanned ware and the like. My father always ensured his employees were well looked after, and Andrew does the same. There is not the sort of poverty I have seen in Sandley Heath."

Anna shivered, and Robert was immediately solicitous. "I thought you would be cold as soon as we stopped walking." He took off his coat and wrapped it around her, and Anna snuggled into the luxurious body warmth.

"You see before you, Anna, a different sort of beauty than that you saw from this same spot in summer."

"It is a wonderful sight, most certainly," Anna agreed. "I never saw anything like it in my life. But how can a battlefield be beautiful? It is not the word I would use to describe it."

"No? What word would you use?"

Anna hesitated. "If it is a battlefield, frightening, I think. You see the lines there, the lines of the canals? They are dark red in the light; they seem to me like veins of blood running through the land."

"Ah, yes. I can see what you mean. But I think your reaction is coloured by what you know of what goes on there, the hard work and the poverty. As an artist, I see it differently. My impression is of a great, heavenly fireworks display. It is the same thing as seeing you dancing on the bellows, when you weren't really dancing at all. You know what it was really like, because you were close to it, but my father, as an artist, saw the beauty in the image, and that was what he painted."

"Yes, I see...or at least I think I do." Anna turned her face to Robert. "Thank you for bringing me up here. It has given me a great deal to think about. When I am hammering at the chain, I shall have the consolation of knowing that from up here I look like a firework!"

Robert laughed, and·after a last look at the great spectacle spread below them, they made their way down to the cottage, where Robert handed in the lanterns. When they reached the carriage, Anna gave Robert his coat, knowing their time together was ending, and that she would probably never see him again. The thought filled her with despair. She glanced at his profile as the carriage rumbled back to Sandley Heath, and saw he had a troubled look. When the carriage stopped at the end of Dawkins Street, he took her hand gently.

"Goodbye, my dear Anna. Thank you for your help." His look held her; she felt unable to breathe. "I should like to paint you again some day. You are a very good model." He smiled gently, and her misery was profound.

"Goodbye, Robert. Yes, if you need a model again, I shall be grateful for the work."

"Perhaps next year. I am off to France for the summer."

"Oh." He would not even be in the country, she thought miserably. The driver opened the door and Anna climbed down from the carriage. She looked up at Robert. "Thank you for everything."

"Goodbye. If ever you need anything, let me know."

The driver closed the door and mounted to his seat. He winked his eye at Anna, picked up the reins, and the carriage trundled away into the darkness.

Anna walked slowly down the ginnel and let herself in at the back door. Doors were never locked in Dawkins Street, as no one had anything worth stealing. As she entered the back room, she stopped short.

"Oh, no!" It was too bad. Her father was sprawled on the floor in front of the fire, sleeping it off. At least his snoring was not the heavy stentorian sound he sometimes made, so Anna decided she would probably be able to wake him and push him up the stairs herself, rather than have to fetch Will. *I'll warn mother first,* she decided, making her way up the scrubbed wooden stairs. As George Gibson was such a big man, his wife always had to get out of bed when Anna brought him up, in case she could not hold him and he crashed down on top of her. Anna entered the tiny bedroom and touched her mother's arm. "It's me, Mom," she whispered. "I'm back. Dad's asleep downstairs. I'm going to have to help him up."

Her mother did not move. "Mom," Anna said more loudly. "Wake up, Mom. I've got to bring Dad up." With sudden dread, she shook her mother's arm. "No...oh, no! Mom? Are you ill?" With trembling fingers, she found the matches at the side of the bed and lit the candle, but her mother's body was quite cold.

Before Anna went to the chainshop on Thursday morning, she walked to the bottom of the road to catch Clancy on his way to work. As he approached, he looked the picture of dejection.

"Hello, Clancy."

He looked up, and said with some relief, "Oh, there ye are! I was just thinkin' about ye. I only heard last night when I got home from work."

"Yes."

"I can't tell ye how sorry I am, darlin'." His face was full of concern. "To think on Saturday I was telling ye all my troubles about Mam. Who would have thought your own mam would be the first to go? What was it?"

"Her heart," Anna said briefly. She bit her lip and then said, "I'll walk along with you." They walked down the bank towards the chainshop where Clancy worked as second hammer. After a moment, Anna said, "Of course she's always been frail and a bit bluish, but I never thought...."

"No."

"She had a nasty turn the day before. I should have known it was serious, but she said she was all right."

Her eyes had a pleading look, and Clancy said gently, "It's nobody's fault, darlin'. Was someone with her?"

"No!" The sound seemed wrung from her body. "She was all alone. I had gone to Dudley Castle for tea with Robert. A goodbye treat."

"I see," Clancy's tone was gentle, but his face seemed suddenly turned to stone. He said, "And your dad?"

"When I got home, he was lying drunk on the floor as usual," Anna said bitterly. "He must have been too far gone to realise anything had happened. He may well have been there when she...when she...." She broke off, fighting back tears.

Clancy asked, "And how is he bearing up?"

Anna looked at him in amazement. "How is he? He? How should I know? I suppose he's all right. He's got his booze."

"Come on now, darlin'," Clancy said gently. "Think how you feel because you were out, and then imagine how he must feel."

"He doesn't care."

"I'm sure that's not true."

"If he cared, he would never have been out drinking in the first place."

A retort sprang to Clancy's lips, but he stifled it. Instead he asked, "Are ye on your way to work?"

"Yes. I had yesterday off, but I have to go in today or we'll never pay for the funeral. I had six shillings saved from my pay from modelling, and another guinea Florence gave me when I left, but that's all, and our Will has nothing."

"It's your dad's responsibility, Anna. He earns a great deal more than you."

"Arr. And spends it," she said bitterly.

"Have you asked him for money?"

She shook her head. "I haven't spoken to him," she said. "I just couldn't bring myself to speak to him."

"That's no good, Anna, not for any of you. If you still feel you can't talk to him, ask Will to do it."

She nodded briefly and then said, "The funeral, it's Saturday at two in the afternoon."

"I'll be there. Is there anything I can do?"

"Yes. I came to ask you...will you come with me to the Clent Hills on Saturday morning? Early?"

"Yes, of course, but...on the day of the funeral?"

"There should be some primroses out. I know it's early, but there are sure to be some in the sheltered places. I can't go alone, and mother loved primroses so."

"I'll call for ye at six-thirty, darlin', to allow plenty of time."

"Yes, thank you. I'm not preparing food for the tea after the service; Mary's doing it for us."

They said their goodbyes and Clancy went to the chainshop. As he put his bottles of cold tea into the bosh to keep cool, he watched Anna making her way up the bank. She looked small and slender, he thought, as if she would not have the strength to make it to the top. He wondered how she would get through the next few days, and then realised that it was the weeks to come which would be the real problem. Working all day, all the domestic duties, and a drunken father to boot. *Poor lass*, he thought, *my heart bleeds for ye, so it does*.

"It's no use looking like that, Robert." Florence brandished the marmalade spoon as her son thrust his head into his newspaper. "If you don't want my truthful opinion, you should not ask what I think," Florence continued, spreading marmalade on her toast. "Leave it alone, that's my advice. Let the poor girl be."

"That's hardly a charitable attitude!" Robert burst out. "You know very well she needs the money, and a change of air would do her the world of good."

"Ah! So it's Anna's welfare you are concerned about now, is it? A moment ago your own needs were paramount, you must have her as a model and no one else would do."

"That's right!" Robert put down his newspaper. "I do need her. If I'm to make a triptych, I need another portrait. Outdoors...in the fields in her flowered dress, perhaps. Then I will have the work scene, the domestic scene, and an outdoor scene."

"And that will take the whole summer?" Florence asked with a hint of sarcasm.

"No, but Anna will have extra work from the other chaps. Jacques usually brings his wife to model for us, but she is not coming this year. She's expecting a child," he added a little self-consciously. "We kill two birds with one stone. We have a model and Anna makes some money and has a good holiday into the bargain."

Florence sighed. "I can see your mind is already made up," she said. "I just want to remind you, Robert...."

"What?" His blue eyes were bland over his teacup.

"You know perfectly well what."

"Mother! You surely don't think...? I'm very fond of Anna. I wouldn't hurt her for the world."

"Your record does not inspire confidence, Robert."

Robert slammed down his cup so that it almost broke the saucer. "You would have to bring that up, wouldn't you?"

"I'm not thinking only of you; there are the others too," Florence said calmly.

"Therese will be there."

"Yes, thank God!" Florence sighed, deciding she had to mend fences. "Look, dear, I'm not accusing you of any ulterior motive."

"I should hope not!" Robert broke in.

"I'm only saying that Anna...well...she is an innocent."

"She's more sophisticated than when she first came here, and who's idea was that? I was going to put her in the servants' quarters...like," Robert searched for a word, "like...an employee. It was you who insisted she be treated as a guest and eat at the table with us. Now you're saying...."

"I'm not saying anything, Robert, but I think, on reflection, that perhaps I was wrong. I may have made it more difficult for the poor girl to accept her lot. And then her mother dying so suddenly a month ago. I told you I had a letter from Anna, didn't I?"

"Yes," Robert said shortly. He had had enough of the conversation and decided to be brutal. "That is a prime consideration," he said. "I happen to know that Anna's father is a real drunkard and she will be alone in the house with him now. My plan will give her a break and an increased income so that she can make a few choices of her own."

Robert gave his mother a curt nod and left the dining room. Florence got to her feet and rang for the table to be cleared. She reflected sadly that it was not perhaps so easy to help those less fortunate than oneself, even with the best of intentions.

It might be better to leave them alone, or just give them a little money to enjoy in their own way. And who was to say whether her world, the world she had tried to introduce to Anna, was an improvement on Anna's own? Materially, of course it was, but in other ways? Even so, a drunken father....

Florence went across to *The Chainmaker's Child* and stood a long time, staring at the dainty image. "I think you may be in between the Devil and the deep blue sea, my dear," she said. She traced her fingers gently across the faint signature in the corner of the painting. "Oh, Andy," she whispered, "I do hope your family doesn't hurt your little chainmaker."

"Gerron wi' it!" Ma Higgins commanded. "Yo' ay got all day!"

Anna regarded her coldly. "This ain't my job," she muttered, as she carefully folded cart traces into a half size barrel.

"Wot did yo' say? I'll tek no mouth from yo', Miss Toffeenose!"

"I only said I don't get paid for this." Anna stood her ground. "I could be working on chain...the dog leads."

Ma Higgins snorted. "Yo' just do as you'm told, ma wench," she said, not unkindly. She did not mention that Anna was the only one of her workforce she could trust to count the correct number of cart traces into the barrel. "Tell yer wot. Yo' get them traces counted out proper, an' down to Tommy 'Oskins, an' I'll put yer down fer a extra dog chain."

Anna raised her eyebrows, thinking Ma Higgins must have gone soft. It was impossible to make even half a dog chain in the time it would take her to do this small job.

"And in case yo' think I'm doolallytap," said Ma Higgins, reading Anna's mind, "there's another barrel to do after this un."

Anna sighed. "All right," she agreed. At least it was something different. It was a lovely spring day outside, and she would be able to breathe in the fresh air as she rolled the barrel down to the cooper for him to seal it.

"Mek sure Tommy 'Oskins does a good job," said Ma Higgins as she turned away. "Them cart traces is goin' all the way to Masser-chew-sits."

Anna could not help but smile. Ma Higgins relished the lovely, long American name and pronounced it with a flourish as often as she could. Lots of their chains went to America, packed carefully in the wooden barrels, which kept them in good condition on the sea voyage and ensured they could be easily moved.

Having carefully counted out one hundred traces, Anna put the lid on the barrel and pulled it onto its side. She rolled the barrel carefully out into the dazzling light, laughing as the other women, infected by the bright spring sunshine, launched into *Rule Britannia* at the tops of their voices, assuring anyone who passed by that "Britons ... never, never, never ... shall ... be ... slaves...." and beating time with their hammers.

Anna rolled the barrel carefully down the lane to the cooper's shop. She had to wait a few minutes before he could attend to her, and so took the opportunity to sit down on a small bank outside, where a few dandelions had pushed their heads through the straggly, unkempt grass. Anna picked off the flower heads and pushed them into the pocket of her baggin apron. *Not enough to make a brew for Clancy's mom,* she thought, *but there might be a few more on the way home.* She had an idea. Why not? Provided she did the washing first.

She got up quickly as the cooper beckoned. "Will you seal this, please? For Ma Higgins, and there's another one to come. They are for Massachusetts."

"Leave it wi' me, ma wench." The cooper gave her a wink. Anna smiled her thanks and then ran as fast as she could down the rutted lane, wrinkling her nose as she caught the stench from the overflowing middens in Tibbetts Yard. She ran down the bank to the forge where Clancy worked and found him hard at it.

"What's to do, darlin'?" Clancy looked quite pleased at the interruption. He took a bottle of tea from the bosh and wiped his brow before taking a swig.

"I must be quick. I only slipped out for a minute," Anna said, breathless from her run. She glanced around the forge, giving quick smiles of recognition to the men who, without exception, had stopped work to look at her. "I thought perhaps we could go to Clent tomorrow as the weather is so good. Just for the afternoon, I mean. I have to do the washing first. We could find dandelions for your mom."

"Sure, that'll be grand. I can do with the fresh air," Clancy agreed. "I'll come for ye about one o'clock." He smiled happily as he watched Anna dash away up the bank. At the top, she turned, breathless, and waved her hand. Clancy waved back, closing his ears to the coarse comments of his companions. He was pleased that Anna seemed to be emerging from the awful depression which had engulfed her when her mam died. He felt a thrill of excitement. Perhaps everything would work out after all.

There were plenty of dandelions, and as Anna said goodbye to Clancy the following day at the bottom of Dawkins Street, she promised to deliver the infusion to his mother that evening, as soon as it was made.

"I've really enjoyed this afternoon," she said. "Thanks for taking me."

Clancy's eyes softened. "Ye know I hope to be taking ye much further than Clent, Anna," he said quietly.

Anna smiled. "I know." She hesitated. "It's...it's such a big decision, Clancy. Let's take one step at a time, shall we?"

Clancy nodded. He felt like kissing her on the cheek but thought better of it. Someone might be watching. He should have done it when they were at Clent, he thought, where they found all those dandelions in the hollow.

"I'll see ye later," he said and then walked slowly home.

Anna was light-hearted after her afternoon in the fresh air. She swung the basket of dandelion flowers and hummed a little tune as she walked up the ginnel and in at the back door. Her father was home, but he got up as she entered and reached for his jacket.

"Yo've been a while," he said, a hint of complaint in his voice.

"Yes, been to Clent with Clancy, collecting dandelion heads." Anna surveyed the fire, which had burned very low. "You could have banked the fire up, Dad. It's nearly out."

"Not my job to see to the fire," he said briefly, pulling on his jacket.

Anna made no reply. She picked up the fire bucket and threw on some small coal. Then she riddled the ashes at the bottom of the grate with the poker to let air in underneath, and the fire began to draw.

"Anyway," her father said crossly, "no need to mek the fire up that much, not in this warm weather."

"I have to cook the dinner," Anna protested, "and make up the infusion for Mrs. Sullivan."

"Yo' needn't mek me any dinner," George Gibson remarked. "I'm off to the Sandley Arms. I wanted me dinner an hour since, but there was none."

"Well hang on a bit, Dad. It won't be long."

"'Ang on? 'Ang on fer yo'? Who do yo' think you'm tellin' to 'ang on? In case yo've forgot it, ma wench, this is my 'ouse, an' I'll 'ave dinner when I say, not when you'm ready ter mek it!"

"I didn't mean that, Dad."

"I'll gerra pie at the pub. A fine thing when a bloke cor gerra meal in 'is own 'ouse after a week's work! When 'is daughter is too busy flauntin' 'erself on the Clent 'ills like any brass-faced tart."

"Dad!"

"Well, it's true, ay it?" he shouted belligerently.

"No, it's not true! I was with Clancy Sullivan."

"Arr. An' everybody knows what yo' was up to!"

Anna's face flamed crimson. "Don't you dare...don't you dare say such a thing!"

"I'll dare what I want in me own 'ouse, ma wench, an' do' yo' forget it! Yo' was off wi' that painter chap Nicholson the night yer mom died."

Anna let out a shriek and sprang at him. Her father swung his arm to fend her off and caught her with a heavy swipe across her cheek. The blow knocked Anna across the room, and for a few seconds, she blacked out as she slid slowly down the wall. George Gibson hesitated for a moment, then went out and slammed the door.

When Will arrived half an hour later, the kettle was singing on the hob and Anna was seated by the fire, weeping quietly.

"What's to do, our Anna?" Will bent over and put his hand under her chin. His face darkened as he noticed the red marks on the side of her cheek.

"'As our dad been at it again?" he asked.

Anna nodded briefly. "He wasn't drunk either," she said, "not this time."

"What was it about?"

"I don't know, really. I think it was because I'd been to Clent with Clancy to get dandelion flowers, but he knew we were going. He was cross because his dinner wasn't ready when he wanted it, but it was only six o'clock."

She raised a tear-stained face to Will. "Oh, Will, he called me names, said I had been up to things with Clancy and Mr. Nicholson, and I haven't! Oh, Will, I haven't, truly!"

"Course you 'aven't, ma wench," Will sighed. "What we'm goin' to do with Dad I do' know. 'E's gettin' worse."

Anna began to weep again. "He said...he said I was off with Mr. Nicholson when Mom died." She broke down into heavy sobs.

"Arr, that's it. That's what's mekin' 'im like this," said Will. "Come on, our Anna. Get a cup of tea on an' stop cryin'. We'll soon sort this out."

Anna put the teapot to warm and got down two mugs. She wiped her eyes. "What do you mean, Will? What is making Dad like this?"

"Guilt," said Will briefly. "'E feels guilty about Mom, so 'e lashes out at whoever's nearest. It just appens to be yo'."

Anna, still sniffing, poured the water into the teapot.

Will asked, "Yo' remember 'ow 'e was, Anna? After the funeral?"

Anna nodded. Would she ever forget, she wondered, but knew that the image of her father's grief on that dreadful day would stay with her all her life. It had been so strange. He had been quiet and morose until the day of the funeral and had seemed pleased and touched when Anna and Clancy returned from the Clent Hills with bunches of primroses for the coffin. He had kept up well through the service and the tea afterwards, accepting condolences and chatting to his neighbours in a matter-of-fact manner. It was only after everyone had gone and Will, Mary and Anna were starting to clear away that George Gibson broke down. He had suddenly put his head down on the table and begun to weep, pouring out his grief in loud, racking sobs which shook his great frame and wrung the hearts of his family. It had seemed to go on for ages, and Anna, who had never seen her father cry, became quite distressed. It was Will who had eventually got their father to bed.

Anna looked at her brother now with affection. She poured the tea, and Will, clasping his hands around the enamel mug, said quietly, "He's took it a lot 'arder than folks think."

"Perhaps."

Will hesitated, trying to choose his words. "The...the cryin'...yo' remember. It wasn't just because Mom was dead."

"No. It was for himself," Anna said. "It was because he didn't know how he would manage."

"No, Anna, yo' don't understand." Will swigged at the mug of tea as if it would help him find the words he needed. "All that grief, all that pain, it was for...for what might have been."

"What do you mean?"

"Yo' know the story, ma wench. Mom and Dad 'ad a real love match. Mom got thrown out by 'er folks an' Dad lost 'is job. They were young then, Anna; they must 'ave 'ad such 'opes, such plans...for what they were goin' to do together. I expect Dad made promises...an' they all come to nothin'. 'E must 'ave felt 'e failed 'er. I think 'e was cryin' for all them things, all them things that never 'appened. For all 'e tried, an' 'e's always been a real worker, yo'll give 'im that...they ended up 'ere wi' next to nothin'."

Anna was silent. She had never heard her brother talk about feelings before, and she was quite affected. After a moment, she countered, "But these last few years, Dad has been earning good wages, and he didn't help, he just spent it all in the pub."

"Do yo' think 'e don't realise that? By the time 'e was gettin' better money, it was too late, the rot 'ad set in, so to speak, an' 'e probably tried to blot it all out wi' booze. We don't know, Anna, 'ow things were between 'em, what 'ad been said, but I do' think 'e really meant what 'e said to yo'. 'E was just 'urt, and lashin' out."

Anna nodded. "You may be right, Will, but it isn't easy to live with."

"I know, ma wench. But it may get better. Summer's comin', God's good, an' the Devil ay altogether ta bad."

Anna smiled, remembering with a pang the last time she had heard the saying. It had been spoken by the woman at Dudley Castle, when she was with Robert. Now Robert was gone, and her mother too.

"I'd best get goin' if there's no tea left," said Will. He got up and gave Anna a wink. "Keep yer chin up, ma wench. There's worse things 'appen at sea!"

"I know," Anna said. "I'll call in later when I've seen Mrs. Sullivan."

When Will had gone, she made the dandelion infusion, thinking carefully about what he had said. She tried to imagine her parents' courtship, but the image of her father as an impetuous young lover did not come easily. Nevertheless she recognised the truth of Will's remarks. *It must have been hard for them,* she thought, *the plans that foundered, the chances that did not come.*

When the infusion had cooled, she took it round to Mrs. Sullivan, and she was horrified to see the wretched bag of bones that the old lady had become. Clancy was not there, and Anna sat with his mother for an hour and read to her the story about the loaves and fishes from the New Testament, whilst the old lady sipped the dandelion broth. When Anna left, she felt depressed beyond words, but calling in at Will's home to play "the farmer wants a wife" with Billy and Dottie in the backyard helped to relieve her spirits, and she felt quite cheerful when she returned home to do the ironing.

Anna was in bed when her father returned that night. She was afraid that after their argument he might be aggressive, but he made his own way to bed with little noise. Sunday passed quietly, and as Anna went to chapel in the morning and the evening, she saw little of her father.

She was on her way to work early on Monday morning when she saw the postman waving to her. She ran across the road to meet him. "Oh, thank you, Jim."

She held the letter tightly in her hand as she walked down to the chainshop. A letter was something of an event and she would open it when she arrived at work. It had to be from Florence, in reply to her own. Anna felt a thrill of satisfaction. Although Florence had asked her to write, Anna had not been at all sure she would receive a reply.

She glanced down at the envelope and her heart missed a beat. It was not Florence's hand, but Robert's.

Anna made four links before she could bring herself to open the letter. She glanced at it again and again as she worked, imagining little stories about the contents until she could stand it no longer. When she finished the next link, she stopped and tore open the letter, reading the contents with ever increasing incredulity.

Maisie Collins at the next hearth was inquisitive. "Yo' got a letter, Anna? Who from?"

Anna did not reply. She just stared blankly, and Maisie watched her anxiously as she finished off a link. Then she came across to Anna and asked kindly, "Bad news, is it, love?"

Anna found her tongue. "No," she said. "It's an offer of work, more work as a model."

"Wi' that lovely Mr. Nicholson?" Maisie laughed delightedly, and she gave a sly grin. "Yo've fell on yer feet there, ma wench!"

"There's nothing like that!" Anna said hotly, feeling the blush suffuse her cheeks. "It's to model for other people as well, other artists."

"Well I never! Yo'll be famous!"

"Stop yer yackin'!" Ma Higgins was on the warpath. "I do' pay yer fer...."

"Anna's gorra job," Maisie interrupted with some pride. "'Er's gonna be a model fer them artists."

"More modellin', Anna?" Ma Higgins was interested. "Well, it's a chance to mek a bit. I do' blame yer, so long as it do' interfere wi' yer work."

"Oh," Anna said, still feeling stunned. "It isn't the same as before, Ma, it's...it's...." She swallowed. It was hard to say it. "It's in France!"

"Yo' do as yer want, ma wench," Will said seriously. "I know there's them as'll say yo' shouldn't go, but tek no notice, nor of Dad neither. It's up ter yo'; it's your life!"

Anna smiled at him. She cuddled Dottie to her as the child began to whimper. "There, my pet, don't cry. Your mom's getting you some lovely sop."

Mary brought over the child's dish and began to spoon bread and milk into Dottie's ready mouth. "Our Will's right, Anna," she said. "Yo' think of yerself fer once. Dad'll be all right. We'll keep an eye..."

"You've got enough to do, Mary, with Billy an' the babby."

Will started to laugh. "I think yo' should go. You'm talkin' stronger Black Country every day since Mom went."

Anna laughed too. "You're probably right. But it's easy to say do what I want. That's the trouble. I don't know what I want."

"But it's only for the summer. Yo'll be back before yo' know it," Mary said. She smiled wistfully. "I just wish we 'ad the chance," she said.

"That's true." Anna gave Dottie back to Mary and rose to leave. "I do want to go if I'm truthful. I suppose I'm just a bit nervous," she giggled. "Going to France is a bit different from going to Dudley Market!"

"Well, do' worry about Dad, that's all I'm sayin'," said Mary as she walked through the yard with Anna. "Old mother Smithson will be glad to do 'is washin' for a shillin', an' I'll be round every day to do 'is cleanin' an' keep the fire up. I can tek Dottie wi' me. 'E can 'ave 'is dinner wi' us on 'is way 'ome from work."

"He won't like that," Anna said. She could see storms ahead. Her father had refused even to listen to her proposals. He had pronounced that she was not going to France and that was that.

"Then I'll tek 'is dinner round," said Mary. She gave Anna a swift kiss. "Tek courage. 'E cor bite yer!" she said with a smile.

That evening, Anna did gather her courage as she prepared dinner. One of their neighbours had killed a pig at the weekend, and in payment for saving all their vegetable peelings for the pig's feed, they had been given a piece of the shoulder meat. Anna had made a rich gravy and had scored and salted the skin to make the crackling crisp and succulent, and her father complimented her on the tasty roast potatoes and spring cabbage. "This is a feast for the middle of the week," he said. "You've got yer mom's touch with the taters an' all."

Anna decided this was the time. "Dad," she said slowly, "there's something I have to tell you. I've made a decision." Her father looked up sharply, and Anna continued, "I've decided to go...to go to France."

"I've told yo'...."

"No, Dad, you don't understand. It isn't your decision; it's mine."

"What?" Her father went red in the face.

"Just for once, Dad, listen to what I have to say before you fly off the handle."

For a moment, George Gibson looked as if he was going to get up and storm out, as he usually did if crossed. However, the pull of the gravy was strong, and he thought better of it. He sat, eating his dinner in silence, as Anna continued.

"You think I'm trying to cross you, Dad, but I'm not. You will be well looked after. If I wasn't sure of that, I wouldn't go. The reason I've decided to go is that I shall never have such a chance again. When you were young, Dad, you would have wanted to do it, you and Mom. Trouble is, you probably didn't get the chance. I have, and I'm not going to let it slip through my fingers."

Her father remained silent until he had finished his meal. Then he pushed his plate away and said quietly, "And this chance, what is it exactly? A chance to do what? Play the fool with that young man?"

"No, Dad! Not at all!" Anna could feel her temper rising but was resolved to stay calm. "It's several chances really, but the first is to make some extra money, the sort of money I can never make at the chain. Mr. Nicholson says there will be several artists there; they rent a big farmhouse every summer. One of the artists' wives used to model, but she is expecting a child and won't be there this year. I shall have a room to myself and all my meals provided. There is a cook there called Therese, and when I am not being painted, I shall help her in the kitchen."

"Does she live in, this woman?" her father asked gruffly.

"Yes, she lives there. But, Dad, more than anything else, I shall travel to another country! Think of it, Dad, to be able to go so far and not have to pay anything for it!"

"Mr. Nicholson will pay your fare?"

"Yes, just think, I'll see the sea!"

"And your fare back home?"

"Yes, of course. At the end of August, they all go to Paris for two weeks, and I shall go with them. They won't be painting then, of course. It's like a little holiday."

"Strikes me it's all 'oliday."

"Yes, I think so too. In Paris I shall have to help with the cooking, but I shall have time to see the sights. Mr. Nicholson said in his letter he will take me to the art gallery to see some paintings by a man called Chardin. I don't really know what he's on about, but it's a painter Mr. Nicholson admires."

George Gibson gave a deep sigh. Anna's remark about lost chances had gone home. Still, he wavered until Anna said, "Won't you read Mr. Nicholson's letter, Dad? I have it here."

She fished in her apron pocket and handed him the letter. George Gibson perused it a long while. Eventually, he handed it back to Anna and said, "Well, it seems all above board. But it still don't seem decent to me, a young woman goin' all that way wi' a young man an' them not wed."

"But, Dad, gentlefolks take their servants everywhere with them."

"Arr, perhaps they do. An' folks do all sorts o' things these days. It do' mean I 'ave to agree wi' 'em." He got to his feet. Anna waited, but he said nothing more.

"Then I can go, Dad? You give me your blessing?"

"Yo' get no blessin' from me, ma wench. Yo' do what yer want, seein' as yo've med yer mind up. But do' come runnin' back 'ere when it all ends in tears."

PART TWO

FRANCE

Brittany

1905

Anna awoke to the pungent smell of coffee. She
lay for a moment, savouring the comfort of the
bed, smoothing the thick, white counterpane with
her fingers. She had never woken up in such a
lovely place, she decided; it was even better than
High Cedars. Not so grand of course, but somehow that made it even more enjoyable. She gazed
around her in contentment at the crudely plas-
tered ceiling and walls, whitewashed in snowy contrast to the heavy, carved chest and clothes press.
In the corner stood a big china jug and washbowl
on a tall stand, with thick white towels hanging
on a rail at the side of it. Anna got out of bed and
crossed to the small window. The cretonne curtains fluttered slightly in the morning breeze, and
she opened the window wide and breathed deeply.
Robert had been right, the rain had gone at last,
and it was a lovely morning.

In the courtyard below, a door opened, and
she saw the stocky figure of Therese crossing to
the open-fronted barn with a bucket of feed for
the chickens.

"Hello, Therese!"

"Bonjour!" Therese turned and waved. "At last
the child awakes! After all the work is finish."

Anna laughed. Although it was only her third
day at the farm, she knew this was a joke. It had

taken very little time to discover Therese hid her kind heart with a sharp tongue, and Anna felt a thrill of excitement as she quickly washed and dressed, for this morning she was to accompany Therese to the local market. On the stairs, she met one of the resident artists, Alphonse, coming up. He spoke little English, but he smiled and said, "*Bonjour, ma petite!*" and although Anna did not understand him, she knew he was being pleasant and smiled back shyly and said, "*Bonjour,*" which was the only French word she knew.

Including Robert there were four artists staying at the farmhouse, a very old building built from local rose-pink stone and known as "La Maison Blanche." Robert had explained the house had originally belonged to a man known as Le Chevalier Blanc, who had been turned out of his home at the time of the Revolution. In English, he said, the name meant "The White Knight", and at this point, Anna had lost the thread of the conversation, for Robert started to talk about teaching her to play chess. The farmhouse now belonged to Therese's father, and the hazily remembered tales of the French Revolution made Anna speculate uneasily as to how he had acquired it. What had happened to The White Knight? Had he lost his head like so many others? Had Therese's ancestors been among the army of sans-culottes who had stormed through the countryside, killing and burning? The possibility that the farmhouse had played its part in such turbulent history gave it added appeal, and tantalised by her own imaginings, Anna had quickly fallen under its spell.

When Anna reached the kitchen, Robert and the other two artists were finishing breakfast at the big, scrubbed table. One of them was Jacques, a big, curly-haired man with an extraordinarily full beard, who spoke very good English. He had brought Anna a letter of advice from his wife, who had modelled for them in previous summers. Shortly after they arrived, Jacques had attempted to translate the letter to her, but had then stuffed it into his pocket, saying, "Don't worry, she only says two things to you. When you are tired, you must tell us because we shall never notice, and do not let me drink too much! She also wishes you luck!" he added, sheepishly. He rolled his eyes and tugged at his beard, "My wife, she don't think too much of us!"

Anna had laughed, and had liked Jacques immediately. She could not say as much for the other artist, a grey-haired, stick-thin woman with enormous dark eyes. She hardly spoke, and struck Anna as being extremely strange.

Jacques immediately poured coffee for Anna and pushed it towards her as she sat down. Robert, looking apologetic, said simply, "Good morning, Anna. You're too late. We've eaten all the croissants."

"Never mind," said Anna. "I've eaten far too much since I arrived." She looked at the woman seated opposite and took the plunge. "Good morning, Sylvie."

The woman started slightly at the sound of her name. For a second her huge eyes looked at Anna above the finely drawn cheekbones. She gave an almost imperceptible nod and then bowed her head; conversation was not a priority for Sylvie. Therese entered and plonked a dish of hot croissants on the table. "*Voilà, chérie,* I know these *cochons* will leave nothing for you."

Later that morning, Anna and Therese visited the market. Although Robert had offered to drive them in the pony cart, Therese refused, preferring to walk, pulling a two-wheeled handcart which she had used for years. The village was about a mile away, and as they made their way along the lane, Anna could hardly contain her delight in the lush countryside, dashing from bank to hedge, from tree to shrub, picking one pretty flower or twig after another.

"Look, Therese! What is this called? Oh, look...how pretty!"

Therese snorted. Secretly, she was enchanted with Anna's enthusiasm, but she said shortly, "Stop dance about; you will be exhaust before market."

Anna fell into step beside her. "But it's so lovely, Therese! You can't understand...it's so clean and fresh."

"Where you live is no green? No flowers?"

"Oh, yes, England is lovely in the spring. We...." She stopped a moment and then continued, blushing slightly, "Clancy...my friend Clancy and me, we go to Clent; it's quite near to where I live. There are hills and meadows and flowers...like here. But we can only go there when we have time, perhaps once or twice a year. Most of the time we are at work."

"And it is not clean? You say clean and *fraîche*?"

"No, it is not clean. Every day I get very dirty; it is hard to keep clean. Here it is wonderful. I wash in the morning and at night, but I am not dirty at all! It feels very nice." Anna laughed and stooped to pick a buttercup. She held it underneath Therese's chin and said, "There, you like butter."

"Silly child! Monsieur Robert tells me your work is very 'ard. 'E say you work very much."

"When did he tell you that?" Anna asked, surprised that she should be the subject of conversation.

"When I ask 'im. I ask Monsieur Robert to tell all about you."

"Oh." In spite of herself, Anna added, "What else did he say about me?"

"'E say you are model...and your Mama is...what is the word? *est morte*?"

Anna swallowed, understanding. "Yes, my mother died a few months ago."

"Monsieur Robert, 'e say you need 'oliday, so you come 'ere."

Anna laughed. "I never had a holiday in my life, Therese. I came here because I will be paid well to model for the artists, Robert and the others. At home I cannot earn nearly so much."

Therese nodded. She understood the economics. "Yes, it will be good for you 'ere."

"Robert has been so very kind to me. He was so good on the journey. I was very nervous when we crossed the Channel; I had not seen the sea before."

"You do not like the sea?" Therese asked.

"Oh, yes, I like it. To look at it is wonderful, but it is frightening to be on it in a boat."

Therese gave a snort. "Poof! They say the English are good sailors."

Anna laughed, "Perhaps they are, Therese, but not where I live. Most of my friends and neighbours have never seen the sea."

"Well, it is no use to be afraid. You 'ave to go 'ome, *n'est ce pas*?"

"Yes, but not till the end of summer," Anna said happily. She twirled around. "Look how my dress flares out, Therese! Robert's mother bought it for me; they have been so kind."

"Yes, you said so before," Therese considered for a moment and then said levelly, "Take care, my pretty one, that you do not allow Monsieur Robert to be too kind."

Anna coloured a little. "Robert is my employer, Therese, nothing else."

"*C'est bon.* It should stay like that, *chérie.*"

Therese sniffed, trundling the handcart behind her as she strode out along the lane. Noticing Anna's discomfiture, she added kindly, "It will not be a problem for you. There is a young man at 'ome, 'ow in English you say? A sweet'eart, perhaps?"

"Perhaps." Anna had a sudden vision of Clancy's despairing look as he waved to her from the bottom of Dawkins Street. She could see his thick curly hair and the long, dark lashes which fringed his blue eyes. "Irish eyes," her mother had called them, sooty and smoky and utterly devastating to the young girls who worked in the chainshops near the forge. Many of them would no doubt be setting their caps at him right now. *While the cat's away*, she thought, with a sudden feeling of panic.

"My sweetheart," she said to Therese confidentially, "he...he is very handsome, nice looking," she explained. "He is waiting for me. He intends to go to America, to try and make a new life there. He wants me to marry him when I get home."

"And go to America?" Therese was incredulous.

"Yes, he has cousins there who will help him to get work."

"And you will do this?"

"I...I don't know. I couldn't decide before I came to France. I could not promise him. It is such a big step."

"Indeed. A very big thing," Therese agreed. "You would leave your papa, and the brother you tell me about, and 'is family. But then, if you love this...this...."

"Clancy," Anna provided with a hint of pride.

"This Clancy...if you love 'im truly, all others are nothing, is it not so?"

"I suppose so."

"Do not suppose, *chérie*," Therese said darkly. "Be sure. In *affairs d'amour*...affairs of the..." Therese struggled for expression, pounding her big hand on her chest, "...affairs of the 'eart...you must be sure."

This was said with some vehemence, but she followed her pronouncement with her most winning smile. "And then, *chérie*, when you are sure, you give all...but all.... *Absolument!*"

"And so you see, it was 'er 'usband all the time!" Jacques finished his story to gales of laughter. "*Son mari*," he added, still laughing, for Alphonse's benefit.

Anna wiped tears of mirth from her eyes. Jacques was such a fool, she thought happily, starting to giggle again. Her ribs ached from so much hilarity and she felt quite light-headed. Even Sylvie was smiling, she noticed as she poured herself another glass of red wine. She gazed contentedly around the big kitchen table; it had been another wonderful meal, perhaps better than any so far, and for the first time, it had been cooked entirely by herself, albeit under Therese's expert supervision. What fine people they all were, and how she had come to love them.

She stopped her thoughts in their tracks. Was it true? Did she really love them? All of them? Even Sylvie? How could she feel so strongly about people she had known for a mere six weeks? It was this place, and the wine, she decided, realising she was a little drunk. Life at La Maison Blanche made you suspend your judgment, made you forget the future and live only for today. It seemed she had become closer to these friends than to any people she had ever known; yet how could that be in only six weeks? She considered them in turn, examining them closely over the rim of her wine glass. Big, noisy Jacques, who had shown such gentleness as he plaited her hair into a thick braid when she sat for his painting called *En Repos*. This was a beautifully executed portrait in soft, delicate hues, with an ethereal quality which made Anna feel the girl in the painting was not herself but some transient spirit which had inhabited her body just long enough to be captured on canvas. Anna admired Jacques's work more than any other, even Robert's.

Then there was the soft-spoken Alphonse, who to her astonishment had asked, with help in translation from Robert, if she would sit *à nu*. When Robert explained this meant without clothes, Anna was horrified, but as soon as she made it plain she would not agree, Alphonse had been quite amenable, deciding instead to paint her in the farmyard holding a pitchfork and in the company of a goose. Jacques had joined the discussion and expressed the view that Anna was too slender to sit successfully *à nu*. "Not enough flesh," he said dismissively, and Anna began to realise that these men truly saw her with a different vision.

It had been pleasant sitting for Sylvie, who remained quiet and reserved. Therese had volunteered the information that Sylvie was from the Balkans, although she didn't know exactly where, and inferred that her strange manner was due to some dreadful events in her childhood. Sylvie preferred to paint outdoors, and Anna had enjoyed sitting in the sun on the terrace, where she prepared vegetables as Sylvie daubed her canvas with strong strokes of vibrant colour. She had created an impression of the courtyard at La Maison Blanche, and Anna saw that the essence of the place had been captured on canvas. During the long, hot days, Anna had felt a sense of mutual understanding and respect grow between them, and although she did not understand Sylvie's painting, when she looked at it, she felt a powerful impact, and she was aware that Robert and Jacques regarded Sylvie as the true genius amongst them.

And Robert...ah, Robert! Anna regarded him gravely over her wine glass as he conversed enthusiastically with Jacques and Alphonse. He was, she decided, like herself, slightly intoxicated. Since they had been at La Maison Blanche she had watched him relax gradually, day by day. As he lounged in a deck chair with a book, or sat painting a still life hour after hour, as his fair hair grew longer and became even lighter under the warm sun, she saw him become slower, friendlier, as if the casting off of his English clothes had unloosed his limbs and his mind from some long constriction.

Robert suddenly became aware of her gaze, and he leaned across the table. "Ah, tomorrow," he said pointedly, "tomorrow at last I shall have you to myself for two weeks. And you," he said, turning to Jacques, "can take your turn at still life."

"No, landscape, I think," Jacques replied, stifling a yawn. "And what do you intend? Where will you paint?"

"I want Anna to sit for the third picture in a triptych. I have already painted her at work and in a domestic scene. This one is to be out-of-doors and at leisure. I thought we might take a picnic and find a good spot for the day." He smiled at Anna. "Would you like that? You have seen very little of Brittany apart from your walks to the village."

"Oh, yes! I'd love it!"

"Right. Then if no one else needs the trap, I'll

show you the Rose Granite coast. It's wonderful huge boulders of pink stone."

"I thought you were going to paint," Jacques commented dryly.

"Of course I am, but Anna is entitled to a little fun, especially after the marvellous meal she cooked for us tonight." Robert picked up the wine bottle and regarded it gravely. "I do believe this is almost gone. Another bottle anyone?"

"Not for me. I'm a little tired. Good night." Sylvie rose from the table. At the door, she stopped and turned, and said in her heavily accented English, "Thank you, Anna, for the delicious food. You have a talent for the cooking." She left the room and the men stared at each other.

"Would you believe it?" Robert commented. "I think that is the longest speech I ever heard Sylvie make."

"Yes," Jacques agreed. He turned to Alphonse and translated what Sylvie had said. Alphonse remarked, "*Oui, c'est vrai!*" and lifted his glass to toast Anna.

Jacques joined in, saying, "Yes, she is right, *ma petite*. The meal was...*superbe!*" He kissed his finger ends with a flourish in Anna's direction, and she flushed with pleasure, for she knew he spoke the truth. She had surprised even herself with what she had been able to achieve. The soufflé had been light as air, and the guinea fowl mouth wateringly succulent, although she was unable to pronounce the name of the recipe, which Therese said was *hachis parmentier de pintade*. The *tarte tatin* which followed had revealed a supreme blend of sweetness and sharpness achieved by using two distinct varieties of apple, heightened by a hint of cinnamon.

"Yes, it was good," Anna admitted happily, "but

it is entirely due to Therese. I realise now I understood nothing at all about food or cooking until I
came here."

"You could not have a better teacher," Robert
commented. "And she has a superb herb garden.
When I am back in England, I often think of the
meals here, and I yearn for Therese's cooking. As
you know, we have a good cook at home, but
French food...ah...this is something different."

Jacques laughed. "We 'ave a different attitude
to food, that is all. The English eat to keep themselves alive; in France, food is life itself and worth
the most detailed attention." He turned to Anna
and his voice became serious. "Take advantage,
ma petite, and learn everything that Therese can
teach you. Make notes so you do not forget. It
seems you 'ave a talent for *le cuisine*. Therese tells
me yesterday that you 'ave an excellent palate, you
know 'ow things should taste. This is something
'ighly regarded in France. To cook well means you
will never be without work."

Anna laughed, but saw with sudden clarity that
Jacques spoke the truth. There would be no opportunity to prepare such food back in Sandley
Heath, but there were other places, and if she could
come as far as Brittany, she could go anywhere.
She began to giggle, and Robert said, "I think the
wine has gone to your head."

"Yes, and I like it. Let's have another bottle."

"Not for you, young lady," Robert said firmly.
"Remember, you have to be up early for our day
out tomorrow. Come on. Time for bed." He took
Anna's arm, but as she struggled to her feet, the
walls of the room seemed to move, and she sat
down again with a jolt.

"Heavens, how much did you have?" Robert
looked quite put out. "You are drunk, my dear,"

He hauled Anna to her feet. "Jacques, I blame you. You always fill her glass too full."

"Me? I did nothing! Anna can please 'erself."

"I'm perfectly all right," Anna said firmly. She took a deep breath and made her way to the door, concentrating hard. "Good night, Jacques."

"Good night, *ma petite*."

Robert followed Anna up the stairs. He was slightly concerned in case she should fall, but she managed to reach her bedroom door safely. She turned. "There, you see? I'm perfectly all right." She giggled again. "I do feel funny, though. I must have had quite a lot, but it wasn't Jacques."

"No." Robert looked at her fondly. She had obviously never experienced a feeling of intoxication in her life and she looked a little dishevelled, like a infant who has been playing rough games.

"What a child you are, Anna," he chided. "I must watch you more closely or you'll get into all sorts of trouble."

"No, I won't," she responded archly as she opened the door. "And I'm not a child." She leaned towards him confidentially. "I'll show you," she said, and the next instant she was kissing him so passionately that, in spite of his surprise, he felt himself respond. Before he knew it, a great surge of feeling engulfed him so that he could not stop the demands of his lips on hers, searching, seeking, exploring, savouring the passion she returned to him, all reason lost.

Suddenly Robert pushed Anna from him roughly. He stood, shocked, his breathing laboured and his heart hammering in his chest. "Go to bed, Anna," he commanded sternly. "Now."

The sweet smile in her eyes told him she understood, told him she had found out his secret, understood the longing he had pushed to the back of his mind since those early days at High Cedars, the desire for her which had been harder to deny every day they spent in each other's company. He had not dreamed she felt it too, that it was the same for her. Her gaze was bright and glowing. He tore his eyes away.

"Good night, Anna," he said gently. As he walked back down the stairs, he could feel her eyes following him, her gaze burning into his back. His mother's words of warning flitted through his mind, but he discarded them instantly. What did she know of a young man's needs, or a young woman's for that matter? This was France. He had enjoyed a wonderful evening and felt good about himself and his life. It was a perfect summer, and tomorrow would be another lovely day.

Robert

The trap bowled merrily along the narrow lane, and Anna, refreshed after several cups of strong coffee, began to enjoy the morning. It was probably just as well that she had only a hazy recollection of the events of the previous evening. Robert felt a certain inward amusement at her lack of any sense of embarrassment. He glanced at her, savouring the freshness of her young cheeks, noting with a painter's eye the tendrils of tawny curls which escaped from under her bonnet.

"Nearly there," he said, as she felt his glance and turned towards him. "Just around the next bend there's a place to stop and rest the pony. We'll walk from there."

Anna felt a twinge of disappointment as she clambered down from the trap. It was obviously the right place, several carts were there already, and a young French boy quickly appeared, offering to take care of the pony for a few sous. If the sea was nearby, it was certainly not visible, and neither was the pink granite coastline Robert had promised.

She followed as Robert took the picnic basket and led the way along a small path which wound between the trees and then across an area of sparse scrub. After only a couple of minutes, the path rounded a huge boulder and suddenly the sea was before them, blue and magnificent. Anna stopped.

"Oh! Oh, my goodness!" For once, her delight

at discovering the sea was overcome by the extraordinary coastline which bounded its white crested borders. As far as she could see, huge boulders of pink granite dominated the view, worn into smooth, fantastic shapes by the pounding seas of centuries.

"Oh, look, Robert. It's like...like...." Her words trailed away on the slight breeze. It was not like anything, she thought, not like anything she had ever seen or imagined.

"It's...beautiful, but so...strange."

"Yes." Robert had visited the Rose Granite coast several times before, but the first sight of the bizarre landscape always disturbed him. "I sometimes think that perhaps the surface of the moon is something like this," he ventured.

"Of course not!" Anna had recovered and was starting to jump with excitement. "The moon is made of green cheese, everyone knows that!" She started to run, calling, "Come on, Robert, down here...."

Robert followed with the picnic basket, watching Anna as she clambered blithely among the rocks, making her way towards the sea. For a moment, he considered painting her here, against this background of weathered granite, the softness against.... No, she must be seen against the greens of the countryside. These hard shapes would destroy what he intended, and anyone who observed the finished picture would not believe such a place existed and would misinterpret his intention.

Anna had climbed up onto the top of a high boulder. "Look there, Robert! That one looks as if it is balancing on a point!"

Robert laughed, "It probably is. If you pushed it, perhaps it would topple over."

He watched surprise and indecision struggle

briefly in her face before she responded, "Oh! Stop teasing. But it does look as if it would topple."

"The sea has worn the granite away over the years so that there is only that small point left to hold it up," Robert explained.

"What happens when the point is worn away completely? Will the boulder just roll down into the sea?"

"I shouldn't think so. It will happen very gradually." Robert put down the basket. "Come and sit down, Anna. This flat rock will be ideal for the picnic."

As she clambered down from her vantage point, he glimpsed a slender ankle, a froth of white cambric lace, and as she neared the bottom, a vision of beautifully rounded calf.

He felt the familiar stirring and smiled at her gently as she began to unpack the basket. *Gently does it*, he told himself. Like the sea had worn away the granite, so he would wear away her reserve, her rigid working class conception of right and wrong, the values she had absorbed because she had no others. He would show her new ways of thinking, open her up to passion, to transports she had never dreamed of. She was already half way there if last night was anything to go by.

"I honestly think I will miss Therese's pâté more than anything else in France," Anna said. She cut a big slice and passed it to him on a plate. She sawed at the bread, speared a thick chunk on the end of the knife and held it out to him. "I never tasted it before I came here, you know," she confessed, helping herself to a slice.

"There are lots of things you have never done, Anna," Robert said gently.

"I know. I certainly was never at a place like this." She spread pâté on her bread, took a bite and chewed contentedly, gazing around her all the while. "That boulder, will it fall eventually?" she asked. "Will the sea wear it away in the end?"

"Oh, yes," Robert said quietly. He smiled. "Eventually it will fall. You can bank on it."

Anna was restless. Her eyes roved the beach below, watching idly the antics of two small children as they dug happily in the sand pools left by the receding tide. She wondered vaguely where the children lived, and let her gaze wander beyond the beach to the few small cottages which straggled out from the village. Perhaps they lived in one of those or in Locquirec itself. She craned forward but still could not see the village, hidden beyond the high rising cliff.

"Keep still, please, Anna," Robert said briefly.

Anna started back into position quickly. She had been sitting in this spot for hours on end, day after day, and although she was becoming a little stiff, she had not tired of the view. *How extraordinary to live here,* she mused, *watching the children playing in the sand.* They had been brought up in the centre of so much beauty, freshness and freedom. She could not help but compare their surroundings to those of her own childhood, when the escape to clean air and fun had been once a year on the day of the chapel outing. Did these children know how lucky they were? Probably not, any more than she had known how meagre and poverty-stricken was her own childhood. It had been how things were, that was all, and in the same way, these children took Locquirec and its surroundings for granted.

Surely it could not be much longer until lunch? Trying not to move her head, she glanced sideways at Robert. She felt again the peculiar intense feeling in her stomach as she watched the assiduous concentration on his face as he worked. *Such a beautiful face,* she thought. *Anyone who gets to know him must surely love him as I do.* She loved his thick, untidy eyebrows, his aristocratic nose, and the plane of his cheekbones which she knew so well from long study. And his lips, so sensual when he laughed, so inviting even when pressed firmly together in painstaking application, as they were now. And his body, his long lean body which she found herself watching each day, devouring every movement with her eyes.

"Not long now, my sweet." The long body moved, brush in mid air, as he contemplated the canvas.

Anna dragged her eyes back to the view, and a faint blush coloured her cheeks. He had called her "my sweet". Surely that meant something? Or perhaps it didn't. Although she could remember little of the night at the farmhouse when she had drunk too much, she knew she had behaved disgracefully, kissing Robert in a very forward manner. She also understood he had enjoyed it as much as she did. Since that day, he had never made a move towards her, and yet sometimes she felt, in that strange current which seemed to pass between them, that he wanted her as much as she wanted him. If that was so, why did he not take her in his arms? Why did he not sweep her away and make love to her, give her the kisses she needed so desperately? In the last two weeks they had become so close, so intimate, but without touching, so that it was driving her mad. In another few weeks they would be going to Paris, and their time together would surely be curtailed.

"There. We'll break for lunch." Robert began to wipe his brush. "I won't pack everything away; we can have lunch here. Tell you what," he continued as Anna stretched her stiff limbs, "let's move round the corner into that little hollow we found the day it was so windy. It was very sheltered."

"It's not windy today," Anna countered, "and we can't see the sea from there." Nevertheless, she followed Robert as he picked up the basket and walked a little further up the steep hillside.

Robert spread the rug in the hollow and Anna unpacked the basket. As usual, Therese had done them proud, with a selection of cheeses and fruit and a Breton patisserie. Robert opened a bottle of wine, and as they enjoyed their lunch, they relaxed into the easy familiarity which had grown between them.

Anna was never sure afterwards exactly how it happened. As he reached across to the picnic basket, Robert's arm brushed her breast lightly. She stiffened, as he murmured briefly, "Sorry." In that second, their eyes locked for what seemed like an eternity, and a moment later she was in his arms, responding to his kisses with abandon, trying to slake the thirst for him which had been denied too long. Her need aroused in her a passion which shook her body through in its intensity, and when he released her at last, she was gasping and breathless.

"My dearest, my little darling...," Robert whispered. He stroked her face tenderly, and in his eyes Anna saw the look of burning desire and felt her heart leap.

"Oh, Robert...." She could not speak, the words would not come.

Robert kissed her face gently, her eyes, cheeks and neck. His lips caressed her shoulders as his hands moved over her body, fondling, caressing and arousing in her a tumultuous wave of desire, a craving which could not be denied.

Even so, there was a moment when she desisted, when her mind sought to gain dominance, and she gasped, "We must not...we must not...."

Robert drew back, and she saw the tortured look as he whispered, "If you do not love me...."

"Of course I do! Oh, Robert, you know how much I do."

"And I love you, so much, my darling. Let me show you how much. We must always be like this, must always be together." His kiss drowned any protest, and Anna gave herself up to the voluptuous enjoyment he gave her, his practised hands rousing her to such a crescendo of passion that, when he entered her, there was only a fleeting second of sharp pain before she was lost in an ever mounting symphony of feeling which swept her to unimagined bliss.

Therese was harassed; it had been a hard day. There seemed no end to the items which had to be completed and crossed off her list. It wasn't just the packing of their trunks. La Maison Blanche was to be closed up for at least a month, as Therese was to accompany the group to the Paris house to act as cook, the artists having decided that to enjoy her food for another few weeks was well worth the expenses of her trip. This arrangement suited Therese very well, as she had a sister living in Paris and would be able to visit her for a few days. Even so, closing up the house entailed a lot of work. She had organised the meals so that food could be either finished up or taken with them, arranged for her friend Albertine to come and feed the livestock each day...and she must leave the place clean.

She looked up from wiping the larder shelves as Anna appeared in the kitchen. *Mon Dieu*, she thought, the girl looks younger and lovelier every day. Therese was no fool and was well aware of the reason. *It's amazing,* she thought, *what love can do for the complexion.*

"Hello, Therese. Still at it? Well, I'm ready, all packed, and I've cleaned my room and Robert's."

It was on the tip of Therese's tongue to say, "I expect more than cleaning 'as been going on in Monsieur Robert's room," but Anna smiled her lovely open smile, and Therese bit back the retort and said instead, "The kitchen floor is to be clean. Then I must prepare for myself. I still 'ave not find my clothes to take to Paris."

"Oh, Therese, aren't you excited? I am. To think of us going to Paris! The only sad thing is leaving here." Anna looked round the large, comfortable kitchen with affection. She knew the memory of La Maison Blanche would remain with her. She had been happier here than ever in her life.

"Poof!" Therese was saying. "Excited for going to Paris? What is Paris? Nothing! And those Parisiens, they 'ave much money to waste but are so...so...."

"Stingy," Anna supplied the word, well aware of Therese's views on Parisiens. "Or mean; you can say mean."

"Yes, mean," Therese agreed. "They will not give you the drip off the nose!"

Anna laughed. "Go upstairs now, Therese, and pack your things. I will do the floor," she added, seeing Therese was about to remonstrate. "You have done enough for today. When the floor is dry, I will make us a nice cup of tea."

Therese nodded, but at the door she turned. "Coffee," she said firmly.

"Tea," Anna responded, just as firmly. "There is enough to make a last pot."

Therese scowled, and left the room muttering, "*Les anglais! Le thé, toujours le thé!*"

Anna smiled; she enjoyed their little arguments about tea versus coffee. She fetched the floor bucket and began to wash the floor. It was a good floor of dark stone tiles and came up well. She was reminded of the quarry floor in the kitchen at High Cedars, although, of course, that was red. There were a few quarry floors in the better houses in Sandley Heath, although her mother had never enjoyed the luxury of such a floor at home; in fact, there probably wasn't a quarry floor at all in Dawkins Street.

What was she thinking of? Where was her mind wandering? She was not going to think of Sandley Heath. The old life was far away, and she would never return to it. Her life had changed so completely since she came to France that she knew she could never again be comfortable in the restrictive poverty of her home. But then, had she ever been comfortable there? She realised she had not. Until she came to La Maison Blanche, she had never known what it was to be at ease, to be free, to have fun. At High Cedars, she had seen something of the sheer delight of conversation with intelligent people, as they pitted their wits against each other in argument, and it was the same here. Every evening, she listened to the artists as they debated every subject under the sun over their dinner and wine. She listened, she learned, and she loved it.

A frown crossed Anna's brow as she finished the floor and surveyed her work. She would have to write to Clancy, and to her father and Will. She had sent a few letters home, letters of the kind they would expect to receive, letters which gave no information other than assurances about her health and comments on the weather.

She went out to the yard to empty the floor bucket. The sun was strong and warm on her face and arms, and she stopped a moment, trying to draw to herself the character of this lovely place. She wanted to keep it, to fix in her memory forever the warmth of the old pink stone, the noisy clucking of the hens, the cheerfulness of the small flower bed, the scent of Therese's herb garden.

Would she ever return here? Surely she would. Robert had spent his summers here for some time, and her life was undoubtedly bound up with him forever. She felt a little thrill of happiness at the thought. For the last two weeks they had made love any way and anywhere they could, any place they happened to be. Sometimes it was in Robert's room or in hers, having crept along the landing, trying not to make the floorboards creak. They had made love with ever increasing passion and variety, in the hayloft and in the fields, in the woodlands under the trees, and yesterday, they had taken a last picnic to the hillside overlooking the beach near Locquirec and had found the little hollow they both remembered with affection. Impressions of their passion filled Anna's mind, and she hugged her secret joy to herself with delight.

For a moment, she wondered with a degree of apprehension what Florence would make of their love, but quickly decided Robert's mother would probably be delighted. She had, after all, spoken of Anna as "one of the family."

She returned to the kitchen and put the teapot to warm, smiling to herself. Eventually, she would get Therese to admit she liked tea in the afternoon.

Paris

The grey stone tower of Notre Dame seemed ethereal in the moonlight, as the boat wound its way slowly down the Seine. As Sylvie had declined to join them, Anna found herself sandwiched between Alphonse and Jacques near the stern and gazed around her in rapturous enjoyment. She still could not get used to the beauty of the city, for she had not realised until she came to Paris that it was possible for a city to be beautiful. In her experience, the more buildings there were, the more ugly and dirty the place became. Jacques had tried to explain to her that many parts of Paris were indeed filthy, poor and overcrowded, but Anna did not wish to listen.

"I believe you," she told him, "but I do not wish to see those parts. I know what they will be like. Where we are living now is so lovely, the trees, and the museums and galleries, and the Tuileries Gardens."

Her enthusiasm for the city had touched his heart, and because Robert had been busy much of the time, Jacques had taken upon himself the duty of escorting Anna to several places she wished to see. To his surprise, he had found himself involved in a personal journey of rediscovery, seeing Paris through Anna's fresh and enthusiastic eyes. Most of all, she delighted in the spacious elegance of the large townhouse the artists had taken for a month, and Jacques often caught sight of her examining a piece of furniture or fabric or even a kitchen implement with undisguised curiosity and appreciation.

He smiled now as Anna tugged his arm, point-ing at the squat tower of Notre Dame. She chatted happily, spilling out details of the long climb the day before, when she had persuaded Therese to join her in braving the steps and their own fright to see the big bell and the view from the top.

"From here you can hardly see the gargoyles," she bubbled. "Look! At the top...there on the corner...I stood right next to that one and gave him a hug. He was so deliciously ugly!" She sighed with contentment, recalling the fun of the ugly faces and strange shapes, the wonderful view over the city and the joy of feeling you were at the top of the world. She turned to Jacques confidentially. "Jacques, do you know what was the best memory of all?"

"What?" he said gravely, his eyes twinkling above the huge bush of beard.

"When we were up there, right at the top look-ing at the view, I suddenly could smell lavender. It was impossible, but I could smell it. Therese could smell it too. Then we realised what it was. There was a lavender seller on the square in front of the church. He had a big cart piled high with it, and the scent was wafting up, all that way to the top."

"I see, and that was your best memory?"

"It was...I can't explain. It was...touching, the scent of lavender up so high."

"And the church itself didn't impress you?"

"The building, yes, of course. So old and so beautiful. But inside...." Anna giggled as if slightly ashamed, "it's a bit...a bit...overdecorated. You must remember I am a chapel person; we do not agree with ornamentation. I felt quite strange in there...quite wicked!"

"Really? How dull chapel must be!"

"No, it isn't," Anna responded seriously. "We do not believe in praying to pictures and statues like the Catholics; we only pray direct to God, from our hearts."

Jacques, who had been brought up a Catholic, felt it his duty to defend the Faith. "We don't worship pictures, Anna, or statues either. They are symbols, that is all."

"Pictures and statues don't mean anything," she replied. "They are not God."

"Of course not. But I can't agree they mean nothing." Seeing she did not understand, he continued, "Have you ever had your photograph taken, Anna?"

"No," she said, mystified. "But I have seen photographs."

"Well, imagine you have a photograph of someone, a person you love dearly, your mother perhaps."

"Oh, yes! I always wished I had a photograph of Mother."

"Imagine you have. It is in a nice frame on a chest in your home, where you see it every day. It is a comfort and a reminder. One day, someone comes to your house, picks up the photograph, takes it from the frame and tears it into pieces. How would you feel?"

"Dreadful, that would be awful."

"Of course. Because the photograph, the image, means something to you. In the same way, our paintings, icons or statues in the church mean something to us, because they remind us of what we love."

Her face was a picture. "Is that true? You don't actually worship those things?"

Jacques laughed, "Of course not, any more

than you chapel folk live on bread and water like the Catholics say!"

"Oh, Jacques!" Anna squeezed his arm. "You have been so good to me, you and Therese. I wouldn't have seen or understood so much if you hadn't helped me. Robert has been so busy."

"Yes," Jacques said dryly, "I suppose you can call it that."

He glanced to the prow of the boat where Robert sat with some English friends, recently arrived in Paris. The party was in full swing and centred around an extremely attractive, fair-haired young woman, who was holding Robert's arm and laughing. As they watched, Robert raised his champagne glass to her and took a sip.

"Delphine is in good form tonight," Anna said a little acidly. She resented the way Delphine Braybrook had monopolised Robert since she and her mother had arrived to take up residence only two doors away from their own house. She seemed to expect him to escort them everywhere, even shopping. "Delphine and her mother take up a great deal of Robert's time," she added.

"Yes...they are old friends I believe," said Jacques. He tugged at his beard. "Anna, you must not take Robert too seriously. He is great fun, you know that of course, but not...not...." He tailed off, dismayed by the look of innocent enquiry in her big eyes.

"How do you mean, not take him seriously?"

Jacques couldn't do it. "I just mean, he's a great one for fun, but...you couldn't expect him to...to ever buckle down to real...work." He gave a slightly nervous laugh. "Perhaps I'm wrong. I didn't think he would finish that picture of you, but he did. It's very good, too. He's never finished one before when he's been in France, at least as far as I know."

"Oh, yes, it is good, isn't it? I can hardly believe it is me! Florence, his mother, will love it."

Anna smiled happily at Jacques and turned her attention to admiring more of Paris by night. She was not worried about Delphine Braybrook. Hadn't Robert come to her room last night and held her in his arms as tenderly as ever? Hadn't he told her that Delphine and her mother were a damned nuisance? Their love affair was as passionate and close as ever, even though since they came to Paris it had become increasingly clandestine.

As the boat drew towards the small wooden jetty where they were to disembark and visit Le Poste restaurant for dinner, Robert made his way towards them, followed by Delphine. He winked at Anna and stopped to chat to Jacques, reminding him of the last time they had dined at Le Poste. Anna could not help but stare at Delphine. Apart from her beauty, she seemed to exude an air of confident condescension, from her perfectly coiffured head to her soft lilac leather shoes. These matched exactly her superbly cut skirt and jacket, and Anna almost gasped aloud as she noticed the diamond brooch which Delphine had pinned at the neck of her lace blouse. Everything she wore was of outstanding quality, and Anna, who had dressed very carefully for the evening in her best skirt and a new cream blouse, began to feel like a country bumpkin.

Seeming to feel Anna's gaze, Delphine met her eyes and a slight frown shadowed the beautiful face. Anna gave a wide smile and said quietly, "Good evening, Miss Braybrook," and Delphine inclined her head regally.

As they began to disembark, Delphine said in a loud clear voice, "Why have you brought servants with you, Robert?" Robert stopped, frozen in the act of handing Delphine from the boat. He said nothing, and Delphine, having gained the wooden jetty, continued in the same tone, "That girl, Anna whatever-her-name-is, surely you're not intending she should eat with our party?"

Robert coloured, and said quickly, "Anna is not a servant, Delphine. She is our model and a friend."

"Oh, really?" Delphine sounded quite amused. "I never understand you artistic types. I thought a model was a servant per se, if not something worse!" Her eyes raked Anna from head to toe and her expression clearly implied that she couldn't be blamed for thinking that someone who dressed like a servant was one.

Anna, trembling with mortification, felt Jacques squeeze her elbow. "Come, *ma petite*. Don't take notice. You are with me." He handed her from the boat and gave a slight bow. "I am very honoured to be your escort."

His kind smile made Anna's eyes brim with tears, and she trembled as she said quietly, "I think...I think perhaps I should go back to the house."

"*Non!* Absolutely not!" Jacques said fiercely. "You must not give way to such..." he searched for a word, "unpardonable rudeness. You must not give her the satisfaction, *ma petite*."

He took Anna's hand and tucked it into his arm. "We shall go in. They have an excellent chef here and you must try something different. You have a good palate and must give me your impressions."

In spite of Jacques's kindness and the relaxed atmosphere and superb food, Anna spent a miserable evening. She could not forget Delphine's snub, which had so obviously been deliberate, and began to wonder what had motivated it. Robert and several of the party, including Delphine, went on to a club after dinner. Anna declined to go, telling Jacques she had a slight headache, and he insisted on escorting her home before leaving again to join the rest of the party.

Anna heard them return very late, but Robert did not come to her room. Was it because Jacques had told him she was not well and he did not wish to disturb her, she wondered, or was it something more sinister?

Anna's misgivings melted away the following morning. She was busy in the kitchen helping Therese with the breakfast when Robert put his head round the door. "Good morning, piglet. Feeling better?"

Anna gave him a winning smile, obviously Jacques had told him. "Yes, fine now, thank you. Have you had breakfast?"

"Yes, and I've come to ask Therese's permission to spirit you away." He looked quizzically at Therese. "I'd like to take Anna to see the Chardin paintings. I did promise her."

Therese sniffed, "You take 'er where you like. I manage."

"Are you sure, Therese? I would like to go." Anna could hardly contain her excitement, and a grudging smile crossed Therese's lips in spite of herself. "Go on...to your gallery," she grumbled. "You think I need you? You talk more than you work."

Anna looked suitably contrite at this admonition, but Robert laughed aloud and said, "Everyone is out for lunch anyway, so no need to feel guilty, piglet." He had taken to calling Anna "piglet" since they arrived in Paris, because of the fondness she had developed for the rich pastries at the Salon de Thé.

Now he said quickly, "Run away and get ready. Put on your best bib and tucker and after the gallery, I'll take you somewhere special for lunch."

Anna threw a pleading look at Therese which was answered by a curt jerk of Therese's head in the direction of the door. Anna dashed out, and Robert sat down at the kitchen table.

"You get on well, don't you? You and Anna?" he said, watching as Therese sorted raspberries into a large white bowl.

"She's a nice girl," Therese responded after a moment, adding a little unwillingly, "She 'as...what is it? *joie de vivre*."

"Spirit," Robert said thoughtfully. "In English, we would say she has spirit."

"*Mon Dieu!* What a language! How can this be?"

"Not the sort of spirit you're thinking of," Robert laughed. "Not like the Holy Spirit, or the spirit you drink."

"What a language!" Therese said again. "One word for many things."

"This spirit means lots of life, enthusiasm," Robert explained. "But I think *joie de vivre* is just right for Anna."

"Yes." Therese fetched a huge kitchen scale and poured the raspberries into the big brass pan. She added a few more raspberries, watching until the pan dipped obligingly, and then said quietly, "It will be a pity if the *joie de vivre* is lost from Anna."

"Why should it be?" Robert asked.

Therese's lips set in a firm line. It was not her place to criticise, but she could not help saying, "You forget I 'ave known you many years, Monsieur Robert."

"Yes, but Anna is different, you must know that, Therese! I am very fond of her, and so is my mother. I would not hurt her for the world!"

"Good!" Therese grunted. "Make sure you don't!"

"I knew 'piglet' was the right name for you," Robert remarked. "How you get away with it without putting on weight I'll never know."

Anna giggled as she finished the last crumbs of a *tourtière Bonaguil.* She sighed happily. "It is because I have to sample as much as I can while I'm here," she explained. "Once I get home I shall never taste anything like it again."

"You could make some," Robert ventured. "You have lots of recipes. You and Therese seem to be talking of nothing but food these days."

Anna fell silent. There was no use explaining that even if she could obtain the right ingredients in England, she could never afford to buy them. She was not sure why she had collected so many recipes, but perhaps one day.... She pulled herself together.

"Do you think the chef would give me the recipe?" she asked. "Therese has taught me how to make *mille feuille,* but this is different."

"I expect so, if you are really interested." Robert summoned the waiter and spoke to him in halting French. The man seemed delighted with the request and hurried away. Robert smiled. "There you are. You will find the French are always ready to talk about food. You are becoming quite a francophile yourself!"

"Yes, and thank you for such a lovely day. I thought the paintings were marvellous. You know," Anna leaned forward confidentially, "when I first went to High Cedars and you wanted to paint me in my working clothes, I couldn't understand why! I had never seen pictures of working people." She laughed. "To be honest, the only pictures I had seen were those in the Dudley Art Gallery when I was a child, when we went to see your father's painting. All the pictures seemed to be of very grand ladies and gentlemen in beautiful clothes, apart from the religious ones and some landscapes."

"There are other forms," said Robert with a smile. "But Chardin has always been very special for me. I remember the time I first saw his work when I came to Paris a few years ago. I knew immediately that I wanted to paint ordinary people, working people, like he did. Now we arc in the age of the machine, and I can paint a different kind of worker, the industrial worker."

"I loved the painting of the kitchen maid," said Anna, remembering the simple domesticity of the picture. "I liked the still life too."

"But do you know what it is that you admire?" Robert asked. "Why did you like the picture of the kitchen maid?"

"I don't know," Anna admitted. "I think...because it's real."

Robert looked pleased. "A good answer," he said approvingly. "You are learning about art, piglet. You see, Chardin painted just what he saw. Many artists tend to idealise scenes or make them more romantic. For example, if they are painting a country scene, the farm labourers will all have rustic apple cheeks, and the women will be shown sitting at a cottage door, surrounded by chubby infants. The reality is often very different."

"Yes, it is," Anna agreed. In her mind suddenly appeared an image of a skinny drone at the door of a hovel, with two filthy children clutching at her skirts. She had seen them on a farm when she had visited the Clent Hills with Clancy. She recalled her misgivings about Andrew Nicholson's portrayal of her in *The Chainmaker's Child* and felt she understood what Robert meant.

"So you are saying art has to be honest?" she asked.

"For me, yes. There are other artists who look at things differently. Some of them like to paint what they *don't* see, but rather what is in their imagination. For me, honesty is everything."

Anna felt a surge of happiness run through her. When Robert talked to her like this, she felt whole, included, as if she belonged to his world.

"Another thing I meant to ask you," Robert continued, "do you remember when we climbed to the top of Dudley Castle at night and saw the fires?"

"I'll never forget it," Anna answered.

"At that time, we talked of beauty. I said the scene had a savage beauty of its own, but you disagreed. How do you feel now? Can you see what I meant?"

His eyes were intense, and Anna had the feeling that somehow her answer was important. "I don't know. I think I feel the same. It was certainly an incredible sight, even exhilarating perhaps, but I still cannot think of it as beautiful."

"Ah." He looked a little disappointed. "Incredible...and exhilarating," he repeated. He began to laugh. "Like us!" he said, his voice dropping to a whisper. "When we are together we are incredible, and exhilarating."

"Yes, but beautiful too," Anna said softly.

"Don't you see, that's it!" Robert said, the whisper becoming intense. "Our love is passionate, even savage. There are many friends of mine, and yours, who would say it is also wicked and sinful. But you and I know it is beautiful, as you say." Robert licked his lips in concentration and the lock of fair hair fell forward over his eyes, to be flicked back with the impatient gesture Anna loved. "It is like the view from the castle," he continued eagerly.

"You could only see it as a battlefield, but for me it had a strange beauty, a savage beauty of its own." His voice became thoughtful. "I can often find great beauty in things that others find repulsive...or sordid even...."

At that moment, the waiter returned with a scruffy piece of paper on which was scrawled the recipe for *tourtière Bonaguil.* He spoke to Robert, who made valiant attempts to understand the fast, heavily accented French. At length, Robert turned to Anna. "I have it at last. The chef is asleep at the moment, but his wife has written out the recipe. She says to tell you it is for a large quantity; it makes twenty-four! She thanks you for your interest and sends you a small gift."

The waiter produced a paper bag containing two *tourtières Bonaguil.* Anna smiled her thanks, and after Robert had paid the bill, they left the restaurant to the accompaniment of much laughter and handshaking and promises to return.

In the carriage, Robert took Anna's hand. "Yes, piglet, it's definitely the *joie de vivre,*'" he said.

"The what?"

"*Joie de vivre.* That is French for 'joy in living' or 'love of life'. Therese and I were saying we thought you had it."

"I do when I'm in Paris or at La Maison Blanche," she said.

"True! How else can I explain the phenomenon of a restaurant in Paris actually giving food away to the customers? It has never happened before in my experience. It must be catching, this *joie de vivre!*"

Anna giggled. "I never had it in Sandley Heath," she said. A frown flitted over her face. "When.... How much longer will we stay here?"

Robert smiled. "Oh, we've a couple of weeks to go yet. In other years I used to go on to Cannes for the autumn."

"And this year?"

"No. Since my father died I don't like to leave mother alone for too long, although Andrew will keep an eye on her." He squeezed her hand. "Anyway, I've got to get my little piglet home," he said gently.

Anna grimaced. *Yes*, she thought, *sooner or later the piglet has to return to the sty.*

"Enjoy yourself!" Anna called when she saw Sylvie at the front door with her easel and canvas. Sylvie looked up, and although it was impossible to imagine her complying with the instruction, at least she smiled as she left the house.

Anna felt at a loose end. Jacques and Alphonse had already left to visit an exhibition, and Therese had gone to her sister's for the day. She had left Anna in charge of the domestic arrangements, which were few, as only Robert was home, entertaining Delphine Braybrook and her mother at coffee in the drawing room. Anna had been aware of a lull in the conversation as she had taken in the coffee, but she had put down the tray and said "good morning," not even looking at Delphine. As she left the room, Robert had given her a heavy wink.

Now she wandered through the lovely house, wondering if Robert would be free later or whether he intended to take his guests out to lunch. She went into the small library, one of her favourite rooms, and perused the shelves carefully; there were a few volumes in English if one could find them.

"Oh, you're here."

Anna turned quickly to see Delphine had entered the library. She was wearing a stunning day dress of caramel coloured lace, with an inset fichu of pale peach silk, and as she moved, Anna was aware of the delicate perfume which surrounded her. She smiled graciously at Anna.

"I was not aware you read French, Miss...er...."

"Gibson," Anna supplied quietly. "Anna Gibson."
She turned back to the shelves. "I don't read French,
but there are some English books here."

"Oh, yes, I believe there are a few. I read very
few novels. When I do, I read in the original French;
one tends to lose so much in the translation."

Anna did not reply. Delphine, however, was
inclined to talk. She took out a slim volume and
offered it to Anna. "Here's one in English which
may be suitable. I have not read it but it seems
very light reading."

The snub was obvious. Anna stiffened, and said
quietly, "Why are you determined to be so rude to
me? I have never harmed you as far as I know."

"Harmed me? Of course you have not, my dear.
It would be very difficult for you to do so, would it
not? The contest would hardly be equal."

Delphine appeared to be enjoying herself.
Anna, trembling slightly but with a high spot of
colour flaming each cheek, stood her ground. "Then
I ask again, why be so rude to me?"

Delphine laughed. "Since we are alone, I will
confess it. I was not trying to be rude, as you so
quaintly put it, I was simply giving you a gentle
warning."

"About what? What have I done?"

"Nothing as far as I know, but you might...."

"Might what?" Anna said hotly, becoming exasperated.

"Become a little too close to my fiancé. I have
seen you talking and laughing together."

"Your fiancé?" Anna began to smile. "But I don't
even know your fiancé." Even as she said it a cold
dread began to gnaw at her.

Delphine, observing Anna's face, said quietly,
"So he didn't tell you? I thought as much." She

turned away as if annoyed, but then said in a more conciliatory tone, "It's unofficial as yet, but Robert and I have been promised for almost two years. We are getting married next spring."

Anna did not answer. She stood, white-faced, staring at Delphine with a look of undisguised shock.

Delphine became concerned. "Come and sit down, Anna. You are as white as a ghost." She propelled Anna towards a chair, and Anna sat down mechanically. Delphine hovered. "I did not mean to upset you so, but I had to say something!"

"Y...yes." It was a strangled whisper.

"I mean, before it became serious." Delphine looked into the wide eyes and read the fear there. "Anna, you didn't...?" She stared at Anna's pathetic face and recoiled with a groan of disgust.

"You little fool!" she exploded, "How could you be so stupid?" She paced the floor angrily, and her lips set into a thin, determined line. "So Robert's had his sticky fingers in the jam pot, has he?" she said, almost to herself. "Again!" she added, and Anna felt as if she was shrinking, crumbling, dissolving slowly until she was an unimportant scrap, a meaningless and insubstantial wisp, who could not think or feel, could not...could not....

How Anna reached her room, she never knew. It was a combination of shambling steps and wild clutching at the banister rail, pushed and pulled by Delphine, who, once Anna was safely on the bed, fetched a glass of water. Anna attempted to sip it but was overcome by a wave of nausea.

After a moment, she felt a little better, and attempted to regain some remnants of dignity. "I'm sorry," she said to Delphine. "I'm alright now."

Delphine sat on the edge of the bed. Her voice was quietly determined. "Anna, I'm sorry to have given you such a shock, but I ask you to understand. This is something of a surprise to me also. I had not realised that...." Her voice tailed off, and Anna took her cue.

"Oh, there was never anything between Robert and I," she lied. "Nothing serious, just a mild flirtation really. It was a shock to find out he is engaged, that's all."

Delphine did not believe her, but said quietly, "Of course. Do you feel better now?"

"Much better, thank you." The conventions were in place again.

"Then I have one last thing to say to you. It will be best if you leave as quickly as possible. I am going to invite Robert to accompany us to Cannes for a couple of months."

Even now Anna clung to a shred of hope. "He may not wish to come," she said. "I think he wants to return to England."

"He is coming to Cannes," Delphine said firmly. "There is no doubt about that. If he doesn't...." She left the rest of the sentence unspoken, but it hung in the air between them.

Delphine rose. "Surely you did not think...? You must have known Robert could not marry you?"

Anna forced a smile, her composure returning fast. "Of course not; it never entered my mind. I told you, there was nothing serious."

Delphine sighed and said, not unkindly, "Go home, Anna Gibson. Go back to what you know and to those who care for you. It is useless to try to be what you are not. Goodbye."

"Goodbye, Miss Braybrook."

Robert found her in the kitchen an hour later, preparing the vegetables for dinner.

"Oh there you are, piglet." He had the grace to appear slightly shamefaced. "Delphine tells me you have decided to go home early."

"Is it true?"

Robert looked slightly startled. "Er...is what true?"

"You are engaged to be married to Delphine?" His manner gave the answer, but she had to hear it from his lips.

"Well...unofficially."

"For two years?" For some unaccountable reason, she wanted to brush the lock of hair back from his eyes.

"About that, I suppose."

"Why didn't you tell me?" She must keep her voice steady.

"Didn't think of it, really. It didn't seem to have anything to do with us." He smiled sheepishly, and Anna realised with sudden clarity that he was speaking the truth.

"You didn't think I would be hurt?" she asked gently, almost as if she spoke to a child.

"Why should you be? It isn't as though...." Suddenly a frown crossed his face and he said slowly, "You didn't think.... Anna, you can't have thought we would ever marry?" His expression showed more clearly than words that the idea was preposterous.

Anna made no reply, and Robert continued quickly, "You can't have thought that. I never gave you the slightest reason to think...."

"Is Delphine rich?" Anna interrupted softly.

Robert was taken aback. "That's not a nice suggestion, piglet. I have known Delphine for years. Her father and mine were business acquaintances."

"I see. But she is rich? As wealthy as you?"

Robert laughed shortly. "She could buy and sell our family a hundred times over, but that has nothing to do with it."

"Of course." Anna smiled. "I just wanted to know, to get things sorted out in my mind." She turned away and cut fiercely into a cauliflower, adding lightly, "I think I'll go on Friday if I can get a ticket."

"There's no reason to go early, piglet. We aren't leaving for Cannes for at least a week. Stay until then."

"No, I must get back." She put the pieces of cauliflower into a bowl and sprinkled them with salt.

"Well, if you must. When I get home, about the end of September, I'll get in touch." He came around the kitchen table and took her hand. "We mustn't lose each other, piglet. There is no need for you to work at chainmaking for the rest of your life."

She looked at him, not understanding. "What else is there?"

He smiled his easy smile. He was back in control and there had been no ugly scene. "Well, I've been giving that some thought," he said. "Why don't I buy a little place for you, a house in Dudley, perhaps, or a cottage in the country, if you prefer it. I'll make you an allowance, not a fortune, but more than you will ever earn from the chain, and then we can see each other whenever I can get away."

His words were like a physical blow; her degradation was complete. She picked up a basket of peas and began to shell them. Controlling the tremble in her voice, she said, "No."

"But why not? We could...."

"No."

"But what else can you do? Make chain for the rest of your life? Or marry that gawky Irish workman...if he'll have you now, of course." He stopped. "I'm sorry, piglet. I shouldn't have said that."

Anna swallowed. "No, you shouldn't have." Her trembling hands would not split the peas.

"It's just that I'm worried for you," Robert said. "I want to see that you have a decent life."

"Decent? Did you say decent?" she almost spat at him.

Robert sighed. "It's a bit late for your chapel Puritanism now. You must face the fact there is nothing for you in Sandley Heath. Your father's a well known drunk...."

"I have a brother too."

"And what can he do? He doesn't earn enough to keep his own family. I'm saying nothing against him, but you know yourself he'll never amount to anything. He's a well meaning clod of earth, that's all, without enough sense...."

"How dare you!" Anna's self control fractured. "How dare you speak of my brother that way?" She was beside herself with anger and her words were torn from her in a frenzied jumble. "My brother is a man...a real man, a decent, hardworking man with more true worth than...than...a hundred of you or your fancy friends! You, who talk on and on about honesty in art. What about honesty in life?" Her words tailed off as the tears came, running unheeded down her cheeks. Robert attempted to put his arm round her.

"I didn't mean anything. I'm sure your brother is a fine chap. I just want...."

"Oh, what's the use?" Anna got up from the table and wiped her eyes. "Robert, this conversation is over. The answer is no, and will always be no. I'll leave on Friday."

"If that's what you want."

Anna walked to the door. She said, "Why did you make love to me, Robert? Why did you bring me to France?"

"You are beautiful, piglet," he said simply. "I've always tried to make you see. I appreciate beauty."

On the day Anna left Paris, the weather broke, and a fine rain drizzled over the grey stone of the city as she drove to the Gare du Nord. She had bidden a tearful goodbye to Therese, who had presented her with a collar of handmade pillow lace, which she had sat up half the night to finish on time. Anna had promised to write to her at La Maison Blanche, and Therese had been distressed.

"It is no use to write, *chérie*, I cannot read the English. I can speak, but not read or write it. Even in the French, I don't write well."

Anna assured her she would not expect a reply. "All the same," she promised, "I shall write to you from time to time. If you have no one to translate, you must wait until Jacques comes; he will do it."

"Yes, *chérie*, that will be good. Or Monsieur Robert."

"Yes, or Monsieur Robert," Anna agreed dully.

She had not seen Robert since the previous evening, when she had made it plain she would not allow him to accompany her to the station. He had handed her an envelope containing her wages for the previous month, together with what he called a small bonus. Anna had remonstrated, but Robert had insisted, and after a moment, she had put the envelope into her purse unopened. In her room later she found he had included an extra ten pounds. Generous though the sum was, she could not control the uneasy feeling that she had been paid off like some common whore.

These thoughts intruded again as the carriage jolted its way to the station. She glanced across at Jacques and Sylvie, who had both insisted on seeing her off.

"Aren't you going to open it?" Jacques asked.

"Open what? Oh, of course."

Still clutched in her hand was a small package Alphonse had given her as she left the house. He had kissed her roundly and said, "*Bonne journée et bonne chance!*" several times. Sylvie and Jacques watched as she unwrapped the package. It was a box of sweetmeats for the journey, and she smiled and asked Jacques to pass on her thanks.

At the station, Jacques took her luggage and they both escorted her to the train. When Jacques disappeared to find the guard, Sylvie spoke. "I 'ave enjoy to know you, Anna. I think you 'ave enjoy, too, at La Maison Blanche."

"Yes, Sylvie, I have enjoyed. I'll never forget you, all of you."

Sylvie put a large folder she was carrying onto the seat next to Anna. "For you," she said, in her heavy guttural accent. "You can per'aps sell one day, if you need money."

Anna stared. "Is it...is it a painting?" She knew Sylvie almost never parted with a picture; she even hated selling them.

"Yes, I think you like."

"Oh, I will.... Oh, Sylvie, thank you."

At that moment, Jacques returned, and the guard blew his whistle. Jacques gave Anna a kiss. His bushy beard tickled her face. "I 'ave arranged for the guard to take care of you," he said. "*Au revoir, ma petite. Bonne chance!*" He leaned forward and pushed a small packet at Anna as the train began to move. "A memory from Paris," he said, waving.

Anna watched and waved until their figures merged into the distance. She sat down and opened Sylvie's folder. It was the glorious painting of the courtyard at La Maison Blanche, showing herself seated on the terrace, preparing vegetables. Anna felt the tears dim her eyes, she would treasure this for the rest of her life. She put it away hastily, trying to hide her emotion from the other passengers.

She picked up Jacques's parcel, and even before she had it open, she knew what it was. A big bag of lavender.

Clancy

Clancy's thoughts were black. He trudged up the hill from the foundry, making his reluctant way to the tiny house which seemed even more prisonlike since his mother's death. The numbing sense of loss which had come upon him then had at least been lightened by the prospect of Anna's return and hopes of their future in America. Now the bleak road ahead seemed to allow no glimmer of light to penetrate his dark solitude, and the horizon was hazy and uncertain.

As he turned the corner, he saw Will Gibson approaching, and felt a small fluttering of hope. "Will, I'm glad to see you." Clancy smiled with relief. "Did ye see her? Did ye ask her?"

Will's face was like a mask. "Arr, I saw 'er," he answered. "There's a deal to it; more ter tell like."

"Well, come in, man," Clancy said as they reached his front door. He opened the door and Will followed him inside. The fire was almost out, but Clancy attacked the compacted lump of slack with a poker, and it soon broke into a blaze. He added some small coal and pulled the kettle across on its trivet.

"There. Kettle won't be long. Have a seat." Clancy smiled as he reached down two enamel mugs from the shelf. He liked Anna's brother; he was a man you could trust.

"No tea, thanks," Will said. He seemed ill at ease, and Clancy had a sudden premonition.

"She still won't see me?"

As Will shook his head, Clancy burst out, "For heaven's sake, man, I don't deserve this! I can understand if she's decided not to marry me or feels she can't face going to America, but why this? What have I done that she won't even speak to me? She's been back a week now."

"It ay that, Clancy." Will's tone was solemn. "Yo' ay done nothin'. It's 'er. Our Anna." He stopped, as if choosing his words.

"Well?"

"I couldn't understand it either. Since 'er's been back, 'er ay said two waerds to anybody." Will sighed and continued, "I was worried, real worried. 'Er said nothin' about France, what 'er's been doin'. Yo'd think 'er would be bendin' our ears, borin' us to death with all 'er adventures."

"Well?" Clancy said again.

"Last night, I went to see 'er when Dad was at the pub. I got to the bottom of it at last. 'Er ay mad with yo', Clancy. Far from it. 'Er's ashamed."

"Ashamed? What about?" A sudden fear began to gnaw at Clancy.

As if in answer to his thoughts, Will said, "That bastard Nicholson, Robert Nicholson."

Clancy's mind screamed in revolt, and he felt a great wave of loss and sadness overwhelm him. He wanted to deny it, to tell Will there was a mistake, but he said simply, "I should have expected it. Your sister is very beautiful and he...he can offer her much more than I can."

"'E's offered her nothin'," Will said bitterly. "Apparently he's gettin' married next spring to some 'igh falutin' lady. 'E's thrown 'er over."

"What?" Clancy was distressed and muttered briefly, "Poor Anna." He turned to Will. "Whatever's happened, Will, it means Anna is still free...and I still love her."

Will raised a tired face. "Yo' don't understand, Clancy. Anna's in the club. 'Er's 'avin' a babby."

The small back room in Dawkins Street was silent as the grave. Anna found the house oppressive, but had not cared to walk out. Only the gentle crackle of the fire and the slight hiss from the simmering kettle broke the quietness as she sat, mending a shirt of her father's. She seemed unable to shake off the heavy feeling of depression which had descended upon her like a thick blanket. Her unhappiness was broken only by occasional moments of sheer panic, when she forced herself to think about what lay ahead.

Even after confessing all to Will a few days ago, she had been unable to bring herself to tell her father. In spite of the fact that they seemed to be getting along quite well, she was sure he would turn her out once he knew of her condition. Will and Mary had already said that if the worst happened, she could move in with them, but they were already overcrowded and Anna hated the thought of putting them to such inconvenience. The worst aspect of all was Anna's dread of the gossip which would undoubtedly surround her. The talk and backbiting would be inevitable once her pregnancy started to show. What a laugh the girls would have, she thought, biting off her thread and surveying her work. The shirt would "count as one" as her mother would have said, although it would not last much longer.

As usual, the thought of her mother brought unbidden tears to sting her eyes, but Anna consoled herself with the thought that at least her mother would not witness her daughter's disgrace.

The girls would certainly enjoy the scandal. "Miss Toffeenose" herself in the club! Ma Higgins

had agreed to take her back to make chain, starting Monday, but Anna knew it was likely she would
be dismissed as soon as her secret was out. Married women often worked right up to the day before
birth, but if you were unmarried it was very different, you were regarded as a sinner likely to corrupt
decent people. Anna could well remember seeing
small children throwing stones and shouting names
at a woman everyone called "Daft Molly".

Anna started when a tap came at the back door.
It could only be Will, but he did not bother to knock.
Her face flamed into confusion as the door opened
and Clancy came in.

"Oh, there ye are. I thought I'd catch ye, so I
did."

The look of him standing there, solid and reassuring as ever, and the soft sound of his Irish
brogue seemed to turn Anna's stomach to water.
She began to tremble violently, but managed to
say, "Hello, Clancy," almost in a whisper.

He came in and sat down in her father's chair.
"You're looking well," he said conversationally.
"Nice and brown after your holiday."

Anna looked at him, but it did not seem he
was being sarcastic. She suddenly remembered
her manners. "I'm not sure why you're here,
Clancy, but could I just say, before you say anything, I was really sorry about your mother."

"Thank you. It was a blessed release for her at
the end."

Anna nodded, and there was a short silence.

"I...er...I came to talk to you," Clancy said hesitantly. "Will told me...about everything...how
you're placed...."

"I know." Anna felt her cheeks burn.

"I think you could have told me yourself,"
Clancy said shortly.

"I couldn't! Oh, Clancy, I just couldn't! I didn't want to hurt you and I knew I had...and I was so ashamed." Her small outburst ended in a whisper of anguish.

"Well, that's as may be," Clancy responded quietly. "Anyway, I want to hear it from your own lips, not from someone else, even Will, good chap that he is. It's taken me a couple of days to think it over, but that's why I've come."

"I don't understand," Anna whispered. "What...what do you want to know?"

"Everything," Clancy said firmly. "Everything that happened to you from the time you left here."

"But why? What good will it do?" Anna's tone was bitter. "Knowing everything will only hurt you more than ever, and I've hurt you enough."

"That's my choice, Anna," Clancy said. "And you owe me that at least," he added quietly.

Anna swallowed. "All right, I'll try to explain."

It was difficult at first. She began hesitantly, with details of the journey and her arrival at La Maison Blanche, but as memory came flooding back, the telling became easier, and details poured out about life at the farmhouse, Therese, the joy of the cooking she had learned, Sylvie and Alphonse and dear Jacques, the local market on a Wednesday, the hens and the ducks....

As her story progressed, Anna found herself trying to make Clancy understand the feeling of freedom she had felt in France. She tried to explain what she herself now dimly realised, that it was not only Robert, but a whole way of life which had seduced her, intoxicated her so that she suspended her normal judgment. She made no excuses, and she told briefly but honestly how Robert and she had become lovers. Her story tailed off in a whisper as she told him of Delphine's visit, and how Robert was due to be married in the spring.

"He ditched ye," said Clancy bitterly. "That's what I find so hard."

"Not really," Anna responded with a little sarcasm. "By his own standards he offered me a good future, a 'decent life', as he put it." In answer to Clancy's enquiring look, she continued, "I didn't tell Will, I couldn't tell anyone...but I'll tell you, Clancy." Her voice dropped to a whisper. "He...he offered to find me a small house in Dudley, or in the country, and to make me an allowance, so he could visit whenever he wanted."

Clancy was on his feet. "The bastard!" His face flushed with anger. "I'll kill the...."

"Sit down, Clancy. You have no reason to be angry with anyone except me."

Clancy sat down, but his face remained flushed.

"It was then, when he said that, that I realised how stupid I had been." Anna hesitated, and then said, "Wait a moment." She went upstairs and returned with the painting Sylvie had given her.

Clancy was impressed and said quietly, "You really enjoyed it, didn't you? France, I mean?"

"Yes. In spite of everything, I was probably happier there than ever in my life."

It was hard for Clancy. He said quietly, "But you didn't let him make love to you simply because you were happy. Why, Anna? Why did you...allow him?" He sighed. "You would never have allowed me to get anywhere near you."

She could not lie to him. "I loved him, Clancy," she said. "I really loved him."

Clancy nodded. "And what now?"

"I have no idea. I am in deep trouble and Dad will probably turn me out. I have a little money but not enough to last long." Anna took a deep breath. "You haven't shouted at me, Clancy, or said all the things I'm sure you want to. You haven't called me dirty names."

"Would it help?" Clancy asked bitterly.

"Perhaps not, but I know I deserve it, so I understand how you must feel."

"Do you?" He did not tell her he had already voiced all the things she imagined and worse, had screamed them into his pillow for three nights in a row, not knowing how to ease his pain. It had not helped. At the end of it all, he knew he still loved her. After he had confronted this fact, and accepted it, the plan had almost formed itself. Nothing in the account she had given had changed his mind. The plan was still valid. He cleared his throat.

"Anna, I wanted you to tell me about it because I am going to America in a few weeks. I wanted to understand what had happened."

"Yes. I am sorry, Clancy, sorry to have hurt you so."

"I have a ticket for you too, if you want to come with me."

"For me?" The shock showed in her face. "But...."

"We shall have to put the banns in right away, so we can be married before we go."

"Married? Clancy?"

"We have both attended that chapel for so many years, it wouldn't be right to be married anywhere else. At least, that's how I see it." He looked at her a little defensively and added, "You know my dearest wish has always been for us to be married and go to America together." His voice became soft. "I know you don't love me, Anna, but I love you, let's hope enough for both of us." He smiled. "Will you have me, darlin'?"

"Oh, Clancy, I feel so ashamed." The tears were

running down her face. "What about...what about the baby?"

"That's my only condition," Clancy said firmly.

"What?" Anna held her breath.

"The child is mine. Completely mine. You say Nicholson doesn't know about it and he must never know, and neither must the child. If we are married before we go, people in America will think the child is mine. That is how I want it. Do you agree?"

"Oh, Clancy...of course I agree, if you're sure."

"It's taken me a few days to think it out, but I'm sure. Are you sure?"

"Oh, Clancy!" Anna wiped her eyes. "You are the dearest, kindest man I ever knew. I'll make it up to you, I swear."

"Then we'll never speak of this again. And if you really mean what you say about making it up to me, it's time you offered me a jar of tea...and a kiss to seal the bargain."

Anna and Clancy were married three weeks and two days later. As it was a Saturday, most of the neighbours attended the chapel, and as Clancy had no relatives in England, Will did duty as best man, looking extremely uncomfortable in a starched collar and a jacket borrowed from a workmate. Anna wore the good grey dress Florence had given her, her only concession to frivolity being a pink cabbage rose pinned to the brim of her wide brimmed hat.

Afterwards in the front parlour, where a tea was provided for the family and a few friends, George Gibson made a speech, short but to the point, saying he was glad his daughter had "come to 'er senses and wed a good sound man, instead of runnin' around foreign parts an' all that malarkey."

"What's America then, Dad?" Will spoke up. "Ay that foreign parts?"

Following the general laughter, George proceeded to explain that "goin' to America was different, because our Anna's wed now."

As soon as tea was over, Anna and Clancy left on the cart for Dudley, where they were to take a tram for Birmingham, their overnight stop. They would then take the morning train to Liverpool to embark that afternoon. They had with them one suitcase each, Anna having carefully placed Sylvie's picture in the middle of her clothes so it would not be damaged. Between them they had fifty-two pounds, the sum total of their savings.

Will and Mary, with Billy running alongside, came to see them off on the cart, both visibly upset. The parting was short, every one of them wanting to say so much, but unable to say it. Will grasped Clancy's hand, saying over and over, "Yo'm a good man, Clancy. I know yo'll tek care on 'er."

He hugged Anna briefly, and with embarrassment. "Write to us, our Anna," he said. "Not just...weather an' that. Proper letters. Tell us 'ow it is, what it's really like."

"I promise, Will. You take care of them all, and yourself too." Anna felt the tears sting her eyes. "Thanks, our Will, for everything. You were always on my side."

After a last kiss for Billy, they were on the cart. As it trundled away, Will shouted, "Do' forget us when yo' mek yer first million!"

After the excitement of the day, Anna was tired by the time they arrived at the small hotel in Birmingham where they were to spend their first night together. Clancy was impressed; it was the first time he had ever stayed in an hotel, and he delighted in showing Anna the small rug on the floor by the bed, the lamp with the Chinese style shade, and the thick, pink eiderdown on the double bed.

Anna did her best to respond enthusiastically, but she could not help but compare the second rate hotel with places she had seen in Paris with Robert, with the simple but classic rooms at La Maison Blanche, with High Cedars.

When Clancy took her tenderly into his arms that night, she responded happily and eagerly, knowing how much she owed him, recognising his worth and integrity, aware she could never repay him for his kindness and generosity. But long after Clancy fell asleep, she lay awake, trying to make sense of it all. Most of all, to her own dismay, she longed for Robert, with a deep yearning which she knew she must always keep concealed.

The longing never left her. It remained a deep, unsatisfied need which accompanied her night and day on the long and uncomfortable sea crossing, when she was sick to the point of exhaustion. And it was to remain with her for years to come.

PART THREE

AMERICA

Beginnings

1905 -1906

Anna strained forward with difficulty. Her scrubbing brush would hardly reach into the dark corner beneath the heavy sideboard, groaning under its load of plates and dishes. Satisfied at last, she leaned back on her heels, relieved that the condition of the floor was slowly improving. When she had started work two months earlier in the dimly lit bar in downtown New York, the tiles had been so heavily grimed her scrubbing brush had hardly made an impression. Gradually, after much hard work, the bar was approaching conformity with the recently imposed hygiene standards, and as she surveyed her work, Anna felt a bizarre sense of grim satisfaction.

Bizarre, because she could not be proud of working in such a place, but a position of any kind had been hard to obtain. Clancy was unhappy that she was doing such menial work, but her now visible pregnancy deterred prospective employers, and Anna had taken what she could get.

She got up slowly and carried the heavy bucket to the back drain and emptied it. Then she returned to the bar, taking care to step only on those parts of the floor which had already been dried by the draft of air which wafted through the open door accompanied by the jumbled sounds and smells of the city.

Intending to close the door against the inevitable tide of men who would wander in if it was left open, Anna hesitated, breathing in air which smelled fresh and sweet compared to the atmosphere of the bar. No matter how hard she scrubbed, it still reeked of stale beer and tobacco. She peered outside; she enjoyed seeing downtown New York come to life each morning. Joe Kowalski was already outside his delicatessen opposite, painting slogans and prices on his window in large letters of whitewash. Other shopkeepers were washing down the sidewalk or opening up their shutters. It promised to be a good day for trade, mild for November, and with a clear sky after the heavy rain which, for the last two days, had driven customers to seek shelter at home.

Anna locked the door. It would be two hours until opening time. She went to the sink and began to wash the mountain of glasses left from the previous night. The bar owner, a balding, heavily set man with a huge belly, looked up from his accounts book as he heard the chink of glass.

"Coffee," he barked.

Anna moved quickly to obey the command. She had become accustomed to the way Ben Brackley spoke; his sentences invariably consisted of only one or two words. She considered Brackley vulgar and entirely lacking in manners, but at least he paid her on time and let her get on with her work in peace. She poured him a cup of coffee and set it down on his desk. He made no acknowledgement, but as she turned back to the sink he said sharply, "Where's yours?"

It was a moment before Anna realised he was referring to the coffee. She hesitated. "I was not sure it was allowed."

Brackley gave a sharp jerk of his head towards

the coffee pot. Anna said, "Thank you," and moved to pour herself a cup. Things were looking up, she thought as she returned to the sink. A few miserable dollars a week for fifty hours of slavery and a free cup of coffee into the bargain. She consoled herself with the recollection that tomorrow was Sunday and Clancy had promised to take her across the Brooklyn Bridge, which spanned the great East River. They would walk to the other side and then take the cable train back, and it seemed it might be good weather for their outing. She smiled happily to herself at the prospect and continued to wash the glasses.

The Brooklyn Bridge, despite its huge size, was crowded with walkers taking the air on what was likely to be one of the last really fine days of the year. The central walkway, elevated so that the carriages, carts and cable trains did not obscure the view, was peopled with a diverse variety of New Yorkers, from the elegant and sophisticated to the poorest new immigrant. Anna had wanted to walk across the bridge ever since her first view of it on the day they arrived in New York, and now she clung happily to Clancy's arm, revelling in the ever expanding scene as they neared the centre of the bridge. She stopped to take in more fully the view up river to Long Island Sound, and Clancy looked at her anxiously.

"Are you tired? Is the walk too much for you?"

"No, of course not. I want to spend a few minutes just looking, that's all."

Clancy smiled. "Yes, it feels good up here in the fresh air. I wouldn't fancy it in a gale, though." He pointed up river. "One day, Anna, when we have made our fortune, I shall take you up there on one of the Fall River steamboats, a really grand one, and we shall have a stateroom."

"Oh, shall we?" said Anna, laughing. "Like the one we had crossing the Atlantic you mean?"

Clancy made a face. "Not the slightest bit like that I should hope. I still feel that life on board can be good if you have the money to do it properly."

"And if you aren't sick all the time," Anna murmured.

"Oh, you won't be sick, I promise. By the time we can afford it, our children will be grown up and off our hands."

"How many?" Anna interrupted.

"Four, I think. No, five," Clancy said seriously. "The last one was a surprise," he explained, watching the dimple in Anna's cheek as she suppressed a smile. "Anyway," he continued, "we shall travel overnight, as all the best people do, leaving the pier on the Hudson at about five in the afternoon, which gives us a few hours to watch the Sound pass by, and then we shall take a good dinner in the saloon. A turn around the deck, and then down to our stateroom to sleep. We wake up in the Fall River and board the train to Boston to see all the sights. Staying at the best hotel, of course," he added quickly.

Anna sighed. "It sounds wonderful, Clancy, but I fear it's a pipe dream." She laughed, "At least I'm glad you have the plans ready."

"One of the fellows at the site was telling me about it," Clancy explained. "Apparently rich folks do the trip all the time. His sister works as a nurse-maid and was taken along with the family. She said it was wonderful."

"That's the sort of job to have," Anna agreed. She took Clancy's arm again and they crossed to look over the bay towards the Narrows, Coney Island, and the wide waters of the Atlantic.

"Look," she said, pointing, "that's where we came in."

"Will I ever forget it?" said Clancy. "Sure 'twas a wonderful sight."

"Oh, yes," Anna breathed, remembering.

Wretched and ill, she would have been happy to make land anywhere, as long as she could get off the ship. But after a week of the stone grey colours of the crossing, the soft hues of the New Jersey Hills had been a feast for the eyes, and the lovely islets and wooded slopes of New York Harbour had gladdened her heart. As the ship had slowly made its way along the Narrows, amid the crowded shipping and past the Statue of Liberty, Anna had gathered impressions so fast she had felt breathless. The main impact was of great vigour and industry, with views of enormous buildings and ferry boats crossing in every direction, and a sense of amazement at the span of the great bridge where they now stood.

Anna squeezed Clancy's arm. "I still can hardly believe it," she said. "That we're really here and have settled in so fast, that...that we're married."

Clancy laughed, "Well, we're married right enough so you'd better make the most of it. But let's have a little less talk of us being settled. We are certainly not settled in that dump we are living in, and the sooner we move out the better."

"It's as good as we had in Sandley Heath," Anna pointed out.

"There may be more space than Mam and I had," Clancy admitted, "but I can't agree it's as good. There's no privacy."

"That's true."

The mention of Sandley Heath brought memories of the family, and after a moment, Anna said, "It was so good to have Will's letter." She laughed.

"I never knew Will to write so much; he made a real effort with all the news. He knew I would be interested to hear about Mrs. Pankhurst and Annie Kenney being arrested in Manchester."

"The women's movement certainly is in earnest," Clancy agreed. "To choose prison instead of a fine shows real courage, but it won't have any effect."

"You think not? You think women will not get the vote?"

"Some day, perhaps, but I doubt in Mrs. Pankhurst's lifetime. Parliament will never agree. Just after you went to France, there was a bill put forward, but it was talked out. Much as I admire your suffragette friends, I have to admit I would rather see every working man get a decent wage to keep his family, than see votes for women."

Anna considered, and then said, "I don't see why we can't have both."

Clancy laughed. "There you go, reaching for the moon again. I agree with you, but it's not up to us, is it?"

They turned and continued their walk across the bridge, both wanting the afternoon to last, to delay as long as possible the inevitable return to the two rooms with sink and gas ring they had taken on the third floor of a brownstone house downtown. Only Sylvie's picture, in pride of place on the dingy wall, lifted the depressing atmosphere.

After a moment, Anna said, "I know you don't like where we are living, Clancy, and neither do I, but I think it would be wrong to move before we can afford it."

"I don't want us to bring up the baby there," Clancy said grimly.

"I know, and you're right. That's why I think we should stay as long as we can and try to save a little. We shall need every penny when the baby comes, but that is four months yet. That will be soon enough to move." She smiled. "You may have a rise in pay before then."

Clancy grunted. "Some hopes. Not on the construction site anyway; there's ten men for every job going."

Anna felt a small pang of unease. "Do you wish you were going? With Dennis and Michael?"

Clancy laughed. "With those two tearaways? Not on your life! Don't get me wrong, Anna, I'm grateful for the help my cousins gave me. I'm sure I wouldn't have found work so quickly without them introducing me to the foreman at Hampson's. But they are youngsters; I'm an old married man, so I am."

Anna looked at Clancy sharply and saw that his eyes were twinkling. Nevertheless, she responded, "That's what I mean. If you weren't lumbered with me, you could go with them."

"With that pair? I've got more sense! They may kid themselves they are going west to seek their fortunes, but what they are really looking for is adventure. They'll probably find it, and if I know them, any money they attract along the way will be spent as quickly as it arrives." Clancy patted Anna's hand. "No, my love, there are fortunes to be made just as easily here in New York. I just haven't found out how...as yet."

They walked on slowly across the bridge, pausing every few minutes to admire the view. When they reached the Brooklyn side, they found a small café, lingering over their cups of dark, rich coffee until the light began to fade and Clancy said they must take the train back. As they settled into their seats, Clancy said suddenly, "I don't really care about making a fortune. I just don't want you to work in that awful place a moment longer than necessary."

Anna laughed. "It's not so bad, and when the baby comes, I'll have to leave anyway."

Clancy smiled, and as Anna met the dark Irish eyes, she could see the love clearly shining there. "I can hardly wait," he admitted softly, "for next April, when I'll have you and the little one all to myself."

Often, during the wintry days which followed their trip to the Brooklyn Bridge, Anna was to recall Clancy's words with happy anticipation. Her body felt cumbersome and heavy, and the work at the bar became more difficult every day. She seemed trapped in a habitual regime of work, fretful sleep and more work. Clancy was attentive and kind, but as the days went by, Anna felt that her whole life was concerned with only one aim, how to push her reluctant body through each miserable day.

The necessity to save every penny meant Anna and Clancy had few treats or outings, and over the weeks, the narrowness of their existence and the drabness of their surroundings took its toll. They spent a meagre but restful Christmas together, and as they played word games on Christmas afternoon, Anna realised she had hardly used her brain for months. She remembered the evenings at La Maison Blanche, where the conversation had been intellectually challenging and full of interest, where she had felt she was growing, learning, becoming more fully alive. She was still growing, she reflected grimly, physically at least. Mentally she was confined even more tightly than she had been at Sandley Heath.

By mid January, the preoccupation with her strict routine had left Anna morose and sullen, as if the daily drudgery had become an end in itself, its completion the only aim or reason for each passing day. As she polished the bar one morning, she was sunk so deeply into vacant introspection that she hardly heard Ben Brackley's staccato voice, and started suddenly as he repeated, "Wake up!"

"I'm sorry, Mr. Brackley, what did you say?"

"Your man," he looked annoyed, "out back." He indicated the rear door with a sharp jerk of his head.

"Clancy? Here? What does he want?"

Ben Brackley's long suffering sigh was the only answer, and Anna went quickly to the back door to find Clancy in a state of some excitement.

"What's happened?" A chill ran through her. "You haven't lost your job?"

"No, darlin'. Nothing like that. You must come quickly. Now."

"But I don't finish till...."

"Never mind. You're leaving here. I've got you another job."

"Another job? But I can't. I'll have to leave when the baby comes...."

"I'll explain on the way." He grabbed her arms. "Trust me, Anna."

Anna, sensing his excitement, nodded. "I'll tell Mr. Brackley. Can I give him notice?"

"No, I'll speak to him."

Clancy went into the bar and returned after a few moments, grinning. "He's not very happy. Offered to pay an extra two dollars a week to keep you!"

"Two dollars! Perhaps...."

"Come on. We have to get the tram quickly."

Clancy bundled her down the road to the tram stop, explaining that the cook at the Hampson's construction site had been dismissed that morning, and Clancy had immediately offered Anna's services as a replacement.

"A cook? I should like that. What does it pay?"

"More than you are getting now," Clancy responded grimly, "But, Anna, that isn't the point."

"Oh? What is the point?" Anna questioned as they boarded the tram.

Once they were seated and had paid their fare, Clancy explained. The cook was not an employee, but had a contract to provide meals at lunch time for four managers and over sixty construction workers for a set fee per head. The contract had only two weeks to run and Hampson's was not going to renew it due to complaints about the meals. There had been a big row and the cook had departed in high dudgeon. "Don't you see, Anna?" Clancy enthused. "It's running your own business."

Anna was bemused. "But how?" she asked. "I don't even know what they want. Are you sure I can do it?"

"Of course. You are the best cook I ever knew. What you learned in France will come in useful, and you'll soon find out which foods are popular. I can help you there. Think of it, Anna! Working for yourself and having complete control, from buying the food and planning the menu to the cooking and serving. As long as there are no complaints, you'll be alright. The bosses at Hampson's don't really want to be bothered about the food; they have too much else to think about."

"I see." Anna hesitated, everything was happening too fast. "I have to buy the food? For so many?"

"Yes, we can use our savings to start you off."

"Our hundred dollars? But Clancy, that is our nest egg! It was for..."

"It was for us to make our fortune, to start us off," Clancy said vehemently. "We won't need to touch any of the money put by for the baby, but

Anna, this is our opportunity. I know it's a difficult time for you, but think of it! If Hampson's gives
you the contract, you can train someone else to
cook, and after the baby arrives, you can concentrate on buying and menu planning and leave the
hard work to your employees."

"Employees?" Anna's eyes widened.

"Yes. Of course you will have to visit occasionally to oversee things. I'll help all I can," Clancy
volunteered, noting her stricken face.

"Clancy, wait a moment. You said 'if they give
you the contract?' I thought you said I had got
the job?"

"Well, you will be on trial at first," Clancy admitted. "For two weeks."

"Only two weeks? That's hardly time to prove
myself!"

"Anna, you must trust me. I have been eating
in that canteen for months now. The food is awful
and the men are heartily sick of it. The cook has
been taking his fat fee and then serving up rubbish, lining his pockets at the men's expense. You
can't fail to do better if you take an honest profit."

"Well, if you say so," Anna said doubtfully as
Clancy indicated they were approaching their stop.
He handed her down from the tram and tucked
her arm under his.

"When I heard the cook had been thrown out, I
knew it was our chance, and I went to see the manager Mr. King right away," Clancy said. "Of course
he didn't want to issue a contract to a female, but I
explained I would be your guarantor. Mr. King was
in a quandary and desperate for someone right
away, so he agreed to give you a trial."

"I see," Anna said faintly.

Clancy squeezed her arm. "Don't worry,
darlin'," he said cheerfully. "You are the finest cook

and the best organiser I have ever met. It may be daunting at first, but I know you can do it. There is an assistant there, a Chinese who will help all he can. I told him to prepare the vegetables for you."

"For me? You mean?"

"Didn't I tell you? That's why we are in a hurry. It's after eleven now and you serve your first lunch at one o'clock."

It was a strange feeling to be working out one's own pay, Anna decided. Seated at the small table in the dingy apartment, she carefully listed all her invoices, then added the wages she had paid to Mr. Sung and the newly employed kitchen girl named Jennie McCormack, who Anna had taken from the local orphanage. She took the total away from the money the company had agreed to pay for the first two weeks, and found she had just over sixty-two dollars left.

"Sixty-two dollars, Clancy. That's thirty-one dollars a week! How much do you think I should pay myself?"

Clancy put down his newspaper. He came across to the table and began to check her figures. Satisfied, he smiled down at her. "Excellent! I didn't think you would make so much right away. It just shows how crooked that swine was." He frowned. "Didn't I see some sacks of flour in the kitchen larder?" he asked.

"Yes, I ordered more than we needed of the basics: flour, salt, spices, potatoes, that kind of thing. I got a better price buying larger amounts," Anna explained.

Clancy smiled. "Then you have made more than you thought. Those stocks should be counted in, as they are items you won't need to buy next week."

Anna beamed. "Then I'll pay myself thirty dollars a week!"

"You certainly will not! Anna, you must stop thinking of yourself as an employee. You are the owner of a business now, joint owner anyway; we are in this together. Pay yourself the same as you were getting at the bar."

Seeing her face fall, Clancy relented. "An extra two dollars a week then, like Ben Brackley offered to pay you. The rest must be kept in the business."

"What for?" Anna asked.

Clancy hesitated. He was not quite sure what for, but a friend at the construction site, whose brother had a small shop, had advised him that they should only take out what they needed, leaving the rest in the business. He realised now that he had no idea what this meant.

"Tell you what," he suggested, "we'll open another account at the bank, one especially for the business. We'll put into it the money we have over and the money we get next week from Hampson's, and we can see how we go."

"All right," Anna agreed happily.

"And something else," Clancy ventured. "Would you like to see the George Bernard Shaw play on Broadway? We could perhaps run to that as a special treat."

"It was taken off, surely?" Anna responded. "Raided by the police as indecent."

"Not *Mrs. Warren's Profession*," Clancy laughed. "The one I should like to see is *Arms and the Man* if we can get tickets."

Anna smiled. "If you like. Why are you so keen?"

"He's a good playwright," Clancy said. "At least everyone says so. I'd like to see for myself." He grinned broadly. "He must be good, he's Irish, so he is."

Anna laughed and turned back to her accounts. Although the last two weeks had been very hard work, she was already feeling comfortable in her new role. It had been a real challenge, and she had been up to the test. Even the first lunch had been successful as far as the men were concerned, as it was an improvement on the daily mush, heavy with lentils and little else, they had been served for weeks. Anna had found they preferred good plain food, served piping hot. She reserved her more advanced skills for the manager's dining room, where the meals were eyed at first with cautious apprehension, but after a few days with wholehearted appreciation. She knew she was succeeding when, during the second week, Mr. King approached her and asked if she could provide lunch for some guests the following day.

"I usually take guests out for lunch," he explained, "but as your fare, Mrs. Sullivan, is so unusual and so excellent, I thought it would be a treat for them. It will also save a great deal of time."

"Thank you. I take it, then, that you will be offering me the catering contract?"

"I shall indeed, Mrs. Sullivan. After I have had an opportunity to discuss it with your husband, of course."

Anna beamed at the memory. She had served up a very special lunch to Mr. King's guests and had been congratulated by the whole party. Only one other innovation had given her more pleasure, and that was her decision to provide a dessert at lunch time after the main meal for the construction workers in the canteen. She had costed it all out carefully and had discussed it with Clancy.

"It is immoral to make quite so much money from the contract," she said. "We can provide a main meal and a dessert for the money we are paid, and still make a healthy profit. If this is going to be our future business, I want to be able to be proud of it."

Clancy agreed and had announced to his astounded workmates that, as from the following week, his wife would be providing a second course in addition to the much improved fare they now enjoyed. The Sullivans' popularity soared, and Anna was looking forward to the work, especially as she had become good friends with Lee Sung, the Chinese assistant, who was delighted with the new arrangements.

Everything was working out well, Anna thought. She put away her papers, walked over to Clancy and kissed his cheek. "Thank you," she said.

"For what? Not that I'm complaining," he grinned.

"For everything. For marrying me when I was in such a mess."

Clancy grimaced. "What's brought this on? We agreed all that was in the past."

"I know, and it is," Anna said softly, kissing him again. "I just want you to know I'm grateful. Not only for that, but for seeing our chance when it came. Not many men would have realised it was an opportunity to start in business."

"Well, you have done the work," Clancy said, slightly embarrassed.

"Yes, I have worked, but I wouldn't have had the chance if you had not thought of it and had confidence in me. I'm really grateful."

"Is that all?" Clancy said softly, not able to help himself.

Anna turned away to the table, gathering up her papers as if she had not heard him. "We shall have to keep proper account books now we have the contract," she said. "I'm not sure exactly what we need, but perhaps the bank manager will advise us. Will you ask him?"

Clancy nodded, and returned to his newspaper, cursing his own stupidity for trying to force things. It was too soon, he thought, still too soon. Her mind was full of that bastard Nicholson, that was obvious. He saw again Anna's tear-stained face as she sat in front of the fire at the house in Dawkins Street, heard again her soft reply, *I loved him, Clancy. I really loved him.*

How long, Clancy wondered, *how long before she forgets?* He wondered why it mattered so much. He had all he wanted, didn't he? Anna, and a child on the way that he already loved as his own, and now a start in business...it was all to play for.

But Anna had never said she loved him, and he had a feeling she never would.

"The timing could not be better, as far as I am concerned," Anna announced. "By the time you are employing workers at the new site, I should be able to take charge of the catering arrangements." She blushed slightly, finding it difficult to refer explicitly to the impending birth of her child, although it must be plain to Mr. King that the time could not be far away.

"Quite so, quite so." Mr. King was similarly constrained and wished for the tenth time that his excellent caterer was male and not subject to the inconveniences of pregnancy. He smiled stiffly. "The new Hampson's site will be operational about the end of July," he said. "Are you quite sure you can take it on?"

"Quite sure," Anna smiled, "and on the same basis as our existing contract. I have been fortunate in Mr. Sung. He is an excellent cook and I have taught him all I know. I can leave him in charge here, and I shall be free to concentrate on the new site."

"Very strange that," remarked Mr. King with a slight frown. "When Mr. Sung worked here with the previous contractor no one thought much of his talents, certainly not as a cook."

"That is easily explained," Anna said sweetly. "Mr. Sung was treated as nothing more than a kitchen boy. He was never allowed to show what he could do, never given any encouragement. In any case, one cannot produce good food without ingredients."

"Quite so, quite so," Mr. King said again. "Well, Mrs. Sullivan, I am delighted you will be catering for the new site. Your food has done wonders for morale."

"Thank you," Anna said, rising to her feet. It was clear the interview was over. "Mr. King, have you any idea how much longer the present site will continue?"

"At least another six months," the manager replied. "And by then no doubt other buildings will be under way. Hampson's is doing very well, Mrs. Sullivan, and there is no reason why you should not expand your business along with ours." His tone held a hint of patronage, and Anna smiled.

"That is good to hear," she replied. "I ask because I have been approached by several business-men with a view to putting in a catering service for their factories, and in one case, for an entire office block. I do not wish to take on too much, and as Hampson's was our first client, it will, of course, always have priority."

A raising of the eyebrows and a decided look of dismay on Mr. King's patrician features made Anna giggle a little as she made her way from the manager's office back to the kitchen. She did not mean to upset Mr. King, but felt he was pompous and condescending. She had not told him that most offers of future work had come from businessmen who had lunched at some time at Hampson's. The manager had unwittingly provided her best advertising as he boasted of the quality of meals served to the Hampson's workforce. His guests had taken the opportunity of testing his claims by sampling the food on their plates. There had been more offers of contracts than Anna and Clancy could possibly consider, especially as the baby was due in under a month. As she entered the kitchen, Mr. Sung looked up.

"You look velly pleased," he said, "like cat which eats the cleam."

"Very good, Lee," Anna smiled, "except we usually say, 'The cat that got the cream.'"

"Got the cleam," Lee repeated. "It is not easy language." He stirred the huge saucepan on the stove and held out the steaming spoon to Anna. "What you think? More pepper?"

Anna fetched a teaspoon and took some stew onto it, tasting it carefully. "Mmmm, that's good, Lee, but yes...I think a little more pepper. I'll get it."

She went to the kitchen larder, a large, deep cellar which was ideal for storage. How or why it happened she was never to understand, but as she began to descend, her foot missed the step. Even as she fell, a reflex twisting action enabled her to protect her bulging belly to some extent, but her shoulder caught a shelf opposite and she crashed heavily to the floor.

Lee Sung was there in seconds, his face horrified. "Oh, Missis! Oh, Missis!"

Anna gathered her wits. "It's all right, Lee, I don't think anything is broken, but I hurt my side." She attempted to rise and a sudden wave of nausea and searing pain overwhelmed her.

Lee Sung rounded on the kitchen maid, who seemed dumbstruck. "Go quick, Jennie. Fetch someone. Quick!" He cradled Anna's head on his arm. "Then fetch Mr. Sullivan. Quick, Jennie!"

The last thing Anna remembered was Lee Sung's anxious face, and the sight of the big spoon still held in his free hand. Then the tearing pain enveloped her, racking her whole body with spasmodic shuddering, which rolled her back and forth like a rag doll, the pain increasing its terrible intensity until at last she sank into sweet oblivion.

Clancy stared at the doctor. It had been a long night and his brain would not function.

"I don't understand," he managed at last. "You said...I thought you said my wife was all right."

The doctor, a kindly man with greying hair and a tired look, explained again. "Yes, Mr. Sullivan, your wife will be fine in a few weeks, provided, of course, there is no infection. And the baby seems very healthy after all he's been through. A fine boy."

"Then what...?" Clancy was still bemused.

"As I explained, there were some injuries which made the birth difficult. We had to take...measures to save the baby and Mrs. Sullivan. Your wife no longer has the ability to bear further children."

Clancy sat down on the hard chair which had been his seat during the horrendous hours of waiting. Their four lovely children...no, five, he corrected automatically, the last one was a mistake.... He put his head in his hands.

The doctor patted Clancy's shoulder in sympathy. "Come on, old chap," he said. "Your wife and baby are both doing well now."

The doctor reflected briefly on the selfishness of men. *After all that poor woman had been through…. Most families had too many children anyway.*

"Your wife needs your support now," he said firmly.

Clancy nodded and said, "Thank you, doctor, for all you did tonight."

The doctor smiled. "Well, you can go in now and meet your son, and remember, his being the only one is not the end of the world. It's not as though you haven't any children at all."

Clancy nodded again, and entered the big ward, where he found Anna in a bed near the door. She had a large bruise on her cheek, and her eyes were bleak and dark rimmed with fatigue.

"There ye are, darlin'. How are ye?" She noticed his accent, stronger now as always when he was upset.

"Oh, Clancy, I'm all right now, but…."

Clancy smoothed strands of hair gently from her face and kissed her lightly.

"Sure ye look as if ye've been in the wars, so ye do! That's a nasty bruise."

"Oh, Clancy."

"And aren't we the lucky ones? A lovely boy, so the doctor said."

He followed her eyes to the small crib at the foot of the bed. He got up and carefully looked in. When he turned to face her again, his eyes were brimming. "Can I pick him up?"

"Yes, I think so." Anna glanced at a hovering nurse, who turned her back and walked to attend a nearby patient.

Clancy picked up the tiny bundle and brought him to Anna. "He's a darlin', so he is. What shall we call him?"

"I had already thought…if you agree…. I had a brother who died. James. I'd like to name him for

James."

"James he is, then."

"Clancy. Clancy, I'm sorry."

He looked surprised. "What for?"

Her face creased. "You know what for. I can't have any more children."

"Oh, that!" Clancy said lightly. "Who would want more when we have this little darlin'? He's just perfect," he added, bending so that Anna could see the child. "Would ye believe the tiny fingers? Just look, Anna."

Anna smiled weakly. "Yes," she whispered, "he's lovely."

And so are you, she thought. *So are you, big Irish lummock that you are. So are you.*

Winning and Losing

1908

The kitchens at the Plaza hotel were beginning to return to some sort of order after the hectic madness of the lunch period. A waiter entered and, after a quick glance around, realised it was now or never and approached the chef with some trepidation.

"Excuse me, Chef, would it be convenient...?"

The great man's eyebrows narrowed, and the waiter readied himself for a torrent of abuse. Instead, the chef simply barked, "What is it?"

"There is a customer, a lady who insists on speaking to you."

"I don't speak to customers." The tone was dismissive.

"I know. I told her. She said she would wait until you could spare her a moment."

A faint memory stirred and a look of enquiry crossed the chef's heavy features. "What is her name?" he asked with some interest.

"Mrs. Sullivan," the waiter replied, pleased that he had not been sent away with a flea in his ear. "I have no idea who she is; she is not a regular."

"No matter," the chef interrupted. "I have been expecting Mrs. Sullivan." He glanced around the kitchen. "Tell her I shall be five minutes."

The waiter scurried away, altering his gait to his usual smooth glide as he entered the restaurant. He approached a small table in the corner, where the elegant Mrs. Sullivan was taking a late lunch.

"Chef will be here in about five minutes, ma'am."

"Thank you so much."

Anna gave him a winsome smile and ordered claret jelly for dessert. As she finished it, the chef arrived.

"Mrs. Sullivan?"

"Chef, how kind of you to spare me a few moments. I know how busy you are. Will you join me?"

"That...would not be quite correct, Mrs. Sullivan." For once, the chef was discomfited. He had been told she was attractive, but was unprepared for such stunning looks.

She turned the smile on again. "Oh, don't be so stuffy, Chef. Sit down."

She indicated the chair opposite and the chef sat down gingerly. It was unfair of her to put him in this position, he thought.

"I wanted to congratulate you on a perfect lunch," Anna said enthusiastically. "The lobster cassolette was superb. Just the right touch of tarragon, and Calvados...I think?"

Her tone invited him to confirm the ingredients, but the chef pulled himself together. "You may be having success at other establishments, Mrs. Sullivan, but not at the Plaza."

"I am not sure what you mean." Her lovely face held a look of polite enquiry.

"I do not wish to appear ungracious, Mrs. Sullivan. I appreciate your compliments on the meal, but I have been expecting you. Why did it take you so long? We are, after all, the best restaurant in New York."

Anna suppressed a half smile. "I did have an excellent lobster thermidor at the Ritz Carlton." Seeing the chef's face change, she relented quickly. "Come now, Chef, I was only teasing; the cassolette was even better. You say you were expecting me? I did not realise I had been...noticed."

One could hardly fail to notice you, the chef thought. Aloud he said, "I do not often meet my culinary rivals," he corrected himself, "or those who believe they are my rivals, but I do have a few friends in the business. I have heard of you, Mrs. Sullivan. You eat in the best restaurants, usually choosing a speciality for which the place is famous. Then you ask to see the chef to congratulate him...and wheedle as many tips and secrets from him as you can."

"Wheedle? Did you say wheedle?" Anna looked quite shocked.

"What would you call it?" the chef asked sardonically. One had to hand it to her, he thought. She was quite an actress.

"I would call it an interesting exchange of information and recipes, of course, among people who are all interested in food."

"And what is your purpose?" The chef was not to be deflected. "I know you are not in the restaurant business, at least not in *haute cuisine*."

"No, I am not. I am interested in good cooking, that is all. I have lived in New York for three years now and have discovered that even the most wealthy people eat out. Any special occasion, even a family dinner party, is held in a restaurant, as the standards at home are just not good enough."

The chef smiled. So that was it, he thought. This elegant lady hoped to climb the social ladder by giving dinner parties at which the food compared with the best the hotels and restaurants could offer. "That is quite true," he smiled. "In any case, women cannot cook, not at the highest level."

"You think not?" Her voice had a steely edge. "Chef, which night do you have off?"

"Me? Oh...er...Mondays."

"Good. To show you I mean what I say, I would like you to come to dinner on Monday evening. I shall cook."

"Oh...that's very kind, Mrs. Sullivan, but I don't think...."

"Come now, Chef, you have handed out a challenge, have you not? Here is my card, be there at seven thirty. We shall eat at eight."

"But, Mrs. Sullivan...."

"You have given me an excellent lunch, Chef. Please, let me return the favour. There is only one condition." She displayed her winning smile again.

"And that is?"

"If you agree I am a true cook, I want that recipe for lobster cassolette."

When Anna left the Plaza, she took one of the new metered taxicabs home. She had enjoyed riding in them since the first fleet had arrived in New York from France a year earlier amid a blaze of publicity. It was silly, she supposed, but she liked to sit in the back seat and know that the cab had also been in France, as she had, and she would dream a little about those long, lost days as she rode around New York like a lady.

When she arrived at the elegant house on 65th Street which was now her home, she immediately went to the nursery, where Lottie Wilson, the elderly English nanny she had engaged for James, was delighted to see her.

"Oh, ma'am, it's you," she whispered, her face beaming with pleasure. "I'll put the kettle on right away. The little one is fast asleep, bless him. He'll be awake soon, no doubt."

Anna took a quick peep at her son, then took off her hat and sat down in a comfortable chair near the fireside. She liked being in the nursery with Lottie; the plain furnishings and simple fare reminded her of home.

Lottie busied herself with the tea things and said quietly, "Did you get what you wanted?"

Anna sighed. "No. The chef knew I was there to pick his brains and wouldn't tell me anything."

"Oh, dear!" Lottie said with concern.

"It's not so bad. I've invited him to dinner on Monday. If he likes my cooking, he'll give me the recipe."

Lottie's face lit up. "Then it's in the bag. There's not a better cook in all New York than you, ma'am." She poured boiling water into the teapot and stirred thoughtfully, saying, "You may not get much more information, though."

"It's no matter, I have all I need," Anna answered. "I shall be making up my own menus when we open our first restaurant." She smiled at Lottie. "And how are you feeling, my dear? Have you heard from your son?"

"No, ma'am. Not since the letter from Philadelphia, when he was trying for a job on the railroad."

"Don't worry; he'll be alright. He was probably right to leave. Things are not easy now for immigrants." Anna's mind went back to her own arrival in New York, and she continued, "It was better when we came. President Roosevelt made it clear that immigrants of the right kind were welcome."

Lottie nodded. "And now we get blamed for every single thing wrong with this country, especially if we happen to be Catholic."

Anna frowned. "Surely not, Lottie. I am not a

Catholic, but I employed you to care for James because I know you are a good woman."

Even as she said it, some trick of memory caught her suddenly, and she was in Paris, and Jacques was explaining that Catholics didn't really worship pictures. Anna tried to concentrate. Was it possible that simple incident had affected her decision to employ Lottie?

"I know that, ma'am," Lottie was saying. She seemed to have something on her mind. "Mrs. Sullivan, there was something I wanted to say to you," she ventured.

Anna waited as Lottie poured the tea. When she had handed Anna her cup, Lottie said hesitantly, "You will recall I told you I would have to leave here as soon as my son sent for me to join him?"

"Yes."

"I want to say that even if he sends for me, I don't need to go until you are ready. It isn't as though Eddie needs me; in fact, I'd be a liability for the first few years, until he's got himself settled. I'd love to look after James until he goes to school, if that's all right with you."

"You know it is, Lottie." Anna was pleased.

"I've become so fond of him," Lottie confessed. "He's a lovely boy and that's the truth."

Anna laughed. "That's not what you said when he tipped the tea leaves into the rice pudding."

Lottie joined in the laughter. "He's mischievous right enough, but there isn't an unkind or ungenerous bone in his body." She beamed at Anna. "Just like his pa," she added.

Anna did not reply. She sipped her tea as Lottie chattered on.

"What I mean, ma'am, is I'm glad you didn't give me that job in the kitchen I applied for. I'm so much happier looking after James. Mr. Sullivan

relies on you for the business, and you need someone to rely on too. All I'm saying is, ma'am, that
someone is me."

"Thank you, Lottie. It's a relief to know you
can stay for another couple of years, for James'
sake." Anna stopped, and then said carefully, "It's
been good to have you here, Lottie, for me as well
as James. Good to have someone to talk to about
the business...."

"What, me? Lord, ma'am, I've no head for business."

"No, but you are interested, and it helps me to
talk over my ideas with someone who isn't directly
involved." Anna smiled sadly. "It helps me to know
someone is on my side."

As Anna kissed her sleeping son and then left
the nursery, Lottie pondered on her words. *Whatever made Anna Sullivan imagine no one was on
her side? Why was everything such a battle for her?
It was plain her husband worshipped her. Surely
he was the one to talk to about the business?*

Lottie got up stiffly as she heard James begin
to stir. Her feeling for Mrs. Sullivan was not simple gratitude; she felt genuine affection for the family and didn't like to think the mistress was unhappy. Perhaps it was because there had been no
more babies, she reflected.

Lottie lifted James from his bed and kissed him
gently. "There we are now. Just woken up, have
we? Come with Nanny and have some milk."

She sat the two-year-old in the small chair,
which his doting pa had made with his own hands,
and went to pour the milk, still considering Anna's
words. *The simple truth was probably,* she thought,
that young Mrs. Sullivan misses her mother.

When Clancy arrived home, he was none too

pleased to hear that the chef from the Plaza was to dine with them on the following Monday. "I don't know why you can't leave well alone," he grumbled. "I don't have the social chit-chat for these people."

"What people?" Anna retorted. "Anyone would think I had invited high society. The chef is a very hard worker, like you and me. I will take care of the small talk," she added. "It will all be about food."

Clancy frowned. "Does he have a name, this culinary wizard?"

"I've no idea. I just called him 'Chef'."

"I can't call him 'Chef' all evening."

"Well, call him 'Maitre', then, if you prefer," Anna said tartly.

Clancy tried a different tack. "When you go to these places dressed up so...so...."

"Beautifully?"

"I was going to say expensively," Clancy retorted. "People will think you have the money to back it up. This chef will expect...."

"He will expect a good dinner, and he'll get it. And I'm sure he has never been invited to a better address."

"That's true. We should never have spent so much on this house. The area is beyond us."

"Of course it isn't. We are as good as anyone else. This is America, Clancy. We are not limited by ideas about what is 'our place in society'. Money is what matters here."

"And we don't have enough to live in a place like this," Clancy retorted.

"Of course we do! It's already worth twice what we paid for it. Property prices are going through the roof!"

"Yes, we're so well off we only have one downstairs room furnished!" Clancy reiterated.

Anna laughed out loud. "Yes, but what furnishing. You must admit we have done it right, haven't we?" She looked around the elegant drawing room with delight, where Sylvie's painting held pride of place over the fireplace. "Honestly, Clancy, did you ever think we should have a place like this? I'm sure it's right to furnish only one room at a time and do it really well. Everything we buy will be of the very best quality."

"Everything *you* buy, you mean."

For once his tone seemed to reach her, and she said slowly, "You don't mean that, do you? You don't really think I'm spending too much money? We are doing so well."

Clancy relented. "It isn't the money, sweetheart. It's just that I don't know where we are going. We have a good business, yes. Over fifty accounts now. But no matter how many accounts we get, we shall never be in the class of our neighbours."

"There you go again! Class!" Anna said vehemently. "I want James to have...."

"I know," Clancy interrupted. "You want a good future for him and so do I. But, Anna, I don't want to belong to so-called high society. I wouldn't be comfortable."

She laughed again. "And neither would I. But when we have our chain of first class restaurants...."

"I've told you I'm not sure about that."

"Well, I am. Why do you think I've been working so hard all this time, picking up tips from the best chefs in town? I am teaching young Jennie McCormack all I know. She's really good, Clancy, and will be ready for responsibility before too long. And as for society, when we have our chain of first class restaurants, we shall make our own society."

Clancy sighed. "You and your big ideas. I didn't know I married such an ambitious woman."

"You did."

He looked at her and then laughed. "Yes, I suppose I did." He crossed to the drinks table and poured himself a whisky. "You want a drink?"

"No, thank you."

Clancy sat down in the large armchair opposite. He sipped his drink and regarded her gravely. "These big ideas of yours. If I agree...."

"Oh, Clancy!"

"I said *if* I agree, it has to be on a proper footing."

"Of course."

"You say of course, but you don't even know what I'm talking about," Clancy said hotly.

She waited for him to explain, and at length he said in a conciliatory manner, "Anna, we don't have the knowledge, enough business expertise, to take on something of this kind."

"But we do! Clancy, we do! I have the most wonderful food planned."

"There you go again. I'm not talking about food!" Clancy was becoming impatient. "I'm talking about business."

"But we are running our business very successfully," she protested.

"Yes," Clancy agreed, "but as much by luck as good judgment. The bank has been very helpful, but the more I learn, the more I realise how ignorant I am, so I do."

Anna was quiet now. She could always tell when Clancy had something on his mind. He smiled sheepishly and then continued. "I was going to talk to you about this, anyway, but now, if you insist on these plans, it's even more urgent."

"What is?"

"Anna, I want to go to college."

"College? Whatever for?" She looked dumb-founded.

"A Commerce degree. I don't think I could get into Colombia, but there are other...."

"But whatever for?" Anna asked again.

"Because, Anna, if we are going to have a really successful business, we must know what we are doing! You understand the practical side, the meals, and training our staff on the sites. You always were a born organiser. But I have to deal with the business accounts, and there is so much to know! Not only the bookkeeping and profit and loss accounts, but the various taxes and the regulations and...."

"But surely we can employ an accountant?"

"Yes, and then we have to believe everything he says! When I had that meeting at the bank last week, I didn't understand half of what was going on!" Clancy said vehemently. "Anna, if anyone wanted to cheat us, we would be fair game."

She frowned. "I never thought of it like that. I see what you mean, but...does it have to be you?"

"Yes. I have to be involved, understand the business side in the same way that you understand the kitchens. You know instantly if someone is trying to pull the wool over your eyes."

She looked at him intently; he was getting through. He pressed his point. "At the moment, they could tell us anything."

"Yes, I see."

Clancy remained quiet, letting the idea sink in. At length she looked up. "If you went to college, would it mean a delay in opening the restaurants?"

"Yes, but we can go on expanding in the business we already have. We know what we are doing by now. The new delicatessen is going well."

"Yes, with Joe Kowalski's help." Anna smiled. "That was a good move. I'm glad he agreed to work for us. But what I dream of is a chain of really top class restaurants."

"I understand that, and I want it to happen one day. But that kind of venture will involve much more risk. It will cost a fortune to launch each restaurant, that is, if you want to attract real society people." He leaned forward in the big chair. "We have to be much more financially secure before we do it, darlin'. And we need to know more. If some cheapskate gangster tries to move in on us, I want to know more than he does."

"What do you mean? We've never had any trouble."

"Not so far. Most of the canteen sites are out of town. But things could change, and the delicatessens may be different," Clancy said grimly.

"But what could they do?"

"Bribe our accountant to hive off some of our profits, that's what!"

"Oh!"

"That's only one of the reasons I need to learn more," Clancy said. "I don't want to alarm you, but we are not in Sandley Heath now. Most of the small businesses in town pay protection money to the mob. I didn't tell you, but it was the main reason Joe Kowalski agreed to join us. He was frightened and didn't want the responsibility of being the boss any longer."

"Oh, Clancy, poor Joe!" Anna was upset. "But the newspapers said last year that Johnny Torrio had moved to Chicago."

"He has, but he has left someone to run his rackets here. A man called Capone."

"I've never heard of him," Anna said doubtfully.

"Perhaps not," Clancy replied. "He may not be so well known, but he has been a friend of Torrio's for years. Things will not get any better, you can be sure of that. We need to be big, Anna, really big, to stand a chance."

Anna sighed. "I know you're right, Clancy. But how long? How long before we have our chain of restaurants?"

Clancy laughed. "How can I know? It will take as long as it takes. Three years, perhaps, for me to be qualified. By then James will be old enough for school, and with luck, we shall have a larger chain of canteens, which Lee Sung can continue to run, with Joe running the chain of delicatessens. You will have extra time to train Jennie for the restaurants, and we should be in a very healthy position."

"Yes." He sensed her disappointment, but her eyes were bright as she began to laugh. "Have you thought, Clancy, we are still making chains?"

"Yes," he smiled, "but these kind pay better. And talking of chains, that reminds me. I increased the monthly bank order to Will and the family, as you wanted." He finished his whisky. "What's for dinner? I suppose it's something exotic again?"

"Of course. You are my recipe tester."

Anna crossed to Clancy and kissed him gently. "I shall enjoy having a top businessman for a husband," she said.

He put his arm around her. "And I enjoy having a good cook for a wife," he rejoined. "Mind you, I do have one complaint about the food."

Her eyes widened. "A complaint?"

"Yes. I wish, just once in a while, you would make us a good bread pudding."

The chef from the Plaza had handed over the

recipe like a lamb, Anna reflected happily. She had been right about the ingredients, but it was good of him to give her the tip about the bouillon. It had been a good evening, and for all his misgivings, Clancy had enjoyed it as much as she had. She glanced across to where her husband lay, deep in slumber. *I'm not surprised you can sleep like that,* Anna thought. *You surpassed yourself tonight.* She turned to him and gazed closely at his face. He looked very young and vulnerable when he was asleep, and for some unaccountable reason, she suddenly felt like weeping. She drew in her breath and considered him, still a handsome man, a little more flesh on the bones, perhaps. His features had a chiselled look, and the thick dark eyelashes, which had inspired so many comments from the girls at the chainshop, were still long against his cheeks. *Not fair for a man to have such eyes,* Anna thought. Irish eyes, her mother had called them, and the look she had seen in those eyes tonight had told her how much he still loved her. He was a passionate man, she thought tenderly, so passionate and so gentle. She had stopped feeling guilty about making love with Clancy long ago. *You couldn't help yourself,* she thought tenderly; there was something about Clancy that made it easy to make love, and she had enjoyed it tonight as much as he had.

Then why couldn't she sleep? Why was her mind going around in circles? She suddenly realised she had felt uneasy for days, since Lottie had made that remark about James being just like his pa.

James was not like his pa. Anna had searched the boy's features for a look of Robert, but apart from the blonde hair, there was nothing. James was more like her family and, if anything, looked rather like Billy when he was small.

Just like his pa. A sudden image of Robert came to her, fair and smiling, as he flicked the hair from his eyes with a quick shake of the head. In an instant, they were in the hayloft at La Maison Blanche, making love with wild abandon in the sweet scented hay. She remembered with a pang of delicious pain the little hollow on the cliffs above the beach at Locquirec, and suddenly it all flooded back, the feeling of freedom, the generous liberality of France, the exuberant joy and the terrible anguish. The rushing remembrance enveloped her and rolled back the last three years as if they had never been.

Anna turned over and buried her face in the pillow. *Why?* her mind demanded bitterly. Why did she still feel so much for someone who had tossed her aside like a plaything, like a summer toy which had served its purpose once the season faded? How could she still yearn for Robert, long for news of him, when he had treated her so badly? *Because,* her heart answered simply, *because of what he meant to you. Because of how he made you feel, how he was, how you thought he was. Because you were young and he was the first, at the time, you thought, the only one.*

Anna got out of bed quietly and went downstairs. She found her reticule and read again the last letter from Therese, written out in Jacques's steady hand. She skimmed through the items of local news until she came to the part she sought. She read: "Robert was not here this summer. We heard he had spent the spring with his mother in England, but then went straight to Cannes. He spends most of the year there now, at his wife's home. They have a little boy, one year old now. Did you know? Jacques says he thinks Robert is not painting much these days."

Why had Jacques sent that message? Did he think she was interested in Robert's painting? At least she had news. In the two letters she had received from Florence, there had been hardly a mention of Robert and Delphine. Of all who were there in France, Anna felt that only Jacques had perhaps understood anything of the passion of that summer.

A slight noise made her start. Clancy stood in the doorway in his dressing gown. "What are you doing down here, darlin'? I woke up and missed you, so I did."

Anna dashed away a tear which she only now realised was running down her cheek. "I...I couldn't sleep," she said lightly. "I didn't mean to wake you."

Clancy was looking at the letter in her hand. "What are you reading?" he asked.

"It's nothing important...just a letter."

He nodded slowly. "Yes, I can guess which letter it is." He came across to her, took the letter and glanced briefly at the signature. He folded it and replaced it in her reticule.

"The past is over, Anna," he said quietly.

"Of course it is. I was only thinking of Therese."

Clancy took her arm. "I know what you were thinking of. Come back to bed."

As they reached their room, Anna saw the dejected droop of Clancy's shoulders and guilt overwhelmed her.

Clancy asked, "Would you like me to make a cup of tea?"

"No, thanks," Anna said. "I'll sleep now, I'm sure." She smiled brightly. "I have a busy day tomorrow. I'm going to start looking at restaurant design."

Paolo

1911

Exactly three months to the day after Clancy qualified, the first Sullivan's restaurant opened. It was an immediate success, and from the outset was heavily booked. Anna felt they should have chosen larger premises.

"Most certainly not," Clancy assured her, as they locked up after a hectic evening. "Part of the attraction of Sullivan's is the special atmosphere you have created. If the restaurant was larger, we should lose that."

"But we are turning away so many customers," Anna complained.

"And the answer to that, my dear, is to open another Sullivan's as soon as possible, but not too near this one."

"Fifth Avenue?" Anna asked hopefully.

Clancy sighed. "You know my views about Fifth Avenue. It is far too expensive."

"Even now? Now you know how successful we can be?"

"Even now." Clancy took Anna's arm and tucked it under his. "Let's walk home, at least part of the way, shall we?"

Anna nodded, and Clancy asked their chauffeur to follow them at a walking pace. It was a lovely evening; the air was fresh and sweet after the oppressive atmosphere of the kitchen, and they strolled comfortably, enjoying the quietness of the streets late at night.

"Imagine," said Clancy, "that our restaurant is on Fifth Avenue. Could you have taken any more money tonight?"

"No," Anna admitted. "Although we could have charged a little more, maybe."

"How much more?" Clancy asked.

"Er,...perhaps ten percent," Anna said.

"Right. If we were on Fifth Avenue instead of just off Union Square, we should have taken ten percent more. But our rent would have trebled. We would actually be taking a loss, whereas our present site will make us a good return."

"I can see that," Anna said. "But I thought Fifth Avenue was the place to be."

"It is if you can make it work," Clancy said. "But it is no use opening something that will not make a contribution to the business. Every canteen and delicatessen we own pays its way, and we must make sure that every Sullivan's does too."

"I suppose so," Anna said a little sadly.

Clancy laughed. "We are still making chains, Anna, as you often remind me, and every chain is only as strong as its weakest link."

She looked at him keenly. "A restaurant on Fifth Avenue would be a weak link?"

"Yes. Not only would it make no contribution to the chain, but its losses would wipe out the profit from a few of the others. The secret is to find sites which are quite near to the best areas, but not in the prime positions, where the rents are beyond us."

"And you think you can find sites like that?" Anna asked.

"Oh, yes. I shall keep my eyes open, and we aren't in any hurry. The customers will always want your food."

Anna laughed. "I must admit I didn't expect such compliments. It's very gratifying after all the time I spent planning. They like the design, too."

They walked on in silence until Anna said, "Jennie has been a godsend. She has worked so hard, I think we should pay her a bonus."

"Yes," Clancy agreed. "I was going to mention it myself. I must say you were right about her. I had my doubts, but for an eighteen-year-old, she has a good head."

Anna smiled. People often underestimated Jennie McCormack. With her slender figure, fair hair and pale skin, she appeared frail, almost wraithlike, but her ephemeral beauty hid a very practical nature and a strong, tenacious will. It probably came from her orphanage background, Anna thought, and having to make her own way in life.

She leaned her head against Clancy's shoulder. "I suddenly feel very tired. Shall we drive the rest of the way?"

Clancy beckoned the chauffeur, and within a few minutes they were home. Lottie, their housekeeper since James had started school, had waited up in case they needed anything.

"I'd love a cup of tea, Lottie," Anna said, sinking into a sofa.

"And something to eat?"

"Not for me," Anna responded, "But perhaps Mr. Sullivan."

"Yes," said Clancy. "Tea for me as well, Lottie, and a slice of that bread pudding I saw in the ice box."

Anna suppressed a smile, Clancy's success had not altered his fondness for bread pudding. He sensed her interest and said defensively, "Well, I like it, so I do."

"I know. That's why I made it."

He smiled. "I'm surprised you had time. You have been working far too hard lately."

For once, she agreed with him. "Yes, I know. Now we are up and running with the restaurant I can relax a little. I was meaning to talk to you about it."

"Well?"

"Firstly, I want to hand over all the cooking to Jennie McCormack."

"I know she's good, but is she that good?"

"She is. I have taught her all I know. With the help of the new chef, she will do well, I'm sure of it. As we are closed on Mondays that will be her day off, and I shall go in to help on the weekends and check the ordering."

"Do you need to do even that much?" Clancy asked.

"Yes. I don't want to lose touch with the business. I must always know what is going on, in that way I can develop new menus."

"Do you have to?" Clancy said gently. "If you wish you need never do a hand's turn again. It's time you put your feet up, enjoyed the money we have earned."

"I could never be idle," Anna responded, smiling.

"But why not? Now we have the first Sullivan's open, it will be a simple matter of copying your ideas for the others, and we have plenty of good people."

"I know, but I need to be involved, especially as James is at school. Perhaps if we had other children."

Clancy fell silent, and neither of them spoke as Lottie entered with the tray. After she had gone, Clancy said, "I sent the money to Will today, by the way. Enough to pay for the house, and some extra for furnishings and moving expenses, as you wanted."

"Thank you," Anna said. "They must be so excited to be moving to the country. I can't imagine our Billy is fourteen now, and Dottie, eight. Little Andrew will be four soon. I'm glad he will grow up away from Sandley Heath." She hesitated. "If ever I feel I can leave the business for a while, I'd like to go home to see them all." She smiled at him. "Wouldn't you like to do that, Clancy? Go home for a visit?"

Clancy shook his head ruefully. "Someone would need to stay here. Anyway, it isn't home to me. Personally, I don't care if I never see Sandley Heath again. It was never really home to me the way it was for you."

Anna nodded. "Clancy, you don't mind sending so much money to my family? The annuity you arranged for Will was very expensive."

Clancy laughed. "Of course not. Will is a good fellow, I always thought so. Anyway, what are families for? If my cousins needed money, we'd help them too, but they seem to have fallen on their feet, heaven alone knows how! We have been so lucky, Anna; it's good to share it around a little."

Anna frowned. "We have not been lucky at all. We have been hard working and imaginative. We made our own luck."

"Rubbish!" Clancy took a large bite of bread pudding. He ate appreciatively, saying, "This is delicious!" before he replied, "We have worked hard, certainly, but can you honestly say you have worked harder than you did at Sandley Heath?"

"No," Anna said, remembering suddenly. "Not as hard as that. But this is a different country."

"Of course. That is where the luck comes in.

We were lucky to be here at such a time, when things were expanding so fast. No matter how hard they work, Will and Mary will never have the chance to do what we have done."

"That's true," Anna admitted. "But they could have joined us here. We asked them often enough."

"I know you would have liked that, darlin'. I think their decision not to come was more because of your dad being left alone than anything else."

"You're probably right," Anna said. "He's seventy-four now and still putting his spoke in. Will said in his last letter they had endless trouble getting him to agree to move with them."

"Yes, and that surprises me," Clancy said. "He always longed for the countryside so much."

"Did he? I never heard him say so."

"Perhaps he didn't talk about it to his family, but I remember once, in the Sandley Arms when he was the worse for drink...."

"Which was very often."

"He told me about Worcestershire, and about his childhood." Clancy hesitated, remembering. "He spoke about it so...so...movingly."

"Dad? Spoke movingly?" Her tone was contemptuous.

"Yes, truly." Clancy smiled gently. "I know you've never really forgiven him, but he had a terrible life, you know."

"What about my mother?" Anna retorted. "It was worse for her."

"Perhaps it was. But he had a point of view as well. He left everything he loved to be with your mother and then found he couldn't provide for her as he wanted to."

Anna's face was tight and closed. "Anyway," she sighed, "it's all water under the bridge now."

"Yes. I only wanted to make the point that it

isn't easy to feel like that. To know that your wife wants something else, something you can't give her, no matter how hard you try."

Something in Clancy's voice touched a nerve, and Anna got up and went over to him. She stroked his temples gently and said, "You have always been so good to me, Clancy. If it wasn't for you, where should I be now, I wonder?"

He caught at her hand, opening her palm and raising it to his lips. Then he said simply, "But it's not what you really wanted, is it?"

"How can you say that? It is due to you that we have the business. If you hadn't got me the position as cook at Hampson's, we should never have got off the ground. I didn't dream we should ever be so well off and able to help Will and the family. It's all due to you."

Clancy was engaged in kissing her fingers one by one. When he raised his head, Anna thought she saw tears in his eyes. He smiled. "Oh, yes," he said, "we have money, more than enough, and we made it together. But as I said before, it's not what you really wanted, is it?"

Anna started. She listened intently, and after a moment she heard the sound again. There was someone or something out there, at the rear of the premises.

She put down her pen and moved quietly out of the office and across the darkened restaurant kitchen towards the window. She could feel her heart thumping in her chest as she peered out into the blackness. At first, she could see nothing, but then discerned a shadowy figure poised on the fence at the back of the restaurant, and she heard the slight thud as he jumped to the ground. Holding her breath, Anna moved across the kitchen, carefully opened a drawer, and extracted a large torch.

Momentarily, she cursed herself for working so late alone; she had promised Clancy to be home an hour ago. Deciding surprise was the best form of attack, with one quick movement she unlocked the door and directed the torch straight at the intruder.

For a few seconds they stared at each other in frozen silence. He was young, perhaps in his early twenties, and in spite of the look of shock he wore, Anna was immediately conscious of his startlingly handsome features. He moved slightly to avoid the beam of the torch in his eyes, but not before Anna had seen the startled look change to one of embarrassment, and a deep flush suffuse his face as he turned away.

"What are you doing here?" Anna said sharply.

"Nothing." The quiet reply was superfluous. In spite of his attempt to hide it, the torch had already picked out the chunk of French bread in his left hand. He saw she had noticed it and said sullenly, "Not doing any harm."

Stealing from the rubbish bin! Anna's heart lurched, and she was back in Sandley Heath, desperately filling a bucket with "sleck" from the waste tip, not exactly stealing, but not really allowed either.

"Are you hungry?"

The young man stared. The light was still in his eyes and he couldn't see properly. "No," he spat out sarcastically, "I do this for fun, I like eating out of rubbish bins."

"Put the bread back and come inside," Anna said.

He hesitated, but only for a moment. He followed her into the kitchen, and Anna motioned him through to the restaurant. The chairs had been stacked on the tables for the night, but she got one down and said, "Sit down. The table isn't laid but you can use a tray. Scrambled eggs alright?"

His look of blank surprise changed and he nodded quickly.

Anna returned a few minutes later with a tray carrying a plate of bacon and eggs, a pot of coffee and a large piece of pie. She set the tray in front of him and said, "There was bacon in the ice box. You're not Jewish, are you?"

"Er...no. Italian." He stared at the tray.

"Well, eat up. I'll get some bread." She caught his eye. "Some fresh bread," she added pointedly.

He needed no urging, and Anna left him and returned to the office. Through the small security window, she watched him eat; he was obviously famished. An immigrant, perhaps, who had been unable to find work? He spoke excellent English, she had noted, with only a faint trace of an accent. She inspected him closely, noting his dark curly hair and broad shoulders; he had the good looks for which the Italian nation was famous. His clothes intrigued her. There was something which did not match with her notion of the penniless immigrant. He looked as if he had been sleeping rough, but his suit was of good quality and his shoes, though dirty, were of fine leather.

As the young man finished his pie, Anna put away her menu book and went to join him in the restaurant. "More pie?"

"No, thank you." As he saw her smile, he added, "Well...yes, that is...it's delicious.... If you don't mind...."

Anna fetched another slice of pie and a cup. "I think I'll join you for coffee."

In an instant, he had placed a chair for her. "Please do!" His smile was a revelation, radiant with charm, and infectious with impish familiarity, as he waved her to her seat with an expansive gesture.

Anna hid a smile, wondering who was doing the entertaining here. He was certainly someone to turn heads, and what was more, he knew it.

"What is your name?" she asked, as he filled her coffee cup.

"Of course! Where are my manners? I do apologise." He rose to his feet; the food had turned him into a different person. He made a low bow. "Vetti. Paolo Vetti. Recently arrived in your great country."

Anna smiled. "It isn't really my country. I'm an immigrant too."

"You?" He seemed amazed. "But you, you work here? When you gave me food, I thought...."

"You thought correctly. I own the restaurant, or at least my husband and I do."

He frowned. "Your husband should not allow you to be here alone, and so late!" he pronounced. "I might have been anyone. A thief perhaps...."

"And you are not?" Anna asked innocently, smiling to herself as she watched outrage and disbelief struggle for supremacy in the handsome face.

"Of course not!" He coloured slightly. "Because someone has...has hard times it does not mean...."

"I know. I was only teasing."

For a moment, he looked resentful, and then the stunning smile lit up his features again. "Well, you are my guardian angel, and I will never be able to repay you. Why are you so kind to me?"

Anna hesitated and then said slowly, "Perhaps because I can remember what it is like to be hungry."

"You? But you own a restaurant! You were never hungry, surely?"

"In my childhood, yes, quite often." She smiled

at him. "And you, Paolo Vetti? How does it come about that you are hungry?"

He did not answer at once, as if considering the question. At last, he said, "I am tempted to lie to you, because I would like you to think well of me."

"I shall only think well of you if you tell the truth," Anna responded gently.

"You are right. I shall tell you. I am hungry because of my own fault, my own stupidity." He took a deep breath and then continued, "Since my father was...died, three years ago, my uncle Vittorio has been in charge."

"In charge of what?" Anna asked.

Paolo looked perplexed. "I mean responsible for me. It is my English," he explained lightly. "Uncle Vittorio has plans to come to America; he will be here in about three months time, and I was to come with him. I couldn't wait. I was not so happy at home. I did not get on well with my cousins, so I begged my uncle to let me come right away. He was against it, but I told him I would be alright."

Paolo took a deep breath and suddenly crashed his fist onto the table "When I think of it now!" he almost groaned, wincing at the memory. "When I think of all the disasters my uncle warned me against, and how I laughed at him and told him such things could never happen to me.... Oh, no! Not me! I was far too smart!"

The bravado of a few moments ago was gone, he looked deflated and bitter as he said slowly, "You can guess, I am sure. Against his better judgment, Uncle Vittorio allowed me to come on ahead, with enough money to last until he joined me. I arrived a week ago, and the first night, I met some men who said they would help me find a good place to stay. They were friendly. I was grateful." His voice was explanatory, pleading with her to understand. He sighed. "I got drunk, of course, and woke next morning in an alleyway. I had a bump on the head and not a penny left."

"Did you go to the police?"

His eyes opened wide. "Of course not." Realising she expected an explanation, he added, "They would have laughed at me."

"Yes, they might have."

"I have been trying to find a job, but I do not have much experience."

"What experience do you have? What did you do in Italy?"

"Do?" He seemed to find the question strange. "Well, I...I was at university, and at language school."

"How old are you, Paolo?"

"Twenty."

Anna sipped her coffee slowly. Twenty years old and obviously this young man had never done a hand's turn. How much chain had she made by the time she was twenty, she wondered? She put down her cup.

"I'm afraid I can't do much to help, Paolo, but if you are prepared to work hard, I can offer you a job as a kitchen hand for the next three months, until your uncle arrives."

"A kitchen hand! That will be marvellous!" He seemed delighted.

"No, it won't. It's menial work and very hard. Washing up, scouring pans, scrubbing floors, that kind of thing."

"Paolo Vetti is not afraid of work," he said proudly.

Anna gave a wry smile. "I'm pleased to hear it. The pay is low, but you will have all your food provided, which helps." She felt in her reticule. "A few dollars advance pay," she said, holding it out to him. "Enough to find a cheap room."

He seemed embarrassed. "Thank you. I will repay one day for your kindness."

"No need. As I say, it is an advance on pay. Report here at two in the afternoon tomorrow. You will work from two until ten or eleven in the evening."

"I have to work in the evening?"

"Yes. It may surprise you, but that is when the customers dine," Anna responded a little acidly.

"Of course. I didn't mean.... I am so grateful."

"Don't be grateful. Just be on time and work hard," Anna said. She got to her feet, suddenly very tired. "I am going to take a cab home now," she said. "You can come with me, and I will ask the driver to take you on to find a room. He will know where."

A few minutes later, as Anna alighted from the cab, Paolo caught her arm. "You have not told me your name," he said, the huge smile lighting up his face.

"Sullivan," Anna said. "Mrs. Sullivan. It's in large letters over the restaurant." This young man needed taking down a peg or two, she thought.

He did not turn a hair. "But you have a Christian name also?" he asked softly, his beautiful dark eyes liquid in the half light.

Anna gave in. "It's Anna."

"Anna." He spoke the name slowly, lovingly. "Yes, it is beautiful, like the lovely guardian angel who bears it."

Anna got out of the cab hastily. The impudence! In spite of herself, she giggled slightly. The front door opened and Clancy stood there, looking anxious.

"I was just about to come for you. Where on earth have you been?"

"Sorry, Clancy. I was delayed."

"Oh?"

"Yes, I was taking on a temporary kitchen hand."

Paolo Vetti proved as good as his word. He performed the most menial of duties with enthusiasm and good humour, and his friendliness and outgoing personality brought an atmosphere of cheerful industry to Sullivan's kitchen. Even the dour-faced vegetable chef, whom Jennie McCormack called "old sourpuss" behind his back, pronounced the new boy "okay, I suppose," which was high praise indeed.

The only person who seemed impervious to Paolo's charm was Jennie herself. She kept him hard at work continually and rarely spoke to him. When Anna entered the kitchen at noon one day and found Paolo scrubbing the floor underneath the ovens, she took Jennie aside.

"What is Paolo doing here? I thought he didn't start until two?"

"He doesn't normally," Jennie said defensively. "I was not satisfied with the state of the kitchen floor, so I told him to come in early to do it again."

Anna frowned. "We cannot afford to pay...."

"No extra pay," Jennie interrupted. "He should get it right in his normal working hours."

Anna looked at her in surprise. Although Jennie was strict, it was unlike her to be unfair. "What is it, Jennie? Why do you dislike him so much? I thought he was doing a good job. He certainly works hard."

Jennie flushed. "Yes, I suppose he does work hard." She bit her lip. "I don't dislike him, Anna, but he's just so...so conceited and arrogant."

Anna laughed. "Yes, he is, I agree. Back home we would say he was full of himself, but that is only on the surface. Think how kind he has been to James, playing football with him and taking him to the park. Come on, Jennie," she added in a conciliatory tone, "Paolo is a young man! He's out to prove himself, to impress everyone."

"Well, he doesn't impress me!" Jennie snapped, a little too sharply.

Anna smiled. "Are you sure?" she asked with sudden intuition, and watched the slow flush suffuse Jennie's pale face, as she raised a nervous hand to tidy her already immaculate fair hair. Jennie remained silent, and Anna put her arm around her.

"Oh, Jennie, my dear girl, you shouldn't feel embarrassed because you find yourself attracted to him! He's the most good looking young man I've ever seen."

Jennie smiled uncertainly. "Yes, he is, isn't he?"

"Hasn't he asked you out yet?" Anna probed gently.

"Yes! The very first day he was here!" Jennie burst out. "I said no, of course," she added primly.

"And he hasn't asked you again?"

"No." Jennie's lips were tight. "He's found other fish to fry. I've seen him talking to that new girl at the delicatessen. Joe Kowalski had to speak to him for wasting staff time."

"But that doesn't prove anything. He's probably a little lonely. He has no one in New York. What do you expect him to do if you sent him away with a flea in his ear?"

Jennie's eyes were round. She thought a moment and then blurted out, "It's too late now, anyway. In a couple of weeks, his uncle will be here. Paolo will leave and I shall never see him again...." Her voice tailed off in despair, and she began to cry.

"What nonsense! I didn't think you were a girl

to give way to such silly imaginings," Anna chided gently. "All you need is a plan of attack. I'll help you."

"How?" Jennie sniffed, wiping her eyes.

"Next Monday evening, come to dinner. I'll invite Paolo too, and you can get to know each other a little better."

"Dinner? At your house? But, Anna, your dinner parties are famous! Everyone says...."

"Everyone won't be there. Just you and Paolo, and Clancy of course. A nice quiet dinner, and I'll cook for you myself."

As Anna made her way home a few hours later, she reflected sadly on the weakness of womankind. *How vulnerable we all are,* she thought, *when we meet that certain man, the one who has the power to make our heart race the moment we see him. Who would have thought that Jennie, prim, practical, down-to-earth Jennie, would have been so affected by a bumptious young Italian with a heavenly smile?*

How well she remembered that feeling, the delicious excitement and anticipation, mirrored by the agonies of self-doubt which inevitably accompanied the early stages of love. How long ago it seemed now, and yet the feeling had never left her, that deep seated longing for...she knew not what. All she was sure of was that it was gone. Gone forever.

With his usual dashing courtesy, Paolo arrived on the following Monday evening bearing a dozen red roses for his hostess. When Anna protested that the flowers must have cost half his wages for the week, he was unrepentant.

"What better way to spend one's money," he murmured, kissing her hand with an extravagant gesture, "than to please a beautiful lady?"

"My beautiful lady," Clancy reminded him. "Just in case you forgot," he added, laughing, unable to resist Paolo's infectious smile. "Will you have a drink?"

"Thank you. A little wine perhaps? Er...I wondered...is James still awake?"

"He was a moment ago," Anna smiled. In the three months since he had joined the restaurant, Paolo had become James's favourite "uncle".

"May I go up, just for a moment? I brought him this."

Paolo took a small wooden humming top from his pocket. "It's just a small one," he explained. "But it makes a grand noise as it spins, and you can keep it going for ages. I got it from the market."

"You spoil James," Anna said. "It's the second door on the right."

Paolo raced up the staircase two at a time and Clancy began to laugh again. "It makes you wonder who is the child out of the two of them, so it does," he said, pouring Paolo's drink.

Jennie arrived at that moment, and by the time Paolo returned minutes later, she was already seated on the large sofa in the drawing room, looking very elegant in her deep blue dress. Paolo's initial surprise at seeing her was replaced by obvious pleasure, and as usual, he soon became the life and soul of the somewhat hilarious party.

By all measures, it was a very successful evening, and Anna was happy to observe Paolo's keen interest in Jennie; when he thought Jennie was not looking, he would steal sidelong glances at her. After dinner, the conversation turned on many subjects, from the international situation to prospective sites for more Sullivan's restaurants.

By ten o'clock, they were completely relaxed, and were listening to Paolo extolling the delights of Rome, when the door suddenly opened and Lottie appeared, a little flustered.

"Mr. Sullivan, there's a gentleman here...he insists...." Before Lottie could finish speaking, a big, heavyset man pushed his way into the room, followed by two equally large companions. He wore a grey suit and a wide brimmed Homburg hat, and as Anna stared in astonishment, she noticed his heavy-lidded eyes, which roved around the room in languid enquiry. Following his look, she saw an almost imperceptible smile touch his mouth as he saw Paolo.

"Uncle!" Paolo, white faced, had risen to his feet.

"Paolo." The big man's voice was soft, with a thick accent. "So I find you at last."

"I thought you were coming next week, sir." Paolo still looked shocked.

The big man smiled. "You know I do not do what others expect," he said, not unkindly. He looked around the room. "It seems I find you in good company after all," he said with an air of condescension. "After seeing that slum you are living in, I am surprised."

Paolo remembered his manners. "Uncle Vittorio, may I introduce my hosts, Mr. and Mrs. Sullivan? They own the restaurant where I have been working. This is Miss Jennie McCormack."

Vittorio Vetti inclined his head slightly, ignoring Clancy's outstretched hand. "I see. You have been working in a restaurant? I heard miracles happened in New York. Now I know it is true." His joke seemed to please him and he gave an expansive smile. Turning to his companions, he made a dismissive gesture, and the two men left the room.

Anna regained her composure. "Mr. Vetti, we

are so pleased to meet you. Clancy, do get Mr. Vetti a drink."

"Glad to," Clancy growled, "if he is staying." He stared at Vittorio. "You haven't removed your hat, sir," he said pointedly.

For a moment, Vittorio Vetti held Clancy's look, and Anna had a sudden impression of menace. Then he smiled again, and removing his Homburg murmured, "My apologies, ladies. I am a little tired after the journey. A whisky would be very good."

He accepted his drink and made a few desultory remarks about his journey and the weather. Paolo seemed struck dumb for once, and the atmosphere remained tense, in sharp contrast to the relaxed intimacy of only minutes before.

Anna said, "I'm sure your friends would like a drink. Please ask them to join us."

"No, Mrs. Sullivan," Vittorio Vetti responded in his soft musical voice. "That is perfectly alright, my...friends...will not wish to disturb you further." He seemed amused, and added quickly, "I came here only to find my nephew. When I went to the address he sent me, I was shocked to find him staying in such a place. The landlady said he had come here, and so I followed. I was anxious to check that he was not in bad company."

"Uncle!" Paolo burst out, "Mr. and Mrs. Sullivan are very respectable people and have been very kind to me."

"Of course! I understand that now." Vittorio Vetti turned to Anna. "Please forgive me, Mrs. Sullivan, but I worry about Paolo. He is a little headstrong."

"I know," Anna smiled.

"Thank you for befriending my nephew. I will take him off your hands now."

"I can't leave the restaurant until next week,

Uncle," Paolo protested. In response to a look of withering coldness from his uncle, he added lamely, "They were expecting me to work next week. I have to give notice."

"That's alright, Paolo," Anna said gently. "We can manage. I can take someone on easily enough."

Vittorio Vetti gave a lofty smile. "I can hardly believe it. My nephew is actually needed at this restaurant?"

"Paolo has worked very hard," Anna said sharply. "We shall miss him a great deal."

Vittorio looked surprised but nodded his head and finished his drink. He put down his glass and said, "Then I'm pleased. Come along, Paolo. We must leave these good people in peace." He nodded to Jennie and Clancy, and said quietly to Anna, "You have been kind to my nephew. Thank you. If you ever need anything, let me know." He picked up his hat and left the room, and Paolo, with a hasty goodbye, followed him.

In the hall, Paolo turned back to Anna as Lottie went to fetch his coat. "Mrs. Sullivan, I am sorry, but you see how my uncle is."

"It's alright, Paolo. Try to keep in touch with us, and with Jennie."

His beautiful eyes blazed. "You think I have a chance?"

"I think so. Yes, I think you have a chance."

The stunning smile lit up his face as Lottie helped him into his coat. "I must hurry," he said, "My uncle is waiting in the car, but...Mrs. Sullivan...Anna?"

"Yes. Anna."

"Anna, I want to say thank you for...everything. Everything! I will never forget and I am always your friend. You understand? Always!"

"Yes, Paolo. Always."

Anna watched the large car drive away and then turned to find Jennie and Clancy in the hall.

"It seems the party is over," Anna said ruefully, "but you don't have to leave just yet."

"I must," said Jennie. "I work for this dreadful boss who will expect me to be bright and efficient tomorrow."

Clancy went to find the chauffeur to take Jennie home, and Anna confided, "It's alright, Jennie. Paolo will keep in touch."

"I doubt it," Jennie responded, "Uncle Vittorio will never let him out of his sight. Did you ever see such a strange person? Poor Paolo!"

"He is intimidating, I agree, but Paolo will keep in touch. He told me."

"Did he?" Jennie asked eagerly. "Are you sure?"

"Yes, I'm sure," Anna said as Clancy returned with the chauffeur.

As they waved the car away, Clancy said, "I hope you aren't encouraging anything between Jennie and Paolo."

"You noticed it?"

"I'd have to be blind not to," Clancy retorted. "They were both so aware of each other and trying to pretend they weren't!"

"I am encouraging it. Why do you think I invited them here together?"

She expected Clancy to laugh, but he turned away quickly and returned to the drawing room. He poured himself a nightcap and then said shortly, "It's not a good idea. Jennie has a good position with us, and we can't afford to lose her."

"I shouldn't like to lose her, certainly, but I would never stand in the way of her happiness."

"Happiness? You think she'd be happy with him?"

Something in Clancy's tone alarmed Anna.

"What is it, Clancy? You like Paolo. I know you do."

"I don't like his family."

"I admit Uncle Vittorio is a bit strange, but...."

"Strange? Anna, that man is Mafia!"

Anna felt her blood run cold. "No! You must be wrong. How can you possibly know that?"

Clancy turned, and his face was tense. "I thought there was something odd about Uncle Vittorio even before I met him, so I did. Twice I have asked Paolo what his uncle's business is, and twice I got fobbed off." He laughed bitterly. "I asked because I thought we might be able to help, give his uncle a start over here. What a joke! Did you see his suit? The car? That man is no ordinary immigrant. He's rich already!"

"But that doesn't mean he's a criminal. Just because he's Italian and has money...."

"What about his two henchmen? They were bodyguards, Anna. I'm sure of it." Clancy downed his whisky. "Anyway, with luck, we'll never see Vittorio Vetti again. He won't want to know us any more than we want to know him." He sighed, and put his arm round Anna. "I know you were fond of Paolo, and I liked him too. After all, the lad can't help his family. But for Jennie's sake, let it go, darlin'."

Anna's face was filled with dismay. "I can't believe it. You have no proof of what you say, and I think you must be wrong." She swallowed. "Nevertheless, just in case, I shall be careful." She stared at her husband. "Oh, Clancy, if it's true, what will happen?"

Clancy shrugged. "I don't know." He smiled ruefully. "There is one thing, though. I wish I hadn't told him to take his hat off."

Best Friends

1915

As soon as James saw Paolo in the park, he began to run. It had been almost a month since he had seen his favourite uncle, and he knew there would be a surprise. His certainty was based on the celebration of his ninth birthday the week before. Paolo never forgot.

James had enjoyed his birthday. Eight of his classmates were invited to his party, which had been great fun, but he had missed Paolo, even though there was consolation in the shape of a new bicycle from his parents.

Paolo was leaning on a parapet, looking at the water. James shouted, and immediately Paolo's handsome face broke into a big smile. "Hello, little brother! How you doing?"

As James dashed towards him, Paolo held out his arms in the way he always did, and James, too late to stop his headlong rush, suffered the indignity of being lifted up bodily and swung around, before being returned gently to the ground.

"Stop it, Paolo," he said, pushing his friend away with an impatient gesture. "People are looking."

"Oh." Paolo pulled a face, pretending to be hurt. "Too grown up for a swing now, are you? Too much the young gentleman for old Uncle Paolo?"

James flushed. "That's for babies," he muttered.

Paolo relented. "Come on. Let's go to the refreshment tent. I expect you're hungry." Amusement played around his lips as he said, "That hasn't changed, has it?"

"No," said James, and he followed Paolo to the crowded tent, where they queued for sandwiches and cake to take away in paper bags for a picnic.

"Can I have coffee?" James asked.

"No. Milk." Paolo said, handing James the paper bags to hold.

"But I am allowed coffee now."

Paolo looked at him closely. "Are you? Are you sure?"

"Well...sometimes I'm allowed. If Mama is in a good mood."

Paolo turned back to the waitress. "One coffee and one milk, please."

"Oh, Paolo!"

"Come on, and stop complaining."

They made their way to the edge of the lake. There were several families enjoying picnics, but as they neared a space near the trees, a man stepped forward and spread a rug. Paolo nodded to him and the man returned the nod and walked away.

"Is that your chauffeur?" James asked.

"Er...yes."

They sat down on the rug and opened the paper bags. It was a warm day, and as he munched his sandwich, James felt his spirits rise. It was good to be with Paolo again, even though there was no birthday present after all. Paolo spoke first.

"I'm sorry about swinging you. I can see you are a bit old for it now you are nine. I won't do it any more."

James was magnanimous. "That's alright," he said loftily. "I know I used to like it when I was little."

"Where are you supposed to be?" Paolo asked.

"Having afternoon tea at Jackson's with Cummings."

"Who is Cummings?"

"A boy in my class. His aunt is taking him out to tea this afternoon, so I got him to tell Matron I was invited too."

"How did you manage that?" Paolo said with interest.

"Gave him my treacle pudding."

Paolo suppressed a smile at the matter of fact tone of the nine-year-old. He handed James another sandwich and said seriously, "Well, old chap, I'm glad you're growing up so fast. I feel I can ask your advice."

James looked startled. "What about?"

"It's...it's a matter of the heart," Paolo said solemnly. Seeing the puzzlement on James's face, he added confidentially, "A love affair, James."

"A what?" James flushed. "Don't be soppy!" He took a bite of his sandwich and said, with his mouth full, "You're always soppy, you are. Girls and all that stuff."

"I'm not soppy this time, James. This is serious. I'm going to get married."

"Married? You? What for?"

Paolo hesitated and then replied, "Because it's time. When you get older, it's quite natural to get married. Everybody does it. Your mother and father for instance. If they hadn't got married, they wouldn't have had you, and then where should we be?"

James considered. "I suppose so. Does that mean you'll have children as well? Be a father yourself?"

"I expect so, in time."

"I don't see why you need to," James said truculently. He held up a chocolate eclair in case Paolo wanted it. Paolo shook his head with a smile and James bit into the eclair with relish. He wagged the remains of it at Paolo. "You've got me. What do you want other children for?"

Paolo looked stunned. "But you're not a child. You're like my brother, a younger brother."

James liked that. It was true, Paolo always called him "little brother".

"I suppose," James conceded. "I wanted a brother but I didn't have one."

"Nor me," said Paolo gently. "I had four sisters."

"Where are they?" James asked. This was news. Paolo had never mentioned sisters.

"In Italy. They are all married now. I was the youngest," Paolo told him. "They were not allowed to come to America."

"Oh. Well...I suppose it will be alright for you to get married. You might as well start looking, but don't get anyone too soppy."

Paolo laughed out loud. "She's not soppy at all, James."

"You've found someone already?" A knowing look crossed the boy's face and he crowed, "I know who it is. I know who it is. Jennie McCormack, I bet!"

"Good guess." Paolo looked at him keenly. "How did you know?"

"I heard Father ask Mama if Jennie was still keen on you."

"Did you? When was that?"

"A few weeks ago. On Mama's birthday, when the red roses arrived, the ones you always send her."

Paolo smiled. "Did she like them?"

"Yes, I think so. Father said...." James stopped himself and flushed slightly.

"What did he say?" Paolo asked. "It's alright, James. I know he doesn't like me."

James hesitated and then blurted out in a rush, "When he saw the roses, he said, 'Wonder Boy is still around, is he?' and Mama said yes and it was kind you still sent her roses every birthday, and Father was grumpy and said was Jennie still keen on you."

"Oh. What did your mama say to that?"

"I don't know. She saw me and sent me out to see Lottie."

James looked at Paolo anxiously. "Don't worry, Paolo," he consoled. "They are very good parents really. Father is very kind."

"But of course he is," Paolo laughed. "James, your parents are very good people, and I admire them both."

"I know. You said before. But they wouldn't let me invite you to my party, well, Father wouldn't, and Mama does what he says."

Paolo sighed. "I have explained many times that your parents and my family have different business interests. It's only business, that's all."

"I know. I think it's soppy, business."

"Yes, it is. Anyway, you will all be invited to the wedding," Paolo said with a flourish.

"Father too?"

"Of course. I think he will come. He is Jennie's employer, after all."

"I think weddings are soppy. All that dressing up," said James.

"There will be lots of good food," Paolo pointed out.

"Will there? Oh, look, here's your chauffeur again."

Paolo got to his feet and took a large parcel from the sweating man. "I wonder what we have here?"

James flushed with pleasure. "For me?"

Paolo laughed. "You knew I wouldn't forget. Open it."

James struggled with the box, and at length, with some difficulty and a little help, he extracted a large sailing boat.

"Oh, Paolo, it's wonderful! Can we sail it now?"

"Of course, that is why we met here." He looked at his watch. "We have an hour before I take you back to school. We must make sure you arrive at the same time as Cummings."

James was already at the water's edge. "Wait a moment," Paolo said, "I have to show you how to trim the sails. There's not much wind today." He showed the boy how to raise and lower the sails, and then watched as James put the boat carefully in the water. "Don't loose hold of the string," Paolo instructed.

He watched James fiddling with the boat, and wondered, not for the first time, how Anna's tawny-haired beauty and Clancy's dark, Irish good looks had combined to produce a child with such fine, fair hair and pale, aristocratic demeanour. In spite of his appearance, however, the boy already showed a fiercely independent will, which Paolo recognised and appreciated. He would never do anything to harm his self adopted "little brother".

He walked over and knelt down beside the boy. "Don't forget our secret, James," he said. "When you show the boat to your father, you must tell him the present was delivered to school, like last year."

"Yes, I know," said James, and he pushed the lovely toy out onto the lake.

The arrangements for Paolo and Jennie's wedding caused the first serious quarrel that Anna

and Clancy had ever had. When Jennie had shyly
asked if Clancy would give her away, he accepted
with alacrity, delighted and honoured by the request. As Jennie was an orphan, Anna and Clancy
had been unanimous in their desire to take over
the parental role and to provide the reception for
the couple. As they now had twenty profitable restaurants as well as the hugely expanded catering
business and a chain of fifty-eight delicatessens,
they could easily afford it.

Apart from their role as Jennie's employers,
Anna and Clancy had watched her develop from a
timid young girl to an accomplished woman under their tutelage, and both of them were genuinely fond of her. As Clancy put it, they "wanted to
give her a really good send-off," but it was here
that the difficulties began. Holding the reception
at their home would mean inviting Vittorio Vetti
and his guests, and it was by now common knowledge that the family were part of what was locally
known as "the mob". Anna had always tried to distance herself from this knowledge, and as she saw
Paolo rarely, only when he picked up Jennie from
her restaurant and Anna happened to be there,
this was not difficult.

Clancy put the problem in a nutshell. "We can't
possibly invite the Vetti clan here," he said. "If we
do, we can't invite anyone else. They won't come."

It was true. Clancy and Anna now had a wide
circle of friends and neighbours who would not be
impressed to find the notorious Vittorio Vetti at
any function to which they were invited, bride-
groom's uncle or not.

"We needn't invite any of our friends," Anna
said. "After all, Jennie hardly knows them. We'll
invite Jennie's personal friends from the business,
that's all, and Paolo's guests."

"All two hundred of them?" Clancy said. "That was the last count according to Jennie. Anyway, that's not the point. I don't want that...that gangster in my house."

"I'm sure he's not as bad as you make out," Anna said dismissively. "You talk as if he's like that Al Capone."

"He's exactly like Al Capone," Clancy snapped. "He's into every racket in this city."

"You can't know that, you can't possibly know that!" Anna cried. "If you will listen to every rumour you hear...."

Clancy lost his temper. It was such a rare occurrence that, when he banged his fist down on the table, Anna jumped, realising she had gone too far.

Clancy controlled himself with an effort. He came across to his wife and pointed to the armchair. "Sit down there!" he commanded, his voice shaking. "Sit down and, for once in your life, listen to me!"

Anna sat down. Clancy, still upset, sat opposite.

"There are one or two things you have to understand, Anna, and I want no arguments about them, because I am in a position to know the facts, so I am, and you are not. You are not!" he repeated loudly, as Anna made to speak. "First, Vetti is a gangster, with a finger in everything. Not just a bit of gambling and a few numbers rackets, but extortion, blackmail, prostitution and every other dirty game you can think of. You say you are fond of Paolo, and I have always liked him, but that doesn't alter the fact that he works for his uncle, doing God knows what. I wish Jennie wasn't marrying into that family, but she is, and we can't do much about it."

Anna sat silent, and Clancy continued firmly, "But there is one thing I can control, and that is who I invite to my home, and that…mobster…will find no welcome here. And that's final!"

Anna remained silent for a few moments and then said acidly, "Have you finished?"

"Yes. And I hope you have understood."

"I have. The plain fact remains that we have a wedding reception to plan. If the numbers are as you say, we couldn't hold it here anyway. We don't have the room."

"Right, that's agreed then," Clancy said. "It will have to be a hotel."

"But that's so impersonal."

"Then impersonal is what it will have to be!" Clancy retorted, and for the moment, that was that.

In the event, it was Vittorio Vetti himself, the subject of their quarrel, who provided the answer to their dilemma. After two days, when relations between them were still strained, Clancy arrived home to find Anna's mood considerably improved. She handed him a whisky and said, "We have to talk about this wedding business. I think we may have a solution."

Clancy smiled to himself. At least she hadn't said, "I have the solution." He sipped his drink and said, "I'm listening."

"This afternoon I had a telephone call. From Vittorio Vetti."

Clancy bridled. "What did he want?" he asked coldly.

"To see if he could help. I think it had occurred to him we might have a problem."

"Oh?"

"Yes. He didn't say so, not in so many words. He said how much Paolo and Jennie appreciated our offer of the reception. Then he asked if we realised the size of the guest list, it has reached two hundred and forty from his side already."

"Good grief!" Clancy said. "I think he intends to invite everyone who pays him protection money! What did you say?"

"I told him we didn't have enough room here and were thinking of a hotel. I mentioned the Plaza or the Ritz Carlton. Then he suggested we hold it at his home, in the gardens. He thought it might be enjoyable for the guests as the weather should be good in May."

"That means we have to go to his place."

"I know, but at least it will be only ourselves and Jennie's friends from the business, and they won't mind. I thought that for such a wicked and vicious gangster it was rather a sensitive suggestion," Anna added pointedly. Getting no response, she added, "According to Jennie, Vetti has a very large country house, and the setting is beautiful. As it is quite a way from the city, it will at least be private."

"Yes, I'm sure. Huge iron gates and armed bodyguards! What did you say?"

"That I would talk to you about it and let him know."

Anna sat down. Her shoulders slumped dejectedly and Clancy saw a small tear run down her cheek. He stared at her with concern. "What is it, darlin'? Surely you're not upset because we had a little tiff?"

"Oh, Clancy, please say you agree. It is the best solution we can get. And even you have to compromise sometimes." Anna wiped her eyes, and continued. "He said we can have the ceremony on the south lawn, and we could provide the food ourselves, so we could do Jennie proud."

"Alright," Clancy said.

"And none of our friends need...." She stopped. "Did you say yes?"

"Yes. Now dry your eyes."

"Oh, Clancy! And you'll come?"

"I have to, don't I? I'm giving the bride away, so I am." He put his arms around her. "I'm not happy about it, but it's better than having the Vetti mob here or being seen with them in public. I wasn't simply making difficulties, Anna. We are in business. We have to be careful, so we do."

"I know. You're right." She began to cry again.

"What now? What is it, darlin'?"

"Nothing," she sniffed, then, "Oh, Clancy, here we are arguing about a wedding, and back home, all those dear lads are dying in France!"

He hugged her close. "Billy will be alright, Anna, I'm sure of it. And we don't even know if he's in France."

She clung to him, weeping openly now. "It said in the paper today that the Germans are using poison gas."

"I know. I saw it." Clancy shared her distress.

"I know he's eighteen, but somehow I can't think of him as a soldier. I always think of him as I remember him, scampering along the ginnel. He was such a little imp." Anna smiled beneath her tears, and then said, "Do you think America will join the war?"

"I doubt it. Not yet, at any rate," Clancy said seriously. "President Wilson wants to keep us neutral." He hugged her again. "Try not to worry about Billy, darlin'. According to Will, the lad has a good head on him. He'll be alright."

The day of Jennie's wedding dawned clear and bright, and even Clancy was impressed by the arrangements. Vetti's large, Palladian style mansion was filled with flowers, and the elegant satin-lined marquee on the south lawn was carpeted and furnished lavishly and had a raised dais for the ceremony.

Paolo was nervous and uncomfortable, but even more handsome than usual. Jennie looked almost ephemeral. The cream-coloured lace dress Anna had helped her choose showed her willowy figure to perfection, and she seemed completely relaxed, smiling around her at the assembled guests as Clancy escorted her down the centre aisle. Anna could not help the thrill of pleasure as she watched her husband. He looked so distinguished, she thought, the handsome good looks of his youth had developed into a maturity which suited him. The slight greying at his temples had added an air of refinement and distinction, Anna decided, and after Clancy gave Jennie's hand to Paolo and resumed his seat next to her, she caught his hand and squeezed it, and she received a reassuring smile from the still magnetic Irish eyes.

In contrast, Vittorio Vetti had not matured so well, Anna thought, studying the man intently. He was older than Clancy, of course, but even allowing for that, it was obvious that his maturity had a fleshy, rather vulgar coarseness. His hair was becoming thin on top, and his large frame had become corpulent under the expensive, grey vicuna suit. His heavy-lidded eyes were somnolent and lazy, but Anna noticed that occasionally his gaze travelled around the scene, wary and snake-like, as if watching for the moment to strike. Anna shuddered, wondering if Clancy's opinion of the man came near to the reality.

An hour later, as the guests strolled in the grounds, enjoying the free flowing champagne and the warm sunshine, Anna was able to put her doubts behind her once more. Vittorio Vetti approached her with hand outstretched, a welcoming smile transfiguring his features.

"My dear Mrs. Sullivan," he exclaimed, and Anna recalled immediately the low, musical voice and heavy Italian accent she had last heard in her own drawing room on the evening Vetti had arrived in New York. "I have been looking for you," he continued. "What a great success! I have received so many compliments. The buffet is superb!"

Anna smiled as she shook Vittorio's hand. "Thank you, Mr. Vetti. I admit I am pleased, but it was not difficult. I have twenty excellent chefs to call upon, and they all wished to impress."

He laughed aloud. "They have done so. But please, Mrs. Sullivan, call me Vittorio. We are not quite family...but almost." He was still holding her hand. Now he tucked it into his arm with a proprietorial gesture and said confidentially, "May I show you my rose garden? It is looking wonderful at the moment, although it is early in the season. I should appreciate the opportunity of a quiet chat, and it seems it must be with you, as I think your husband is carefully avoiding me."

Anna felt a momentary alarm, and stammered, "I...I think Clancy has taken James to find Paolo," but her companion appeared to be quite at ease. He steered her through a small arbour and along a walk covered with climbing roses, pointing out differing varieties as they went. He seemed knowledgeable about his subject, discussing flower form at length, and Anna found it hard to imagine this man could combine such an interest with the horrors Clancy had described.

"Yes," Vittorio concluded, as they entered the formal rose garden, "fragrance is the most important thing in my view. A rose is not a rose without fragrance." He smiled softly. "As a woman is not a woman without perfume," he added. Anna smiled, wondering what was coming next, but Vittorio had serious matters on his mind. He said quietly, "I expect you and your husband were very much against this marriage?"

"We...er...it is really no business of ours."

"Not legally, no. But you are Jennie's closest friends. Actually, I have never understood that. Surely Jennie is only one of your cooks?"

"Much more than that," Anna explained. "Jennie joined us when she left the orphanage. At that time, we only had the catering business. She was so intelligent and adaptable that she soon became my right hand and used to help me run the business, including finding new menus. She was with us all the time we were building up the delicatessen chain, and when Clancy was at college, I don't know what I would have done without her."

"Yes, Paolo told me about that," Vittorio said speculatively. "Your husband seems to be quite a man, Mrs. Sullivan. It is a pity he dislikes me so much."

Anna coloured. "Vittorio, I assure you...."

"Don't worry about it," Vittorio said lightly. "I understand his feelings completely. Unfortunately, he has believed some very silly stories about my business interests."

They stopped, and Vittorio reached up and picked a perfect, deep pink bloom from the hedge and handed it to Anna. "This is the best perfume of all, Mrs. Sullivan. It is called Madame Isaac Periere, one of the old Bourbons." He sighed. "You know, Mrs. Sullivan, there are those who are simply jealous of my success. They do not think it acceptable that a poor Italian immigrant should do quite so well, and so they insist he must make his money illegally."

Anna was unsure how to reply. She hesitated and then plunged in. "I do not know what your business interests are, Vittorio. What do you do exactly?"

Vittorio Vetti's mouth dropped open. Then he let out a great shout of laughter. "Yes...oh, yes! Mrs. Sullivan, I can see why Paolo finds you so refreshing!" He steered her to a garden seat and then explained, "Most people would not dream of asking me such a question! But since you have, I shall tell you," he said, still laughing. "My business interests are very varied. I have laundries, a whole chain of them, and a very large transport fleet." His voice became smug and self congratulatory; he was almost preening himself. "I was one of the first to capitalise on motorised transport, Mrs. Sullivan, while others were still saying we should stick to the horse and cart!"

He waved his hand dismissively, and then said, "We have changed the subject, have we not? I asked about your opposition to this wedding. I do not blame you. I was also very much against it."

"Were you?" Anna said, genuinely surprised.

"Yes indeed, my nephew and I have had many quarrels about it."

"I can't understand why you should object." Anna was slightly nettled. "Jennie is...."

"Jennie is a very lovely girl, intelligent and charming, and she loves my nephew dearly. I have no doubt of that."

"Then why?" Surely not because she is an orphan?"

"No, not really. It is not what she is; it is more what she is not, if you see what I mean."

"I don't," Anna responded a little tartly.

Vittorio sighed. "I suppose I am old fashioned, at least that is what Paolo says. I am a traditionalist and always imagined that Paolo would marry a nice Italian girl from home."

"Surely it is up to Paolo who he chooses to marry?"

"Yes, of course, as has proved to be the case, and I will give him all the help and support I can, but between us, Mrs. Sullivan, I admit to being disappointed. It's nothing to do with Jennie; I like her, truly I do. But she is not Italian and so will not understand Paolo's background, and she's not Catholic either. Hence that hotchpotch of a ceremony you saw today."

"I thought it was very beautiful," Anna said.

Vittorio shrugged. "I suppose it was alright, for New York. But his sister's wedding two years ago, and the others, all in Rome of course, they were superb. Have you ever been to a full Catholic wedding, Mrs. Sullivan?"

"No," Anna admitted, for some reason thinking of Notre Dame in Paris. Clancy had to be wrong about this man, she thought. Could a mobster care so much about a wedding ceremony?

As if he read her thoughts, Vittorio said, "Of course, I can't pretend I am an especially religious man, but it is the tradition in our family, Mrs. Sullivan. These rituals, they are important."

"Yes, I think I understand. However, I don't think you will be disappointed in Jennie."

"I'm sure I won't," Vittorio said. He seemed to pull himself together and added, "Paolo is like a son to me. I am a little overprotective, perhaps."

"You have no children of your own?"

"No. My wife died in childbirth, our first, and the child too."

"I am so sorry," Anna responded gently.

Vittorio smiled at her. "There is no need to be. It was all a very long time ago. Paolo's mother died when he was only a few months old, and when his father...died...a few years later, I inherited a ready-made family."

"You took on a big responsibility," Anna observed.

"Yes, but I have enjoyed it, and as I said, family is important." He hesitated, adding, "There is one thing you may be able to help me with, Mrs. Sullivan. I want Paolo and Jennie to live here with me, but Paolo will not hear of it."

"But they have bought the little bungalow out towards...."

"I know!" Vittorio interrupted fiercely. "To think of Paolo living in a dump like that!"

"It's hardly a dump. It's a very nice little bungalow," Anna said.

"You have seen it?"

"Of course," she replied. "I helped Jennie choose some of the furnishings."

Vittorio threw his hands in the air in frustration. "I give up. I thought you would be on my side, and it seems you are helping them in this nonsense."

"There aren't any sides, surely?" Anna said gently. "We are both on the same side, Paolo and Jennie's side?"

Vittorio sighed. His shoulders slumped and he said glumly, "Of course, you're right, and of course, I'm on their side. It's just that I can offer them more here. It's safer for them."

"Safer?" Anna was mystified.

"More secure," he corrected himself. "I would like Jennie to be protected from all the noise and bustle of the city, and if they have children, there is space here."

"It's a very nice area they have chosen," Anna reassured him. "And I have a complaint of my own. I understand that it is due to your influence that I have lost Jennie from the business."

Vittorio smiled. "It was the only concession they made to me, Jennie giving up work," he said. "The only point I won!"

"It wasn't a battle, surely?" Anna said. From the look on his face, she saw that it had been exactly that.

"On that point, I would never give way," Vittorio said. "Married ladies do not work when their husbands can support them. It's not right. It would be a disgrace."

"What about me?" Anna asked. "Am I a disgrace?"

"Certainly not. But you are a New Yorker, not Italian."

"No, I'm not. I'm an immigrant from England. And, Vittorio, remember this. Jennie is not Italian either."

He smiled ruefully. "I'll do my best. Shall we go back?"

Anna took his arm, and a few moments later, as they left the rose garden, they saw that a large number of guests had gathered on the terrace. There seemed to be some sort of commotion, with everyone talking at once. Clancy extricated himself from the throng and came down the terrace steps towards them.

"There ye are, darlin'. There's terrible news. The *Lusitania* has been sunk by a German submarine. She was off the coast of Ireland, so she was. Twelve hundred souls drowned, many of them were women and children."

"Oh, how dreadful!" Anna was aghast.

Vittorio was quick to agree. "And on our happy

day, too," he said sadly. "It is most distressing. I expect like me, you are glad to be out of Europe, Mr. Sullivan, so this dreadful war does not affect us so directly."

"I'm not so sure of that," Clancy said grimly. "A hundred and twenty eight of the passengers were American citizens. This may be what was needed to make President Wilson decide to take America into the war."

President Wilson stopped short of declaring war, but in the aftermath of the public outcry, he issued a strong warning to Germany, as well as initiating what was called a "preparedness campaign" at home.

For Anna and Clancy, however, the war in Europe came suddenly near. Only three weeks after the wedding, Anna arrived home to find Lottie looking anxious.

"What is it, Lottie?" The two women had grown so close that Anna noticed immediately if Lottie was troubled.

"Oh, it's nothing, I'm sure. You know me, always looking for trouble before it's here." Lottie fussed, as she carried a tray of tea into the drawing room.

"Goodness, what service! You had tea ready, I can see...." It was then that Anna noticed the letter on the tea tray, and picked it up with an expression of delight. "Oh, look! It's from Will." Her expression changed suddenly, and she stared at Lottie with apprehension.

"Oh, Lottie, I had a letter from Will last week."

"I know, my dear." Lottie said. "I've been able to think of nothing else since it came. I know he only writes about once a month."

The two women stared at each other, the envelope trembling slightly in Anna's hand.

"Best open it," Lottie said. "It's probably nothing much."

Anna sat down and slowly opened the letter. She knew the contents before she read it, because unlike Will's normal letters, it was only a page, written hastily in the familiar copperplate handwriting. Anna let the page flutter to the floor, and Lottie picked it up and read it quickly.

Lottie bent and kissed Anna, feeling her heart clench as if in a vice. The face Anna turned towards her was white and stunned, full of pathetic pleading. "Not our Billy. Oh, no, dear Lord...not our Billy."

"I'll telephone Mr. Sullivan," Lottie said.

Half an hour later, rocked in Clancy's arms, Anna cried, "It can't be true, it can't. We didn't even know he was in Gallipoli."

"I know, darlin', but in wartime, they can't tell you where the soldiers are going."

"I read about it, Clancy! I read about the landings at Sedd-el-Bahr and the terrible loss of life there...and I didn't know...I didn't know Billy was one of them." Anna's voice was an anguished wail.

"I know. It takes a long time for news to get through, and then Will had to let us know."

"Poor Will and Mary! Oh, Clancy, I must go home for the funeral."

Clancy rocked her gently. "Hush, darlin', hush."

"I must book a passage."

"No, darlin'. Quiet now. You don't have to go anywhere."

"But I must."

"No, darlin'." Clancy looked into her brimming eyes with compassion. "I'm not allowing you anywhere near the Atlantic with those German subs about, and anyway," Clancy hated himself but finished the sentence quietly, "there isn't going to be any funeral, darlin', not for Billy, not for a lot of our boys."

She stared at him a moment, not comprehending, and then he watched her crumple, become smaller somehow, and she said wonderingly, "Vittorio...Vittorio Vetti, he said rituals are important. He was right." A thought struck her and she raised a tear stained face to him. "Oh, Clancy! We were at the wedding, enjoying that lovely day...and our Billy was already dead!"

"You mustn't think of it like that, darlin'. It's the war, that's all. It turns everything upside down."

His words did not help. Anna's brain held on to the image of a small, cheeky boy, running down the ginnel at Sandley Heath to visit the corner shop for a pennyworth of Hudson's soap and a ha'penny blue. "And a bag o' boilers from your rich auntie," she whispered before her grief broke, and she sobbed her misery into Clancy's shoulder. Clancy did all he could, but she would not be comforted.

The traffic was heavy at the end of the working day and Clancy sat in the back of the car, fuming at the delay. After a hectic afternoon, he had been about to leave for home when the telephone call from a downtown delicatessen had sent him in the opposite direction to deal with what was described as an emergency. What kind of emergency was not clear. The manager had seemed almost incoherent, insisting only that Mr. Sullivan must come right away. It was amazing how problems seemed to arise when Joe Kowalski was on holiday. Clancy recalled that the manager of the deli, a man called Hopkins, had been with the company for several years. Surely he should have been able to cope until Joe came back from visiting his sister? It was particularly annoying to be delayed tonight, because for the first time since Billy's death, Anna had agreed to accompany him out to dinner.

Reaching the delicatessen at last, Clancy's temper was not improved by seeing the shutters down and the shop closed. Telling his chauffeur to park around the corner, he alighted and angrily rattled the door.

"That'll do you no good," said a poor-looking woman with a scarf around her head, who was standing in the doorway. "I've been knockin' five minutes and 'e won't open, although 'e's in there. I seen 'im lookin' out."

Clancy rattled the door again, and as he was doing so, it was opened a few inches and Mr. Hopkins peered out. "Oh, it's you, Mr. Sullivan. Thank goodness!" He opened the door and Clancy entered, only to see Hopkins quickly shut the door behind him.

"Hopkins! Why are we closed? There's a woman out there wants to buy something."

"Sorry, Mr. Sullivan, I had no choice."

It was only then that Clancy noticed the extent of Hopkins discomfiture. His face was ashen, and he was wringing his hands together as if terrified.

Clancy moved forward into the darkened shop. "What is it Hopkins, what's wrong?"

He was answered by a gruff and rather uncouth Brooklyn accent. The voice said, "Nothing wrong. Nothing at all, Mr. Sullivan," and Clancy was just able to discern a heavy figure moving at the back of the premises.

"Who is that?" As he said it, Clancy saw the

gun. It was pointed straight at him.

"It's the mob, Mr. Sullivan. They want money." Hopkins voice came from beside him, whining, pleading. "I said I couldn't give them any, and Joe was on holiday. They said they wanted the boss."

Clancy stared in amazement. He had thought the business was immune to such pressures because of its size. "It's alright, Hopkins," he said.

"I didn't know what to do," Hopkins whined. "They had a gun on me."

"You should have given them the money," Clancy said, "and then telephoned me."

The gunman came out of the shadows and Clancy saw he was a thickset man, heavy and dark, with stubble on his chin. He was followed closely by his accomplice, a wiry, ferret-faced man who was holding an axe. The first man pushed his trilby hat to the back of his head with the gun and smiled broadly, showing his bad teeth.

"That's what I like to hear," he said. "A boss man with sense. You can call me Peters. Mr. Peters."

"Well, Mr. Peters, I don't intend to pay protection money. I don't like my staff to be threatened, that's all. As soon as my manager had got rid of you, I should have telephoned the police." Clancy managed to sound firm, convincing.

Peters laughed out loud. "Would you now? And what do you think they would have done?"

"Put you in jail for threatening decent citizens," Clancy said. He had recovered from the shock and was becoming angry. "Just go, please. Get off my premises or I'll ring them now, so I will."

The gunman was surprisingly quick, and the revolver was under Clancy's chin in an instant. He pushed Clancy's head back. "Shut that mouth or I'll blow your head off."

Clancy froze, but managed to mutter, "Then you'll never get any money." His heart pounded in his chest as he watched the gunman's face. After a moment, the gun was lowered and Peters stepped back.

Clancy swallowed. "Can we let Hopkins go? You don't need him, surely. He won't say anything."

Peters considered. "I'm a reasonable man. I don't need him when I have the boss man." He turned to Hopkins. "You say a word to anyone," he said, "and you'll be killed. Certain."

Hopkins flinched, and looked desperately at Clancy, who said as calmly as he could, "Don't worry, Hopkins. No one is going to be killed. Go home now and don't speak to anyone about this, you understand? I'll come and see you tomorrow."

"That's right," Peters said in a soothing tone. "Nobody gets killed because everybody plays ball and does what he's told." He turned to Hopkins again. "You probably think being killed means being shot." He put the revolver to Hopkins' head. "You're wrong. There are better ways," he threatened softly, almost whispering, as the ferret-faced man came forward and raised the axe to within inches of the manager's terrified eyes.

"Stop this!" Clancy commanded. "He won't say anything."

Peters nodded and ferret face opened the shop door. Hopkins gave a quick glance in Clancy's direction and hurried out.

"That was all most unnecessary," Clancy said.

Peters faced him. "Are you going to play ball?"

"No," Clancy said.

Peters smiled. "I know your problem, Mr. Sullivan. Didn't want to talk in front of your manager did you? You're going to tell me you already pay protection to Vetti's mob." He made an expansive gesture, "I have good news for you, Mr. Sullivan. You need never pay another dollar to Vetti. He's on his way out." He grinned evilly. "You pay me instead."

"I pay no one," Clancy said. "I've never paid anything to Vetti and I'm not paying anything to you."

Peters grinned. "You think after we've gone you can ring Vetti and he'll send his boys to deal with us. It's reasonable you should think that way. That's what you've been paying for after all, protection."

"I've told you I don't pay anyone!"

"But you're wrong," Peters continued, as if Clancy had not spoken. "I've told you Vetti is finished. We are taking over this area."

Clancy remained silent.

"Fifty dollars a week," the gunman said. "That's what I need from each of your delicatessens. We shall collect every Friday evening about this time. We have a list of your branches, and a list of your restaurants too."

"You'll get nothing from me," Clancy growled.

"I haven't been given a figure for the restaurants, but I'll let you know the amount soon. If you don't want your staff involved, we are prepared to accept one weekly payment from you personally, covering all the outlets. Cash, of course."

"I've told you, you're wasting your time."

The gun was under Clancy's chin again. "Fifty dollars. Now! From the till!" He pushed the gun so that Clancy was forced back until he was behind the counter. "Open the till!"

"No."

The revolver butt crashed into Clancy's face and he staggered back, his hands clutching air, blood coming from his nose. Peters attacked again, but this time Clancy was ready for him and landed a huge, round armed blow on his jaw, which knocked Peters sideways and sent the gun spinning across the floor. As ferret face sprang at him with the axe, Clancy caught his arm and twisted it up behind his back. "Drop it!" he commanded, and the axe clattered to the floor. Then Clancy's head seemed to explode, and he dropped like a stone.

When the mists began to clear, Clancy thought at first he was alone. He was lying on the floor of the shop, and as he tried to marshal his thoughts, he became aware of voices in the office. His head was throbbing, and as he tried to rise, Peters appeared.

"He's awake."

Clancy stared at Peters, gratified to see he had a split lip. Ferret face came out of the office and was joined by two other men, both holding guns.

"That's right, Mr. Sullivan, they were in the office," Peters said. "Did you really think we would have no assistance?" He bent down and took hold of Clancy's hair, forcing his head back to face him so that Clancy could smell his rotten breath. "You're dealing with organised people here, not amateurs!" Peters hissed. "You had your chance and you didn't take it. We don't give more than one!"

He dragged Clancy to his feet by his hair. "Watch!" he ordered. Ferret face went to the till and opened it. He counted out fifty dollars and put it into his pocket.

"You see? That's all we needed, but you wouldn't play, would you? You had to be a hero."

Ferret face reached inside Clancy's jacket and found his wallet. He took all the banknotes from it and counted them. "A hundred and twelve dollars," he announced importantly.

Peters snatched the money. "Mine!" he said.

"For this...." He pointed to his split lip. "It's not enough, Mr. Sullivan, not anywhere near enough. You are going to be taught a lesson."

Clancy tried to fight back, but it was impossible. The gun was held at his head by ferret face as the others administered a systematic beating. They enjoyed their work, and long after Clancy had lost consciousness, they continued kicking viciously at his prostrate body, until suddenly there was a rattling at the door, and a voice shouted, "Mr. Sullivan, are you there?"

"Out back," said Peters.

The mobsters darted through the office, out of the back door, and over the wall. At the same time that they reached their waiting car, Clancy's chauffeur was breaking into the delicatessen.

"Does Clancy know you are here?" Paolo asked.

Anna's lips were tight. "No," she said, "he forbade me to get in touch with you."

"But you came anyway," Paolo smiled his beautiful smile. "I'm glad you did, Anna."

"Then you can help? You will tell me where to find them? Where to pay the money?"

"No. You must go home and forget all about it. Just leave it with me. I will take care of everything. You do not have to pay any money."

"But I must! You haven't seen what they did to Clancy. Three broken ribs, and not an inch of his body without a bruise. Paolo...please...he almost lost his eye!"

"Anna, listen carefully. You do not know how to deal with these people. I do...or at least my Uncle Vittorio does."

"Your Uncle Vittorio is as bad as they are!" Anna cried. "They thought Clancy wouldn't pay them because he was already paying Vittorio! Your gangland wars are no concern of mine, Paolo; I just want my husband safe."

"Of course you do, and I will see to it that he is," Paolo said soothingly, his dark liquid eyes regarding her with compassion. "I'm so sorry, Anna, that this has happened, but you mustn't blame me for it, or my uncle Vittorio. It has nothing to do with us."

"Gangsters are gangsters," Anna said sullenly. "Your uncle told me that he had laundries and...and a big transport company."

"He has," Paolo said simply. "I run them for him. Anna, you must understand that in my family it has always been like this. We have always made our money this way. I am trying to persuade my uncle to give up the old ways and to concentrate on the genuine businesses we have, but he is slow to change."

"And the genuine businesses, Paolo? Were they started with honest money?" Anna asked.

Paolo flushed. "I do not expect someone like you to understand, Anna. It is a family thing. I cannot allow you to speak ill of my uncle. He has been very good to me."

Anna was silent, and after a moment Paolo spoke again. "My father was killed by a rival group in Rome. He was strangled with piano wire and left hanging on the gate at the front of our house. I was only six, but I can still remember the horror of it. My Uncle Vittorio took me and my sisters away to live with him. He cared for us all, and he put me through language school and university. He loved us, Anna, and I love him."

"I understand your loyalty, Paolo," Anna said quietly, horrified at this revelation. "But I can never understand why you choose such a life when you could live honestly. It seems we must agree to differ." She leaned across the desk. "Tell me one thing. Was it on your orders that we were never approached before to pay protection money?"

Paolo looked away. "I've told you to leave everything to me. There is no need to go into this."

"Was it, Paolo? Were we under your protection and didn't even know it?"

Paolo sighed. "I asked my uncle to make sure that your businesses were let alone. He agreed."

"Why? Why did he agree?"

"Because I asked him. Why else?"

"I see. You allowed us to trade in peace for all these years. Thanks, Paolo," Anna said bitterly.

"Don't be silly. It's not like that."

"Isn't it? Isn't it? Do you know what a fool I feel?" Anna cried. "All these years Clancy and I have been congratulating ourselves on how clever we were to build such a good business, and now I find out we were successful only because you allowed us to be."

"It's not like that at all. Your business acumen is obvious. It's never been in question and you know it," Paolo said. "You're just upset about Clancy."

Anna's eyes blazed. "Yes, I am! And you're right about the business. Clancy and I do have business acumen, and we've worked hard to build something to be proud of. I'm damned if any tin pot gangster is going to help himself to a slice of it." She pulled on her gloves. "Paolo, I came here to beg you to tell me where and how to pay the money. I see now that Clancy was right. He said we mustn't pay a penny. I'd sooner close the whole lot down than give in to those bullies." She stood up. "I wish I didn't have to rely on you, Paolo, but I do. I don't know how you can stop them but...but I'm grateful to you, for Clancy's sake." Her lip trembled. "He insisted the shop stay closed until he was better, in case they came back. For the first few days, when he was so ill, I didn't understand what had happened. I only got the full story yesterday when he came home from hospital. I thought...I thought if Peters found the shop closed he might come to the house."

Paolo came around his desk and gripped her shoulders firmly. "What is this? Where is my strong, brave Anna?" He kissed her forehead gently. "Leave everything to me. I promise you will have no more trouble. Best not to let Clancy know you came here."

Anna looked uncomfortable. "Alright." At the door she stopped. "Paolo, the roses you send me every year on my birthday, they are lovely, but...perhaps you should not send any more."

Paolo's smile lit up his handsome face. "Clancy is jealous?"

"No, of course not. But perhaps it is not a good idea."

"I think it is a good idea." He took her hand and raised it to his lips gently. "I shall always send you roses, Anna, every year on your birthday until the day I die. Remember, Anna, we are best friends. Always."

Anna looked into the smiling eyes and could not help but respond. "I remember, Paolo. Best friends."

When Paolo returned to his office after escorting Anna downstairs and out through the laundry, he found Vittorio waiting.

"You heard?" Paolo asked.

"Yes."

"You didn't have to listen," Paolo said shortly.

Vittorio sat down at his nephew's desk. "If you didn't want me to hear, you shouldn't have bundled me out of sight next door when your unexpected visitor arrived." He took a cigar from his top pocket and bit off the end. "You could have allowed me to pay my respects to Mrs. Sullivan and then make my apologies and leave. You create your own problems if you attempt to hide me." He struck a match. "Slow to change, am I?" he asked.

"I said nothing I haven't said to your face plenty of times," Paolo said, reddening.

"I think you did. One or two things," Vittorio said. He puffed slowly at the cigar. "You know, nephew, we have had so many arguments about business lately that I was beginning to believe you had forgotten your roots, forgotten what we were all about. I was wrong." He looked at Paolo, and a slow smile spread over his face, and for once it reached his eyes. "Yes, I'm glad to say I was wrong. You'll be alright."

Paolo leaned across the desk. "Why didn't you tell me you were having problems, that someone was trying to muscle in?"

"You're always telling me you don't want to know about the rackets. Anyway, I wasn't having problems. Nothing I can't handle."

"They're not Capone's men?"

"Heavens no! Capone and I have an agreement. He doesn't want my bit of territory. He's got his hands full already. No, these are a new group in from Chicago, big on muscle and low on brains."

"And you're sure they are not a problem?"

"Of course they're not. It's just unfortunate they picked on the Sullivan's deli as one of their first attempts." Vittorio took a long pull at his cigar. "You want me to deal with them?"

Paolo was looking at the ground. "Yes," he said, stony faced.

Vittorio heaved his bulk out of the chair. "Then it's done, my boy," he said. "The old fashioned ways do come in useful sometimes, don't they?"

Two days later, Clancy was sitting up in bed reading the paper when he saw the photographs. After staring at them for a moment, he dragged himself painfully across the bed and pulled the bell cord.

Anna answered it herself, still in her dressing robe. "What is it dear? More toast?"

"Look at this," Clancy said, pointing to the article. "It's them. Anna, it's the men who beat me up."

Anna took the paper, transfixed by the two faces which stared out at her. A fleshy looking dark man and a thin-faced man with shifty eyes. The caption said "Two Men Found Shot," and Anna read the short paragraph with mounting horror. It said the men had been identified as Joseph Peters and William Sedgewick, who had recently arrived in New York from Chicago. Two eyewitnesses described how the victims were gunned down by someone in a passing car, and the murders were attributed to a rivalry between underworld gangs.

Anna sat down on the bed, trembling violently. "How dreadful!" she said.

"Yes, I suppose it is, but I'll bet they asked for it," Clancy said. "Do you suppose Vittorio Vetti had something to do with it? They said they were taking over from him. It's obviously some kind of gangland war."

"I don't know, and I don't want to hear about it," Anna snapped. She picked up the paper and pulled out the page, tearing it into shreds and flinging it in the waste paper basket. "I don't want to hear about it!" she said again, and burst into tears.

Clancy was all apologies. "I'm sorry, darlin'. I shouldn't have showed it to you. I know you have been upset about all of this. I'm a thoughtless brute sometimes, so I am. Come and give me a kiss, but carefully. Mind the bruises."

Anna kissed him gently and assured him she was all right. She went into her dressing room and sat down before the mirror. Her face stared back at her, guilt ridden and red eyed. Was it her fault? In spite of what they had done to Clancy, and she hated them for that, they were dead because she had asked Paolo for help. Perhaps it was not that, she reasoned, clutching at the thought. Perhaps Vetti had them killed because they were trying to take over his territory. Surely not, it was unthinkable. Not that nice man who had showed her his rose garden and talked about fragrance.

Anna buried her face in her hands. "Oh, Paolo," she whispered. "Oh, Paolo...how can we be best friends? Do I know you at all?"

Prohibition

1920–1922

Lunch at the Plaza was always a treat, and Anna's spirits lifted as she was shown to her table and saw that Jennie had already arrived. They kissed, and Jennie handed Anna a menu. "I've already chosen. I'm having the sole and the soufflé," she said.

Anna glanced at the menu, made up her mind quickly and ordered *bisque d'Etrilles* to start. "I'll have the soufflé as well," she informed the hovering waiter, "And something to drink. What do you suggest?"

"We are recommending our freshly made lemon drink at lunch time, madam," the waiter replied. "It would be admirable with your choice of menu."

Anna sighed. "That will do." As the waiter turned away, she caught Jennie's eye and they both began to giggle. Anna pulled her face into a haughty expression in mock imitation of the waiter. "We are recommending our freshly made lemon drink," she mimicked, and collapsed into giggles again. "Admirable indeed! Whatever they like to call it, it's lemonade. It makes one feel like a child. Oh, Jennie, I'd love a nice glass of Chablis with this lunch, or a dry Vouvray."

"You won't get that at the Plaza," Jennie said, still laughing. "Oh, Anna, it is good to see you. Did you enjoy your birthday?"

"Yes, although it's hard to believe I'm thirty three and James is fourteen." She smiled. "Paolo's roses were beautiful, as usual, and Clancy and I took a trip to Boston. It was a surprise. I think he was trying to mend fences between us."

"Are you still having problems?" Jennie's face was full of concern.

"Not really. No more than usual, anyway. He's always felt strongly about law breaking, especially since he was beaten up a few years ago. It took him months to get over it. He still hasn't forgiven me for continuing to serve liquor in the restaurants. We had a blazing row about it."

"I know. Paolo said he thought you were upset when he met you a few months ago."

"Paolo has been marvellous," Anna said. She leaned across the table and said in a low voice, "He has seen to it that we get our supplies delivered each week with the laundry, and no-one is the wiser. Our regular customers have been coming to us for years, and I don't see why they should be deprived of a drink with their dinner just because the government has decided to go back to its Puritan roots."

Jennie agreed. "I can't imagine how they think Prohibition can work," she said. "Already people are finding so many ways to get round it. I'm surprised Clancy can't see that."

"Oh, he's against Prohibition," Anna explained. "When the Volstead Act was passed he was furious. He thinks it will lead to all kinds of trouble."

The waiter arrived with the lemon drink in a glass jug. He poured it into their wine glasses, and as he drifted away Anna took a sip. "Lemonade," she said. "They have added something." She sipped again. "A little ginger and mint I think, but it's still lemonade. Anyway, Clancy doesn't agree with Prohibition but says everyone should obey the law. He says you can't choose which laws to obey and ignore the others."

"But it's such a stupid law."

"I know, but Clancy says we have to get the law changed if we don't like it. He thinks it will be eventually."

"You sound as if you're coming round to his point of view," Jennie said, smiling.

"No, I'm not, but I understand his argument and I always have. To be honest, I think I would have agreed with him if it wasn't for the restaurants. We sell very little liquor in the catering business apart from beer, and none at all in the delis. But we have always served wines and spirits in the restaurants, and I was not prepared to lose most of our best customers. If they can't buy a drink at Sullivan's, they will simply go elsewhere."

The first course arrived and they ate for a few moments in silence. "The sole is very good," Jennie said, and Anna smiled.

"Did I ever tell you about the first time I lunched here? I was trying to collect menus. It was when James was small. I used to go to the best places, choose a speciality, then send for the chef to congratulate him. They would be so flattered they usually gave me the recipe." She laughed. "The chef here rumbled me. It was most embarrassing."

"What happened?"

"I invited him to dinner on his day off so I could convince him I was a serious cook, on condition that if he was sufficiently impressed, he would give me the recipe."

"And did he?"

"Yes, and several others too." Anna's expression changed, and she added, "Those were good days, really. It seems we were happier when we were struggling to build the business than we are now we are successful."

Something in her tone made Jennie look up sharply. "Come now, Anna, it can't be so bad. Clancy is a lovely man; you know he is. You have just been telling me how you defied his wishes," she lowered her voice, "I mean about the liquor. In most marriages you wouldn't have got away with it. He would have put his foot down and that would be that."

"He tried to," Anna said, "but I would not allow the restaurants to go under. I admit I dug my heels in; after all, I am an equal partner. In the end we agreed Clancy should have his way with the catering business and the delis, and I should do what I wanted with the restaurants. He," she bit her lip, "he hasn't set foot inside a Sullivan's restaurant since that day."

"Oh," Jennie said, hardly knowing what to say. She knew Clancy had always been fully involved in all aspects of the business, and this seemed serious.

"He still does our accounts," Anna continued. "As we don't officially sell drinks any longer, we enter all the income from them under 'puddings and desserts'. Last week over breakfast he told me he was pleased to see we had made three hundred and twenty percent increase on 'puddings and desserts' already this year." They both began to giggle again. "I know it sounds funny, but it's not like Clancy to be sarcastic," Anna said.

Jennie considered. "I don't think he was being sarcastic," she said. "I think he was trying to point out that you should put the income under other headings too, so it isn't queried when your books are audited. Anyway," she said, seeing the look of surprise on Anna's face and wanting to change the subject, "tell me about your birthday treat, your trip to Boston."

"We had a lovely time," Anna said. "It was something Clancy promised me years ago when we first arrived in New York. We were very poor, and one Sunday afternoon, we walked across the Brooklyn Bridge, and Clancy told me that when we were rich, he would take me on one of the steamships. We would have a stateroom, he said, and a wonderful dinner, and wake up in the Falls River and get on the train to Boston to see the sights. You know, Jennie, at the time it seemed like an impossible dream, but we did it all last weekend. I enjoyed every moment, especially Boston, and we didn't speak about business once."

"There you are, then. I told you Clancy is a lovely man. How romantic that he remembered and made your dream come true."

"Yes," Anna said. "Clancy is considerate, and was trying very hard, but somehow it didn't work. We studiously avoided mentioning the business, or Prohibition, and it all became stilted and false. We have always been able to talk things over together, and suddenly we can't."

"He knows you are getting supplies from Paolo?" Jennie asked.

"We haven't discussed it, but I expect he's guessed," Anna said. "And I'm afraid he's never had much time for Vittorio."

"Neither have I, to be honest," Jennie said, as she watched Anna's face cloud with worry. "Give it time, Anna. It will be alright, you'll see," she sympathised.

"Of course it will," Anna said, a little too brightly. "And here's the soufflé. Doesn't it look good?"

She waited until the waiter had served them

and then prompted Jennie. "Now for your news. I want to hear about you and Paolo. Is love's young dream still alive?"

Jennie blushed. "Yes, it is," she whispered. "Oh, Anna, you have no idea. He is so kind and so good to me."

"And so passionate and so handsome and such fun," Anna interrupted, laughing. "I know. I've heard it all before. I never knew two such love birds. Paolo said just the same about you last time I spoke to him." She pulled a prim face. "It's hardly proper, Jennie, to be so much in love after being married for almost five years."

As their laughter ended, Jennie said seriously, "You remember, surely, Anna, what it is like to be in love? You must have felt like this at one time?"

Anna had a momentary vision of the beach at Locquirec. Two children were playing, and she saw Robert's face above her, his eyes filled with love and desire. She found her voice. "Oh, yes, Jennie," she said softly, "I know what you mean."

"Well, then," Jennie said happily, "try and concentrate on that time, how you felt. I know you and Clancy are having a difficult time, but thinking back to the beginning may help."

Anna smiled and murmured that she would try, and then asked quickly, "Is Paolo getting on any better with Vittorio?"

Jennie nodded. "Yes, and we have to thank Prohibition for it. Six months ago, things were almost at breaking point. You remember I told you Paolo had refused to have anything to do with...the...shall we say the more controversial side of Vittorio's business?"

"Yes. I know Paolo runs the legitimate side," Anna said.

"He does help with the gambling too," Jennie

admitted. "He says that doesn't hurt anyone...well not much. Six months ago, Vittorio was really putting the pressure on Paolo. It became very difficult. When Prohibition came in, Vittorio wanted to run bootleg liquor, and Paolo agreed to do it. Vittorio was overjoyed. He felt that Paolo had come back into the fold, so to speak."

"Why did Paolo agree so readily?" Anna asked. "After all, he's running a great risk."

"Risk never worried him," Jennie said. "He just feels that some of his uncle's activities are morally wrong and he doesn't want to be part of them." She lowered her voice. "The rackets, and the girls," she said quietly. "Paolo has never had anything to do with those things. If he hadn't been Vittorio's nephew, he would never have dared to defy him. But Prohibition is a different matter. Paolo feels that people should be free to decide for themselves what they drink. He sees himself as helping them to have a choice."

"I agree, but that's not how the law sees it," Anna said. "And the same applies to me if they catch me serving it."

"I don't think the law is the main problem as far as Paolo is concerned," Jennie said. "It's the rivalry between the bootleggers which worries him."

"You don't think it will get really bad?" Anna asked.

"Perhaps not, now that Al Capone has gone to join Torrio in Chicago."

Anna shuddered. The newspapers had been full of the gangland murder of Big Jim Colosimo in Chicago, which had been attributed to Capone. "I'm sure there's no real risk," she said reassuringly. "I've never had the slightest problem so far."

"But you aren't typical, Anna," Jennie reminded her. "Your order is mainly for the higher quality wines and spirits which are quietly smuggled in from Europe. The trouble comes from the bootleggers running booze from Cuba and moonshine from the distilleries for the speakeasies and beer flats."

"But Paolo isn't involved in that, is he?" Anna asked.

"I think so. You must remember he has a huge transport fleet at his disposal, so it seems to make sense to him."

"I see."

Anna felt a strange premonition, as if she had heard some bad news, but Jennie appeared unconcerned. "We have one thing to be thankful for, Anna. You and I cannot be blamed for any of this. As we are just silly women, we could not possibly understand what is going on. It is a good defence, one which most men would believe even now that we have the vote."

Jennie expected Anna to laugh, but she appeared hardly to have heard the remark. "I couldn't admit it to him, Jennie," she said slowly, "but perhaps Clancy is right. When you decide to break the law, you don't know where it will end."

James made his way cheerfully along the sidewalk, happy to be going home for dinner. He boarded at school during the week, and as he grew older, he felt the restrictions of school life more acutely. He looked forward to the relative freedom of the weekends, and especially to his mother's cooking. His enjoyment of home life made him even more determined to win the current battle with his father. *After all*, he thought, *I am sixteen now, not a child any more.*

He bounded up the steps to the house and turned his key in the front door. As he opened it, he heard the sound of raised voices from the drawing room.

James stood quietly in the hall; they were making so much noise they hadn't heard him come in. He looked around anxiously, and then remembered that Lottie had gone to her sewing bee, and the daily woman would be gone by now. James moved towards the partly open door to the drawing room, mesmerised by the sound of his parents' anger. They never argued, he could not recall them ever being angry with each other. His mother was in full flow.

"How could I have told you?" she cried. Her voice was almost a shout. "How can I tell you anything when you cut yourself off from what is happening? You never come near...."

"What do you expect me to do?" his father yelled back. "To carry on as if nothing is happening? As if I agree with all your dirty, back street deals?"

"I expect you to be realistic," Anna said more quietly, although her voice was steely. "We've had over two years of Prohibition and all your prophesies of doom have come to nothing."

"Nothing?" Clancy exploded. "Give me strength! The woman's blind, so she is. There have been murders on the streets and gangland warfare."

"Not near any of our restaurants," Anna shouted back. "There has not been a single incident. Our profits are excellent, and that is largely due to Paolo."

"I see," Clancy interrupted, his voice becoming intense with anger. "And to protect your profits, you are willing to risk James' future."

"How dare you? How dare you say that?" Anna was beside herself.

James walked in. It took a few seconds for his presence to register, and then his father said gruffly, "So you're here."

"Yes. What's this all about? What's the matter?"

His mother made to speak, but his father held up his hand sternly to stop her and said, "It's about you, James."

"About me? About my not wanting to go on to university?"

"Not exactly, but I expect that is part of it." James watched his father as he walked over to the desk. He took a cigar from a leather box and motioned James to a seat. "Sit down, James, we must talk."

His mother stood up as if to leave, but was stopped by a stern glance from his father. "Stay, Anna, if you please. We will get to the bottom of this." James took a seat opposite and waited.

His father was making a business of lighting his cigar, but eventually it was done. He looked James in the eye. "Where," he said carefully, "where have you been this afternoon?"

So that was it. James swallowed. For a moment, he was tempted to lie, but then knew he could never lie to his father.

"I...I went to see Freddie's new car," he said truthfully.

"And then?"

"I went to Jackson's for tea."

"With Freddie?"

"No." It was obvious he knew.

"Who did you go with?" His father asked calmly.

"Uncle Paolo."

His father turned towards his mother. "You see? Uncle! He calls him Uncle!"

James felt himself becoming angry. "Father, Paolo is my uncle...not really of course...more like an older brother."

"A brother, now, is it? Heaven preserve us!" His father's face was flushed and angry. "James, you know perfectly well what I feel about Paolo

Vetti and his family, don't you?"

"I know you don't like his uncle Vittorio, but you're fond of Auntie Jennie, aren't you?"

His father gave a snort of disgust. "Don't try to wriggle out of it, young man. You are well aware I don't want you to associate with Paolo Vetti, are you not?"

"But Paolo is my friend, Father, he's great fun and...."

"I'm not asking for your opinion!" his father roared. "Will you answer the question? Do you know I don't want you to associate with Paolo Vetti?"

James flushed and looked at the floor. "Yes, Father."

"How often have you been seeing him?" his father asked.

"Not very often. I'm at school and he's very busy."

"How often?" his father persisted.

"Well, always for my birthday. He takes me for a treat usually. And Christmas of course, and in the summer holidays."

James looked up. His father looked quite shaken. "This...this deception," he said slowly, "it has been going on for years, hasn't it?"

"It wasn't intended as deception, Father."

"No? What would you call it? I suppose you thought that what I didn't know wouldn't hurt me, was that it?"

James remained silent. When his father spoke again, his voice was scathing. "I am ashamed of you, James. You have deliberately flouted my wishes, so you have, and shown very bad judgment in your choice of friends."

"There's nothing the matter with Paolo," James burst out, his eyes filling with tears in spite of himself. "You can't make me hate him just because you do."

"Quiet!" his father roared. "You will not see him again. Ever. Do you hear me?"

James did not reply.

"Do you hear me, James?"

"Yes," James said sullenly. The tears were now running freely and he despised himself for his weakness.

"Go to your room," his father ordered.

James turned. His relief at being dismissed was almost overpowered by the sense of injustice. At the door he stopped, and flicked back his fair hair with a truculent toss of his head. "You hardly know Paolo," he said. "How can you know what he's like?"

"Go to your room, James," his father snapped.

James tried to remember what Paolo had said to him at the teashop. "You're sixteen now and can be your own man."

"I'm going, Father," he said, "but you can't cut me off from my friends just because you don't like them. You can't make me study, either, and I'm not going to university no matter what you say."

As he left the room, Clancy turned to Anna. "I hope you're satisfied," he said.

"You have brought this on yourself," Anna replied. "There was no need to be so hard on him. He was only being loyal to his friend, after all."

"Friend? You think Paolo Vetti is a suitable friend for our son?"

Anna sighed. "Clancy, let us please try to talk about this without...without shouting at each other." She came across the room and sat down opposite her husband. "Do you remember when James was small? Paolo used to play with him and take him to the park for me? They became friends then. Paolo is a lot older than James, but they have always been friends. They are very close."

"Thanks to you," Clancy said shortly.

"I agree with you that if we lived in an ideal world, James would perhaps not be friends with Paolo. But it is not an ideal world, and James has lots of other friends too."

Clancy's expression showed no sign of softening. "Have you known they were keeping in touch all these years?" he said accusingly.

"I...I suppose I turned a blind eye," Anna confessed. "I suspected it."

"You suspected our son was friendly with a gangster, that he thought of him almost as a brother...and you turned a blind eye?" Clancy was incredulous.

"No!" Anna said vehemently. "I didn't think my son was friendly with a gangster. I thought he was friendly with a nice young man who happens to be married to a close friend."

"And happens to have an uncle who is a gangster, a racketeer and a pimp," Clancy retorted angrily. "And don't say Paolo isn't a gangster, he's running cargoes of bootleg liquor all over this city, so he is."

Anna sighed and got up. "If we're back to that again, there's obviously no more to say," she said. "But be careful, Clancy, that you don't drive James away completely. You have probably made him even more determined not to go to university."

"It's all my fault, now, is it? Have you thought that his friend Paolo may have put the idea in his head?"

"Hardly," Anna snapped. "James has views of his own. Anyway, I happen to know Paolo advised him to go to college. He went to university himself, you know."

"How do you know what Paolo advised?" Clancy queried. His tone was sarcastic.

"I know because I asked him to talk to James," Anna responded hotly.

It was a mistake. Clancy flushed with anger. "Are you telling me you discussed our son's future with that...that hoodlum?"

"He's not a hoodlum. And yes, I did, and I'm not ashamed of it," Anna cried. "Can't you accept that Paolo is actually very fond of James? That he was concerned about his education?"

Clancy gave an incredulous laugh. "I don't believe what I'm hearing."

"Well, you had better believe it. I wanted to support you in this, but you are too prejudiced to see anything clearly. I had to talk to someone, Clancy, and let's face it, I can't talk to you anymore."

She left the room, and Clancy, thoroughly disconcerted, went to his club.

Paolo's mood was black. Nothing was simple, he reflected, no matter how hard you tried to make it so. Just when he had thought the demarcation lines were accepted, when he thought his uncle was coming round to his ideas, Tony Cavellini had to appear on the scene and begin to throw his weight around.

Paolo had thought he was making progress. His uncle was growing older, and his hold on the rackets and brothels was weakening, and added to that was the simple matter of economics. Thanks to much hard work and a little doctoring of the accounts, Paolo had managed to convince Vittorio that crime did not pay so well these days, and that perhaps the risk was hardly worth taking when the legitimate businesses and the bootlegging were bringing in such a good return.

Paolo sighed as he reached the large van. He

unlocked the door and climbed up into the driver's seat. He could have done without this trip, but with one driver in hospital and another running scared, he had no alternative. Damn Cavellini. If he'd only waited a few months more, he could perhaps have picked up some of Vittorio's business for the asking. But then perhaps not, he reflected. It was one thing for Vittorio to give up his activities in response to a reasoned argument from himself, but quite another for him to be forced out by a rival gang. Even as he considered it, Paolo knew his uncle would never give in to threats. He had seen off predators before, of course, but he was younger then, and Cavellini wasn't simply out for the rackets and the girls. Much as he hated to admit it, Paolo knew Cavellini's real target was the lucrative liquor business, the business upon which he himself had spent so much time and effort.

Paolo started up the engine. He did not want to confront the issues which now weighed so heavily on him, but he knew he must. For the first time, he questioned the instinct which had persuaded him to defy the Prohibition laws so readily. He still felt that the law was wrong, that people should be entitled to take a drink if they wished, but suddenly things were getting out of hand. An incident the previous week, when a driver was beaten up, had thoroughly shaken Paolo, and he did not want to think of the consequences if Tony Cavellini decided to meet his uncle Vittorio head on. *Who knows, perhaps that stiff-necked Clancy Sullivan was right after all,* Paolo thought. Perhaps he had foreseen all this mayhem, although it was not as bad in New York as in Chicago by all accounts. Paolo grinned to himself. Perhaps it was a pity that Capone had moved to Chicago, after all, he would have seen Tony Cavellini off quickly enough.

Paolo drove the van toward the yard gate. There was only one thing he was sure of. When his son was born, he must not be brought into this situation. His son would not have the childhood he himself had suffered. If Vittorio would not agree to give up all but the legal businesses, he would take Jennie and the baby and move away to a new life, anywhere. California perhaps.

Paolo swerved suddenly as a figure sprang into the road, waving. He recognised the slight form and boyish fair hair immediately, and pulled onto the shoulder. James dashed up as Paolo wound down the window.

"Hello, little brother! What brings you here?" Paolo was delighted to see him.

"Looking for you. I was coming to the yard. I have to talk to you."

Paolo frowned. "All right, but it will have to be tomorrow. I have to go somewhere now and I'm late already."

"No, Paolo, now." James opened the door and climbed into the passenger seat. "I have to talk to you. It's important."

"But I told you, I have to go."

"I'll come with you. We can talk on the way," James said firmly.

Paolo hesitated. "You better not, James. I shall be a couple of hours at least."

"That's all right," James said lightly. "I'm not expected home until dinner." Seeing that Paolo was still hesitant, he added quietly, "If you're worried because you're going to collect booze, don't be. I know all about it and I shan't be in the way. I can help you load the van."

Paolo's face darkened. "I'm not happy about it, little brother, but if it's important, you can come. It will perhaps get rid of those schoolboy ideas you have about running liquor. You will see it is not exciting at all, just rather boring, hard work."

As the van bounced back onto the road, Paolo said, "Right. Now tell me what is so important."

James, hesitant at first, outlined the details of his argument with his father the previous evening, explaining, "Someone must have seen us having tea in Jackson's and told him. When I got home, he and Mama were having the most dreadful row. I don't think it was entirely about me, I think it was...."

"Yes," Paolo said, "I understand what it was about."

"Well, anyway, I told him you are my friend, and I told him I'm not going to university, whatever he says."

"What are you going to do?" Paolo asked in a conversational tone.

"What do you mean?"

"You say you are not going to university. What are you going to do?"

"I don't know, really. Get a job of some sort, perhaps."

"What sort?" Paolo asked. "What experience do you have? Do you know how difficult it is to get work now?"

James flushed. "I...I could do a job in our own business. After all, it will be mine one day."

"Why should your father give you a job when you have defied his wishes?" Paolo asked quietly. "Why should he take on a sixteen-year-old boy, when he can choose from qualified people who will jump at the chance to work for him?"

"You don't know that," James said sullenly. "I don't think people will jump at the chance to work for him. He's a tyrant."

Paolo laughed. "You have a lot to learn about

employers, little brother. Your father is certainly no tyrant. He's known as a good employer. Ask Jennie. She worked for him long enough. You say the business will be yours one day. I wouldn't count your chickens if I were you. Why should your father leave it to you if you defy him? If you don't go to university, you won't have the qualifications you need to run the business."

James was silent for a few moments, as the van wound its way out of the suburbs and into a dusty lane. Eventually he said, "Father's forbidden me to see you at all."

"Then what are you doing here, little brother?" Paolo said softly. "Your first duty is to your father and your mama."

"Why are you on his side? Don't you want us to be friends anymore?" James burst out, tears starting in his eyes.

"We shall always remain friends, little brother, whether we see each other or not. Nothing can alter that. I am on no side but yours, James, but I can see your father's point of view. If I were in his place, I would feel the same."

"He called you a gangster and a hoodlum," James said.

Paolo pulled the van into the side of the road and stopped. After a moment, he said quietly, "Little brother, I think perhaps it's time I was honest with you. You are sixteen now; it is time for you to grow up. Can you take it?"

Paolo's beautiful, dark eyes were grave, and James felt a pang of apprehension. If his father was right, and Paolo was a hoodlum, James didn't want to know it. "Yes, I can take it," he said.

"It is true that my uncle has done bad things...does bad things...and some people might describe him as a gangster. I don't approve of all

he does and I have told him so. We have disagree-
ments, like you and your father. But Uncle Vittorio
has been very good to me. I love him dearly and
could never hurt him."

"I understand," said James. He was not used
to Paolo being serious and found it disconcerting.

"I break the law, too, James. At this moment, I
am going to pick up some illicit booze."

"But that isn't really wicked. Everyone thinks
Prohibition is stupid."

"Not everyone, James. Some people felt very
strongly that it would make America a better society. Perhaps it would have, if everyone had obeyed
it." Paolo turned to face James and said earnestly,
"Because I didn't agree with the law, I decided I
could break it, but I'm beginning to think I'm
wrong."

"You're beginning to think...like Father?"
James faltered.

"When a good man like your father calls me a
gangster and a hoodlum, it makes me ashamed."
Paolo's voice became soft. "You know, of course,
that Jennie and I are expecting our first child?"
he said.

James flushed, this was becoming embarrassing. He nodded.

"Think of it, James. In a month I shall have a
son of my own."

"Or a daughter," James interrupted.

Paolo looked surprised. "Or a daughter, I suppose," he said. "I do not want my son to grow up
hearing people call me a gangster and a hoodlum.
I intend to leave New York, move somewhere else,
California perhaps, and start afresh with my family."

"So we shan't be seeing each other anyway?"
James said, trying to mask his disappointment.

"Think of it this way, little brother. If you go to university as your father wishes, by the time you have your degree, Jennie and I will have made a new life." He laughed, and a glimpse of the old Paolo showed itself. "I shall have a boring job in a boring place, but we shall be so happy," he said with a flourish. "And we shall not be breaking the law. I'm sure your father will be happy for you to come and stay with us for holidays when we are so respectable."

James laughed. "And we can write while I'm studying?" he said.

"I should think so," Paolo said. "I will ask your father for permission. When I explain to him what I'm doing, I think he will agree. Now," he said seriously, "how do you feel?"

James thought for a while. "I'll tell Father I'll go to university," he decided.

"It is a good decision. Once you are there, you will realise you have done the right thing," Paolo said. He started the engine. "Now let's collect this moonshine. It isn't far."

Five minutes later, they pulled up at a run down farmhouse. Paolo reached behind his seat. "Here," he said, "put this on. I don't want you recognised, or me either, for that matter." It was a bag-shaped head cover made of dark material with two slits for the eyes and a hole at the mouth. Paolo pulled one over his head and laughed as James did the same.

He got down from the van. "Stay here until I've arranged things," he said, "and then you can help me load up."

James sat in the van and watched Paolo walk up the drive and enter the farmhouse. He felt a little silly with the bag over his head, but rather important all the same. Suddenly, he heard the sound of an engine, and there was a swirl of dust and the screech of brakes as a large car pulled alongside.

It was all over in seconds. James hardly had time to realise what was happening as he was bundled unceremoniously out of the van and into the back of the car. He was pushed down onto the floor, and through the slits in his head cover, he saw the gun pointed at his head.

"Make a sound," a voice hissed, "and you're dead."

Kidnapped

1923

"But don't you understand? They took him instead of me," Paolo cried.

Vittorio Vetti regarded his nephew solemnly. "Of course I understand, and there is no problem. They know they have the wrong person."

"They know?" Paolo was frantic. "How do you know that for sure?"

"Because Cavellini has been in touch."

"Already?"

"Yes. I admit that at first I thought they had taken you. But Cavellini said right away they had a young boy with fair hair." Vittorio gave a short laugh. "He was furious. Perhaps we have overestimated the threat. His team can't be so sharp to have made such a mess of a simple lift."

"We were wearing masks," Paolo said. "What are they going to do with James?"

Vittorio smiled. "Oh, you know, the usual threats. I told them to go ahead and do what they liked. The boy has nothing to do with us."

"You told them what?" Paolo sprang around the desk and caught hold of Vittorio by his lapels. His dark eyes glittered savagely and his tone was venomous. "If they harm one hair of James Sullivan's head, I'll hold you responsible, you old goat."

"Paolo!" Vittorio struggled to release himself

from Paolo's grip. "Don't get so excited! They won't harm him. Why should they? They'll probably drop him off on some street corner when they realise I won't play ball."

"And what if they don't? What if they kill him before they drop him off?" Paolo pulled the lapels across as if he would throttle Vittorio. "And if it had been me, Uncle? Would you have played ball then?" he demanded viciously.

"Calm down, my boy. Don't take it out on me. I am not responsible for the boy's problem. In fact, if anyone is to blame, it is yourself. You had no business having him in the van with you."

Paolo released his uncle with a shake. Vittorio smoothed his lapels and adjusted his diamond tie pin. "As for what I would do if you were taken, how can I say?" he said. "I do what I must, depending upon the circumstances."

"And what are you going to do now? In these circumstances?"

"Why nothing! I regret this has happened, but the boy is not our responsibility."

Paolo grabbed the telephone and held it out to Vittorio. His face was white with anger and his breathing was fast. "Here," he commanded, "phone Tony Cavellini now."

"And tell him what?" Vittorio asked calmly.

"Make a deal. Whatever he wants you give him. Now!"

"I don't respond to threats, Paolo," Vittorio said coldly. "Not from Tony Cavellini and not from you."

"Is that your final word?" Paolo asked intently.

"You know it is."

Paolo leaned across the desk, his voice choked with anger. "Then let me tell you something, Uncle. I was going to tell you next month, after the baby is born. I was going to choose the right time, and the right words, so it would not upset you too much. I realise now there is only one right time and that is this moment."

"What is all this? Are you practising your part in a melodrama?" Vittorio sneered.

"No melodrama, Uncle, just a statement of fact. I'm getting out. I'm going to take my wife and child as far away from you as I can."

"All this just because of that stupid boy," Vittorio grumbled. "Paolo, come back here! Where are you going?"

At the door Paolo turned. "Someone has to tell his parents," he muttered. He went out, slamming the door behind him.

Anna tried to make her tone light. "There's a letter from Will," she said. "He's bought himself a car, an Austin seven. He says, 'When the sun is hot you can fold the roof down.' I think he means it's a convertible."

Clancy nodded. Realising some effort was needed on his part, he said, "A car will be useful, so it will, living where they do now."

"Yes, indeed, although apparently the trams are much more frequent now," Anna said. "Things have changed so much since we left. It's a pity Dad did not live to see it. He would have been amazed, our Will with a car."

Clancy nodded again, and silence fell. *Heavens*, Anna thought, *how long can this dreadful atmosphere last?* The doorbell rang.

"I expect James left his key behind again," Anna said. "He's awfully late."

The door opened and Lottie came in. "There's someone to see you," she said, and Paolo entered the room behind her.

As soon as she looked at him, Anna knew something was wrong. Paolo's face was white and he looked distraught.

"What are you doing here?" Clancy's voice was icy.

"I've come to tell you...there is bad news."

Paolo spoke quietly and precisely. He gave them all the facts, told them everything he knew, except that his uncle had refused to intervene.

Anna sat, white and horrified, taking no part as Clancy, sick with fear, questioned Paolo intensely. "What can we do? Do you know where he is? Shall we get the police?"

"No. That might be worse for James."

"You mean to say I have to rely on the likes of you to get my son away from these...these...."

"I know you don't like me, Mr. Sullivan, but you can rest assured I will get him out. I'm on your side, you know."

"I'm not on the same side as any hoodlum," Clancy said fiercely. "What was he doing in your van anyway? Only yesterday I told him he was not to see you, so I did."

"I know, he came to tell me. If it helps at all, he came to talk about it...about going to university."

"It does not help and I do not need your assistance to bring up my son," Clancy said bitterly. "This is all your fault, can't you see that?"

Paolo flinched. "Yes...yes, I do see that."

He crossed the room to Anna. She looked up at him with eyes that were uncomprehending, beseeching. "Paolo...?"

"Don't worry, Anna. I will get him out, I promise you." His beautiful face was tragic as he whispered, "Best friends, Anna. Remember?"

She nodded.

Clancy barked, "What can I do?"

"Nothing, Mr. Sullivan. I will telephone you

shortly, as soon as I know anything."

At the door, Paolo turned, hesitant. "Please forgive me," he whispered, and went out.

There was silence. Anna sat, shocked, unable to take it in. She turned to her husband. "Clancy...."

The face he turned to her was terrible to see. "You have sowed, Anna," he said grimly, "you have sowed, so you have, and now you see what you have reaped."

Paolo stopped his car at the first bar he could find. He went in and ordered a coffee and asked if he could use the telephone. He dialled a number. "Put me through to Tony Cavellini, please. Tell him it's Paolo Vetti."

Anna sat in front of her dressing mirror and stared vacantly at her image. She was still a good-looking woman, with hardly a hint of grey in the thick, tawny hair which she wore dressed into a chignon. Despite the recent years of good living, or perhaps because of them, her skin had a healthy glow, and her figure, although still slender, had a womanly maturity.

The eyes which stared back at her in the mirror were wooden, lifeless. She was suspended in time, in limbo, and not even her fevered imaginings could impinge upon the impression of unreality.

The telephone rang downstairs. In an instant she was alert, straining, intense, and yet she seemed unable to move. She could hear Clancy's voice, low and quick, and then his footsteps on the stairs. He opened the door.

"That was Paolo. I'm going out."

"Where?" Her voice was a mere whisper.

"I don't know. I'm meeting Paolo on the corner

with our car. He says I'm to drive him to pick up James."

"Oh, Clancy!" Anna got to her feet, and hurried across to him. "Has he got him out? Is James safe?"

"I don't know. He wouldn't say any more. I must go."

They stared at each other for a moment and still the words would not come. As Clancy left the room and made his way downstairs, he thought he heard Anna whisper, "Take care," but then told himself he had imagined it.

James started. He had been wallowing in the depths of introspection, and the sharp knock at the door startled him. Terrified, he tried to remember his instructions. He grabbed the bag-shaped hood which he had been wearing when they took him and put it over his head, twisting it back to front so that he could see nothing. "If ya see us, and can tell about it, we'll have to kill ya," the voice with the heavy New York accent had said.

The same voice came now from outside the door. "Ready?"

"Yes," James said, turning to sit with his back to the door as instructed.

The door opened. The voice said, "Hands behind ya' back." James obeyed and felt someone tie his hands together. The cord was tight and bit into his flesh. The same person began to bind his feet, but the voice said, "Leave that unless you want to carry him to the car."

"Where am I going?" James ventured.

"A drive into the country," the voice said, not unkindly. "Don't worry, kid, somebody loves ya after all. In a coupla hours, this'll be over."

James was yanked to his feet and marched

toward the door. The voice asked, "Will ya be quiet or do I gag ya?"

"I'll be quiet," James assured him, his voice high pitched with fear.

"Right. One peep and there's a bullet in ya' head." They pushed him through the door and began to give him directions as he attempted blindly to negotiate the stairs.

"Repeat the instructions back to me." Paolo's voice was sharp, uncompromising.

"I don't see...," Clancy began.

"You don't need to see. Repeat the instructions," Paolo snapped. As if to emphasise the point, he added, "You are not the boss here, Mr. Sullivan. Not this time. Do as you are told if you want James to be safe."

Clancy swallowed the retort which sprang to his lips. He huddled down into the seat of the car and shivered. It was a filthy night, cold and wet, and they had been parked on waste land in the middle of nowhere for almost an hour.

"When you get out of the car, I open the passenger door and then slide across into the driver's seat," Clancy began. "I wind down the driver's window and push this damned thing," he gesticulated with the shotgun he held on his lap, "out of the window to cover James until he gets here."

"Yes. Then?"

"As soon as James is in the car, I tell him to get on the floor and I drive away. I take him straight home and we talk to no one about what has happened."

"Yes, it is important they know James is no threat to them. Whatever you do, don't go to the police."

"How will you get home? Why aren't you coming with us?" Clancy asked.

Paolo smiled. "That wasn't a note of concern I heard, was it, Mr. Sullivan? Don't worry about me. As I told you, I have traded James for information. They know better than to trifle with me." His fingers drummed on the steering wheel impatiently. "How much longer? They are late."

As if in answer, car lights appeared in the distance. The car made its way slowly towards them and stopped about a hundred yards away. The lights turned on and off twice, and Paolo turned his on and off in return.

Paolo opened the car door. "This is it. Follow the instructions to the letter and everything will be all right."

Clancy suddenly realised what was happening. "Paolo, are you exchanging yourself for James?"

"The instructions, Mr. Sullivan."

Then Paolo was walking slowly towards the distant car, and Clancy watched, torn between admiration for Paolo's courage and fear for James's safety. Suddenly aware, he opened the passenger door and moved across into the driver's seat, pushing the shotgun through the window so it was clearly visible. "God only knows what I'll do if I have to fire the thing," he muttered to himself. It was the first time in his life he had had a gun in his hands.

When Paolo had covered about thirty yards, Clancy could discern the slight figure of James making his way towards him. The glow from the distant car headlights caught his fair hair, and Clancy felt his stomach tighten with tension. As James and Paolo drew closer together and passed each other with barely a change of stride, Clancy let out his breath at last, and a minute later James was in the car.

"Lock your door and get down on the floor," Clancy commanded, as the engine roared into life. He could not resist a glance at the other car and was just in time to see Paolo knocked to the ground. Cursing under his breath, Clancy let out the clutch and the car moved away at high speed.

Vittorio Vetti was angry. Not only with Tony Cavellini but with Paolo too. He could hardly believe that his nephew had willingly engineered this situation, but most of all he was angry with himself. He had handled it badly, he reflected, ever since he had known of James Sullivan's abduction.

It was not as if there had been no pointers to Paolo's feelings for the boy. For years, Vittorio had known of the friendship between his nephew and James Sullivan and had marvelled at it. He recalled what Paolo had told him of his early days in New York, and how Mrs. Sullivan had given him food and work. Vittorio realised for the first time that perhaps Paolo had not told him everything about that time. The bonds were stronger than he had realised, and of course, Jennie was almost part of the Sullivan family.

Vittorio clenched his fists in despair. That was the worst thing. The child was due within weeks and his father was being held by that thug Cavellini. He could not think of telling Jennie the truth, and yet how could he explain his nephew's absence? Jennie knew Paolo was anxious to spend as much time as possible with her in the coming weeks. It was no use trying to pretend he was on a business trip. Vittorio felt his gorge rise when he thought of Jennie. After all, he was almost the child's grandfather, particularly as Jennie had no parents of her own.

Vittorio sighed. There was no point in prolonging the agony. He had much experience in fighting off predators, and he knew when he was beaten, when it was time to deal.

He picked up the telephone and rang Tony Cavellini.

They met in a quiet suburb, each driving his own car. Around the corner in both directions, their henchmen waited, armed and nervous. Cavellini got out of his car first, and Vittorio joined him on the sidewalk.

"You look older than when I last saw you in Rome, Tony," Vittorio remarked. "You are almost grey."

Cavellini shrugged his big shoulders. "At least I have not put on weight like you, Vittorio. You know," he said, looking around him at the peaceful avenue of bungalows and green lawns. "This is nice. Quiet. I like that. I could just shoot you here and now and have done with it."

Vittorio gave him a basilisk-like stare. "Not if you are unarmed, as we agreed."

Tony Cavellini smiled, showing gold fillings which glinted oddly against his swarthy face. "I expect I'm just as unarmed as you are. Shall we walk?"

"Yes, but not in the direction of your back up," Vittorio said.

"And not yours either," Cavellini responded.

There was a small side street at right angles to the road and by tacit agreement they turned into it.

"I've said I'm prepared to deal," Vittorio said, "but only if my nephew is returned to me unharmed. Damage one hair of his head, and I'll fry your balls for breakfast and have the rest of your carcass made into dog food." This was said in a conversational tone and appeared to have no effect on Cavellini.

"I want the lot. Numbers, protection and brothels, and the four gambling houses." The gold teeth glinted. "Yes, I said four, Vittorio, we know about the one across the river." The teeth showed again. "And of course the booze."

"I have some legitimate businesses also. You're sure you wouldn't like them too?" Vittorio asked sarcastically, and Cavellini laughed.

"I'll let you keep those. After all, questions might be asked."

"You can have the protection and the brothels," Vittorio said. "Paolo wants me to be rid of them anyway. That's the deal."

Cavellini gave a snort of impatience. "Look, Vetti, I didn't have to come here. You want your nephew back alive or not?"

A young woman was walking towards them wearing a soft pink wool coat and pushing a perambulator. The two men moved aside to let her pass, and both raised their hats.

"Paolo tells me he and his wife are expecting a happy event," Cavellini observed. "He should be around to take care of them. If he isn't, who knows what could happen to them?"

"Harm any of my family and...."

"You know the deal!" Cavellini snapped.

They walked on a few yards. Vittorio said, "Alright, the numbers and the four gambling houses as well."

Cavellini waited, and after a moment, Vittorio added, "Yes, all right, the booze. Provided Paolo is returned and we hear nothing else of you."

Cavellini's tone was laconic. "But of course, Vittorio. Why should I bother you again? You will have nothing left I want."

"There's one condition," Vittorio said.

"No conditions," Cavellini said flatly.

"It is that it happens fast. Tomorrow latest."

Cavellini frowned. If Vittorio was planning to double-cross him, he would need more time than that to arrange it. As if reading his thoughts, Vittorio said, "It's because of Jennie, Paolo's wife. I haven't told her. I can get away with saying he is delayed for one night perhaps, but no more. Paolo would not want her worried, not now."

Cavellini relaxed. "You're going soft in your old age, Vittorio. I've done you a favour, after all. It's time you retired."

They turned as if by mutual consent and began to walk back. Vittorio said, "You'll want to see the books?"

"Yes, and be sure it's the right set."

"You needn't worry about that. As you say, I'm retiring. Paolo wanted me to anyway. What about the handover? On waste ground, like the Sullivan boy?"

Cavellini laughed. "If you think I'll walk into that one you're mistaken. You get Paolo and I get a set of books I don't have time to examine. No deal."

"All right. Come to my office above the laundry tomorrow at eleven."

"And get gunned down?"

"Bring as many men and guns as you need. We won't be armed. You can inspect the whole building to make sure of that if you want. Then take as long as you like on the books."

After a moment, Cavellini said, "Okay. When I'm satisfied, you vacate the office, and I'll telephone and have Paolo released."

"No. When you're satisfied you'll have Paolo released to my driver, and when he calls in to say Paolo is safe, I will leave the office and the books to you."

Cavellini considered. "How do I know you'll go?"

"You will be armed and I will not, as I said before. Look, Tony, I'm sick of this, and I want out. I'm thinking of going to California with my family. I want your guarantee I will leave the office in one piece."

Cavellini smiled grimly. "Keep to the deal, and you can count on a quiet old age in California. Cross me, and you and Paolo will feed the crows."

They stopped as they reached the road where the cars were parked. Cavellini shivered. "Damned cold!" he remarked.

Vittorio nodded. "They say it's warm in California," he said, and held out his hand.

After a moment's hesitation, Cavellini shook it briefly and the two men returned to their cars.

As soon as Vittorio reached his office, he sent for his chief clerk. "I want all the books made up to date for tomorrow morning."

"But, Mr. Vetti, tonight's takings don't get here until after midnight."

Vittorio glowered. "Then work late. I want them up to date for tomorrow. Work all night if you have to."

"Yes, Mr. Vetti." The clerk turned to go. "And get me a joiner," Vittorio barked.

"A...what, Mr. Vetti?"

"A joiner. Are you deaf?" Seeing the clerk's puzzled face, Vittorio explained as if to a child, "A joiner, a carpenter, you savvy?"

"Yes, Mr. Vetti."

"Then get on with it."

Vittorio picked up the telephone, and a few minutes later, four men, the same men who had accompanied him for the meeting with Cavellini, entered his office. Vittorio gave detailed instructions, moving from his desk to the window and back to his desk as he talked. When he was sure all was in order, he dismissed them and sent for coffee. It was time for serious thought. He needed an honest man.

Before he had finished his coffee, he picked up the telephone again. "Get me Clancy Sullivan."

Backlash

Anna checked James's luggage for the tenth time. "Are you sure he has enough socks, Lottie?" she said, frowning.

"Anna, I took the list to the store myself," Lottie soothed. "James was lucky to be able to leave right away, and he has enough here to last at least six months. If he finds he needs anything more, he can always let us know."

Anna nodded. Lottie put her arm around her. "It's the best thing for him. You know it is."

Anna nodded again. "Yes, Clancy is right. His education is the most important thing."

At that moment, James came in and caught sight of the two large trunks. "Gosh, Mama, is that all mine?"

"Yes. We don't know what the weather will be, so we have packed something of everything."

James frowned. "I shall only have a small room, you know."

"If your room is too small, you can always take an apartment in town," Anna suggested.

"I don't think Father would agree to that. He was keen for me to live in college."

"Oh."

James came across to his mother. "It's alright, Mama," he said. "I want to go, really I do. Father is right; he was right all along. Paolo made me see that."

He hugged his mother tight and said, "The car is here. I don't want to miss the train." He hesitated. "As soon as you hear anything...."

"Yes. I'll let you know as soon as Paolo is free."

"You're quite sure he will be alright?"

"One thing I do know for certain, James," Anna said earnestly, "is that whatever Vittorio Vetti may be, he loves Paolo. He will make sure he is freed."

The chauffeur appeared to help James downstairs with the trunks, and a few minutes later, Anna and Lottie were waving James away.

Anna went back into the drawing room. She stood in front of the fireplace and stared disconsolately at Sylvie's picture, as if to gain some consolation from the sunny scene. The last few days had been the worst time in her life, even worse than that time in Paris when Delphine had told her she and Robert were to be married....

Lottie came in. "No mooning about, Anna. It won't do any good. College will be good for James; he needs the discipline."

"Yes, you're right." After a moment, Anna said quietly, "I thought Clancy might be here to see him off."

Lottie understood instantly. "It's not what you think, Anna. Clancy isn't angry with James anymore, not since they had that heart to heart. Everything is alright between them."

Yes, Anna thought, things are right between them. It's me he can't forgive. "Even so, he could have been here," she said.

"I don't think so," Lottie replied. "He told James he was sorry not to see him off but he had something important to do. I heard him give instructions to the chauffeur to take the car to the office as soon as he has put James on the train."

"Oh? And what is this important thing he has to do?" Anna asked.

"I've no idea," Lottie said, "but he's been very

preoccupied since he had the telephone call from
that monster Vetti."

It was just after two o'clock the same afternoon when Clancy received the awaited telephone
call at his office. Leaving immediately, he ignored
the protests of his chauffeur and got into the driver's seat of the car, telling the surprised man to
take the rest of the day off. Fifteen minutes later,
he was driving along the dusty road to the neglected
farmhouse where James had been held. He
stopped the car at the entrance to the driveway,
little more than a cart track, and checked his gold
hunter watch. Paolo should be free at about two-
thirty if all went as Vittorio had outlined. Clancy
settled back to wait, wondering, not for the first
time, what on earth he was doing there, and why
he was doing it.

It was exactly two-thirty-one when Clancy saw
a dark-suited figure emerge from the farmhouse
and begin to walk up the long cart track towards
him. Two minutes later, he recognised the figure
as Paolo Vetti, and he noticed that Paolo's walk
was less jaunty than usual. He held his head down,
and moved with a shambling limp, and as he
neared the car, Clancy saw that Paolo's suit was
crumpled and dirty, and his handsome features
were disfigured by a black eye and several yellow
and purple bruises.

Clancy opened the passenger door. "Welcome
back. Your hotel wasn't too comfortable, I see."

Paolo stared at him. "I didn't expect it to be you,"
he said. "What are you doing here?" He got into the
car, moving painfully, and Clancy started up.

"Your uncle asked me to collect you," Clancy
said. "I don't really know why. He said something
about not wanting to use one of his own men."

Paolo smiled grimly. "He's under pressure from Tony Cavellini, the man who took James. Cavellini is trying to take over the Vetti interests and is quite capable of bribing our men. My uncle wanted someone he knew he could trust."

"In case you think that's a compliment, I don't regard it as such," Clancy said shortly, driving away quickly towards the main road. "I don't want to know the details and I don't want anything else to do with this after I've taken you home."

"Fair enough," Paolo said, feeling his face gingerly. "All the same, thanks for agreeing to collect me."

"How did you get the eye?" Clancy asked. "Did they beat you up?"

"Yes, but it was my own fault. I was trying to escape. I thought...." Paolo hesitated, and then continued ruefully, "I wasn't sure my uncle would be able to get me out, or would want to."

Clancy drove on for a few minutes in silence, until they came within sight of the suburbs. He pulled up outside a bar and said gruffly, "I was wrong to tell James not to see you. You have proved a true friend."

"In your shoes, I should have felt the same," Paolo said. "But you needn't worry. As soon as the baby is born, I am taking Jennie to California to start again."

"I know. James told me." Clancy took a deep breath. "You and your family will always be welcome at our home, Paolo."

Paolo hung his head. When he looked up, Clancy saw there were tears in his eyes. "What a day!" he said lightly, trying unsuccessfully to recover his composure. "First I am released and now...this." He laughed briefly. "I don't suppose the invitation extends to my Uncle Vittorio?"

"No, it doesn't, you cheeky pup," Clancy returned. "And after I've telephoned him from this bar, I hope I never hear of him again, so I do."

Vittorio Vetti put down the telephone. "That was my driver," he said. "He has Paolo." He fixed Tony Cavellini with a penetrating stare. "He says Paolo has a black eye and is badly bruised."

Cavellini shrugged. "He tried to escape. When he was caught, he laid into everyone around him. A couple of my guys look worse than he does."

Vittorio smiled briefly. "Okay. Are we all set?"

Cavellini nodded. "I'm happy with the accounts."

He signalled to his two beefy minders who lounged near the door, bored and hungry after three hours watching the boss pore over Vetti's ledgers. The largest of them opened the door and checked with his two colleagues outside. "Okay, boss," he said.

"You can go, Vittorio, but don't try anything," Cavellini said warily. "And remember, this is for keeps. No comeback."

Vittorio stood up. "How could I try anything? You went over the place with a fine-toothed comb," he said. "Don't worry, Tony. I know when it's time to quit." He walked to the window and picked up a small statuette from the ledge.

"Would you believe it? I almost forgot this," he said. "My mother gave it to me thirty years ago. I took the rest of my stuff out last night." He returned to the table. "You know, Tony, I'm not sorry to be going. The only other thing I have to take care of is..."

It was over in seconds. The revolver appeared in his hand and fired into Tony Cavellini's heart at the precise moment that his men opened the door and shot Cavellini's two henchmen in the back.

Vittorio Vetti surveyed the carnage. Cavellini lay back in his chair, his mouth open in surprise, he had died instantly. One of his minders was also dead, but the big one moved and screamed. Vetti put the revolver to his head and fired. It was suddenly very quiet.

"Good job, boys," Vetti said to the two men in the doorway.

"Worked like clockwork, boss," said one of them.

"Yes," Vetti said.

He walked back behind the table. "This was excellent," he said, pushing back into place the wooden flange which had been fixed along the edge of the table. "That carpenter deserves a bonus. They never suspected a thing." He worked the flange again, "I think I'll keep this. You never know when it might come in handy."

The tension was eased and all three laughed, a little too loudly. One of the men said, "You don't want your desk back in here?"

"No. I'll keep the table." Vetti said. "But you can put back my good rug. You'd better burn this one." He kicked at the bloodstained rug and walked to the door. "Get everything cleaned up. You know what to do. I won't be in tomorrow, I'm going to see Paolo. Make sure the decorator does a good job." He felt in his jacket pocket and extracted two envelopes. "Here we are, boys," he said, handing an envelope to each of them. "The bonus, as promised."

He left the office and surveyed the scene on the landing, where two more of Cavellini's men lay in their own blood. "Good work, boys," he said to the two men standing guard over the bodies. "You know what to do now." He took two more envelopes from his pocket and handed them out. "Are the laundry baskets ready?"

"All organised, boss."

"Good. Then I'll leave you to it."

Vetti went downstairs and through the laundry to the street. One more envelope to go and then he could put this sorry business behind him.

On the corner a man selling newspapers looked up as he approached. "Alright, Mr. Vetti?"

"Of course. Well done." He gave the last envelope to the newspaper seller, who smiled happily as he accepted it. "It wasn't that easy to see, Mr. Vetti. I nearly missed you at the window. The sun was in my eyes."

"I'm glad you didn't," said Vittorio, and hailed a cab.

"Tony Cavellini," Anna said, poring over the newspaper.

"What's that?" Clancy was not really listening. Although a week had passed since the day of Paolo's release, the coolness between himself and Anna was still there. He reached for another slice of toast and returned to his own paper.

"Tony Cavellini. Wasn't that the name of the gangster who took James, the one who was trying to take over Vittorio Vetti's business?"

"Anna, will you never stop?" Clancy said with some irritation. "You know I don't wish to discuss...."

"Clancy, was it? Was it Tony Cavellini?" Her tone was urgent.

"Yes, I think so. What now?"

"His body has washed up at Greenwich. He had been shot." She perused the paper. "It says here, 'This is the third victim of New York's current gang wars to be washed up in the area this week.' Further down it says...."

"Let me see that."

Anna handed him the newspaper and Clancy read the piece with mounting dismay. "Will it never end?" he said at last, his face ashen.

Anna stared at him with dawning realisation. "You don't think it was Vittorio?" she said, aghast.

"Of course it was Vittorio! Oh, God!" Clancy put his head in his hands.

"You can't know that for sure."

Clancy's fist thumped down on the breakfast table so hard that the crockery rattled. "There you go again. Defending that murdering gangster."

"I'm not defending him, Clancy," Anna said, startled at the violence of her husband's outburst. "I just thought...."

"You didn't. You didn't think, that's the whole trouble, so it is." Clancy's voice was quieter now. "Anna, does it ever occur to you to defend me instead of the Vetti family?"

"You?" The surprise showed in her voice. "Why should you need defending?"

"You still can't see it, can you?" Clancy said, exasperated. "Anna, Vittorio used me. He used me to get Paolo out, and when I rang him...yes, Anna, I...when I gave him the signal that Paolo was free, he went ahead and did this...this terrible thing."

Anna stared at him in horror. "Oh, Clancy. Do you really think that is how it happened'?"

"Yes, I do. God forgive me, I do."

"But you didn't know! How could you know he would do something so dreadful?"

"Whether I knew or not doesn't alter the fact that I was an accessory."

"Of course you weren't. You only went to drive Paolo home."

"That is what I thought, Anna. But I should have known that nothing is simple when you are dealing with these monsters." Clancy sighed, and looked at his wife a long time. "Are you at last beginning to understand, Anna, why I wanted to steer well clear of the Vettis? Do you see how easy it is to get drawn in to their world?"

"Yes," she admitted, "if you are right and Vittorio did this dreadful thing." In her mind she was back at Vetti's home on the day of Jennie's wedding, and the man beside her was talking of his concern for his nephew and discussing his roses. It seemed impossible that Clancy was talking about the same person, and yet these events had happened, James had been kidnapped, Paolo had been badly beaten, and now...?

"It's not a question of being right," Clancy was saying. "Do you think I care about being right? This is too serious for either of us to score points, so it is."

"I have already told you," she said, "that I intend to stop selling any alcoholic drinks in the restaurants."

"It's a bit late for that, now the damage is done," Clancy retorted bitterly.

"Well, shall we say I have seen the light at last? Does that satisfy you? What else would you like me to admit to? Being a bad mother?"

"There's no need for sarcasm, Anna." Clancy got up from the table and walked to the door. He turned. "Do you really think you can stop this thing, like turning off a tap? It has its own momentum; it goes on and on."

"Now you're being melodramatic," she said.

"Am I? What do you think will happen now?" Clancy demanded. "Do you imagine that Cavellini's friends will let it be?"

She stared at him, her eyes round. "Perhaps you're right. We must warn Paolo and Jennie."

"Don't you dare!" Clancy yelled, finally losing his temper. "It is nothing to do with you. Do you think they aren't capable of reading the paper? That they don't know what is going on?" He came back to the breakfast table and caught Anna's arm. "Never in all the years we have been married have I ordered you to do anything, Anna, but this is different. You will not get in touch with that family."

"Not even Jennie?"

"Not even Jennie. Not until this has quietened down. Do you understand me?"

"Yes, Clancy. I understand."

In the back of his car on the way to the office, Clancy went over the whole affair again and again. He fumed at being dragged into Vittorio's duplicity; he fumed at Anna's acceptance of Vittorio Vetti at face value; and he fumed at James for deceiving him over his friendship with Paolo. But most of all he fumed at himself, for he felt such a bully.

A further week elapsed before Tony Cavellini's brother Giovanni arrived in New York from Chicago. Despite his diligence, he was never able to ascertain exactly what had happened to his brother, but he was certain of the identity of his murderer, and of the reason behind the killings. He was in no hurry to extract his revenge on Vittorio Vetti's person, as he explained to the thin-faced little man who sat next to him in the booth at Selby's bar.

"That comes later, Dino," he said. "Don't be so impatient." He glowered into his beer; he had begun to brood again. He had always disliked his brother, but in death, Tony seemed to have acquired a more likeable personality. In any case, he reflected, family was family. He took a swig from his glass.

"The first thing," he said, "is to show Vetti we mean business." He smiled evilly at Dino. "You know how we shall convince him of that. Then, when he's convinced, I shall finish what Tony started. And if Vittorio hasn't blown his brains out by that time, you can have him."

He motioned to the waiter for another beer. "Not for you," he admonished Dino gently, "not until after the job is done. You have the stuff?"

Dino nodded. "No problem, boss. There's still lots of war surplus around."

"Grenade or bomb?" Giovanni asked.

Dino grinned. "Both."

"Good. There must be no mess up, Dino. This time he must be killed. Mind you, I quite like the idea of Paolo Vetti suffering a bit before he dies."

In the event, Paolo did not suffer. When Dino threw the bomb into the bedroom of the bungalow at two in the morning, Paolo died instantly. Jennie, lying in his arms in the big double bed, survived until the ambulance arrived, but was dead before she reached the hospital.

Anna Sullivan woke with a start. The rug had slipped down to the deck and it was almost dark. For a moment, she hardly knew where she was, then realised she had fallen asleep in the deck chair. She shivered, the night air had a chill to it, and her dreams, if dreams they were, had disturbed her.

She got up from the deck chair wearily and made her way to her stateroom, meeting the cabin steward in the corridor. On impulse, she asked him to bring her a whisky and soda and waited while he opened her cabin door. Once inside, she assuaged her guilt at having ordered such an un-feminine drink by telling herself that the whisky was medicinal. She had asked for it because she had become cold on deck. She liked whisky and drank it occasionally at home in New York, but never in public, although she had noticed that some of the bright young things on the ship seemed to drink whatever they liked.

Bright young things. She sat in front of her dressing mirror and looked at herself minutely, realising she had not done this for a very long time. *Bright young things*, she thought again, *so sure of themselves and so frivolous, like that awful Betty Neville.*

I'm not a bright young thing. Thirty-seven now, and a month ago most people would have said I didn't look it. I do now. Strange how grief and stress affect one's looks. I don't think I ever was a bright young thing, not even in France. I was young, and a bit silly perhaps, but I never...no, not in all my life...never was I frivolous, I always had to work too hard.

Perhaps that was the problem. What was it Clancy had said that awful night when they heard of the bombing, and she had screamed at him, yes, screamed like a fishwife, that it was all his fault, that Paolo and Jennie would be alive if only he hadn't stopped her from warning them.

She sighed. *There you go again. There's no point in going over it, it always comes out the same. You know it wasn't Clancy's fault, it wasn't anyone's fault, except perhaps Vittorio and all he stood for.* But if she knew it wasn't Clancy's fault, why did she still blame him? Why had her bitterness led her to suggest this trial separation? She could hear herself, hear her own voice tight and controlled, proposing this trip as a way of their avoiding each other for a while. She stared at the mirror but could see only Clancy's face, the hurt in the Irish eyes, then the cool response, "If that is what you wish, I've no objection."

She started as there was a knock on the door. It was the steward with her whisky and soda. "Will that be all, ma'am?"

"Yes, thank you. Good night."

"Good night, Mrs. Sullivan."

She sat down at the dressing table again and sipped her whisky. What had she been trying to remember? Oh yes, what it was that Clancy had said that awful night...about her being obsessed by money and putting the business before everything else, dealing with gangsters in spite of the risk to James' safety.

And then that awful moment, when she had screamed how dare he say that, he was not even James's father. She could still hardly believe she had uttered those dreadful words, and the look of shock on Clancy's face still haunted her. She knew now that she was so stung by his accusations that she had been trying to hit back in any way she could, but she would never forgive herself for those words and she could not take them back.

Was it true what Clancy had said? Perhaps it was. She had certainly insisted on continuing to supply liquor at the restaurants when Prohibition came in, but she had never realised it would lead to James becoming involved. She gave a rueful smile at her reflection. She had not realised, any more than Clancy had realised, what would happen when he forbade her to get in touch with Paolo and Jennie.

What a mess. And afterwards...well, whoever was it that coined the phrase "gentlemen of the press"? Gentlemen they certainly were not. Neither were the police, with their questions about Paolo and Jennie meeting at the restaurant, and the endless digging into how much she knew about Vittorio's activities.

Anna sipped her whisky, wondering again why she was making this trip. It had seemed logical at the time; she could hardly wait to get away. Clancy's presence made her nervous. They needed to talk but didn't seem to know where to begin. Perhaps she had been trying to escape from the whole situation, the press, the police, James' grief, her own grief at having lost her dearest woman friend and, of course, her grief at having lost Paolo. Dear, funny, handsome Paolo, she thought, with his overactive ego and his charming good manners. There would be no more red roses on her birthday ever again.

It wasn't simply escape, even if that was part of it. She longed to see Will again. She wondered if her brother would still be the same. Was he still so calm and dependable or had his stoicism been destroyed along with Billy in Gallipoli? She thought of Mary, and Dottie, now married herself, and Andrew, who she had never seen, and whom she thought of as "little Andrew" although he was seventeen now.

And Florence. How strange it would be to visit High Cedars again and see the old lady, now in her seventies, and to hear news of Robert perhaps. Anna began to undress, wondering if Florence had received her letter. She had written that she would call at High Cedars first, as she would be staying in Birmingham overnight and could easily call at Edgbaston before making the final journey to Will's new home.

I wonder if my picture is still on the wall in the sitting room, she thought, and she had a sudden desire to see *The Chainmaker's Child* again. It was as if in looking at the picture she might find a clue to herself, who she really was. Had she truly become what Clancy said, an obsessive businesswoman who put money and success before everything else, even her own son? Another thought struck her. Was it her experience of the good life at High Cedars and her rejection by Robert which had made her so determined to succeed?

At least she was thinking about things at last, she realised with some surprise. Perhaps the trip was doing her good after all. For weeks her brain had seemed turned to jelly and her thoughts nothing but an incoherent jumble of contradictory emotions, but today, at last, she was able to think more clearly.

She got into bed and turned out the lamp, still considering Clancy's hurtful words. In spite of their recent troubles, she had to admit Clancy had been a good husband and friend. She felt tears sting her eyes as she remembered the daily kindnesses, his loving care of herself and James, and the freedom he had always allowed her, so unlike the husbands of some of her acquaintances in New York.

She snuggled into her pillow. She missed Clancy, missed his physical presence; it felt so strange to be alone. She suddenly remembered a quiet moment some years before, when after making love, she was lying in Clancy's arms and he had told her how much he loved her. She had smiled and snuggled into his neck, and he had said softly, "And you, Anna? You have never told me you love me."

She recalled the moment of sudden panic his words had caused. She had smiled and said, "Don't be silly," but she could not say the words she knew he needed to hear. In all the years of their marriage she had never said, "I love you, Clancy."

How strange to recall that feeling here, in her lonely bed in the stateroom aboard the *Ocean Star*, and to know, if she was honest, that nothing had changed. Why was that?

The answer came, like icicles dripping the cold truth into her numbed brain. She had never been able to say "I love you" to Clancy...because he was not Robert.

PART FOUR

RESOLUTIONS

Illusions

Anna stared fixedly at the picture. *The Chainmaker's Child* seemed less impressive than she remembered, and to her surprise, it had little effect upon her. If she was truthful, she had to admit it was well painted, although the brushwork could not compare with Sylvie's. It was the subject matter which was all wrong. It was untruthful, she thought, an idealised version of the event, as she had tried to explain to Robert so many years ago when they had toasted muffins at Dudley Castle. The beautiful, apple-cheeked child bouncing on the bellows, her golden hair flying against the sparks of the chainshop, bore little resemblance to her memory of herself at that age. And yet, she reflected, who was she to say the image was untrue if that was what the painter saw?

She smiled, remembering how excited she had been when the whole family had trudged off to Dudley Art Gallery to see "our Anna on the wall." Then, her young eyes had revelled in this false portrayal of herself, but since that time, her critical faculties had been developed, and she had Robert to thank for that, for lighting her first spark of interest. In New York she had attended many galleries and exhibitions, (often in the company of Jennie, she recalled with a pang) and she had been privileged to see some of the best work of both early and modern painters. She suddenly realised that she still considered Sylvie's painting to be superb, whereas *The Chainmaker's Child* now seemed self-indulgent, amateur.

The sitting room door opened and Florence came in slowly, leaning on a stick and attended by a hovering maid. She seemed to have shrunk to two-thirds of her original size. She peered carefully at Anna through a lorgnette, secured around her neck by a black velvet ribbon. Her eyes, however, were as blue and lively as ever.

"Anna? Anna Gibson? Is it really you?"

"Yes, Florence. After all these years, it is me. You were expecting me, of course?"

"Oh yes. I had your letter almost two weeks ago. I was so delighted, so happy."

They embraced, and then the maid helped the old lady to a chair, and said, "I'll make some tea for you and your visitor, Mrs. Nicholson."

Florence smiled sweetly, and as the maid departed, she said, "Come and sit near me, Anna, so I can see you properly. My, what a grand lady you have become. Look at this...and this." Her frail old fingers smoothed the rose velvet of Anna's walking suit, lingering on the braid trim, and then travelling to the exquisite cameo brooch on Anna's lapel. She stopped. "Oh, my goodness! How rude of me to comment on your dress. What will you think of me?" Her tone became confidential. "It's not often I have such an elegant visitor these days. My manners are deserting me as I grow older."

Anna laughed. "Oh, Florence, it is so good to see you. And as for manners, do you remember the first time I came here, and you had to tell me I didn't have to clear everything on my plate at dinner?"

The next hour was spent in happy recollection for both women. As they enjoyed their tea, Florence was anxious to fill in the gaps concerning Anna's life in New York, her knowledge being limited to the news contained in the annual letters they had always exchanged at Christmas. Her questions reassured Anna that, although physically she was frail, Florence's mental abilities were unimpaired. Anna found herself immediately at ease, as had happened when she met Florence so long ago. For the first time since Jennie's death, Anna felt that particular empathy which arises unbidden between close women friends, and she had to fight the urge to pour out all her troubles to the old lady. She resisted this impulse, realising that the pressures of Prohibition would be hard for anyone in England to understand, and instead turned the conversation to Florence and her family.

Florence chatted amiably about her eldest son Andrew and his success in the family business, and Anna noticed that she seemed reluctant to mention Robert.

Eventually Anna took the initiative. "And Robert, how is he? Is he still painting? His family must be quite grown up now."

"Yes, his boy is seventeen this year. He is also called Robert, you know."

"Yes, he is just a little younger than James," Anna said faintly.

"Yes. He has two girls, as well. I think I told you in one of my letters. Cressida is fifteen this year and Beatrice a year younger, both at such a lovely age." Florence's eyes misted as she added, "Of course, I don't see them any more. I haven't seen them since they were quite small."

"Oh?" Anna said with concern. "Do they not travel to see you? Perhaps you could have gone to Cannes."

"No, Anna, you don't understand," Florence interrupted gently. "Robert and Delphine do not live together now, not for some years." She hesitated. "I did try to put it in a letter to you, but I tore it up. It's not the sort of thing you can write down somehow."

The subject was obviously distressing, and Anna said gently, "I'm so sorry, Florence. It must have been painful for you, and not to see your grandchildren."

"Yes it was, but to be honest, I can't blame Delphine. After she and Robert separated...well, perhaps separated gives the wrong impression, she threw him out, Delphine wanted to sever all links with Robert, and that included his family. She wrote me a long letter explaining what had happened. Of course it was only her point of view, but in all the circumstances, I can't blame her." Florence looked up, and Anna saw her eyes were full of tears. "He is my son, Anna, and you know I love him, but he has always been such a...such a...libertine."

It was not the word Anna had expected, and she felt a momentary shock. "Oh, I'm sure not Florence," she soothed, and was astonished at the old lady's bitter response.

"Don't try to make excuses for him, Anna," she said. "I have heard them all, over and over again, and from his own lips. You knew him for a short time when he was young, and even then I was worried about him. He has never been able to leave the ladies alone." Her mouth twisted. "Ladies is the wrong word. I mean women...or worse."

"Florence!" Anna said, genuinely perturbed. "You don't mean that."

"Oh, yes, I do." Florence gave a rueful smile. "You know, Anna, when Robert said he was taking you to France that summer, I thought the worst even then. I thought he intended to try to take advantage of you." She smiled again. "I should have known you had too much sense to allow yourself to be compromised." She sighed. "I knew him so well, you see, even then." She hesitated, and then asked quietly, "Was I right? Did he try...?" Her eyes met Anna's, and there was more than a question there. It was a plea.

Anna was merciful. "You were wrong," she said. "Robert was always a perfect gentleman toward me."

Florence's smile was of relief as well as gratitude. "I'm really glad," she said. "I was always a little worried about that. You probably think I shouldn't talk of Robert this way, but since he came home he's been such a trial."

"Came home? You mean he's in England?"

Florence looked surprised. "Of course, didn't I tell you? He came home about two years ago. He had nowhere left to go, you see, nowhere he would be welcome. After years of racketing around France, pretending to paint."

"Pretending?" Anna interrupted.

"Yes, I call it pretending because he always said he was painting but he never completed anything. The paintings he did of you here and that summer when you were at La Maison Blanche were the only real paintings he ever did."

"I see." Anna found these revelations astonishing. She attempted lightness. "Well, at least you must be able to see Robert more often now he's in England," she said.

"See him? Sometimes I wish I didn't. Men are such dreadful patients, and Robert must be one of the worst."

"Patients? Is Robert ill then?"

Florence looked embarrassed. "Oh, Anna, I'm

sorry. I thought you understood. Robert has come home to die. He's upstairs. I'll take you to see him if you wish."

Florence got slowly to her feet, and then she caught sight of Anna's anguished face. "I'm sorry, dear. Perhaps you would prefer not to see him, but he has so few visitors apart from Andrew and me. It will be quite proper. I shall come with you."

Anna found her tongue. "Yes, of course. I'd like to see him."

Florence moved so slowly that the journey up the well remembered staircase seemed interminable, but at last they were outside the heavy oak door to Robert's room, and Anna's heart was thumping so hard in her chest that she thought she would surely suffocate.

The huge bulk lying in the big double bed lay inert, turned away from the light streaming in from the bay window, and at first Anna thought they must be in the wrong room. Florence went over to the bed and said, "Robert dear, you have a visitor." There was no response and she repeated, "Robert dear, a visitor for you."

The bulky mass under the bedclothes moved, and from beneath the quilt, a large face appeared, blotchy and ravaged, the fleshy jowls hanging heavily over a thick flannel nightshirt. Anna stared. This was not Robert. Not only was it not him, it was nothing like him, or like he had ever been.

Florence said, "Come on, dear. I'll help you sit up." She put her hand under his arm and attempted to help him pull himself up, but it was painful work, and in spite of her revulsion, Anna went to the other side of the bed and put a hand under his other arm, and they hauled him up onto the pillows.

The grotesque figure in the bed relaxed his head

back, panting with effort, and said, "Who's that?"

Anna stared at him and he stared back. There was not a hint of recognition from either of them. It could not be Robert, she told herself, those piggy eyes, almost hidden in the fleshy, swollen eyelids, that patchy grey hair which seemed not to have thinned evenly but to have come out in clumps, leaving areas of baldness interspersed with tufts of sparse, wispy thatch.

"It's Anna, dear," Florence was saying, "little Anna Gibson. You remember. I told you we had kept in touch. She's been living in America." The small eyes glinted, but there was no change of expression. He stared at Anna again. "Anna," Florence went on earnestly, "the chainmaker's child, who Daddy painted. You remember, dear, you painted her too. She went to France with you many years ago, to La Maison Blanche."

Anna began to feel she was in some sort of horrific nightmare, from which she must fight to wake up. This was not Robert, she told herself. It couldn't be. Suddenly the man in the bed turned, a small gesture, a movement of the head as if to flick back a lock of hair which was no longer there, and she knew at last that this bloated creature was indeed Robert.

To her embarrassment, he appeared to have completely forgotten her. Despite Florence's encouragement, his expression remained vacant and disinterested. Anna was beginning to feel slightly sick, partly from the shock of Robert's appearance, but also from the heavy, putrid smell which emanated from the bed.

She turned towards the window, her stomach heaving, and saw the picture on the opposite wall. She caught her breath. It was Robert's painting of herself, seated on the grass above the beach at

Locquirec. The freshness and beauty of the scene was out of place in the fetid atmosphere of decay and death, and Anna approached the picture, drawn as if by a magnet. She feasted her eyes on the well remembered details, as if she would gather its cherished secrets to herself. The deep rooted treasury of half forgotten moments came suddenly to the fore, and on impulse, she grasped the painting with both hands and took it down.

"Look, Robert," she said, balancing the canvas on the bed so he could see it. "This is me. At Locquirec. Remember?"

The vacant eyes wandered over the picture for a few moments. Slowly there was a glimmer, a second of recognition, then a horrible, leering grimace which split the livid face and revealed the slack, slavering mouth. "The little...chainmaker," he gasped, his words slurring with effort. "Was good fun...plump little bosom." He gave a kind of involuntary snort, as if he would laugh if he could. He wagged a pudgy finger at the picture. "Ignorant as hell," he wheezed, "but I taught her." The wheezing became worse and degenerated into a coughing fit as he spat out, "I had 'em all. Every one I ever wanted...and they loved it...all of them." The fat hand grabbed at the quilt as the paroxysm increased. When at last it subsided, he gasped, "Molly Fleming...what a doer!"

"Robert, be quiet!" Florence demanded. She turned to Anna, and her face was quite serene. "I'm afraid he doesn't remember you, my dear. He has you mixed up with someone else. I'm so sorry. We had better leave him to rest."

Florence rearranged Robert's pillows as Anna, trembling slightly, replaced the picture. A wave of nausea swept over her, and she hastened to the door, unable even to turn her head for a last sight of the pathetic figure who had once been her lover. Her numbed mind could cope with only one thought, *Get away, get away,* and once back in the sitting room, she feigned surprise at the time, and explained to Florence that she must leave. The old lady was apologetic.

"I am sorry, Anna, I realise now it would have been best for you not to see Robert. I have grown used to it, of course, but his appearance is a shock to anyone who hasn't seen him for some time. And his memory...it's the illness of course, the brain damage is progressive."

Anna nodded. Her knowledge of such things was very limited, but already one word was invading her teeming brain. She kissed Florence goodbye, climbed into the hired car which the hotel had arranged for her, and instructed the driver to go to Sandley Heath. As she waved goodbye to Florence, and left High Cedars for the last time, the vile word still resounded over and over in her head. Syphilis...syphilis...syphilis.

Will

As the hired car made its way to Sandley Heath, Anna was in turmoil. Her mind kept returning to the big bedroom at High Cedars, to the foul-mouthed, revolting shambles that Robert had become. She still could not believe it, and yet....

The indicators had been there all the time, she now acknowledged bitterly, if only she had possessed the wit to see them. How could she have been so wrong, so deluded? In spite of all the evidence to the contrary, she had clung to the idea that Robert had felt as she did, that their love affair had been something very special. She now saw with devastating clarity that for Robert their affair had been nothing more than one in a long series of such liaisons, and she felt shamed and degraded by the knowledge.

As she began to recover her equanimity, Anna realised it was perhaps understandable that she had been taken in as a young and inexperienced girl, but since then? Could she ever forgive herself for holding on to her girlish dream for so long, and not only holding on, but cherishing it, nurturing it, until it became more real than reality itself? Reality?

Reality was Clancy, and James, and the business and New York, and the beloved family she was going to see very soon. Her preoccupation with the past had caused Clancy unhappiness, she knew that, and now it was too late to put it right.

The driver stopped the car, and turned to speak to her. "Are you sure this is the right place, madam?"

"Yes, we are almost there," Anna said. "Take the next turning right and go down the hill into Sandley Heath. Drive slowly, please. I want to look."

The driver raised his eyebrows but complied with the request. *Yours is not to reason why,* he told himself. *If this fine lady wants to go slumming in a rough area, it's her business, I suppose. I only hope the kids don't throw stones at the car. This may be the first car ever to drive down here,* he thought, noting the grimy ramshackle terraces and the general air of neglect.

As the car made its way down the hill, Anna opened her window. The familiar smell of home drifted in, an odour of smoke, mud and soot, but there was something missing. Anna smiled as she realised the middens in Tibbetts Yard had been pulled down.

A few more buildings had gone too, she noticed. Most of them had been small forges run by individual families; many of the larger premises remained. As the car passed the chainshop where Clancy had worked, she drew in her breath, almost expecting him to appear in the doorway and wave to her as he had done so many times. She could see him now, striding up the bank in his working clothes. *I thought I'd catch ye, so I did.*

"Is this far enough, madam?" the driver asked.

"Er...yes. Pull up on the left and wait for me, please." Anna got out of the car and surveyed the scene. Apart from the loss of the smaller forges, not much had changed. She looked across to the chainshop where she had worked for Ma Higgins. It was the same as she remembered, but smaller somehow. On impulse, Anna walked down the roughly cobbled road and picked her way across the waste ground to the chainshop. Inside, several women were hammering and striking, and suddenly it was as if she had never left.

The girl at the first hearth inside the door caught sight of Anna and stopped hammering to gawk. A stout middle aged woman approached and asked if she could help.

Anna stared at her. "Maisie? Maisie Collins...?"

The woman eyed her suspiciously.

"It's me, Maisie. Anna...Anna Gibson."

She watched Maisie's expression change from suspicion to delight. "Anna? Is it really yo'?" Maisie turned to the other women, who had all stopped work to watch the encounter. "Look girls, this is Anna...Anna Gibson as was, 'er who married an Irish lad an' went off to America."

The other women nodded their heads slightly and Anna smiled back. Maisie told them to get back to work and they did so, stealing an occasional glance at the well dressed stranger as they hammered. Anna and Maisie walked outside to talk.

"Yo've done well fer yerself," Maisie said.

"Yes, Maisie, we have been very lucky in America. We had to work hard but we have done well."

"'Ave yo' come 'ome fer good?"

"No, just a visit, to see Will and the family."

"Arr, I 'eard they 'ad gone to live in the country. Real gentlefolks now, so they say."

"And you, Maisie? What has happened here?"

Over the next few minutes, Anna learned that old Betty Potts was dead and Ma Higgins had retired some five years earlier. The chainshop now belonged to a man called John Sampson, who visited rarely and left the day to day running of the forge to Maisie, who was now in charge.

"Oh, Maisie, I'm so pleased. You were always a good worker," Anna said.

For some reason, this appeared to anger Maisie. "Oh, yes?" she said acidly. "An' 'ow would yo' know if I'm a good waerker? One of the bosses now, are yer?"

"Of course not, Maisie. I only meant...."

"I know what yo' meant. Yo' always was Miss Toffeenose, an' now yo've turned into Lady Muck. Yo' come 'ere fer a look at what yo' escaped from. Well now yo've 'ad yer eyeful, bugger off!"

Anna stared at her in amazement and decided to leave. After only a few steps, she turned back, saying, "Maisie, how much do the girls make now? In a week?"

Maisie eyed her narrowly. "It depends."

"I know, but how much in a good week?"

"A good wik can be as much as sixteen shillin's."

Anna fished in her purse. "And how many girls are here?"

"Eight, with me it's nine."

"Here's ten pounds," Anna said, holding out the money. "A pound for each girl and two for you. For old time's sake, Maisie," she added, as Maisie's mouth dropped open. "I haven't forgotten what an extra week's pay can mean."

"But...it's so much," Maisie said.

"I can afford it," Anna said tartly. "As you say, I'm Lady Muck now." She turned to go. "If you don't want my friendship, perhaps you'll take my money."

Maisie caught her up halfway across the waste ground. "Anna...Anna, I'm sorry. I dae mean it...about Lady Muck."

Anna regarded her sadly. "Maisie, because I

went to America and got lucky doesn't mean I've forgotten my past."

"I know. I shouldn't 'ave said what I did. It was just...well...look at yo', Anna, dressed up like a real bobby dazzler, an' look at me. These am the on'y shoes I got an' they'm stuffed up wi' cardboard. Yo' got out, Anna. Yo' 'ad the chance wi' Clancy Sullivan. Not many of us got a bloke like 'im."

"I know, Maisie. I was lucky and I know it. Are we still friends?"

Maisie nodded. "The money, do yo' mean it?" She held it out in her hand. "All this?"

"Yes," Anna laughed. "Tell them it's from one of their own who went to America and got rich."

On impulse, she kissed Maisie and then made her way back across the waste ground to the road. As she turned into Dawkins Street, she looked back, and Maisie waved.

Outside number twenty-two, Anna hesitated. She had intended to knock at the door, knowing that when she explained who she was, the new tenant would certainly invite her inside for a look at her old home and probably a cup of tea and a chat as well. Now she regarded the peeling paintwork and the dingy net curtain with sadness and a feeling of futility. Maisie had made her see there was no going back. Suddenly it all seemed irrelevant: the tiny terraced house, the chainshop, Sandley Heath itself...and High Cedars.

She turned and walked quickly back to the car, trying not to notice the few old wives who had come out onto their front doorsteps to look at her. She only allowed herself one slight detour to look at the tiny hovel Clancy and his mother had shared, so she could truthfully report to him she had seen it. Then she got into the car and gave the driver Will's address.

As they left the grimy suburbs and turned toward the countryside, Anna relaxed. This was the England she had known on Sunday school outings and walks with Clancy, and she had forgotten how beautiful it was. Even the skies seemed to lift, and the sun shone weakly through small scudding clouds, as the car bowled along the leafy lanes bordered by banks heavy with the scent of yarrow and wild thyme.

Anna felt her excitement mount. "It's on the road to Wombourn," she said to the driver.

"Yes, I know where it is," he responded. "Very nice countryside out that way."

Anna wondered suddenly whether Will and Mary had changed. It was clear she had changed herself. Perhaps, like Maisie, they would think she had become Lady Muck. Everyone must have changed over the years. She couldn't expect otherwise. It was true Florence was the same, but Robert and Maisie...Robert was a dying wreck, and Maisie had become embittered and cynical, and no wonder.

What a day it had been, Anna reflected. A day of surprises, and not all pleasant. She did not think she could cope with any more. If Will had changed, if dear, lovely, dependable Will had changed, she could not bear it. Her nervousness increased by the mile, and when the car eventually stopped she was reluctant to get out.

It was a square detached house, with five Georgian style windows and a porch over the central front door. There was a path bordered by colourful plants, and a small wooden gate.

The driver opened the car door. "You go on up, madam. I'll unload the luggage."

Anna opened the gate nervously and started up the path. She had only gone a few steps when the front door burst open and a young man came flying down the path toward her. He skidded to a stop a few feet in front of her, a huge grin on his face.

"You're my Aunt Anna," he said excitedly. "I can tell from your photograph, although you're even better looking than I thought. I was watching from the window."

Anna looked at him closely. "Andrew? You must be Andrew." It was heartbreaking to see him standing there, with such a look of Billy.

"That's me. May I give you a kiss, Auntie?"

Anna smiled at him and Andrew kissed her on the cheek. Over his shoulder, Anna could see another figure had appeared in the doorway, and a moment later, Will was ambling down the path towards her, as big and handsome as ever, although a little grey. The smile on his face was as large as his generous heart. Suddenly, the years rolled away, and Anna knew for certain that Will would never change. He would always be there, solid and dependable as a rock, sane and practical and kind. Will opened his arms wide, and with a shriek of pure joy, Anna flung herself into her brother's arms.

Getting to know her family again proved to be a healing experience for Anna, and her welcome was such that it became necessary for her to insist that she not be waited on, but be treated as she should be, as one of the family. Nevertheless, she was awakened by a cup of tea in bed each morning and found that numerous little treats had been devised for her, to everyone's mutual enjoyment. Dottie visited with her new husband Jack Drew, who had recently qualified as a chemist, and the young couple confided to her their plans to open a small shop as soon as they could find the right site. Anna found she was able to assist with much practical advice, and the knowledge that she had helped Dottie and Jack diffused the sadness she felt when they had to leave.

It had not occurred to Anna that she had become something of a folk hero to her family in England, but she now discovered this was the case. Dottie and Andrew had been brought up on tales of their Aunt Anna and Uncle Clancy's success in New York, and there had been much excitement when letters arrived. Then there had been wonderful presents at Christmas and birthdays, and the gifts of money which provided new shoes and warm coats. Finally there was the extraordinary day when Aunt Anna and Uncle Clancy had sent them money to move to the country and buy this house.

For each member of the family, the move had meant different things. For Dottie and Andrew, it meant a better education locally and clean fresh air. For Will, it meant release from the drudgery of chainmaking and from the stress of trying to earn enough to feed his family. For Mary, it meant never again having to share a copper for the washing and having a spacious kitchen in which to work. For the whole family, it meant a private closet and washing facilities, which they had never known before.

For the first few evenings of the visit, Anna, Will and Mary sat around the fire and talked until the early hours of the morning, bringing each other up to date with the details of their lives, the background impossible to include in letters. Anna talked about her early days in New York and how the business had developed, and Will and Mary explained they had chosen this particular house because it had over an acre of land, which had enabled them to develop a small business growing vegetables for the local markets. They had received much help and advice from George Gibson before his death, and the vegetable business was now firmly established and showing a profit.

At length, they were able to speak of Billy, and Will and Mary filled in the details which they had found too harrowing to put down on paper.

"Some o' the forces landed virtually unopposed," Will said. "But at Sedd-el-Bahr, they walked into a wall o' fire, an' they was just mowed down, an' our Billy was one of 'em. There was bad mistakes made, an' some o' the generals lost their jobs over it, but that don't 'elp our Billy or any o' the others. There was thousands of Anzacs killed an' all."

"Arr," Mary agreed. "It wouldn't be so 'ard if yo' felt it was summat worth dyin' for, but it was just a waste...an awful waste. At least that's what we think."

And so they talked of Billy, and wept a little together, and Will showed Anna a faded photograph of his son in uniform, and told her that just before Billy left, he had joked that when he had seen off the Boche, he would be back home for a quick visit before he set off for America to see his Aunt Anna, who he remembered well from childhood. He had a mind, he had told them, to make his fortune in America as well.

After a week, Anna felt sufficiently at home to take Will and Mary fully into her confidence. The gangland killings had not made the British papers, and as yet Anna had not even mentioned the problems which Prohibition had brought. One evening when Andrew had gone out to a local meeting of the Wireless Society, Anna told them the whole sorry tale. She took her time, and began with Jennie, explaining how she had joined the business from the orphanage, and how fond she and Clancy had become of her. She told them of Paolo's arrival, and of the wedding, and of Vittorio Vetti. As her story unfolded, she spared them nothing, recounting the events as they had occurred, including her own mistakes. When she had finished, Will and Mary sat for a few moments in horrified silence.

"That's a terrible tale, our Anna," Will said at length. "Yo' must 'ave bin out o' your mind when James was took. An' that poor young couple, an' a babby on the way.... My, what wickedness!"

"Arr," Mary agreed. "We 'eard about Prohibition, o' course, but I never thought it would affect yo'."

"It wouldn't have done if I had listened to Clancy," Anna said bitterly.

"Well now, it's easy to be wise after the event, as they say," Will said. "Yo' couldn't 'ave known what was to 'appen. Mary an' me, we thought summat was worryin' yer. We said as much."

"Arr we did," Mary agreed, "but I never thought o' anythin' like this. No wonder yo' wanted ter get away fer a break."

"It wasn't only that," Anna said. "For years I have been wanting to come home for a visit, but I kept putting it off. When all this happened it seemed the one sensible thing I could do."

"Well, I'm glad yo' told us, our Anna," Will said. "A bad thing like that needs airin', not bottlin' up."

"Yes, that's true," Anna responded. "I feel better already for having talked about it. It has made me face it."

Will smiled. "There's one more thing yo' 'ave to face, our Anna, while yo' are 'ere. Every time I mention our dad yo' change the subject. Yo' never 'ave forgiven 'im, 'ave yer?"

Anna's face was closed. "It isn't a problem. He's dead now."

"Yes, an' it's time yo' visited 'is grave," Will said gently. "It's a nice walk to the church, so if it's fine termorrer, I'll tek yer there. We'll 'ave a picnic. Our Mary will put one up, won't yer love?"

"Arr, that'll be grand," Mary said, realising that Will wanted to have some time to talk to Anna alone.

"I don't mind," Anna said. "I shall enjoy the walk."

The weather proved fine and sunny the following day, and Anna and Will set out to walk to the village around noon, after Will had finished lifting vegetables. Will explained they would go across the fields, a private route which had been devised by the family as a short cut before they had the luxury of the car. Anna was slightly amused by the family attitude to the car, which was only used for special occasions and trips into Dudley for shopping. It seemed to Anna that the family gained as much joy from washing and polishing the already gleaming vehicle as from riding in it.

Will took the picnic basket and Anna carried a rug, and they made their way along the edge of Will's vegetable field as he talked about his crops and explained his plans for the future. He seemed very happy with his new life, Anna thought, surprised at the knowledge her brother seemed to have acquired.

They left Will and Mary's property and walked through a small wood, climbing quite steeply as they went. As they left the trees and came out into a field of pasture, Will pointed out the church spire in the distance. "That's where we're goin'," he said. "It's a nice little church. It'll tek us about an hour."

They set off across the field, and Will said directly, "That tale yo' told us last night, what's the rest of it?"

"What do you mean?" Anna said.

"Yo' cor kid me, our Anna. There's summat else. Is it Clancy?"

Anna felt a slight panic. "Oh, Will, we had the most awful row. We said dreadful things to each other."

"And yo' dae mek it up before yo' left?" Will asked.

"No. We had already disagreed about the business, and when James was taken it got worse. When Paolo and Jennie were killed it all came to a head."

"Do yo' love 'im?" Will asked.

Surprised at such a question from her brother, who rarely spoke of feelings, Anna said quickly, "Oh, yes, Will. Yes, I do. Clancy has been very good to me."

"Oh. I only wondered...because of what 'appened when yo' went away. I wondered if it 'ad worked out for yer."

Anna felt a wave of relief flood over her. Will was the one person in the world who might understand. Before she knew it, she was telling him of her years of obsession with the past, of the way she had kept memories of Robert Nicholson locked in her heart. She told him of her visit to High Cedars, and Will's face darkened as she described Robert's condition.

"'E was a bastard then and 'e's one now," Will said, "beggin' yer pardon fer the language, Anna."

"I know that now, Will, but I...how can I explain? He made such a difference to my life at that time. I truly loved him."

Will smiled. "Did yo' think I dae realise that?"

he said gently. "Anyone as knows yo', knows it 'ad ter be summat special fer yo' ter go off the rails, as it were. Clancy knew it too."

"Yes, and that's what I regret so much. Clancy is worth a hundred Robert Nicholsons, and now it's too late."

They came to a stile, and Will swung his long legs over it in one movement. "Come on, our kid," he said, "I'll give yer a leg up." Anna negotiated the stile, and Will pointed ahead. "There's a stream there," he said, "where we'll 'ave our picnic."

Anna spread the rug, and they sat down. Will opened the picnic basket and they helped themselves to Mary's pasties with a dollop of homemade chutney.

"So that's it?" Will asked. "That's what yo' are worried about?"

"Yes. When I left New York, Clancy and I were barely civil to each other. Things have gone so far, I don't think they will ever be right again." Anna poured some lemonade. "It's only since I came home I realise how much Clancy means to me," she admitted. "Will, what do you think?"

Will considered, munching a pasty appreciatively. Eventually, he said, "Well, if yer want the truth, I think yo'm doolallytap. Clancy was always potty about yo' an' I reckon 'e 'asn't changed. Yo' 'ave ter go 'ome an' tell 'im what yer just told me, that's all."

"But it's too late."

"No, not fer Clancy, it ain't. 'E's a good bloke, always was. It'll be all right, our Anna. In any case that's all yo' can do. Go an' work in the garden."

"Work in the garden?"

"Yes, at least that's what Voltaire says."

"Voltaire? What's he got to do with it?"

"Well, 'e reckons that at the end o' the day,

that's all any of us can do: go an' work in the garden, whatever our particular garden 'appens to be.
Your garden is Clancy, an' James, an' your business in New York, an' yo' just 'ave ter gerron wi'
it." Will bit into a second pasty, pleased at the effect his philosophy was having.

Anna began to laugh. "So that's all there is
to it?"

"When yo' come down to it, arr," Will said.

"And since when have you been reading
Voltaire?"

"Since I joined the W.E.A." Will said, and seeing the query on Anna's face he expanded, "The
Worker's Educational Society. We 'ave some really
good lectures, an' it meks yo' think. When I started
to read Candide, I thought it was daft at first. This
bloke Candide gets killed so many times, but no
matter what 'appens to 'im, there 'e is again, on
the next page." He laughed. "The tutor explained
it. It's just like life. No matter what 'appens to us,
we 'ave ter go on. At the end, Candide decides the
only thing to do is go an' work in the garden."

"I see," said Anna. "At least, I think I do."

Will began to pack up the picnic basket and
Anna was left reflecting on his words. Could it
really be so simple? Could she go home and start
again? Would Clancy allow her to pick up the
pieces? She looked at her brother with affection.
Trust Will to take any new piece of information,
even philosophy, and turn it to some practical
use. She began to laugh. Will quoting
Voltaire...times were changing indeed.

It took them only another fifteen minutes to
reach the tiny village and make their way to the
church. George Gibson's grave was towards the
back of the churchyard, where a crumbling wall
looked over to a row of straggling labourers' cot-

tages. Anna bent down and cleared a few dead flowers and tired twigs from the flower vase, evidence of Mary's last visit.

"Yo' wouldn't 'ave known 'im, Anna, 'e changed so much after we moved 'ere," Will said. "We 'ad a job to convince 'im to come, but once 'e was 'ere 'e loved it, 'ardly ever went to the pub."

"Really?" Anna said. She could not think of her father without thinking of him drunk.

"I never realised 'ow much 'e knew about country life," Will said, "but o' course that is 'ow 'e was brought up. 'E taught me a lot, especially about the vegetables." He laughed, remembering. "I couldn't beat 'im. 'E would be up before dawn an' 'ad two rows lifted before I was even stirrin'. That was until 'e got too frail, o' course."

Anna was intrigued in spite of herself. "And what did he do in the evenings," she asked, "if he wasn't in the pub?"

Will looked at her narrowly. "Do yo' want the truth?"

"Of course."

"'E used to sit by the fire an' read your letters, an' Clancy's, over an' over again. I think 'e knew 'em by 'eart. 'E was that proud o' yo'."

Anna's eyes opened wide. "Are you sure?"

"Course I'm sure. Per'aps yo' don't realise it, but yo' an' Clancy 'ad done everythin' fer the family that 'e wanted to do, an' couldn't. Providin' for us while we was at Sandley 'Eath, an' then buyin' us this place, an' the annuity. 'E could 'ardly believe it. I tell yer, 'e was real proud o' yo' an' Clancy."

Anna stooped and pulled out a small weed which was pushing its way through the gravel on the grave's surface. "I should have brought some flowers," she said.

"Yes," Will said, "yo' should 'ave."

"Tell me, Will...about when he died. Were you with him?"

"Yes, me an' Mary. 'E 'ad been sleepin' all day, an' we knew 'e 'adn't long. When 'e woke up, I saw 'e was lookin' at the side o' the bed. 'E 'ad your photograph there, on a little table. I knew what 'e was lookin' for, so I got it an' give it to 'im. 'E kissed the photograph, an' then 'e breathed out, 'eavy like, an' 'e was gone. It wasn't too bad, a death like that, in 'is bed at 'ome, with 'is family round 'im."

Anna turned away, feeling hot tears sting her eyes. She stared over the churchyard wall to the cottages beyond. After a moment, she called to Will. "Look, Will, that cottage down there, the one with the good show of dahlias in the back garden. Do you think they would sell some to us?"

After her walk with Will to the village, Anna knew it was time to make plans for her return to New York, and she booked a stateroom on the *Ocean Star* for a crossing two weeks later. She decided that for her last evening with the family she would cook a celebration dinner for them all, giving Mary a well deserved day off, and the luxury of a meal she had not helped to prepare. Anna chose the menu with care, to provide some surprises, but nothing too demanding on palates which were unused to the food she usually cooked for guests in New York. Dottie and her husband were sent invitations, and a few days before she was due to leave, Anna travelled to Dudley to buy ingredients not available locally. When she returned, Mary and Will came out to help unload the car.

"Goodness me, what a lot o' packages!" Mary exclaimed. "Yo'll need two cabins, not one."

"Presents for Clancy and James," Anna explained. "They must have presents from England.

That one isn't going," she said, nodding at the cardboard box Will was unloading from the car. "It's a family present. Come and see."

"What is it, Will?" Mary asked her husband as they reached the kitchen.

"Search me," Will said, depositing the box on the table. "Anna bought this while I was visitin' a couple o' greengrocers. I think I may 'ave another customer," he added with a wink. "They'm tekin' some greens this weekend as a try out."

"Oh, that's good news, our Will. Fetch our Andrew an' we can open this box. Yo' did say it was for all the family, Anna?"

"Yes, for everyone."

Andrew joined them, delighted by the prospect of a present. Will opened the box and took out some small packages. He put them on the table and began to open them one at a time.

"Whatever is it?" Mary said, slight disappointment in her voice.

"I know what it is!" Andrew said suddenly. "It's a wireless, isn't it, Auntie? A crystal set!"

"It never is?" Will said, as his mouth dropped open.

"I know how to put it together," Andrew said excitedly. "We do it at the Wireless society." He began to sort out the pieces of equipment. "This is a good one, Auntie."

"The best they had," Anna said, beaming.

"A wireless," Will said slowly. "It don't seem right somehow, a set just for ourselves."

"Of course it is," Anna said. "Soon everyone will have them, and now that the B.B.C. is broadcasting every day you'll be able to tune in to the news."

"Good 'eavens," Will said. He watched Andrew fiddling with the equipment. "Do yo' know what you'm doin', lad?" he asked nervously. "We don't want it broke."

"Of course I do," Andrew said crossly. "I've learned all about 'em at the Wireless Society." He looked at the clock. "I don't think there's a broadcast on now," he said, "but at six o'clock there's the news, and sure to be some music tonight." He held out the headphones to Will. "You can be the first one to listen, Dad," he said loftily. "I've heard it before."

The crystal set was such a success that Anna began to wish she had not bought it. The problem was that all the family wanted to listen at the same time, and some arguments ensued. Eventually, Andrew partially solved the problem by putting the headphones into Mary's large china mixing bowl, so that the sound reverberated and they could all hear the music as they sat around the table. When the news came on, Will insisted that as head of the household he should be the one to listen. As the items were broadcast, he sat making notes on a sheet of paper put ready for the purpose. When the newsreader said "good night", Will would reply gravely, "Goodnight, and thank you," before removing the headphones. Then he would relate the news items one by one, as far as he could remember them, sometimes with embellishments and comments of his own as he thought fit.

When Dottie and Jack arrived three days later for Anna's farewell dinner, they were immediately summoned to try the crystal set, and there was much hilarity. At last the whole family were gathered around the big dining table, and to Anna's delight, the meal was a great success. The family were not accustomed to taking wine with their dinner, and had agreed to drink it only to please Anna, but as their cheeks became pink and their tongues loosened, they decided to a man that, as Mary put it, "The French 'ad it right after all, per'aps."

Will got to his feet. "'Ang on, everybody, I've got summat to say. I want yo' all to drink a toast, to our Anna an' 'er husband Clancy, an' their lad James, o' course, wi' thanks fer everythin'." The toast was drunk and there was much clapping, but Will was not finished. "Yo' don't need me ter tell yo' what they've done fer us in the past, but now we've 'ad Anna 'ere, 'ome wi' us, an' that was the best thing of all."

Mary said, "'Ear, 'ear," and everyone clapped again.

"Our Anna's give us a few surprises over the years," Will went on, "but now me an' Mary is goin' to give yo' one, Anna. Since we began to do well with the veggies, we've been puttin' the money by..." Will paused and looked round the table for effect, "an' by this time next year I reckon we'll be on our way to America, to visit yo'!"

Anna was overcome with happiness. She had been dreading leaving them all, but it would be so much easier if she knew she would see them before too long. "Oh, Will," she said, tears springing to her eyes, "how wonderful...and we shall have a year to prepare. Clancy and I will plan such a holiday for you."

Andrew interrupted, asking, "What about me? Can't I go?"

Will considered, but Anna saw him wink at Mary. "I should think we should 'ave enough for a ticket for yo' an' all," he said at last, to Andrew's delight.

Anna hugged her nephew. "You and James are quite near in age. I hope you will be good friends," she said happily. She knew Will and Mary were aware that they only had to mention they would like to visit New York and the tickets would have been provided. But this was something they wanted to do for themselves, something to work and save for, and Anna understood that.

Andrew was desperate to discuss the details, but Will would have none of it. "Yo'll 'ave ter wait," he said, rising from his chair. "It's time fer the news."

Victoria

Clancy was exhausted. After a hectic morning, and meetings with Lee Sung and Joe Kowalski in the afternoon, he had felt obliged to carry out his normal visits to two Sullivan's establishments before going home. He had intended to dine at the restaurant, but suddenly he had felt unable to face food and made his excuses, to the consternation of the manager.

He leaned back into the luxury of the car interior and closed his eyes. He seemed unable to cope with the terrible depression which had assailed him since Anna left. It was a feeling of lethargy, as if nothing mattered, as if all his efforts could make no difference. He recognised he had a problem because he had never felt this way before, and he had even consulted his doctor, who had talked about working too hard and prescribed a holiday.

Some hope, Clancy thought to himself. Perhaps later, when Anna came home, they would both go away for the holiday of a lifetime. When she came home. *If* she came home. If she was not so anxious to escape, both from himself and their recent troubles, that she decided to stay in England.

No. She would never leave James, he realised. *Hold on to that thought.* Anna might want to leave him, but it was unthinkable that she would desert her son.

"Mr. Sullivan, we're here, sir," the chauffeur's

concerned voice broke into his reverie. They were home.

"Oh, sorry, Jackson. I must have dropped off."

"You're tired, sir."

"Yes, I am. You can put the car away. I won't need you tonight."

Clancy got out of the car stiffly and walked up the front steps, fishing for his key. Before he found it, the door opened, and Lottie looked out.

"Oh, Mr. Sullivan, thank goodness you're here." She seemed agitated.

"What is it, Lottie? Is something wrong?"

"Not exactly. You have a visitor; he insisted on waiting. I've put him in the drawing room."

"Well, that's alright, Lottie."

"You don't understand, Mr. Sullivan. It's that man...that Vittorio Vetti."

Clancy's face darkened. "It's alright, Lottie. Leave it to me."

When he opened the door to the drawing room, Vetti was standing with his back to him, examining Sylvie's picture of Anna. He turned. "Ah, Sullivan. Good of you to see me."

"It seems I didn't have much choice," Clancy said shortly. He crossed to the side table and poured himself a whisky.

"Are things so bad between us you aren't going to offer me a drink?" Vetti asked.

"They are, and I'm not," Clancy retorted.

Vittorio sighed. "How sanctimonious the winners can be," he said acidly.

"Winners? How can you talk of winners in this sorry business?" Clancy said angrily.

"You misunderstand me, Mr. Sullivan. Perhaps it is the wrong word, it is my English...."

"Your English is perfectly good."

"What I meant was, you are not a loser. You

still have your son. I have lost my nephew and his lovely wife," Vittorio said quietly.

Clancy hesitated. He walked back to the drinks table. "Whisky?"

"Thank you," Vittorio said.

As he handed him his glass, Clancy met the mobsters eyes, and realised the man had indeed suffered. The heavy eyes revealed a look which was lifeless and vacant, and his face had an unhealthy pallor. He had lost weight, Clancy noticed; his expensive suit hung on him loosely, and his necktie was awry.

Clancy sipped his drink. "Say what you have to and go."

Vittorio sighed. "I do not intend to apologise for my life, Mr. Sullivan. It has been what it has been. Do you mind if I sit down?" Not waiting for an answer, Vittorio lowered himself into an armchair. He looked across at Clancy. "If you had been born me...."

"If I had been born you, I'd have shot myself," Clancy said.

The heavy eyelids flickered. "I have considered that option, but there is still unfinished business, and anyway, others are pressing for that privilege."

Vittorio took a gulp from his glass, and Clancy said, "Do you expect me to feel sorry for you?"

"No. Just don't be pious." Vittorio took another gulp of whisky, finishing it. He handed the glass to Clancy, who, after a moment's hesitation, refilled it.

"Don't misunderstand me," Vittorio said. "I believe in good. There are saintly people in the world. They are largely confined to monasteries and nunneries, or working for the poor in some God forsaken hole. Most people, Mr. Sullivan, obey the law because they are afraid to do otherwise. I have only done what others do not dare to do."

"Are you saying it takes courage to live a life like yours?" Clancy burst out. "To take a percentage from decent folk by intimidation? To exploit women? To cater to the most depraved in our society?" He gave a dismissive snort. "That does not need courage. In my book it is cowardly and evil."

"Then it is good we do not all have to live by your book, Mr. Sullivan," Vittorio responded without rancour. "In any case, you don't have to put up with me for long. I intend to return to Italy, that is if I live long enough to get on the boat."

"I see." Clancy finished his drink. "Then, before you go, I will put you straight, so I will. You were wrong to assume Anna and I were not losers. Jennie was almost like a daughter to us, and we were fond of Paolo too, in spite of...."

"I know. In spite of his relationship to me," Vittorio interrupted. "That is why I am here. There is one important matter which must be settled before I leave New York."

"You've got five minutes," Clancy said.

Anna leaned on the ship's rail as the *Ocean Star* approached New York Harbour. It had been a good crossing and the ship would dock almost two hours early. She felt sick with apprehension at the thought of seeing Clancy again and hoped that her telegraphed message had arrived safely. If so, he would be here to meet her, she was sure. Although she was nervous about her reception, she was determined that given the slightest hint of encouragement, she would show Clancy how much she cared.

When the ship docked, Anna secured the services of a porter and disembarked, confident that, by the time she had cleared the Customs building, Clancy would have arrived. The formalities

were few, but when she was ready to leave, there
was still no sign of Clancy. Disappointed, she summoned a cab, and as the driver loaded her luggage, Anna took in the scene around her, unable
to help comparing her arrival in New York today
with her first reception twenty years before. Then,
sick and exhausted from the crossing, she had
joined the long queue with Clancy, under the
canopy which stretched from the ferry landing right
out to the Reception Centre at Ellis Island. It had
taken two hours to reach the Centre, she recalled,
and then the queue went on up the central stairs
to the Great Hall. That was the most terrifying time,
for she had been separated from Clancy for the
medical examinations. Everything had been thor-
ough and impersonal, and she recalled feeling like
a piece of meat as she was quickly processed from
one desk to the next. Anna shuddered as she recalled the moment when someone turned her eyelids inside out with a buttonhook, and suddenly
realised that since that day, she and Clancy had
never been separated until she took her trip home
to England.

Home. Anna sat in the back of the cab and
pondered on the word. She looked out at the now
familiar sights of New York as the cab made its
way homeward, and felt that perhaps, after all,
home was here in New York. But with Will and
Mary in England she had felt completely at home
too. What was it the song said? "Home is where
the heart is...." In that case, home was here in
New York, with Clancy. She smiled at the familiar
sight of the Sullivan's restaurant near Union
Square, and settled back, hoping Clancy would be
at home when she arrived.

He was not. A maid answered the doorbell, a
pert young girl Anna had not seen before.

"I'm Mrs. Sullivan. Who are you?" Anna said, as she entered the hallway.

"Millie Robinson, Madam." The girl smiled nervously. "I recognise you from your photograph, Mrs. Sullivan."

"Good. How long have you been here?"

"Two weeks, madam. Lottie...I mean Mrs. Wilson, took me on."

"I see. What happened to Jane?"

"Got married, madam." Millie held open the door as the driver unloaded Anna's luggage.

"Oh, yes, I remember," Anna said. "Is Mrs. Wilson in?"

"Went out, madam."

"Oh, I see. And Mr. Sullivan?"

"He went out a while ago, madam."

Anna paid the driver and Millie closed the front door. "Would you like some tea, Madam?"

Anna smiled. "Yes, I would, please, Millie. In the drawing room."

As the girl bustled away, Anna took off her coat and hat. She went into the drawing room and the first thing to catch her eye was Sylvie's picture above the fireplace. She examined it with fresh eyes. It was indeed a splendid painting, she decided, even if the memories it revived were now less intense.

What a homecoming, she thought dismally. No-one here, not even Lottie. Perhaps Clancy had gone to meet her after all and they had missed each other. She hoped so. Suddenly it seemed vitally important that he should have made the effort. It was like playing hopscotch when you were a child and not landing on the cracks. If he hadn't gone to meet her, it meant he didn't want her home, was not interested.

The door opened, and as Millie entered with a tray, the front doorbell rang. She put down the tray and went to answer it, and Anna heard voices in the hall. A moment later, the door opened and Clancy came in, a look of delight on his face. He opened his arms wide.

"I missed ye, so I did! The boat was early." He flung his arms around Anna and kissed her soundly. "How are ye, darlin'? My you're prettier than ever. The English air agrees with ye, so it does."

Anna felt a wave of relief flood through her. "Oh, Clancy, I've missed you so much."

He seemed surprised, and said softly, "And I've missed you too."

"Clancy, we have to talk. There is so much....."

"I know, darlin'," Clancy interrupted. "And I want to hear every word, all about your trip, but first things first. You have to say hello to someone."

He went into the hall, and a moment later James came in. "Hello, Mama." He came across and kissed Anna.

"James! What a lovely surprise. I thought you were at college." Anna saw a look of conspiracy flash between James and Clancy.

"Er...Father came to fetch me, so I could be here this weekend, to welcome you home," James explained.

"But that's wonderful, and was that Lottie's voice I heard in the hall?"

"Yes," Clancy said. "James, go and ask Lottie to come in."

"What? Now?" James asked.

"Yes." Clancy seemed nervous. "You can...you can take care of things for a while."

"I'm not sure," James said.

"Of course you can. Stay outside." Clancy ushered James out of the room.

Anna was mystified. "What is going on? Why does James have to stay outside?"

The door opened again and Lottie came in. "Oh, Anna, how good to have you home."

The two women embraced, and Clancy said, "Anna, we have a surprise for you."

James came in carrying a bundle in his arms. Clancy took the tiny baby from him and carried it to Anna. "Look at this little one, Anna. Isn't she a beauty?"

Anna regarded the tiny child with surprise. The baby blinked her long lashes and wrinkled her nose. "She's beautiful," Anna said, entranced. She took the child from Clancy and looked up at him. "Who does she belong to?"

"Anna, it's Jennie's baby. Jennie and Paolo's baby."

Anna stared at him. Clancy bent over and stroked the baby's hand. "It's true, darlin'. When Jennie died on the way to hospital, they managed to save the baby. They didn't think she would survive, but she did. God bless her, she did."

It was a few moments before Anna could speak. "But...we weren't told."

"No. Vittorio asked the hospital to keep it secret. He was afraid the baby might become a target."

"Oh goodness, no." Anna cuddled the child to her and suddenly was engulfed in a wave of happiness. "Oh...it's wonderful, Clancy, wonderful. Jennie and Paolo's baby. How long have you known?"

"Just over a week. It was too late to let you know before you left England."

James bent down and allowed the baby to clutch at his finger. "She did that in the car. Look, Mama, how her fingers hold on." He laughed delightedly. "That's where we were, why we missed you at the ship, we were collecting her from the hospital. Lottie came too, to buy her some things.

Father and I didn't know what to get."

"But why did you have to collect her?"

"Anna," Clancy said, "Vittorio wants us to take her, adopt her as our own. He came to see me. He said that is what Paolo and Jennie would have wanted. They were going to move away and make a new start. Paolo had finished with the mob."

"But doesn't Vittorio want her?"

"Yes, very much. But he knows Paolo was right. Vittorio is going back to Italy and wants the child to have a good family in America. He begged me, Anna, to take her."

"And what did you tell him?"

"That we must wait until you came home, that it was a family decision."

Anna looked at James. "What do you think?"

James smiled. "I could be her elder brother, like Paolo was for me."

Anna smiled. "Yes, it's good for a girl to have a brother."

Clancy stroked the baby's tiny hand. "Will ye look at the little fingernails? Vittorio says Jennie had decided to name her Victoria, after the old queen, if she had a girl. Paolo was going to choose the second name, but he hadn't decided."

"Rose," Anna said, thinking of Paolo's red roses and Vittorio in his rose garden. "Her name is Victoria Rose."

Victoria Rose yawned and then blew a small bubble.

Anna looked up at James. He laughed and flicked back his fair hair in a characteristic gesture. She gazed into the violet eyes of the baby and then into the Irish eyes which regarded her with passionate concern, and she knew they were a family at last.

"I love you, Clancy," she said.

978-0-595-44765-7
0-595-44765-1

9 780595 447657